WALTZES
AND
WHISPERS

Also available from Pumpkin Books

Peter Atkins
WISHMASTER AND OTHER STORIES

Ramsey Campbell
GHOSTS AND GRISLY THINGS

David Case
BROTHERLY LOVE AND OTHER TALES OF FAITH AND KNOWLEDGE

Hugh B. Cave
ISLE OF THE WHISPERERS

Dennis Etchison
DOUBLE EDGE

Stephen Jones
DARK OF THE NIGHT
NEW TALES OF HORROR AND THE SUPERNATURAL

WHITE OF THE MOON
NEW TALES OF MADNESS AND DREAD

Stephen Jones & Jo Fletcher
HORROR AT HALLOWEEN

Nancy Kilpatrick
CHILD OF THE NIGHT
POWER OF THE BLOOD VOL I

NEAR DEATH
POWER OF THE BLOOD VOL II

REBORN
POWER OF THE BLOOD VOL III

Sylvia Starshine
DRACULA: or THE UN-DEAD
A PLAY IN PROLOGUE AND FIVE ACTS

WALTZES AND WHISPERS

Jay Russell

PUMPKIN BOOKS
NOTTINGHAM

Published in Great Britain by Pumpkin Books

An imprint of MeG Publishing Limited
PO Box 297, Nottingham NG2 4GW, ENGLAND.
Also at http://www.netcentral.co.uk/pumpkin/

First edition, October, 1999.

Hardback edition limited to 750 copies.

ISBN 1 901914 16 X

A CIP catalogue record for this book is available from the British
Library.

Printed by Creative Print and Design Group.

Contents

ACKNOWLEDGEMENTS

"Limited Additions" Copyright © 1994. First published in *The King is Dead: Tales of Elvis Postmortem* edited by Paul M Sammon.

"Virtual Uncertainty" Copyright © 1991. First published in Science Fiction Review.

"Sous Rature" Copyright © 1997. First published in *Dark Terrors 3: The Gollancz Book of Horror* edited by Stephen Jones and David Sutton.

"Waltz in Vienna" Copyright © 1997. First published in *Dark of the Night* edited by Stephen Jones.

"Lily's Whisper" Copyright © 1996. First published in *Dark Terrors 2: The Gollancz Book of Horror* edited by Stephen Jones and David Sutton.

"Sullivan's Travails" Copyright © 1998. First published in *Dark Terrors 4: The Gollancz Book of Horror* edited by Stephen Jones and David Sutton.

"City of Angels" Copyright © 1990. First published in *Splatterpunks* edited by Paul M Sammon.

"Undiscovered Countries" Copyright © 1992. First published in *Still Dead: Book of the Dead 2* edited by John Skipp and Craig Spector.

This book is dedicated to Louis Schechter
and
J P Rheems, unsung hero of twentieth century literature

My thanks to the editors who originally bought some of the stories contained in this volume: Jessie Horsting, Paul M Sammon, Elton Elliott, John Skipp and Craig Spector, David Sutton and, most of all, Stephen Jones.

I'm very grateful to Michael Marshall Smith and Kim Newman for their generous lies (I'll let the hostages go now), and to David Marshall for taking a chance on this project.

And, as usual, love, thanks, and everything else go to Jane.

An Introduction To
Jay Russell

THE PROBLEM WITH INTRODUCTIONS IS THAT they tend to be somewhat predictable. You know what's coming. If someone's written something to go at the front of a book by somebody else, then it's unlikely to be "Hey — this is crap. Let's go hunt the author down with knives. I'll pay for the cab." If he's gone to the trouble of doing a piece, the chances are it's because he likes what's inside.

This introduction is sadly no exception.

When I was asked if I'd like to do it, an image briefly popped into my mind. I saw myself as Frankie Lemon, that golden-haired introducer-extraordinaire of prestige heavyweight boxing bouts. I imagined standing in a ring, in a neat little dinner suit, surrounded by howling fans and leather-faced celebrities, and bellowing: "And, in the strange corner, weighing in at an even six hundred pounds, writing out of Walthamstow, England, the Denizen of Darkness, the Nemesis of Noir, the Master of Marcusian Macabre . . . Jaaaaaaaaaaay Ruuuuusssss-ellllllllllllllllllllllllllll!"

But then it was politely explained to me that I had to write it down. Which I think shows a regrettable lack of vision.

In fact, a degree of predictability is endemic to books which feature only one author's work. With most such collections, once you've read maybe two or three stories, you form a sense of the style, of the milieu in which the stories will unfold, of the author's wares and pitch. You know pretty much what you're getting.

Not with this one, you don't.

This book doesn't work that way at all, which is why the predictability of what I'm going to say pains me. I'm willing to bet that every two people who read these stories will pick a different favourite. You'll find straight-down-the-line horror, gothic fantasy, cyberpunk and splatterpunk, literary fiction and noir. It's a smorgasbord of words, an all-you-can-eat Mexican buffet of fiction. We've got searing-hot chilli over there, tasty enchiladas up front, some kind of weird gunk whose ingredients I don't want to even know about, and soothing guacamole on the side. The only thing that ties it all together is that they've all been produced by the same cook, and he knows what he's doing.

He has a voice.

My favourite writers are voice writers. The Ray Bradburys, Stephen Kings, Kingsley Amises of the world. The people who use words like a musical instrument, rather than as dry equations for manifesting a story. If you see Eric Clapton playing live, it doesn't matter whether it's blues, rock or ill-advised reggae. It still sounds like him. Maybe for you that's a bad thing. Doesn't matter. The point is that it's unique. You hear a guitar used as it should be, as a way of expressing an individual's emotions and thoughts and momentary state of mind, in ways that the human throat simply can't.

It's the same with writers. So many seem to regard words and sentences as a kind of necessary evil, something both they and reader have to put up with for the sake of the story. Recently, in the interests of trying not to be a prejudiced asshole — a long-term project of mine, apparently doomed to failure — I bought a couple of airport-style thrillers in paperback. Both had sold by the cartload, and the blurbs on the back were hysterical in their praise. Truly, I felt, my life would be a small, crabbed thing if I hadn't heard what these authors had to say. So I read them, or tried to.

I have no idea how good the stories were, because I didn't get past the first chapter of either. The sense of duty in every sentence was so palpable, the prose so turgid and uninspired, that frankly I couldn't be arsed. It was like being forced to memorise the ingredient list on the side of a can of Dr Pepper before you're allowed to drink what's inside — and then finding it's warm and flat anyway. Books by the airport guys are a basic expense, in accounting terms. You hand over the money, get given something, and that's it. Once you know how everything pans out, you've received all the book has to give. It becomes merely an encumbrance, taking up room on the bookshelf and gathering dust — until you work up the energy to take a box-load of them down to the charity shop. Books by voice writers are an investment, because you can come back time and time again, and they only get better. They earn their place in your life, because they change it, they tell you things worth knowing, and they won't blurt out all their secrets at the first meeting. And the really cool thing is that they cost exactly the same as the bad books. As your literary investment strategist, I think it's clear what my advice is going to be.

It doesn't matter how good a tale you're telling if you don't realise that every sentence also tells its own story. You give me a Jay Russell, or a Jim Thompson or a Joe R. Lansdale, and frankly I don't give a damn what they're writing about. I'm going to read it come what may. The fact that they're telling great stories as well just goes to prove that you really can have your cake and eat it.

Voice writers tend to have much more freedom in their subject matter, because their storytelling ties it all together. It doesn't matter how far out on a limb Russell goes, because somewhere in each story will be a line which makes it real. So in this collection you get stories like "Down", an everyday tale of murdering folk, but also "Sous Rature", a horror story structured around post-modernist nonsense thought. You get an update on what Dracula's been up to, bare pages away from a revisionist baseball romance, and smooth cyberpunk right next to the engagingly bizarre "If Happy Little Bluebirds Fly . . .". You even get exuberantly psychotic tales like "Revenge of the Zombie Studpuppies" — surely one of the all-time great story titles — in the same collection as the measured, emotionally-charged "Lily's Whisper". A good short story can make even novels by the good guys seem thin and drab. "Lily's Whisper" is one of those. It is dark, haunting, painful — but about as difficult to read as your own name. That's what voice writing is about. Getting you to listen to new things, or even the same old things from a different angle — because you love the way you're being told.

Russell knows how to be funny, too. Not the anaemic one-liners which pass for comedy so often these days, but genuine, this-is-how-you-use-words-properly funny. The kind of funny which means you bid a fond farewell to each sentence, confident that the next one will be just as good. This is most evident in "Sullivan's Travails", the welcome return of supernatural sleuth Marty Burns, but it's there in all of the other stories too. Sometimes on the surface, sometimes hiding just behind, just as there is often darkness shadowing the lighter moments of both these stories and our lives. Good writing is about making things real, whether it's virtual worlds or zombies', heroes or losers, happiness or grief. *Waltzes and Whispers* makes all of these real, sometimes uncomfortably so.

If you like words, you're in for a treat. If not, come see what you've been missing. With Russell, you're in the safest of hands.

So it's just a shame that on a personal level he is a reprehensible scumbag, a vile excrescence whose very existence undermines any claim our species might have to value or worth, a despoiler of the clean sheets of purity and truth, a putrid flibbertigibbet of a man.

Who'd have thought it?

— Michael Marshall Smith
London, July 1999

Introduction to "Dracula's Eyes"

Writing is a funny business. Hear the squeals of giddy laughter in the background?

Okay, so maybe it's less "Say, have you heard the one about . . . ?" than it is "Say, what's that funny growth on your neck?" But you gotta take your jollies where you can get them. Really. You gotta.

Part of what makes writing such a thigh-slapper of an enterprise is that delightful little thing known as "the market". Now, you might think that there could be nothing more quantifiable and subject to study and dissection as the market for a product. God knows, most businesses spend millions trying to understand and analyse their markets in order best to exploit them, serve them, make them bigger and happier.

Not publishing.

As a one-time social scientist, I know as well as anyone just how suspect market research techniques can be — a clever methodologist can make a survey spit out any answer at all — but there is something to be said for the idea, if not the specific processes, of understanding who your market is and what and why it wants what it wants. You can't always be certain of those answers because people don't know or they lie or they tell you what they think you want to hear. But they can — and will — tell you something, if you'll only ask.

Publishers never ask; they always just *assume*.

One of the assumptions made is that short story collections and anthologies don't sell. Fortunately small press publishers work under very different sets of assumptions; otherwise, you wouldn't be holding this lovely book in your hands right now. (And just what is that under your fingernails? You march straight into that bathroom and wash those hands . . .) These days, when big publishers do deign to risk a volume of short stories, they generally insist it have a *theme*. (Christ, it's like being back in junior high, isn't it? Can't you just hear Miss Crabapple asking the class what the main *theme* of the book you're supposed to have read is? No wonder the Cliff Notes guy got rich. I half-suspect that the publishing biz is full of teacher's pets whose hands shot up when the English teachers of the world asked that moronic question. I digress therefore I am. Sorry.) Now, a theme anthology doesn't have to be bad. Sometimes the themes are clever and lend themselves to bold ideas. Sometimes, especially if you're in a funk, the hook of a theme book can get you started when the creativity engine is sputtering. Sometimes it's just a good way to pocket some cash. (Usually a *very* small amount of cash. Sigh.) The thing is that, *as a rule* theme books tend to impose strict limits on imagination. Sometimes great stories appear in theme anthos — Joe Lansdale's "Night They Missed the Horror Show" from David Schow's *Silver Scream* leaps to mind like a frog with a V2 up its ass — but my own, admittedly subjective and unscientific sampling, suggests that the best short stories originate elsewhere.

Stephen Jones, who is a wonderful editor (as well as a friend), sometimes assembles theme anthologies, and he does them as well as anyone can. Unlike some of the assembly-line volumes which litter the shelves, Steve edits his books, themed or not, with great thought and care. But at risk of putting words into his mouth, I think he'd rather not do the theme books; I'm pretty sure he prefers unthemed anthologies like the multi-award winning *Dark Terrors* series. But for all the accolades such volumes garner, the publishing world has its assumptions and top of the list under the heading Anthologies is: unthemed doesn't sell. (Actually, top of the list is: anthologies don't sell. Never mind that publishers undermine any possible success of such books by their very assumptions and self-fulfilling prophecies. But you know that, present company excluded, publishers are scum.) So, because he wants to get good work published — and like the rest of us, he has a peculiar need for food and shelter — Steve edits the occasional theme volume. And because I, too, like to eat and sleep under a roof without leaks, I sometimes write stories for them.

"Dracula's Eyes" was written with a theme anthology in mind, but didn't make it into the finished book. Several of the stories in this collection have a similar history and I'll tell you about them as we come to them. The danger of writing a theme antho tale is that if it does not get into its intended volume it's got no place else to go. "Dracula's Eyes", written for Steve's *The Mammoth Book of Dracula* (sadly the tale was about two times too long and six months too late), never found another home, possibly because I never bothered to send it to anyone else. See, I'm almost as useless at marketing as the bad old publishers themselves. I like the story, though, and I think its mix of horror and humour and interminable pop culture references provides a pretty good introduction to the collection and to my style of writing.

Though I have a funny feeling that neither John Travolta nor Tom Cruise will be buying up the film rights.

Dracula's Eyes

THE ROOM HAS NO WINDOWS.

There is a door — *a* door — but it locks from the outside. It's not a particularly sophisticated lock, nor is it a very strong door. There's no need.

Not these days.

The room is a nice room. And why shouldn't it be? Rather more than a room, really, it takes up most of the 71st floor of the Rhymer Building. Officially, of course, in the blueprints and plans, there is no 71st floor of the Rhymer Building; no stairs or public elevator to take you there. Just as there are no windows in the room on the 71st floor. If there were windows, the view would be magnificent (at least on those rare, clear days when you can actually see through the grit that passes for air in Los Angeles). But there aren't, so it isn't.

No matter.

To eyes that have seen so much, the sprawling post-urban expanse of the L.A. basin isn't all that special. Especially to eyes that looked upon that self-same view before the air had become fetid, before the cars and leaf blowers and fatty burger joints mucked it all up, leaving a sky the colour of dirty oil.

Eyes red as blood, but bleary with stupor. Eyes that have beheld the profoundest of beauty and the most profane of decadence. Eyes of power — which hold a trace of that power still — but weakened by age and exhaustion and apathy.

Dracula's eyes.

The decision to make the voyage across the ocean was the best he'd ever made.

No small thing.

Dracula possessed the vampire's natural aversion to water, especially that terrifying expanse of bottomless and deadly blue that is the Atlantic, but there was no avoiding it. He'd investigated the possibility of flying to America, but quickly discovered that such exploits were for daredevils and fools. And while Dracula was not a creature to turn in fear from anything, the centuries had taught him that the very thinnest of lines separates pride from foolhardiness. So he would risk the week at sea — a week, when all was said and done, aboard a luxury ocean-liner — rather than expose himself to the madness of flight.

Though to many, whether by sea or air, flight was what his self-imposed exile from the Old World would seem.

A vampire possesses many superhuman abilities. There are those, of course, who call these talents super*natural*, though Dracula regarded the very notion as absurd. Nothing can exist beyond nature, though one needs understand that nature herself may take on myriad forms. Yet, for all *his* extraordinary nature, Dracula had no innate ability to see into the future (however much a boon such a talent would be). There were some who attributed the Count's success and longevity to such a presumed power of precognition, but Dracula's knack for anticipating events — and capitalising on that anticipation — was purely a result of a keenly-honed intellect. For while he had devoted no small part of the centuries to accumulating *things* — houses, paintings, slaves, gold — Dracula devoted always an equal effort to the development of his mind. He understood art and science, poetry and prose to be sure; but more than anything, Dracula understood *people*.

Which was why, in the year of their Lord nineteen hundred and thirty six, in the 505th year of his immortal existence, Dracula was at last taking leave of his native soil, abandoning almost all of his treasures, to begin a new life.

"You are mad, Zrinyi, do you know that?" Leni had told him.

"A little madness is good for the soul. Or so I am told," Dracula replied, and pressed her head back down to his lap.

"You taste like no other man I've ever known," she said afterwards.

"And you've known a few, I'd judge."

"Practice makes perfect." She smiled. A trace of Dracula's dark seed dribbled down her chin. She wiped it away with a finger, licking it clean. "I'm a perfectionist, I should know."

"Ach, are you still shooting that god-awful film?"

Leni bobbed her head and took a playful nip at Dracula's thigh. "The Olympics go on for another week. You know that. And it's not awful. It is magnificent. Or it will be when I've cut it together. It will be *art*, darling."

"Art is not what you make," Dracula said, pushing her away, "Art is how you live."

She laughed. "What a peculiar thing for a movie producer to say! Take you no pride in your work, man?"

"I produce garbage. To be consumed by swine."

"So why not give it up?"

"And quit show business?" he asked with a smirk.

"Surely you don't expect better moving to *Hollywood?* Here, at least, you have the resources of UFA. There is Harlan, Hippler . . . *me!*"

"Harlan and Hippler are idiots. I am surrounded by hacks and patsies. Where is Lubitsch? Wilder? Siodmak? UFA is a shadow of what it was."

"And me?" Leni asked.

"You have an eye, I admit. But even more, a very lovely mouth."

"Hmmmph," Leni sulked.

"And I have plans," Dracula mused.

Leni dropped back to her knees and hugged Dracula's legs. She rested a cheek on his thigh, pressed her boyish breasts against his cold skin. "And those plans don't include me any more."

"No," Dracula said. "There is nothing left for me in Berlin."

"*Everything* is here," Leni insisted. "The future . . . "

6

"Tomorrow belongs to me?" Dracula teased.

"It could. Goebbels likes you, he always has. Better, he *fears* you. The Reich . . . "

"Has no future. Or a short-lived one at best."

"How can you say such a thing?" Leni whispered.

"The *führer* is an ass. And a lunatic. What possible future for a country cleansed of Jews and homosexuals? Who will be the thinkers, the dreamers, the artists? No-one *likes* yids or fags, mind, but you cannot hope to sustain a civilised culture without them. No, the sun now rises in the West."

"But you *hate* the sun, Zrinyi. I see you always, only after dark."

Dracula just laughed.

"Take me with you?" Leni asked. She pressed her cheek back to his thigh, squeezed his legs a little tighter.

"Your place is here," he told her. "Your . . . destiny."

Leni looked up at him with tears in her eyes, her lips in a pout. Dracula felt himself stir again. She opened her mouth to speak, but Dracula filled it before she could say a word.

"But such a mouth," he sighed.

Koontz held the only key. Or so it seemed to Dracula. Koontz was always there when the door opened, though occasionally he brought others with him. Today it was a young boy, doped to the gills as usual, lifeless as a zombie. And naked.

"Blood in Spirit," Koontz intoned.

Dracula belched in response. His bleary, ancient eyes turned immediately to the boy's neck, the carotid pulsing with life. Dracula weakly raised a hand, pointing a jagged nail at the boy, He inarticulately growled his desire, his belly rumbling at the sight and smell of his dinner.

"Hrrraaauughh," Dracula moaned. He waved his hand spasmodically, like a baby clutching desperately for his mother's teat.

Koontz smiled. The old man, he thought, sounded *exactly* like Karloff playing the monster in one of those old movies. And, of course, he was *looking* more and more like Lugosi every day, albeit the formaldehyde Lugosi, circa Ed Wood. Koontz had a keen sense of irony.

"In a minute, Father," he said. Dracula slowly lowered his hand, but a line of drool spilled from the corner of his mouth. "I need your thumb print first."

Koontz removed a sheaf of papers from a folder and carried them over to Dracula. The documents authorised the Mission's lawyers to pursue a new phase in their campaign for certification of tax-free status from Internal Revenue. The tax agency had been fighting them tooth-and-nail for years, refusing to accept that the Heuristic Mission was a bona fide religious organisation. The Mission had lost several rounds in the courts, but their attorneys were gearing up for yet another challenge. Every time Koontz thought he had wrested full-control of HM from the old man, he stumbled over another hitch in the paperwork requiring Dracula's personal approval. The vampire had been careful in establishing the Mission, to ensure that nothing of consequence could be changed without authorisation verified by his thumb print. Including the ability to ever countermand that directive.

On any number of occasions, Koontz had considered cutting the old bat's thumb off and getting rid of him once and for all. But he wasn't sure that the thumb could be kept in a viable state on its own, and he was afraid to take the chance. Besides, Koontz harboured hopes that sooner or later the old man would make him *protégé* in more than just the Heuristic Mission. Eventually, Koontz would position himself on the receiving end of eternal life.

And deep down, despite the vampire's increasingly decrepit condition, Koontz remained just a little bit afraid of Dracula.

Dracula tried to sit up as Koontz placed the papers in front of him, but half fell off the bed in the process. He made a pretence of looking at the pages, but the words were just black smudges in his blurred vision. He tried, really tried, to bring them into focus, but he was so hungry and too distracted by the smell of the naked boy's blood. The coppery richness of the scent made his head swim, and with a resigned shrug he allowed Koontz to ink his thumb and press it against the various pages.

It would be all right. Koontz knew how to look after things.

"Thank you, Father," Koontz said, He pulled a baby-wipe from the container on the table beside Dracula's bed and cleaned the ink off the old man's thumb as best he could. He carefully placed the papers back in his folder, then walked back over to the boy.

Koontz put his arm around the boy's bare shoulders and walked him slowly across the room to Dracula's bed. The old man's tongue hung out of his mouth and saliva dripped down his now fully extended fangs. Koontz forced the boy down to a kneeling position, then pressed his head down on the bed next to the vampire. Koontz brushed the boy's long blond hair away from his neck. The old man immediately buried his face in the boy's neck, but seemed to be having a problem. Again.

Koontz sighed.

Fishing a paring knife out of a drawer, Koontz made a small cut in the boy's neck. He twirled the blade back and forth until blood gushed out, opening the wound wide enough so that the old man could get a grip on his own. Dracula smiled at Koontz like a retard, then bent down to his dinner. He slurped away happily.

Koontz watched briefly as the old vampire messily sucked the life out of the boy, who had started to convulse, but who offered no resistance to death. He walked back to the door, shaking his head.

"Pathetic," he whispered. He locked the door behind him.

"No, no," Hughes said, shaking his head fiercely. "They just ain't big enough. Haven't you got eyes, man? Can't you see that? When I say *big* ones, I mean big ones."

Dracula rested his chin on his palm and sighed. He looked over at Hughes, the millionaire's weaselly features exaggerated by shadows from the flickering light, then back up at the screen. The actress in the screen test wasn't top of the A-list, but she was a star nonetheless. She hadn't been too happy about having to strip to the waist for the screen test, but she'd done it because, after all, the picture *was* a Howard Hughes production and everyone in town knew of Hughes' . . . fascinations. Dracula was all *too* aware of it, though he'd never shared nor really understood his partner's tit fetish.

Dracula only had eyes for the girl's neck.

"We need an actress, Howard, someone who can perform. By which I mean act. We do not need another circus freak," Dracula said.

"What d'ya mean 'freak?' There are girls in poo-berty with bigger knockers than that. I know. Hell, I've *had* 'em! Dozens of 'em."

"You could have *her*," Dracula yelled, pointing to the screen. "Just say the word." The actress was nervously tweaking her nipples in a fruitless attempt to make them hard.

"I'm a sexual *ad*venturer, Kurt, you know that. Hell, you've shown *me* a thing or two, I'm embarrassed and not a little surprised to admit. So you must understand my concerns here."

Dracula pressed a button on the panel beside his chair. The screen quickly went dark and the lights in the screening room came up slowly. Hughes continued to stare at the blank screen.

"So you're certain: that's a definite no, then?" Dracula asked.

Hughes had his hand down his pants. He pulled it out, sniffed his fingers and shook his head. "A *definite* no."

Dracula sighed again. The thought of killing Hughes then and there flashed through his mind, but he still needed the man too much. Or his money, at any rate.

Besides, he wasn't that hungry at the moment.

"Kurt," Hughes said, "let me explain a little something to you."

Dracula took a deep breath and tried to keep his temper. Hughes was always 'explaining' things — usually the discourse entailed Hughes' rather singular observations on the subject of female sexuality — and it was only by reminding himself about Hughes' bottomless bank account that Dracula was able to stop from ripping the lunatic's heart out of his chest and stuffing it down his throat. He'd done it to countless others before, and with far less provocation.

"You're a stranger here, Kurt. I mean no offence by that, I welcome the immigrant, but you don't always grasp the nature of what we here call the American psyche. Now don't get me wrong, I know you've seen and done a few things, heh-heh, but you're a long way from, ah, where is it again?"

"Bistritz. Transylvania."

Hughes laughed, "Righty-o you are. Just like that vampire fellow. Heh-heh. Say, you ever think of making one of them old-fashioned monster pictures? I mean, now that Universal's given up the ghost, so to speak."

"Not interested," Dracula said, looking the other way.

"Well, sure. I can understand. Tough to pick up the ball after that Abbott & Costello nonsense. And you've been working on that sophisticated guff with Lewton at RKO. Very subtle, very nice. Shame it don't make no money. You know *I* love it, especially that *Cat People* number. Hell, I swear on a stack of titties I'd marry that Simone Simon if only she had a big girl's rack on her. Well, and if she was a better lay. I've *had* her, you know.

Dracula smiled obligingly.

"But that's my whole point, you see. Those Lewton films are Jim Beam-dandy for what they are, but, well, don't tell Val I said this, they just think too damn small. And whether it's bazongas, airplanes or goddamn motion pictures, Howard Hughes thinks big."

Hughes was up and moving now, pacing back and forth in front of the gleaming silver screen. Once he started talking there was no stopping him. Dracula knew that you just had to wait until he wound down, like a little toy soldier with a key in his back.

"You see, Kurt, sometimes you think a little too much like a European, no offence. Nothing wrong with that, of course, you can't help being what you are. Who can? But here in the good old US of A you just got to be thinking big *all* the time, keeping up with the audience. That's what made this country great, the kind of thinking that's put Hitler and them nasty Nazis on the run. Take my word, the war'll be over by summer. By the by, Kurt, you ever get a gander-loo at that Eva Braun *fraulein*? 'Cause I got a fellow on the other side sent me some special pictures, if you know what I mean. Hooo-weee, come to Papa! Now I got no truck with fruity old Adolph, but two-three more inches on Eva's bouncing baby boys and I might have taken Stalingrad. Heh-heh."

Actually, Dracula found Hughes somewhat remarkable. It wasn't that he hadn't seen, heard and impaled his share of blowhards over the centuries, but there were moments when Dracula believed Hughes to possess a spark of divine madness. Hughes was generally so wrapped up in his own petty sexual compulsions as to be a mind-numbing boor. The only comparison, in Dracula's amazing experience, to Hughes' all-consuming breast obsession was his first-hand observation, during his years at the Royal Court, of batty Queen Victoria's compulsive devotion to her dead Albert. But every great once-in-a-while, Hughes demonstrated a kernel of insight, usually found in the midst of some greater tirade, like a pearl in the slimy gizzards of a raw oyster. Dracula had only been half-listening, but something Hughes said sent a sudden electric shock through his system. He turned his full attention to the crazy rich man.

" . . . religion," Hughes was saying. He wasn't even looking at Dracula, just pacing up and down, delivering his monologue as was his wont. "The movies, I mean. It's a gosh-darned, goddamned, titty-licking *re*ligious experience. The masses of people, all sitting there in the dark, going back week after week. You think the church don't know its business? Believe you me, brother, the business of the church *is* business. I should know, I've paid some bills there myself. That's what got me into the movie game you know. It's practically a calling for me, just like a priest. I thought about the priesthood once, you know. No titty, though. Point is, if some scrawny little eye-tie in a big funny hat can have all that wealth and all them treasures and a nice painted ceiling to boot, well, you just imagine for yourself what an ambitious and intelligent *American* can do. Yessiree Bob, Kurt, there's something to this God game. The damn Christians have got a corner on the market, sure, but I see that same potential in the movies. Hell, you think it's a coincidence that there's such a strong Jewish element there? But unlike your actual church, there's room to expand in Hollywood, to elbow your way in. I know you think I just care about the titty, that's what they all think. Why, do you know just yesterday . . . "

Hughes continued his rant — he was off again about the intellectual deficiencies of small-breasted women — but Dracula tuned him out.

He had a vision. An epiphany even. It astonished him that he'd never thought of it before. The Church had certainly had its uses for Dracula over the centuries — the notion that vampires couldn't bear to look upon a cross or crucifix was pure pulp fiction — but the possibility of . . .

Howard Hughes raved on while Dracula sat deep in thought.

"Father?"

Dracula's bed was empty, the duvet in a tangle, the blood-soaked sheets half-stripped, revealing a battered, urine-stained mattress. The room positively reeked, the smell of spilled blood competing with the odours of fever sweat and body waste. A trail of smeared blood ran from the edge of the bed, across the beige shag carpet and stopped at the half-open bathroom door.

"Blood in Spirit! " Lydia whispered.

The small, pert woman closed and locked the door behind her and dashed across the room. The smell got worse as she neared the bathroom. She took a deep breath and slowly pushed the door fully open.

"Oh, Father," Lydia moaned,

Dracula lay on the dirty tile floor, his head wedged in the toilet. He was naked from the waist down, but he wore a filthy, Sonic the Hedgehog pyjama top. Koontz's idea of a joke, no doubt. The old man was lapping at the water in the bowl with his tongue, but he had trouble supporting his head, and every few seconds his whole face would plop down into the filthy water with a splash.

Lydia went over to him and carefully lifted him out of the toilet, leaning the old man against the wall. He immediately slid down the tiles, so that he lay with his neck propped against the wall, his head bent at an awkward angle. Dracula's tongue lolled out of his mouth and an eighteen inch length of dental floss dangled from between his retracted fangs.

"I don't drink . . . wine," Dracula slurred and laughed to himself, until the chuckles degenerated into a hacking cough. He finally spat up something wet and red onto his pyjama top. Whatever it was took the dental floss with it.

"What has he done to you, Father?" Lydia asked.

She desperately wanted to clean him up and get him back into bed, but she knew she couldn't do it without Koontz finding out. And she knew she didn't have all that much time. She unzipped her fanny pack and withdrew a hypodermic needle. The hypo was filled with a viscous, red liquid. She tapped the needle and tested it.

"This is for you, Father. For your own good." *And for mine,* she thought. *I hope.*

She jabbed the needle into a spot at the back of the old man's knee. He howled as the tip pierced his cold flesh and Lydia cast a nervous eye toward the front door. She pressed down on the plunger, making sure that every drop entered the old man's corrupt system. When she was done, she stuffed the needle back in her pack and started to leave.

She couldn't stand it.

Lydia grabbed a swath of toilet tissue and leaned over Dracula. She wiped his fangs clean and threw the paper in the toilet before flushing it. She looked sadly at the old man.

"Remember who did this for you," she said.

She ran out.

*   *   *   *   *

Staked by a big chunk of Howard Hughes' money, Dracula bought the Rhymer Building for cash in February of 1952. He established it as the world headquarters of The Heuristic Mission of the Divine Brotherhood, complete with a state-of-the-art television studio for use with the Mission's weekly broadcasts.

When he'd first arrived in Hollywood, Dracula's presumed status as a refugee from Nazi persecution worked in his favour. Lubitsch and Freund and some of the others in the film community had always looked suspiciously at him — none of them seemed to remember a Kurt Veidt at UFA — but by and large the identity helped him carve a nice niche for himself in the Hollywood pecking order. And once he'd proven his ability to produce successful films, no-one really cared much about his background. In Hollywood, money talks and fascism walks.

But things changed with the onset of the paranoid fifties. The Red Scare meant foreigners were automatic subjects of suspicion, and Dracula's eastern European accent drew the kind of attention that he didn't want. Especially for someone with an eye on television. So overnight Kurt Veidt became Charles S. Williams, and with a good dialogue coach and a lot of practice, Dracula's harsh Transylvanian intonations were flattened into a solid approximation of pure Mid-western patois.

Charles S. Williams' Divinity Hour was only broadcasting on a local L.A. station for now, but Dracula had much bigger things in mind. The numbers on the show were boffo. No-one could figure out why audiences seemed to flock to this particular religious programme, in prime time yet, when all the others struggled for audiences in the nether hours of Sunday morning. When asked, Charles S. Williams simply chalked it up to the show's deeply affecting inspirational message. A scribbler at *Variety* said the show was almost *hypnotic* in its appeal, and wondered if it didn't suggest some possibly dangerous implications about the effects of this new and powerful medium.

Dracula framed a copy of the article and put up on his wall. It made him laugh every time he saw it.

But newspaper critics weren't the only ones who were eyeing the success of the Heuristic Mission with suspicion. The established churches were jealous; they never much liked competition of any sort. With the aid of a few strategically loosened lips, word soon began to spread that the Mission was a communist front. And in the hysteria of the moment, people were only too happy to believe. Charles S. Williams went on the air to denounce the charges *and* the red menace, but the Mission was caught in the crosshairs of the times. If not for Hughes' intervention, the entire project might have collapsed under the scrutiny, but Dracula had imposed on his crazy friend to arrange a very special meeting. A meeting for which Dracula had been preparing for some time.

For obvious reasons, they couldn't meet at the Rhymer Building. Hughes suggested a neutral site and arranged the necessary security, though Dracula was careful to ensure that several of his own operatives were on hand as well. The house was in a run-down-but-not-quite-slummy section of West Hollywood, on a quiet, dictionary-definition inconspicuous street. The only furnished room in the place was an upstairs bedroom, and that contained nothing more than two straight-backed chairs, and a cum-stained king-sized mattress and box spring. It was one of the many hideaways around town that Hughes maintained for purposes of screwing starlets and other big-breasted babes. The smell of sex lingered in the halls like old cigarette smoke.

Dracula carried the chairs downstairs, deposited them in the front parlour and sat down to wait. He'd been there just over an hour when the front door opened.

A big man, muscle-bound, wearing a grey fedora and a tiny bow-tie came in and looked around. He nodded at Dracula, who didn't respond, then searched the house from top to bottom. He went out and a second fellow, with a small, round head and a face like a vole entered, followed by a corpulent watermelon of a man, with sallow, pockmarked skin, wearing an ill-fitting herringbone suit.

"Williams?"

Dracula nodded. "Thank you for coming, Senator." He gestured at the other chair and the fat man sat down. The vole stood just behind the Senator and whispered something in his left ear. Dracula, of course, had no problem hearing his words. "He's a fag," the man had said. Dracula could smell the fear and excitement oozing from the vole's pores. There was no fear at all in the Senator.

"Howard Hughes is a man who always talks sense," McCarthy said. "A good businessman, a good friend, a fine American."

Dracula nodded his agreement. The little man whispered again. *I want to fuck him in the ass.* Dracula pretended not to hear. McCarthy nodded. "My assistant," the Senator said, "Roy Cohn."

Dracula nodded again and winked at the little man. He could hear Cohn's heart begin to beat faster, and he had to swallow a rush of desire to bleed the man then and there.

"I've been led to understand you have something for me," McCarthy said.

Dracula reached into his jacket pocket and pulled out an envelope. He held it out to the Senator, but Cohn dashed around to intercept it. The little man's fingers brushed Dracula's palm as he took the envelope. He tore it open, glanced at the paper inside, then passed it to the Senator. McCarthy had to hold the sheet at arms length to read it.

"List of names," McCarthy said.

"Communists," Dracula said. "Party members, or ex-members, all working in prominent positions of influence in the film and television industries. The starred names are also homosexuals." Cohn's eyes lit up as he glanced again at the list. "No extra charge," Dracula added and smiled.

"Some mighty big names on this list. Of course, we already know about most of them."

Dracula could *smell* the lie. Also the excitement that was now wafting off the Senator.

"I'm sure you do, but do you have the proof."

McCarthy had been staring at the list, his eyes alight, an ugly smile on his jowly Wisconsin face. "Do you?"

Dracula offered a slight shrug of his shoulder. "It can be arranged."

"Whaddaya want for it?" Cohn panted.

Dracula smiled. "Only the friendship of the Senator. And his committee, of course."

"That's all?" McCarthy asked.

"That and an expression of support for the good, *American* works of the Heuristic Mission."

"Support?" Cohn wheezed.

"Just an understanding that we're all on the same side," Dracula said. He turned his full gaze on the Senator, who nodded his head. He couldn't seem to look away from Dracula until Cohn whispered again in his ear,

"I'm gonna come in my pants," the little weasel rasped.

McCarthy looked down at the list, then up at Dracula. "You're sure about these names? That they're all certified reds?"

"All reds," Dracula said, nodding. "Red as . . . blood."

Dracula seemed no more with-it during Lydia's next two clandestine visits. A week later, having administered a fourth injection to him as he lay on the floor half under his bed, he reached out and took hold of her ankle as she started to leave.

"Father?"

The old man tried to pull himself up, but he didn't have the strength. Lydia had to grab him under the armpits to haul him to a sitting position. As soon as she let go, he tilted to the left and started to fall, so she squatted down to support him.

"Wh . . . wh . . . when?" Dracula sputtered.

"When? You want to know the time?" Dracula shook his head. He tilted the other way and she grabbed him again. "The date?"

Dracula nodded.

"It's, uh, the 23rd. Of November." Dracula managed to

raise one hand and beckon with fingers. Lydia understood. "1999. It's November 23, 1999."

Dracula's head lolled back, but Lydia saw just a glint of awareness in his eyes. And something else . . .

Pain?

"Father . . . "

"Who?" he gasped, raising his hand again.

"Lydia," she said. "I'm Lydia. I'm trying to help you."

His eyes had gone blurry again and she couldn't tell if he understood her, but then he reached out for her hand. She held it out to him and he grabbed for her wrist and tried to press it to his lips. She felt his fangs clumsily scrape her skin and knew what he wanted.

Lydia had hoped that the mixture of blood and drugs she'd been injecting him with would be sufficient, but suspected — and feared — that this moment might come. She knew this couldn't be what she was after, this wouldn't be a Dark Kiss, but she also knew she had to take the chance. She didn't think he'd be strong enough to do her any serious damage anyway.

Bracing Dracula with her knee so he wouldn't fall, Lydia tore open the flesh of her wrist until blood pumped out of the open vein. She pressed it to Dracula's lips, felt him suck hungrily.

She nervously glanced at her watch. She'd been in the room too long, but there was nothing for it but to see it out now. She let him suck until she began to feel faint. She pulled out of his grasp with ease.

The old man slumped to the floor, apparently asleep. Lydia took a hanky out of her bag and pressed it to the open wound in her wrist. As she gathered her things, Dracula's eyes opened, and for a just a second, they looked clear. He kept mumbling something as she ran for the door. She thought, at first, it was her name, but the old man must not have heard her right.

"Lucy," she thought he said.

Dracula had never had much use for fashion as such — it was one of those fundamentally human trivialities that simply didn't impinge on his consciousness — but he'd long understood the relationship between appearance and perception, the importance of looking the part that you played. It was every bit as true for a Magyar prince as it was for an Angelino religious leader,

Thus his Nehru jacket.

Ridiculous clothing notwithstanding, the 1960s had proven to be a rewarding time for Dracula and the Heuristic Mission. The decade had not begun well, the Mission was still under the cloud of Charles S. Williams too-close association with the late Senator McCarthy, but the Vietnam War had proved a blessing indeed. The rise of the protest culture, with its hedonistic youth hungry for experiments with drugs and sex, and desperate to find a radical philosophy that sanctioned their wanton ways, had been made to order. In this Summer of Love, the Mission was hip-deep in long-haired, unbathed, tie-dyed, red-blooded young men and women craving spiritual sustenance and willing to give anything — and everything — to get it.

Dracula could not remember a time of such rich and easy pickings since the good old, bad old days of the Black Death.

The Mission had grown phenomenally over the course of ten years. Dracula kept his headquarters in Los Angeles — the city felt *right* to him in a way that no place other than his native Bistritz ever had — but missions and offices of HM could now be found in every major city in America and a dozen foreign capitals as well. 'Donations' from devoted followers came in faster than the money could be spent. Dracula had even, finally, paid off the last of the money borrowed from Howard Hughes, though Hughes himself had gone entirely mad years before upon learning of Dracula's true nature. In his fevered craziness, Hughes had sought refuge among the Mormons, who regarded the Heuristic Mission with a fanatical contempt. Dracula suspected this contempt was rooted in nothing more than deep-set fear of superior competition, but he had greater concerns than a bunch of tabernacle crazies from Salt Lake City.

There was a knock at the door before Koontz walked on in. "Blood in Spirit, Father," he said, bowing his head.

"Blood in Spirit," Dracula responded. He couldn't decide which set of love beads went best with the Nehru jacket. It was an absurd decision to have to make. In the end he just put them all around his neck. What did it matter?

"He's here," Koontz said.

"Why don't you show him to the garden. I'll be there shortly."

Koontz nodded, but he didn't move. He undid the clasp which held his pony tail, shook out his hair, then gathered it up again and resecured the clasp.

"Problem?" Dracula asked.

"Are you sure that this is a good idea, Father?"

In times past, Dracula would have taken a man's head off for such impudence. Now he just stared at Koontz, who shuffled nervously, but stood up under the vampire's gaze. Dracula was impressed. "Why not?" he asked,

"It's just, I mean Timothy Leary does not make for good PR right now. Have you seen this morning's *Orange County Register*? There's another editorial. They have totally got it in for us, you know."

"They are insects. Fleas on a dead rat's ass. Nothing."

"It's just that we've got that hearing coming up before the County Commissioners. They are *after* this building. Linking up with Leary just gives them more ammo to use against us."

"Such enemies are of no consequence. This PR you worry about will be more than offset by the cachet that an association with Leary will grant us among those we need to reach, who need us."

"I suppose," Koontz said.

Dracula took a long look at his young aide. Koontz had come to the Mission three years before and had impressed the vampire from the start with his devotion and his intellect — a most unusual combination. As the Mission had expanded, Dracula found that he needed someone to help him manage things. Many others had been tried and found wanting — they no longer existed — but Koontz had passed every test and was

21

proving himself to be indispensable. Dracula found that potentially worrisome, but knew he could always deal with the problem when and if it arose.

"There's something else," Dracula said.

The young man looked down at his feet. "Yes, Father."

"Speak," Dracula commanded.

Koontz didn't want to look up at Dracula, the vampire could tell, but he forced himself to do so. Dracula was even more impressed.

"*The Times* is going to run a story about me," Koontz said. "I've tried to dodge them, but they've been after me. It's just to get at you, Father, at the work of the Mission, but . . ."

"Is it about Manson?" Dracula asked. Koontz nodded, but he had to look away.

Charles S. Williams had not been the first messiah in Koontz's life. Dracula knew that the man had been part of Manson's 'family' for a time before finding his way to the Mission. Since the Tate-LaBianca killings, the press had been obsessed with Manson, those associated with him, and anyone else in Southern California who could be tarred with the brush of 'cultdom'. Dracula *could* just cut Koontz loose, but to do so because the media had compelled him to rankled against his proud nature. And he sort of liked Koontz. In a pet-like way.

"I'll handle *The Los Angeles Times*," Dracula said.

"But Father, I . . . "

"Did you hear me?"

"Yes, Father," Koontz whispered.

"Then think no more about it."

"Thank you, Father. I'll escort Mr. Leary to the garden. Blood in Spirit."

"Blood in Spirit," Dracula said to the closed door.

Koontz shut the door behind him. He had a funny look on his face.

"Something wrong?" Lydia asked.

"I don't know," he said. "Something . . . isn't right."

Lydia slid up the bed, propping herself up against a pile of pillows. Koontz sat down on the edge of the bed and distractedly ran his hand in slow circles over the blanket. "Is it . . . Him?" she asked.

"Yeah. He seems, I don't know . . . different."

"Maybe he's sick or something. When's the last time he saw a doctor."

"He doesn't need doctors," Koontz said. "Trust me."

"Right. I forgot. He's a *wempire*, one of the undead, heh-heh-heh," she teased.

Koontz raised his hand from the cover and pointed a stern finger at her. "I've told you never to use that word again. Never."

Lydia stopped laughing, "*You* used it."

"I was drunk. I told you to forget it."

"*Forget* that Our Father, the founder and spiritual leader of the Heuristic Mission, is a bloodsucking fiend?" she said with a smile. Koontz's dour expression didn't change. "I don't believe it anyway. Christ, you must think I'm an idiot."

"Hardly. But something is wrong with him. He's looking . . . stronger, more alert. Younger, even."

Lydia was desperate to know more, but careful to hide her excitement. "Maybe it's just you. Maybe you've lost perspective being alone with him so much. If you'd let someone else see him once in a . . . "

"No. Absolutely not. He's made it clear that he won't see anyone else. Ever."

Koontz glared down at her. "Those are his direct orders."

Lydia shrugged and slid back down the bed. "Maybe . . . "

"What?" Koontz snapped.

Lydia threw the covers aside, revealing her naked body. She slithered on top of Koontz's lap. "Maybe," she whispered, "he's turning into a *verevolf!*"

"Very funny," Koontz said. He pushed her away, though not very hard. Lydia slipped around and attacked him from the other side. She unzipped his pants and he offered no further resistance.

"I *vant* to *suck* your *dick*," she cackled.

But her mind was somewhere else.

They were good.

They had to be to penetrate so far into the Mission. They took out half-a-dozen guards as they went, along with three disciples who happened to be in the wrong place at the wrong time. Professional kills: throats slit, single knife thrusts through the heart. No guns. Messy, but quiet.

But not quiet enough.

"You are going to die," Dracula said. "That is a fact as sure as sunset. But *how* will you die? That is still to be determined."

The taller of the two assassins looked scared, as well he might, having been nailed to the wall by Koontz with a series of twenty-penny spikes through his arms and legs. He'd already shit and peed himself and his olive skin had gone an ashen grey. His partner knelt below him on the floor, his hands bound, his lips sucking on the cold steel barrel of Koontz's shotgun. Dracula saw nothing but anger in the second man's eyes. And perhaps resignation. Dracula knew that the smaller man would never talk. He would have to be the example.

The smell of the blood dripping from the crucified man's spike wounds fed Dracula's anger, winding him up toward a state of frenzy. He hadn't eaten yet that day, and had to exert no small degree of his considerable will to keep control of his actions.

The heady, sanguinous odour overwhelmed even the powerful smell of garlic that wafted off the oily skin of both men. That smell, and the gear the men had been carrying — crucifixes, vials of holy water, wafers of the Host — told Dracula most of what he needed to know about them, where they'd likely come from. He'd just gone to considerable trouble to have one Pope killed and now it looked like he'd have to take care of another almost immediately. Still, Dracula wanted to hear one of the assassins *say* who sent them.

If they even really knew.

Dracula waved Koontz away from the kneeling man with a slight nod, Koontz withdrew the gun barrel harshly, cutting a gash in the man's lip as he pulled it away. The coppery smell grew stronger, sending a flow of current up and down the vampire's spine.

The moment Koontz took a step back, the assassin sprang up and straight at Dracula. Hands still bound behind him, he aimed his head at the vampire's midriff and let out a terrific scream.

Dracula sent the man flying off in the opposite direction with a flick of his wrist. He stumbled face first into a glass coffee table, shattering it into a thousand sharp slivers. Dracula casually walked over and picked the man up by his hair. He dragged him back across the room and threw him at the feet of his partner. The man's face was a pincushion of glass. A finger-length shard poked out of the gloppy remains of his left eye.

"This is how you *could* die," Dracula said.

The vampire reached down and grabbed the small assassin by the throat, raising him to his feet. He twisted his hand and held the man up under the chin, his fingers brushing the killer's bloody lips. The injured man opened his mouth and Dracula pushed his fingers inside. The man tried to bite down, but he didn't have the strength. Dracula tightened his grip, digging his nails through the killer's tongue, forcing his thumb up through the soft, fat flesh under the chin.

Dracula swivelled his wrist; right, left, right, left.

The assassin screamed at a dogs-only frequency as Dracula ripped the man's lower jaw from the rest of his head. His partner screamed along at the sight, forgetting his own agony in the horror of the moment. The killer convulsed in Dracula's grip, the jagged remnants of his tongue flapping in the air as blood gushed from the ruins of his face. Dracula tossed the asshole's jawbone aside and grabbed him by the crotch. With prodigious strength, he lifted the man off the ground, high above his own head, and flipped him upside down. Dracula opened his mouth to let the blood that poured from the killer's dismembered jaw flow straight down into his own gullet.

He held the killer there, draining him, chug-a-lugging the blood, until nothing more dripped out. Then he tossed the dead, spent husk away.

"Now," Dracula said to the screaming man on the wall, "let's talk."

"Lydia," Dracula whispered.

She gasped and turned around. The old man lay in his bed, the covers neatly tucked under his chin. He looked worn and tired, but better than for ages. His skin had been a kind of pale grey that first day she'd seen him, now the flesh glowed a pure white.

"Father," she said. She knelt back down beside him and bowed her head. "Blood in Spirit."

"Forget that bullshit," he said. He lifted a hand out from beneath the blanket, grunting as he did so, and raised her chin up with one long finger. "You don't believe a word of it."

She hesitated, but only for a moment. "No, Fath . . . no."

"Good for you." He tucked his arm back beneath the cover. "What have you been doing to me? The injections what are they?"

"It's beta interferon. I stole it from . . . I stole it. I didn't know if it would work, I just took a chance. I read about it on the Net."

"What? What has he done to me?"

"It's . . . you know that it's Koontz?"

Dracula narrowed his eyes, his face briefly alight with fury, but he still lacked the strength to even sustain his anger. "Of course. Who else?"

"It's hepatitis," Lydia said. "He's infected you with hepatitis-C. Seven years ago. He told me all about it. Bragged about it. It happened by chance, he said, but when he saw the effect it had on you, on your . . . faculties, he spied an opportunity and made his move. Ever since, he only brings you . . . food that's already infected. There's not supposed to be any cure for Hepatitis-C. For humans, I mean. But I read that they're trying interferon.

They say it has promise, so I gave it a shot. Thought it might maybe work on you. I've been mixing it with clean blood and shooting you up."

Dracula closed his eyes, but his voice was stronger when he spoke. "You know what I am then?"

"Koontz told me."

"You must mean a lot to him,"

"He fucks me," Lydia said. Dracula opened his eyes and looked her over again. She shrugged at him. "I'm good. Koontz says I was built for fucking."

"Koontz always had . . . an estimable sensibility."

"We'll see who fucks who."

"Is that why you're doing this, helping me? Is it scorned lover's vengeance?"

"No." she said. "Koontz is all right. I mean in his fucked-up way."

"Why then?" Dracula insisted.

Lydia glanced toward the door for a moment. The old vampire followed her gaze, expecting Koontz to walk in at any moment, but the door stayed closed. Lydia stole a glance at her watch.

"I want to be like you," she said at last. "I want . . . the Dark Kiss."

Dracula started to laugh. It began as a coughing rasp, but despite his weakness, blossomed into a hearty, chesty guffaw until he ran out of strength. Lydia felt herself turn a bright red.

"What?" she demanded, the blood rushing to her cheeks.

"The Dark Kiss! Where did you get that from? It must have been a Hammer film. God, I loathe that Jimmy Sangster. Almost as much as Stoker." He started laughing all over again.

"You mean you can't do it?"

Suddenly Dracula was very serious. "I did not say that."

"*Will* you do it?" she whispered.

"It is no small thing that you ask. No simple bite on the throat as the movie portrayals would have it. The process of becoming is long and painful, and often it ends in failure."

"But will you do it?"

"Why would you want such a thing?" With great effort, Dracula reached out again and touched her wan flesh with his death-cold hand. "Why would you want *this*?"

Lydia tried to ignore the chill that his touch sent through her body. She had to clear her throat to speak. "I . . . I don't want to change. I don't want to grow old and sag and wrinkle and droop. I . . . maybe Koontz is right. Maybe I am built for fucking." She ran her hands down her taut body. "But I like being this way. I'm only twenty two, but already I can feel myself starting to fade, losing some of *me*. I don't want that to happen. I don't want to . . . decay any more."

"There are worse things than death," Dracula rasped.

Lydia cocked her head and squinted at him. "Now that's *definitely* from a movie," she said.

Dracula closed his eyes and laughed.

Koontz had been preparing for the moment for some time. Just in case. It was a terrible risk to get rid of the old man, but Koontz couldn't take the much greater chance that the vampire was somehow regaining his strength, coming back to himself. No-one but Koontz had seen Father in years, so suspicions would not be aroused by his continued absence. Koontz would just have to figure a way around the lawyers and the legal problems. It might cost, but then there was always money to be found.

Given the Mission's connections and resources, it hadn't been all that hard to gather what he needed, unusual though it might be, and if any of the acolytes had ever wondered about his requests, none dared to challenge Koontz's authority.

He was Father's right hand, after all.

Koontz didn't know if it would work, but he knew what *didn't* work. He had, himself, seen Dracula drink holy water, swear on a bible and touch his lips to a cross with not the slightest ill effect. The old man had a positive craving for garlic bread and possessed sufficient vanity to spend hours adoring himself in mirrors. Koontz wasn't sure if silver would have any effect, but certainly the vampire had no obvious aversion to gold or platinum.

None of the classic methods seemed to mean much.

But then who would have guessed the damage that could be wrought by a little old virus? The hepatitis-C had laid the old man low where the holiest of religious icons had failed. So Koontz had his minions gather for him a vial of the pure stuff. Along with some Hepatitis-B. And some HIV. And to top off the cocktail, though it had been the toughest by far to come by, an unhealthy *soupçon* of Ebola.

Stirred, not shaken, and decanted into the hypo he now held in his left hand.

A Glock 21 was clutched in his right.

Lydia had just come out of the bathroom pressing something against her wrist, when Koontz fired six shots. The first caught her in the right shoulder, spinning her round. The next five formed a perfect quincunx in her bare midriff. Koontz spent a fair bit of time at the practice range.

Lydia fell to the floor, shrieking and clutching her butchered belly.

Koontz hadn't fed the old man for days, though he didn't know if Lydia had snuck him any snacks. He didn't think so, because the vampire was looking weak again. Dracula's tired eyes were riveted by the sight of the blood pouring out of the dying girl. He was trying to drag himself out of his bed to get to the red stuff, ignoring Koontz's cautious advance. Koontz fired off a few shots, just for the hell of it, tearing dark chunks out of the vampire's flesh and knocking him the rest of the way off the bed. Still impelling himself toward the source of nourishment, Dracula looked up, and Koontz was almost stopped in his tracks by the venom in the old man's eyes.

So he shot them out.

The vampire didn't scream, didn't even moan. He just continued to work his way across the floor toward Lydia, whose shrill cries provided a kind of beacon for him. Koontz stepped in front of him and pushed Dracula over with the toe of his boot.

He emptied his gun into the vampire, but the bullets didn't do much other than make a mess on the wall.

Dracula lay on his stomach, flailing out blindly with one hand. Koontz tossed the gun on the bed and knelt down beside the old man. "Blood in Spirit, Father. I've got exactly what you need right here. A final tribute."

Koontz held the needle out before him. He wanted to watch the vampire die, so he roughly flipped him over.

And found himself staring into Dracula's eyes.

Koontz froze — for just a second — but a second was too long. Just like that, the old man was inside his head.

Koontz saw things. Things he didn't believe. Things he couldn't imagine. Things he didn't believe anyone *could* imagine.

He started to scream.

Lydia knew she was dying, but so horrible was the sound Koontz made that she was distracted from her own pain. His scream started high and ascended to a glass-shattering squeal. She heard other sounds, too: ripping and tearing and sloshing and mulching. It was a near-epic struggle, but she managed to open her eyes.

Little red pieces of Koontz littered the room. In the middle of it all stood — *stood!* — Dracula, lapping blood off his hands with his long, pink tongue. He saw her watching him.

Dracula, his back straight, the effort visible on his face, strode over to Lydia's side, falling to his knees beside her. She took one hand away from her bleeding gut and held it out toward the vampire. His fangs descended as he licked his chops. His eyes glowed from within.

"The . . . kiss," Lydia wheezed. "Father . . . "

Dracula shook his head. He reached down and gently ran the back of his hand along her cheek, closed her eyes lightly with his finger tips.

He devoured her.

The flames from the Rhymer Building lit up the Los Angeles night. A third company of fire engines came roaring up Wilshire

Boulevard, sirens wailing. The usual crowd gathered in the street, watching the firemen's futile efforts to tame the blaze.

The fire leaped to an adjacent building as glass exploded outward into the street. The crowd gasped as one, all eyes watching.

A single figure, an older man who moved with the vigour and purpose of one much younger, strode off in the opposite direction without so much as a glance a back at the inferno, the ruins of the Heuristic Mission.

Dracula ventured into the night to see what he could see.

Introduction to "Limited Additions"

Here's another theme anthology story, albeit one which did see print. "Limited Additions" was written for Paul M. Sammon's *The King is Dead: Tales of Elvis Post Mortem*, a hideously unwieldy title for a little-seen book. The anthology was *supposed* to be called *Dead Elvis*, but unfortunately Greil Marcus beat Sammon to the punch. When Paul asked me for a contribution, he explained that there were two prerequisites: that Elvis Presley must appear somewhere in the story; and that he must be dead. Now that leaves a pretty big thematic range in which to graze. The result is a story which has nothing much to do with Elvis *per se* — having been born in 1961, I'm one of the many for whom the appeal of Elvis is an utter mystery — but which does consider the industries and death cults that are built around dead celebrities. (I steer the interested reader — wake up, that's you! — to my essay "Di/Crash" in *The Media in Britain* edited by Jane Stokes and Anna Reading (Macmillan) for a slightly more serious discussion of such matters.) I've always been a collector myself — though thankfully I seem to be breaking the habit — and I also wanted to explore aspects of that truly bizarre world. It's a theme I returned to recently in "The Man Who Shot the Man Who Shot *The Man Who Shot Liberty Valance*", not contained herein, but published in Steve Jones' *Dark Detectives: Adventures of the Supernatural Sleuths* (Fedogan & Bremer). I know, I know: enough with the commercials.

I believe that this is the third story I ever sold, and it shows a few signs of the over-the-top style I was more inclined to in those days when I was young and foolish.

Now I'm not young.

Limited
Additions

I AM A FUGITIVE FROM A CHAIN GANG PLAYS ON TV in the background. I've always loved Paul Muni. As an actor, I mean. From a business point of view, he's no damn good at all.

I sit with my back to the wall, stealing glances through the curtain at every set of headlights that flashes by.

Waiting.

I've tried three times to get to sleep, but my brain won't let me. Overtired, I think they call it. It's usually kids who are overtired. Babies. Isn't that what people say when a baby's cranky? Am I cranky? I'm not sure. I'm all alone here, so there's no-one to be cranky at but myself.

The negatives sit in their little metal box on top of the television. I really should do something about them, but I haven't the slightest idea what.

Next to the box is the white envelope. With her pictures. They make an interesting pair in their way. Him in the negatives, her in the positives. That sounds like it should have some deep meaning. Too bad it doesn't.

Another set of headlights, another glance. It passes by.

On TV, Paul Muni's in trouble. In real life, so am I.

Nothing to do but wait.

Kimodo had a friend who had a friend. You know how it goes.

The mansion was built on the palisade above Malibu, at the end of one of those winding, canyon roads with a seemingly impossible slope. I braced myself against the dash, certain that the angle was too steep and the Porsche would go tumbling end over end all the way back down to Pacific Coast Highway. Kimodo just laughed and inched the tach closer to the red. I swore I could feel the front end start to lift off the ground just as the road finally levelled out and a bald valet in a kilt came running up on the driver's side.

Kimodo gave the engine a final, noisy rev and hopped out. A second valet, also bald but wearing a different tartan, opened the passenger door. I grabbed my briefcase from behind the seat and trotted to catch up with Kimodo who was already walking toward the house. It was one of those postmodern monstrosities with jutting angles and contrasting facets that looked like it had been put together by three blind guys speaking different languages. It couldn't have been worth more than four or five million.

"Remember," Kimodo said again as we approached the door, "No names."

"Hey, what'd I? Fall off a lettuce truck? Chill, Sunshine."

Kimodo nodded and reached for the bell, but it opened before he could press the buzzer. We were greeted by a small Asian man in a French maid's skirt. Death's-head nipple rings dangled from his naked, golden chest and a brilliant tattoo of Curly from the Three Stooges was etched on his belly. His navel formed the Stooge's lips. It was an 'outie', lending the curious impression that Curly was wagging his tongue in a quasi-obscene manner. 'Nyuk-nyuk-nyuk' was tattooed up the man's rib-cage.

"Kiss-kiss," he said and wandered back into the mansion, wiggling his butt as he walked.

"Welcome to Wonderland," Kimodo said. He licked his lips, rubbed his hands and set off after the Asian. I felt a tug at my pant leg and looked down. A toothless dwarf of indeterminate gender was rubbing against my leg like a cat in heat.

"Blow job?" s/he gummed.

"Giving or getting?" I asked.

It shrugged and smiled.

Wonderland indeed.

*   *   *   *   *

Hollywood is everything you imagine it to be.

And less.

And more.

I could name names — I mean, how much more trouble could I be in? — but I won't.

You'd know them, though. Some were the faces behind the faces, the powers behind the throne, but most of the guests that night would be all too familiar to you. Like the beloved and avuncular network anchor with a penchant for prepubescent girls and concentration camp footage. Or "The Sexiest Man Alive" from a few years back who tithes a third of his earnings to a black coven and shells out another quarter to strange fat men for the privilege of giving them enemas. Or the teenaged sitcom starlet who can't have sex without a live audience *and* a laugh track.

I mingled for a while, exchanging small talk and nods and smiles. I spotted two of my competitors hovering at the fringes, also clutching briefcases and looking as uncomfortable as I felt. I imagined that breeders of thoroughbreds must often feel this way: the fact that you had a professional interest in the business didn't mean you wanted to actually watch the horses fuck.

I ran into an old acquaintance I hadn't seen since the Cincinnati convention back in '89. He was a mountain of a man, but his head was too small for his massive frame, like a lime set atop a watermelon, and he lisped like Daffy Duck. He was known around as The Zookeeper because he specialised in animal shots; mostly dog and pony shows, but you'd be surprised.

"Hey, what it is Keep?"

"I don't know about thith group, I gotta tell ya," he said. "It'th crowdth like thith maketh me wonder thometimeth."

"How do you mean?"

"Don't it ever make you a little nervouth?"

"'A place for every fetish, and every fetish in its place,' my mother always said. She wore fur underpants, you know."

"Live and let live, I know. But . . . all thoth bodily fluidth being exthchanged. Ithn't it dangerouth? Doethn't anybody read the paperth?"

This struck me as perhaps overly judgmental coming from a man spraying saliva filaments about his immediate vicinity, and who made a living selling photographs of women and dogs having sex, but I let it go.

"Well, there's a heaping bowl of condoms on the table there for what it's worth. And I have seen less discreet crowds than this. Christ, Keep, they're just customers and besides," I said, lowering my voice to a whisper, "they're mostly actors."

He shuddered slightly and nodded, then walked off shaking his little head.

I don't know what it is exactly that pushes people out over that edge, or why show biz types seem to go so far over the top, but I know it's something that those of us who don't lead our lives in the spotlight can never entirely understand. For me it was just a hobby and then a business, but for them it seems to be something more. It's not so much that polymorphous perversity is reserved as a lifestyle for the rich and famous — I have clients who are plumbers and stockbrokers and college professors — only that they seem to be so damn good at it.

Truth be known, the bodily fluids thing bothered me, too, but from the stories I've heard, these parties aren't anything close to what they used to be. Maybe it's all a part of the same syndrome, though; a sense of superiority and invulnerability that goes hand in hand with an elevation in stature above and beyond we lumpy proletariat. How else to explain it? I mean, these days I don't even like flushing the toilets in public rest rooms.

"Hey! Mr. Fantastic!"

I was approached by a young man wearing pre-torn jeans and a pink T-shirt emblazoned with a likeness of Angelyne, a local legend. I didn't recognise him at first, until he turned his head and I saw the gold, hammer-and-sickle earring.

"Oh, hi," I said.

"What the fuck are you doing here, my man? You're not here for the fucking auction?"

"Yes, as a matter of fact I am."

"I ain't seen you here before."

"Well, I'm branching out. Going where no man has collected before."

"No shit! Man, I wish I had known. I'm here for the auction, too. Not that I mind the other action, you understand. Heh-heh."

The kid had once been a regular customer at my old store, Fantastic Comix. None too bright as I recalled, but his father was a big mucky-muck at one of the talent agencies and the kid was spoiled rotten. I'd sold him a complete run of *Wolverine* comics at better than double the guide price and the kid never batted an eye. I didn't know his collecting habits ran in other directions.

"So, uh, what'dya got tonight?"

"Well, a variety of items actually." This really wasn't the place to discuss it. I had photos of several of the people in the room.

"Yeah, like what?"

I glanced around cautiously. "I specialise in fifties materials."

The kid grabbed me by the arm, nearly pulling me off-balance.

"Betty Page?" he whispered.

Lord spare me, I thought, *from the Betty Page freaks*. She had a hell of a rack, sure, but I could never figure out all the fuss over her. *Page-ination*, Kimodo calls it.

The kid's eyes had gone all wide and his hammer-and-sickle earring suddenly looked more like a dollar sign to me. Maybe I didn't much care for Betty Page, but I recognised a cash machine when I saw one.

"Nothing tonight," I said, and I saw the dollar signs taking wing and quickly added: "But I may have a line on something coming up."

I didn't really, but wasn't about to let the flounder slip off the hook. He patted me on the back and handed me a business card: no name, just a Valley phone number and a tiny Betty-in bondage picture.

"You call me first," he said, "and we'll do us some business. She's still alive, you know."

"I've heard the stories."

"Yeah, I got fucking detectives looking for her."

I nodded appreciatively. I didn't really care.

"We're getting a line on her. Gonna do some things when we find her, too. You bet."

I didn't much like the sound of that and feared he was about to expound when Kimodo caught my eye from across the room and waved me over.

"You call me first," the kid said as I pried his fingers off my arm. I nodded again and pardoned and excused my way through the guests to Kimodo. He was still eyeing the kid when I came up beside him.

"You know him?" he said.

"Old customer from comic book days. He recognised me."

Kimodo was squinting. "Stay away from him. He's a major freak."

"In this crowd? How can you tell?"

"I hear things. Anyway, it's show time."

I followed Kimodo up the hall to a small elevator which led to a screening room downstairs where the auction would take place.

"I still haven't met our host," I said as we rode down.

"Sure you have. In the playroom. The dude in the gravity boots with the hooter twins."

"With the *bratwurst*?"

"Uh-huh."

"In the Reagan mask?"

"No. Quayle."

"Ohhhh," I said. "Will he be joining us?"

"He doesn't attend the auctions. He just provides the facility in exchange for a small . . . consideration."

"The twins," I said.

"The *bratwurst*," Kimodo corrected.

* * * * *

I did okay at the auction, not great. Sold a nice Sal Mineo fellatio and a Mama Cass autopsy series. The Martin Luther King stuff didn't fly at all — old fashioned racism, if you ask me — but I hit pay dirt with a Jayne Mansfield nut who overbid for a rare, colour beaver shot, and a Garland queen who went apeshit over a Dorothy/Cowardly Lion doggy-style candid. So go figure. I almost bid myself on a stunning Errol Flynn wet shot. (Nazi or not, that boy was hung but the price went stratospheric because you could sort of make out Clark Gable and George Cukor in the background.)

The phone call came the following week.

"Mr. Fan-fucking-tastic!" The kid again.

"Yeah, hi," I said.

"Any skinny on the goddess?"

"Come again?"

"Four times a night, babe. Once in each hole. Heh-heh. I mean Betty. The pictures."

Actually, I *had* reached a contact in the Betty trade, but the pipeline was dry and the prices were inflated.

"Ummm, still working on it. I've got your card so I'll let you know if anything turns up."

"Whoa! Listen up. Are you doing the Vegas thing?" Vegas thing? I hadn't heard about any Vegas shows.

"Err, which Vegas thing would that be, exactly?"

"Shit, Mr. F., are you a player or what? Elvis. Vegas. Saturday. The birthday thing."

"Oh, *that*," I didn't have a clue. "I haven't decided yet, to tell you the truth. There's that other Vegas show coming up and I don't know if I want to do them both." When in doubt, vamp.

"Jesus Jerk-off Christ! Listen, dude: I need you to be there. I need a — whatyacallit — an in-between."

"You mean a go-between?" I asked.

"Yeah! A go-between. There's gonna be some people at the show. Connected people, if you know what I'm saying. People who can help me with this Betty situation."

"Sounds like a done deal. What do you need me for?"

"Ahhhh, these people. They say that I irritate them the wrong way. They want to do business, you understand, 'cause I got something to offer. But they're what you might call on the hinky side. Yeah, definitely hinkitudinous."

"Ummm, listen, kid. This really doesn't sound like my kind of deal. I just sell to collectors, you know? Not a lot of haggling in this trade. I want to do business as much as the next guy, but this doesn't smell so good to me."

"Hey, Mr. F! This is me you're talking to here. And I understand what you're saying. You got every right to see some profit margin on this action. You still got that I-Have-A-Wet-Dream crap from the other day?"

"Ummm, yes, I believe the King material is still available."

"Still available like my grandma's cunt. You can't give that shit away. Name a price."

I thought for a moment and said triple what they were worth.

"Fine," he snapped. "I'll *double* that if you come to Vegas with me. Not to mention the connections you make at the show."

It was an awesome amount of money and he was right about the possible extra action, but I was still dubious. "What exactly is this deal all about?"

"I'll fill you in on the way. I got a plane chartered for early Saturday. Out of Burbank. You're in, right?"

"I . . . I'd like to think about it."

"Shit. What's to think? It's *eeeasy* money."

The duck should always come down at the mention of those two words, but what can you do? I'm as greedy as the next guy.

"Can I call you back?" I asked.

"Listen. I'm just gonna assume you're coming. It's private hangar 23-L. Saturday morning, 7:00 am. I'll be the man with the cash."

He hung up.

I spent the rest of the day making calls and finally managed to confirm that there was indeed an event in Vegas on Saturday

— Elvis' birthday — but that it was very selective. Invitation only. Big money. I was suddenly very interested.

I tried to get in touch with Kimodo, remembering his warning about the kid, but was told he was 'in retreat', which meant he was off with a gaggle of boys and a couple grams of coke. I called the agency where the kid's father had been head honcho to make sure he was still there. He was, so I figured the kid had insurance against serious trouble.

Finally, I found the card the kid gave me and dialled the number. His phone message was a recording of flesh being whipped and orgasmic female grunts. Just before the beep a voice — the kid's — said: "Betty. Then. Now. Forever."

"I'm in," I said, sealing my fate.

ELVIS DIED FOR YOUR SINS was stencilled in red on the receptionist's tee-shirt. Below the words was a photo of the dead king on his porcelain throne. I'd once sold a not dissimilar shot for ten thousand dollars.

The kid was puffing on a Tiparillo and wearing one of those gaudy Hawaiian shirts with little neon-pink pineapples and topless Hula girls. The essence of Vegas-wear. He bragged about the fact that he had only paid two hundred dollars for it at a vintage clothing store on Melrose. I smiled and nodded and realised I should have hit him up for more for the King pictures.

"Name?" the dead Elvis guy asked.

"Buchmeister," the kid said and winked at me. On the plane, the kid had told me it was German for 'Page Master', and that it was the name he always used. I started to ask him why German, but caught myself and did another smile and nod. "And associate," the kid added.

Dead Elvis flipped through a sheaf of fanfold paper until he found the name and drew a line through it. He handed over a couple of badges which ostensibly identified us as participants in a shareholder's meeting for American Marmite. I was embarrassed to note that my badge was also made out in the name Buchmeister, but with 'Guest' in parentheses.

"All business will be conducted in the Penthouse Suite," Dead Elvis recited. "Please display your badges to the penthouse elevator operator and wear them at all times in convention areas. Viva Las Vegas. Next!"

The kid's big deal wasn't supposed to go down until late afternoon, so I had all day to wander the show while he was off doing God knows what. The penthouse suite was no bigger than your average concert hall, but there were only about 100 attendees. Except for the fact that the crowd was about three-quarters male, it couldn't have been more different from the Malibu scene. This group was all Italian suits and silk ties, with nary a nipple ring or tattoo in sight. The obligatory sex rooms were set up for all preferences, but they were discreetly set off from the dealers' area. This was a genuinely professional gathering and I was impressed.

The first panel, "Autopsies and Airbrushes: Ethics or Aesthetics", was quite interesting. I missed the "Elvis: Friend of the Animals" slide show, but it was worth it to swing a deal for some exceptional Natalie Wood nudes from her *Searchers* period. The "Kids Suck the Darnedest Things" exhibit was a bit of a disappointment — although the Buffy and Mr. French shots were sort of cute — and I'm so sick of Jim Morrison ephemera that I just skipped down to the casino for a few hands of Red Dog.

I was just settling in for the show-stopper, an Elvis Passion Play, when the kid tapped me on the shoulder.

"Pssst. Mr. F! Let's do it."

The kid was about as subtle as a tractor pull, so I hustled us out of the suite just as, on the stage, Colonel Parker was denying Elvis for the third time.

The kid had been pretty vague so far regarding the details of this deal. He told me it was a simple exchange, but kept changing the subject when I tried to pin him down. All he would say for sure was that he had once had some action go sour with these contacts and needed a beard to make the new deal work.

"Do they know *you're* involved in this?" I asked, suddenly nervous.

"Ahhhh . . . not exactly," he said, looking everywhere but at me. "As far as they know, my name — which is to say *your* name — is Mr. Piaget. That's French for Page, you know."

I didn't have the heart or stomach to break it to him. "And these pictures are of what exactly?" I asked.

"Not to worry," he said, "just some unusual Elvis material. Something I lucked into." He wouldn't tell me any more about the merchandise, either what he was giving or what I was supposed to be getting.

"You mean you want me to accept the stuff blind?"

"It'll be all right," he nodded. "I trust these guys."

I had a queasy gizzard about this transaction, but accepted that it was too late to back out now. It wasn't until the kid pulled up in front of *Circus, Circus* that he handed me the manila envelope.

"Remember," he said, "sit at the revolving bar on the arcade level."

"How will I know them?"

"Not to worry. *They*'ll know *you*. I'll meet you back at the hotel."

And he was gone. I looked over the envelope, hefted it. It felt like there were maybe half a dozen 8" x 10" photos. I flipped the envelope over, but the flap was sealed with wax, embossed with a likeness of Betty Page. No way to open and reseal it. I thought for a moment that the contacts probably wouldn't know if I looked at the photos and then resealed them in a regular envelope, but decided I was getting good money for the job, so I might as well just do it right.

If Vegas is America's glowing neon monument to the grotesque, then surely *Circus, Circus* is the zircon in its navel. I know that *Caesar's* is tackier, and *Mirage* and *Excalibur* are gaudier and goofier, but there may be no place in the world which better lives up to its name than *Circus, Circus*. On the one hand you've got throngs of little kids milling around the games and arcades, while just below, hordes of greed-crazed 'adults' pull onanistically on the one-armed bandits. What kind of parent would bring their kids to Vegas to begin with, I don't know; but to drop the kids amid the tawdry plasticity of this would-be carnival and then run downstairs to lose their college money at the craps tables qualifies in this bad boy's book as felony child endangerment.

I elbowed my way through the munchkins toward the revolving lounge, which was itself somewhat out of place amidst the clowns and calliopes, and sat down at the only empty stool at the bar. I ordered a beer and was given some amber coloured water that only cost me four bucks. This was another of the many wonderful Vegas perversities: sit at the tables and they'd comp you Heinekens till Bugsy Siegel came back from the grave; sit at a bar and they charged you like it was a Paris disco. They don't like people sitting at the bars.

A fat guy to my left was hitting on a good-looking hooker and laughing uproariously. He would alternately jostle me with his bony elbow and then apologise for the pokes. I just nodded and repeatedly said it was all right. The easiest way to deal with a drunk. I was a little surprised the bartender didn't have him tossed.

I was on my second watery brew, when the guy to my right got up and the seat was immediately taken by a tall, thin man in a navy blue suit. He had on a white shirt with a plain tie and wore dark Ray-bans. His wavy, dirty blonde hair was neatly parted on the left and he was immaculately shaved. I caught a whiff of talc and thought that he must have just come from the barber. He held a small white envelope.

"Mr. Piaget," he said.

I nodded. He didn't say anything else, nor did he look at me. I wasn't sure what to do. Exchanging envelopes with a man in dark glasses in a casino bar struck me as a not entirely inconspicuous thing to do. The fat guy poked me again, laughed some more and apologised again.

The Ray-ban man reached over and plucked my envelope from the bar. He slid his packet over in its place. It, too, was sealed and I quickly thrust it into my jacket pocket. He half-turned away from me and popped open the seal on the kid's envelope, slitting Betty's waxen throat. He didn't take the photos out, but peered down into the envelope and thumbed the pictures the way you'd leaf through a stuffed file drawer. I tried to look over his shoulder, but I couldn't make out any of the images.

"S'all right?" I said, trying a smile.

He resealed the envelope as best he could and turned back around, but still didn't look at me. He nodded, it seemed, to his own face in the mirror above the bar. Just then, the fat guy poked me again, very sharply. He didn't laugh this time, or apologise. And his elbow stayed wedged in my side.

It took a few moments before I realised that it wasn't his elbow, nor was he just happy to see me. I glanced down at the dull barrel of a silencer. It was attached to a .45 that was hidden from prying eyes by the thick folds of the man's bulging gut.

"Uh-oh," I actually said.

I looked up for the bartender, but he was crouched by a freezer at the far end of the bar. I started to get up, but Fat Boy nudged the barrel a little deeper into my ribs, laughing and throwing his right arm around my shoulders to disguise his actions.

"Easy, pilgrim," Ray-ban said. "We're about to take a walk."

The entire lounge jutted out from the arcade level and was suspended over the casino several floors below, spinning in slow, graceful circles. They could have just walked me across the diameter of the lounge and exited back on to the arcade, but I got the feeling they were waiting until our spot on the circle came back around by the entrance, to minimise visibility.

I looked for a security guard, but they were all down on the floor below. The bartender was still busy restocking beer and as I scanned the faces in the bar for someone who might be able to help me, I suddenly realised there were at least three other men strategically positioned around the room, all wearing sunglasses and plain blue suits, with their hands conspicuously nestled inside their jackets.

The lounge had turned another quarter revolution and Ray-ban slid off his stool and nodded at Fat Boy. Just at that moment the house lights dimmed and a thundering, musical "TAAAA-DAAAA" burst from hidden loudspeakers. A spotlight flared on, illuminating a sequined acrobat several levels above us. He was about to ride a tiny bicycle down a thin cable strung from the high ceiling, past the spinning lounge and down to the casino floor.

Show time.

Both Ray-ban and Fat Boy were distracted by the blare of lights and music. It was only for a moment, but it was long enough. I went limp and collapsed to the floor while their attention was focused on the performer. A second after I dropped I heard the muffled whump! of Fat Boy's .45. I started to roll as soon as I was down, but glanced up in time to see a bright red flower blossom across Ray-ban's white shirt. Fat-boy was already lowering his sights toward me, but I scurried off on hands and knees between the muu-muued legs of a blue-haired lady clutching a paper cup full of quarters.

I saw Ray-ban collapse onto the bar and heard Muu-muu shriek behind me. The other blue-suits were edging toward me with guns drawn. Fat Boy waved at one of them to cut off the exit to the arcade. Security guards from below were pointing up toward the lounge. It would only be a matter of seconds before they were all on me. Just then I saw the cyclist start his ride down the cable.

There was really no other choice.

I took a running jump across the revolving floor and hopped the low rail just as the cyclist was zooming by on his downward trajectory. With a breathless leap, I was airborne, and a moment later I found myself dangling from the handlebars of the tiny cycle. The cycle was actually attached to the cable — everything in Vegas is fake — and my weight flipped the bicycle upside-down, sending the surprised rider crashing to the gambling tables below.

The floor was coming up fast now. I let myself drop at the last minute and landed with a painful thud. I risked a glance up and saw Fat Boy standing at the rail of the lounge, slack-jawed.

A team of hotel security guards came up behind him and knocked the gun out of his hand.

Smiling gamblers helped me up and patted me on the back for a job well done, and the crowd was whistling and clapping at what they assumed was another great *Circus, Circus* show. I spotted more guards coming my way and, without stopping to bow, wound my way through the dense crowd and out a side door.

I could hear the lingering applause as I jumped into a cab.

I kept glancing out the rear windshield as the cab proceeded up the Strip. My heart was still pounding when I got out at our hotel, but I felt a crazy kind of elation, too, and thought that maybe I now understood the thrill of sports like skydiving and mountain climbing.

The thrill dissipated as soon as I entered the lobby and saw a crowd gathering around the immense fountain that stood in the middle of the atrium. It was one of those hotels with the rooms set in cantilevered walls around an empty, central cylinder. From the lobby, you could look up and see the cascading levels of rooms all the way up to the great skylights in the roof

I elbowed my way through the rubberneckers until I saw the body that floated in the now reddish water. I instantly recognised the pink pineapples on his Hawaiian shirt. I looked up and spotted a couple of blue suits scanning the crowd, pressing earpieces into place and talking into their collars. Cautiously, I made my way back toward an exit.

I didn't need a closer look at the kid; our room had been on the 18th floor.

I sauntered slowly through the parking lot, head down but eyes peeled for signs of blue. I had to get out of there, but didn't know where to go. My stash of buy-money was back in the hotel safe and my belongings were still up in the room. I thought it best to walk away from the Strip and call a cab from some secluded pay phone somewhere.

I was nearly out of the lot when I spotted the kid's Mustang. I worked my way over to it, but didn't have the keys. I took a shot and felt around under the fenders for a hide-a-key and nearly whooped with joy when I found a little metal box attached near the rear wheel-well. The joy quickly faded, though, as I flicked open the latch and saw there was no key inside.

It was filled with photographic negatives.

A convoy of dark, late model sedans was pulling up in front of the hotel and I dropped to my knees. More blue suits got out and quickly spread across the area. At a furious crawl, I worked my way off the lot and jumped down into a drainage ravine that was concealed behind some brush. Thankfully, the ravine was dry and out of sight of the parking lot.

I got to my feet and ran like hell.

I've collected so many things in my life, it's sometimes hard to keep track. A strange compulsion, collecting. Coins and stamps. Comic books and baseball cards. Rare books and prints and lithographs. Signed and numbered with certificates of authenticity and always — especially — in limited editions.

The motel is well off the Strip. It's pretty run-down, but nothing is too grungy in Vegas. It's simply not allowed. On TV, Paul Muni's on the lam, nearing the end of his rope.

I didn't have time to examine the merchandise until I checked-in. I registered as Mr. Verso. For the kid. My little joke.

I can't for the life of me — you should pardon the expression — figure out why Ray-ban handed the white envelope over to me or why he even brought it along. He obviously had no intention of letting Mr. Piaget get away.

I've been staring at the pictures for hours. I know I said that I never much liked her, but she does sort of grow on you. It's something in the eyes; a visible weakness, a tender fragility that's hard to resist. The kid would have died for these shots.

Oh.

From what I know, she must be about 70 now, but she looks younger. Not young, but attractive middle-aged. There are wrinkles and spots on her face and sags and stretch marks in her once taut flesh. Her tits look surprisingly good, though, and her hair is still dark. She wears it short, now. Befitting a woman of her years.

They're classic bondage shots. She's sitting on the floor in front of a nondescript backdrop. Her manacled arms are thrown back over her head, the chain draped across her shoulder and secured again at her ankles. Her legs are spread and you see all the things that you couldn't back in the fifties. The things that you so wanted to see, that were all the more exciting for being only suggested. Her head is tilted back and that beguiling Betty pout is strained, but it's there. As is the fragility.

Did they already have the pictures, or did they get them — get her — just for the kid? I'm sure they could have found her if they wanted to. No problem.

Maybe they let her go after. She's just an old lady now. Maybe one of them was a fan.

Yeah. Right.

Quite an interesting little package the kid was trading for his goddess. The negatives look authentic to me, but then you can't really tell with the naked eye. I can't imagine where the kid got them, but he must have known or believed that they were fake. He was a pretty good salesmen, though. He sold me and more importantly, he sold *them*.

I'm not entirely sure who *they* are, but I can guess. The negatives pretty much give it away.

There's only five of them and they're near-identical shots. Poorly taken with an obviously cheap camera. Russian, probably. Slightly overexposed, but in focus.

Elvis always looked good, at least he still did at that point in his life — 1960 or '61, I make it. Lean and hard, he was, with the haughtiness of a sovereign in his prime. The curled lip was still a dare and not just a parody.

Lee Harvey, on the other hand, always photographed as the weasel he was. Even with his arm around the King, posed and posing before the exquisite, bulbous minarets of the Kremlin, Oswald still looks like a creep.

Cameras don't lie.

Were the negatives worth killing for? I don't know. I don't know what they really mean or who would even believe them. I've tried thinking about the possibilities, but it just makes my head hurt.

I've collected so many objects and images. I've collected what I've dreamed about and what I've feared, living vicariously through my treasured things. And when I finished a collection, I always found a new one to begin. Limitless, like desire. Sealed in mylar and under glass, stored in acid-free boxes in vaults and cool, dry places.

Always owning, but never owning up.

"I'll steal," Paul Muni hisses and the movie is over. I turn off the TV. I look again at the negatives and positives, and sigh.

I wait to be collected.

Introduction to "Poets in New York"

Okay, this is a strange one. It was not written for any theme anthology, though for some years now I have very much wanted to edit a collection of fantasy/horror baseball stories — sadly, no publisher seems to be interested in the idea. ("No market," they insist. Bastards.) W P Kinsella, author of *Shoeless Joe*, the basis for *Field of Dreams,* writes the best fantasy baseball stories in the world. Baseball fan or not, you owe it to yourself to pick up his two brilliant collections, *The Thrill of the Grass* and *The Dixon Cornbelt League*, because he is a writer of exceptional grace. It is somewhat ironic that this tale should see print in a book from a British publisher, because if anyone in the UK has ever even heard of Lou Gehrig, it's only because of the disease named after him. Baseball is regarded with great derision in Britain, seen as a comical offshoot of the 'girl's game' known as rounders. I admit that baseball is not cricket. Thank god. (Cricket players look like a punch of prissy ice cream men standing out there.) Baseball is one of the things I miss most about not living in America. The rise of the web and the growing internationalization of media has cushioned the blow a bit, but it's not the same without the box scores in the morning paper or hot dogs at the ballpark. Or a ballpark period. Kinsella's 'thrill of the grass' is not felt only by those who glide across it in spikes and cletes.

"Poets in New York" may seem an overly romantic view of the game in an era in which millionaire players and billionaire owners vie neck-and-neck in Most Loathsome contests, but for all its would-be heresy, I think the tale taps into something at the heart of my love for baseball. Oh yeah: and alternate history stories. Like most kids, I not only wanted to be a ballplayer when I grew up, I also always wanted to be Howard Waldrop (but without the fishing).

Confused British readers are invited to write to the author for detailed annotations.

Or just rent *Pride of the Yankees*.

Poets in New York

"FREDDIE, *DARLING*, DON'T BE SUCH A MOPEY-dopy poopy face. Turn that frown upside-down and let's have some fun."

Santa Maria, Garcia Lorca thought, *I hate it when he calls me Freddie.*

But he didn't say anything. Lorca was a moody son of a bitch, but his mother raised her son to be polite and he could not bear to resort to rudeness. Gritting his teeth, he forced a thin smile to unfurl across his handsome face.

"That's so much better," Tomaso said. "Now, really, I absolutely promise that you are going to love it. And it couldn't be a more perfect day to spend at the ballpark. Even if it is up in the nasty old Bronx."

Lorca resigned himself to the situation. He had no particular interest in baseball; didn't understand the American obsession for the deadly-dull game with its lumpy, graceless 'athletes' and even more vulgar partisans. Federico was not much of a sports enthusiast at all (though he always did fancy an athletic build), but *baseball*, ai-ai-ai. It was bad enough the American newspapers wasted precious columns of prose on the lowly enterprise, and the city's squalid subways and saloons were rife with fans exuding endless discourse on the vapid sport. Now to have to actually attend a live performance. And with *Tomaso*, yet!

It was this last that was most upsetting, Lorca considered. He supposed he could bear an afternoon in the sun — the local colour might even help him polish off the final poem for the new collection that was already so late to the publisher. But Tomaso was just . . .

It wasn't that he *disliked* Tomaso. The boy was certainly attractive enough in that slick, New York manner. He was just more *obvious* company than Lorca usually cared for. Federico had no problem with *flash* — god knows, he'd never have gone around with Dali were that the case — but Tomaso was just a bit overdrawn. They had been introduced because of Tomaso's supposed Spanish ancestry, though Federico doubted the boy could even locate old Espana on a globe. Now he was stuck with him, at least through the weekend.

I knew I shouldn't have slept with him, Federico thought.

"It's on to the A-train, dearie," Tomaso said, taking Federico by the arm. "Then it's crackerjacks and peanuts and root, root, root for the home team."

Federico forced another smile. *Ai-ai-ai, Mama*, he thought, *why did you have to raise me so well?*

Don't stare. Lou repeated it to himself as he undid his pinstripes. He'd said it so often it had become a mantra, though following through became a little harder everyday and tranquillity was nowhere near at hand.

The clubhouse was abuzz with half-naked young men — *my teammates*, he reminded himself — and Lou had a particularly difficult time keeping his eye off of wiry Lazzeri as he sauntered bare-ass across the grimy, tobacco-stained floor. He glanced briefly at the picture of Eleanor taped to the door of his locker. His wife's photo always reminded him of a painting of the Virgin Mary that hung above his mother's bed. Cursing his diseased thoughts for the millionth time, Lou sighed, wrapped himself in a towel and headed for the showers.

When he heard the low sizzle of running water, Lou knew it could only be the Babe. No-one else showered *before* the game — hell, half the guys didn't bother to shower afterward. Lou, on the other hand, liked to feel clean when he put on the uniform. Out on the field he could forget the sick thoughts and fantasies that ate at his soul. Not that the rookie often got to play, but there was a kind of escape to be found just in sitting in the dugout, watching the action, waiting and hoping for the manager's call. The shimmering, emerald expanse between the white lines was an enchanted garden that the traumas of the outside world couldn't despoil. And his pre-game shower was a kind of purifying ritual that made it possible to gain entrance.

The Babe was another story. He was usually so hung-over that a steaming hot shower was the only way to leech the poisons from his decaying flesh. Sure enough, as Lou turned the corner, he saw the legendary Sultan of Swat plopped in a wooden folding chair beneath a slow-running stream of near-boiling water.

The slugger's eyes were closed and the butt of a soggy stogie protruded from his chancred lips. His enormous belly spilled over his lap and his fat ass drooped like wet clay over the edges of the chair. In one hand — out of harm's way — he clutched a can of beer, in the other his stubby penis. He kneaded the organ slowly, not actually masturbating, but as one might absently pet a sleeping dog. His teammates and some of the sports writers referred to it as 'The Little Bambino', leading to an endless stream of jokes and *double entendres* at the unknowing expense of the hero's multitude of fans. The Babe didn't seem to care one way or the other. Not as long as there was a full can of beer in the clubhouse.

Like everyone else, Lou was slightly in awe of the Babe, in spite of the man's repulsive personal habits. No-one could quite figure out how the drunk, fat slob could hit a ball with such perfection and power, but as long as he continued to lead the Bronx Bombers to pennants, no-one particularly cared.

Lou cleared his throat as he walked in, and the Babe forced open a bloodshot eye. He grumbled unintelligibly and dropped the heavy lid shut again. Lou pointlessly nodded at him and turned on the shower. The cold water was a shock, but just the bracer Lou needed. He soaped himself up quickly, careful not to touch anything sensitive down below, then washed the scummy film off his body. He refastened the towel about his waist and was nearly out the door when he heard the Babe's throaty rasp.

"Nice equipment, Columbia," he said and belched.

Lou blushed straight down to his pubis. He hazarded a look over his shoulder, but the Babe's eyes were still shut.

As fast as his dignity would allow, Lou Gehrig scurried back to his locker.

The game, much to Federico's surprise, proved to be an entirely pleasant experience. The fans *were* a bit loutish and the names of the teams a tad confusing — Tomaso had to explain three times why the opposition's socks weren't actually red — but the sheer festiveness of the event, unlike anything else Federico had experienced in the United States, was positively carnivalesque.

And the hot dogs went down a treat.

He didn't entirely follow the subtleties of the game — the players seemed to wander on and off the field at random — but with the help of Tomaso and some garrulously inebriated fans in the surrounding bleachers, he thought he had a sense of the action by the time the bottom of the ninth inning rolled around.

The score was tied at 2-2, with Ruffing still on the mound for the Sox and Bob Meusal at the plate. Long Bob popped-up weakly to second, then Collins whiffed on three straight pitches, all out of the strike zone.

"Looks like extra innings," Tomaso muttered, but just as Federico turned to ask him what *that* meant, the crowd let out a fearsome roar. Jumping Joe Dugan had slapped a single into left field past the diving third baseman.

The pitcher was due up next, but as Federico understood this was a bad thing, since for some reason the best thrower was also the poorest hitter. He began to remark on this to Tomaso to demonstrate his newfound mastery of the game, but was interrupted by the booming voice of the invisible announcer.

"Your attention, please," came the thundering echo, "now batting for Pennock, number 4, Lou Gehrig."

Tomaso cheered and began to clap. As Federico joined in, Tomaso whispered to him, "He's the cutest one. Check out that package."

To modest fan approval, Gehrig stepped up to the plate. Federico was too far away to get a good look at the batter's face, but not even the baggy, grey uniform, could disguise Gehrig's lean, muscular form. Federico clapped and shouted encouragement to the young pinch hitter who, he thought, looked just a little nervous.

The first pitch was a brushback: fast, high and well inside. The fans gasped, then booed as Gehrig stumbled back off the plate.

"That hardly seems sporting," Federico said.

The second pitch was a slow curve that caught the outside corner and Federico saw the hitter shake his head over the umpire's call. Gehrig's fine, honey-coloured hair seemed to glow in the warm sunlight.

"He is cute," Federico said a bit too loudly.

The third pitch was a gopher ball: a hanging curve that floated up to the plate big and round as a Florida grapefruit. Gehrig uncoiled like a darting anaconda.

He pulverised it.

The outfielder never even moved, just watched the ball sail over the famed expanse of Death Valley and on out over the left-centerfield fence. Caught up in the thrill of the moment, Federico jumped to his feet, whistling and screaming with the crowd, clapping his hands till his palms turned red. Gehrig slowly circled the bases like an eagle soaring above its aerie. As he completed his circuit of the infield, the deafening noise seemed to fade for a moment. For a magical instant, the batter looked up into the crowd and Federico felt Gehrig staring straight into his eyes. Then the spell was broken and the noise level resumed as Lou was swamped by his rapturous teammates.

"So what'd you think?" Tomaso asked as they filed out of the stadium.

"When do they play again?" Federico said.

The bar was dark and seedy, tendrils of smoke drifting around the patrons like pickpockets. Lou had been deathly afraid that he might be recognised, but decided the clientele were unlikely baseball fans. *Besides,* he rebuked himself, *no-one knows who you are, anyway.*

He'd first heard about the speakeasy from Meusal, who told countless clubhouse stories about the easy scores he had toted up among the ladies here.

"It's full of them artsy cunts," Long Bob had said. "A lot of Reds yapping about the revolution this and the workers that, Me and Poosh 'Em Up went in and hit the pink jackpot, I tell youse. We played it like was a couple of working stiffs railing against the evils of capital, and before you can whistle the national anthem we're balls-deep in sob-sister gash. Them rich bitches is just dying for it, you know, especially for anything smells like a real man. Don't let nobody tell you no different, the pink always comes ahead of the green. 'Course you gotta wade through the Hershey packers to get at the cooze."

"What?" Lou said a little louder than he meant to. Meusal looked at him oddly.

"That's right," he said, holding his gaze on Lou a beat too long. "Most of the fellas there are bent as rusty nails. More pansies than at the botanical gardens. That's why there's more gash than you shake a stick at. Hey, that's pretty good, huh? More gash'n you shake your stick at. I like that."

Looking around the place for the umpteenth time since his arrival, Lou was less certain of Meusal's assessment. He had not been approached by any women, though there were certainly plenty of lookers about. And while the men seemed especially well-groomed, Lou couldn't figure out which ones might be homosexuals.

He stared into his once-again empty glass and thought about going home, but Eleanor was visiting her mother for the weekend and he couldn't abide the idea of another evening pacing the floor of their tiny Brooklyn tenement.

He ordered another drink.

Federico spotted him immediately. He couldn't believe the beautiful young ballplayer was really here; had been certain that Tomaso's information would prove as dubious as his character.

"Are you certain?" he had asked Tomaso.

"Freddie, *dear heart,* I have a friend who has a friend and he absolutely assures me. Though what you expect to happen positively *escapes* me."

Federico didn't know what he expected, either. He had no reason to believe that Gehrig would respond to his interest — "He's married to a woman, for heaven's sake," Tomaso had said — but ever since that afternoon at the stadium Federico had been unable to get the first baseman out of his mind. In a flurry of inspiration he had finished off the overdue volume of verse — *A Poet in New York,* he decided to call it — but had since grown so moony-eyed as to drive-off even the petulant Tomaso.

Federico thought that the young man looked nervous, out of place. Not at all the image of confidence and strength that the papers liked to paint of the city's athletic Adonis. Gehrig's eyes darted constantly around him, though he didn't appear to be on the make. And while the saloon was chock-full of busty, platinum blondes and leggy brunettes, Federico hadn't seen the ballplayer put the touch on a single one. In fact, Federico thought he caught the man gazing his way once, and felt again the thrill of that moment — or had he dreamed it? — when they locked eyes as Gehrig rounded the bases.

Shrugging his shoulders and straightening his tie, Federico walked over and sat on the high stool next to the handsome Yankee. At the exact same instant, the two men raised their hands to order another drink and the backs of their fingers lightly touched. For a moment they glanced uncomfortably at each other, then smiled. They began a conversation with mirthful apologies.

When Lou awoke the next morning he saw Federico still asleep in the bed beside him, tendrils of Lou's dried semen laced down his chin. He let out a long heavy sigh.

And he smiled.

"Motherfucker," Miller Huggins said.

Eleanor's reaction had been much the same, although she had opted for a ten-letter word that was a more clinically accurate summation of Lou's new relationship. Of course, Lou hadn't told his manager precisely how Garcia Lorca figured into the picture. He felt that he owed his wife the whole truth, but not the New York Yankees.

"Lazzeri put you up to this, right? I mean, this is some kind of sick fucking joke."

Lou had always been intimidated by the two-penny tyrant who ran the team, but was determined to stand his ground. His voice quavered a little and his knees felt like runny custard, but thinking about Federico gave him strength.

"I'm sorry, coach," he said, "but some things are just bigger than baseball."

"Aaack! Flpppthh!" Huggins blurted. Lou feared the man was a hair's breadth from pitching an embolism.

"Bigger than baseball? You no-good, bastard, son-of-a-bitch. There ain't nothing bigger than baseball. And even if there is, sure as God loves the Yankees," — Huggins crossed himself — "it ain't fighting for a bunch of Reds in some goddamn spic war. Jesus on toast, man, you ain't even Spanish!"

But Lou had rehearsed the argument with himself a hundred times and was not about to be frightened or persuaded by the little man. He knew he could never completely explain it to a lumbering dolt like Huggins, but he knew that he was right.

"Out on the field," Lou said, "you always say how we got to stay within ourselves, not try to do more or less than we're capable of doing. How we've got to be part of the team. I don't know how many times you must have told me not to think too much out there, just to do the right thing."

Lou was staring hard at the manager now, not a trace of uncertainty in his voice.

"Well, this is the right thing to do. There's some bad stuff happening over there. I know it seems far away, but it's closer than you and everybody else thinks. Feder . . . This guy I know showed me some pictures and told me stories about what these Fascists are doing and believe you me, this Franco fellow is serious bad news. And it ain't going to stop there. Maybe today it's only Spain, but tomorrow . . . "

Huggins was looking at him like he had an extra nose. "I'm sorry," Lou said again and started out of the small office.

"Hey, Gehrig," he heard Huggins say and he paused in the doorway. "You really might've been something in this game. Something special."

Lou never turned around. He just closed the door behind him.

Lou breathed smoke and dust, but he thought of lush, green grass and hot summer afternoons. With Federico gone, he found that baseball once more occupied his thoughts. For a time he tried mentally reciting lines of the poet's verse, but it was just too painful to remember.

He closed his eyes and the sounds of Escalante's death rasps became the roar of the stadium faithful as he stepped up to the plate. He dug his spikes in at the edge of the batter's box and tightened his grip around the smooth, perfect hunk of ash. A mustard-stained hot dog wrapper fluttered above the infield and the air was sweet with the scents of pine tar and spent chewing tobacco. His eyes were riveted to the small white sphere in the pitcher's hand as the faceless nemesis went into his wind-up. The spinning orb expanded in his vision as it sped toward the plate, the red seams bulging like varicose veins against the pale horsehide. He lifted the bat from his shoulder, started to swing, sensed the contact about to occur . . .

"Incoming!"

Lou rolled off the mat and sprang instinctively for the window. The mortar exploded behind him, the force of the blast propelling him out through the empty frame and face-first into the dirt street of the smouldering village. The shell of the building collapsed behind him under the barrage, entombing Escalante and the other injured in a jagged crypt of rubble. Lou quickly inventoried himself for damage and finding none, got to his feet and ran down the road as the Doppler scream of another shell announced itself.

Lou scurried to the relative safety of the woods to watch the final devastation of the innocent town. The mortar barrage went on for another fifteen minutes, until no structure was left untouched. Incredibly, he saw Dominguez crawl out from beneath a fallen door that opened up from the ground like a gateway to Hell. But a Nationalist regular spotted him as he crawled toward a small pool of rancid water and blew off the back of his head.

Lou nearly screamed. It was too much like Federico.

The horrid loop threaded itself through the projector in his head yet again. Federico tied to a chair, the Falangist corporal pounding his beautiful face into raw meat with his immense gloved hands. The poet's once perfect teeth lay scattered on the floor about him like a pocketful of dropped coins. Lou remembered how Escalante had to lie on top of him, stuff a strip of cloth in his mouth to stop him from screaming, from running in to be killed himself. He replayed that final, unspeakable moment as they leaned Federico back against the wall, the three-man firing squad laughing as they checked their guns. Then the corporal gave the signal and Federico's head was so much crimson pulp dripping down the plaster.

Lou ran.

He raced through the woods only to emerge in an immense, cratered meadow. He didn't stop, but pressed his aching muscles even harder. He ran with his eyes closed, his lungs struggling to compress the air quickly enough to feed oxygen to his roiling blood.

As he ran, he saw not the scarred terra of dying Spain, but the flawless green of the stadium grass. He saw a ball arc high above him, sailing toward the approaching stands. He gave it everything he had, the ball coming within reach as the unyielding fence grew ever closer. He timed it and leaped, extending every tendon and sinew, stretching his muscles to their limit.

The bullet hit him and he crashed into the wall as the ball smacked the well-oiled leather of his glove.

When he opened his eyes he saw a soldier standing over him, a pistol aimed at his head. A red blotch spread slowly from a point in the middle of Lou's belly. He closed his eyes.

The soldier drew back the hammer.

(Lou heard the roar of the crowd.)

The soldier squeezed the trigger.

(Lou saw the ball in his glove, laughed knowing that he made the catch.)

From *The N.Y. Daily Mirror* (8/23/39)

"PRIDE OF THE YANKEES" SALUTED ON PIPP DAY

(New York) Baseball great Wally Pipp was honoured today by a standing-room only crowd at Yankee Stadium. Pipp was known to admiring fans as the 'Iron Horse' for his feat of playing in 2131 consecutive games, a record that many believe will stand forever. The lanky first-baseman was forced into retirement earlier this season following a diagnosis of amyotrophic lateral sclerosis, a rare degenerative nerve disease. A teary-eyed Pipp told the cheering throng, "Today, I consider myself the luckiest man on the face of the earth . . . "

Introduction to "Code Warriors"

I've been into comic books since the age of twelve, when my friend Kent Greene opened up their peculiar world to me by way of Marvel superheros. My specific interest in comics has waxed and waned over the years, but I remain a devotee and defender of the form, if not a great deal of the content. Superhero tales meant a lot to me as a kid, and I can still recall the excitement of that weekly visit to the newsstand to see what was out and to pick up the latest chapter in the saga of *The Avengers* or *The Defenders* or my favourite, *Dr. Strange*. And god how comics appealed to my collector's instinct — I still have boxes and boxes of the damned things I can't bear to part with. I didn't read comics for some years, but returned to them in the mid-eighties amid the excitement of *Watchmen* and *The Dark Knight Returns* and *Maus*. There has been some great work done in comics since then, but the medium seems destined never to break free of its superhero roots. For every *Sandman* or *Acme Novelty Library* or *Palookaville*, there are fifty dreadful superhero titles. Adults will read comic strips in newspapers, but efforts to convince sophisticated readers that the greater form is worthy of their attention inevitably founder in the shallow waters of caped crusaderdom. More's the pity.

"Code Warriors" is my own decidedly playful contribution to the revisionist trend in superhero stories and pop culture. Revisionist popular culture, you ask? Read my doctoral dissertation, is my reply.

If you can find a copy I haven't burned.

Code Warriors

S TEAM WHISPERED FROM THE WOUND OF THE
night's fresh kill. It lasted but a moment, like a rising soul,
before dispersing into the frigid air.

As I knelt closer, I felt the chill roll down my spine. Though
my nano-augmented exo-suit envelops me, protects me —
meticulously regulating body temperature against even the coldest
touch of The City winter — it could not shield me from the
sight of wretched evil.

Nor would I leave it do so, were it within my power.

She was dead, of that there could be no doubt. The wound,
deep and wide, extended up her belly from the 'V' of her legs in
a sick exaggeration of her mutilated sex. Her delicate neck, black
and bruised, had been twisted in an impossible, awful way. A
quick x-ray scan revealed a rack of cracked ribs and two fully
severed vertebrae. One broken arm lay bent beneath her, but the
other reached out, the delicate fingers groping for a helping hand
that never came. A single fat drop of blood dried upon her cheek.
I closed her silver eyes.

Her name was Patti Pike and I knew her all too well. Her
smile lit up a million screens every night when she read the local
news. What was she doing alone in Helltown at so ungodly an
hour? And who could have performed such an atrocity on her? I
vowed upon The Code that I would find out.

I scanned the dirty street and dingy slum roof tops, bringing
all visual enhancers on-line. I started in infrared then cycled
through all available wavelengths.

Nothing. No movement, no sign, no trace.

I patched through to NyXus, initiating access to Night Eye spinning in geosynchronous orbit so high above The City. My thoughts were relayed as instantaneous commands to the satellite. Its cameras locked and zoomed in on a ten-block-square zone around the corpse. NyXus analysed the area sector by sector, but detected nothing out of the ordinary.

Just The City. Quiet. At rest.

Lethal.

I sighed, felt the exo-suit immediately compensate with an adjustment in blood oxygen levels. Clearly, Bartleby had been fiddling with the damn thing's sensitivity again. I'd have to remember to re-initialise the wetware when I got back to the Night Den. I'd have a word with Bartleby as well, if it wasn't a waste of breath. There was no talking to him when he thought he was working in my best interests. He's been with me for years, God love and protect him, but his obsessive devotion can be as annoying as it is inspiring.

I glanced again at the dead woman. The blood on her cheek had run as it dried, streaking her face with a red clown-like tear. Crimson ice crystals were already forming at the ragged edge of her wound. I touched the transmit button on my utility belt.

"Nyx," I said. As if it could be anyone else. "Corner of Sterrett and Opper."

I waited there with her in the darkness and cruel silence, until a squad car nosed around the corner. I raised a gloved hand to the patrolmen as they rolled to a stop.

I stole into the night.

The light was on and a window cracked open in the great office atop Police Headquarters. John never heard me come in. Or perhaps he did and chose not to acknowledge. The Commissioner has been acting strangely of late.

He sat at his desk looking old and drawn, the bags under his eyes as big and black as The Raccoon's fleshy mask. His fine silver hair was crudely plastered across his bald spot and his bushy white eyebrows reminded me, as always, of dancing silverfish.

An unaltered cigarette smouldered between the third and fourth fingers of his right hand.

"You shouldn't smoke," I whispered.

He started, tipping a shot glass over onto his desk blotter. A single amber drop spilled over the lip, a trace scent wafting my way. My visor read-out reported bourbon and not a particularly good brand at that.

"Shouldn't be drinking, John. Sets a bad example to the youth."

"Hello, Nyx," the Commissioner said. The rasp in his voice told me that he'd smoked more than one cigarette this night, the odour on his breath that the tipped glass wasn't his first drink. "I didn't think anyone was watching. No youth, at least."

"You never know who's watching, John. You should know *that* by now."

"Yes, I suppose I should."

He righted the shot glass and took a last, long drag on the cigarette. He held the killing breath in his lungs as he stubbed the butt out. As he exhaled the smoke through his nose, a brief look of rapture shaped his lined features. Weakness in an ally is always painful to behold.

"You recognise her?" he asked.

I nodded.

"Any ideas?"

"Too soon to be certain," I said. "It could be the handiwork of our old friend Professor Gash."

"I thought she was safe in Derleth Sanitorium."

"Evil can never be truly confined, John."

"Evil everywhere, right Nyx?"

"That's right, John."

"And?" he said. I thought I detected the faintest hint of a smile dancing at the corner of his lip. Even the enhancers couldn't tell me for sure.

"And justice will be done," I said.

"Of course," he said. "Justice will . . . be done." He smiled broadly now, but there was little mirth in his eyes. They looked

. . . dead. I realised John had grown old and soft. I wondered when it had happened, how I had failed to notice. Had even John grown inured to the evil? Perhaps we were both suffering from the lateness of the hour.

"Justice must ever be done," I said. "The Code is inviolable." I decided it was best to leave, lest John embarrass himself any further.

"Don't you ever get tired?" he asked before I could clear the window. "Doesn't it all ever just wear you the *fuck* out?"

"Justice never sleeps," I said. "Not as long as there's darkness." I perched on the sill, relishing the sight of The City in the dying moments of the night. Dawn threatened as a blonde hair on the horizon. "Language, John. You never know who's listening."

I rode the decaying darkness.

"Nigel! What brings you here?"

"Hello, Donna," I said. "I came to express my sympathies."

Donna Hale rushed to shake my hand and lead me by the elbow. She was a typically obsequious media underling, but she ably handled the day-to-day operation of the television station. It was Hale who'd discovered Patti Pike at a forty watt operation in Nowheresville and brought her to The City, sculpting her into the leading anchor woman, and taking KNYT to the top of the ratings in the process. She led me to a chair as I folded my cane.

"That's very kind of you, Nigel. I'm sure everyone on the team will appreciate the gesture."

"The least I can do," I shrugged. "It's a terrible, awful tragedy. So young and talented. So beautiful."

"Don't I know it," she said. Hale picked her nose and perused the morning paper on her desk. It never ceases to amaze me what people think they can get away with when they're alone with a 'blind' man. I had to let it pass.

"Any idea what she was doing down in Helltown so late at night?" I asked.

"No idea at all." Hale had extracted a particularly messy booger from her nostril and looked for a place to wipe it. She settled on the underside of her expensive chair.

"Was she on assignment?"

"Heavens no, Nigel. Do you think I'm crazy? She was far too valuable a property for anything like that. The police have been interviewing absolutely everyone, but no-one seems to know what she could have wanted in that awful neighbourhood at that hour. Not even Michael."

"Michael?"

"Grove. Her co-anchor. They were an item, don't you know. Supposed to get married later this year. It would have been a killer ratings-grabber." She sighed, then added: "He's very broken up."

"Is he," I said, feeling a tingle.

"Of course. They had that magical thing happening on camera. Like Bogey and Bacall."

"Or Bonnie and Clyde," I said.

"Oh, Nigel," Hale laughed, "you're positively evil."

"Not positively," I said.

I allowed Hale to take my arm and lead the way down to the studio. The normally bustling set was uncommonly, if understandably, subdued. I recognised a pair of John's detectives taking statements from the crew. I could tell from their breathing patterns, the chemical composition of their sweat that they'd struck out. I shook hands and expressed sympathies as we made our way across the floor. Hale escorted me to Grove's dressing room.

Grove was staring at himself in his darkened vanity mirror as Hale gently knocked on the half-open door. With his red eyes and death-pale complexion he reminded me a bit of The Screaming Revenant. He stood up as we came in and quickly put on his camera face. The transformation was as dramatic as any I'd ever seen performed by The Martian Morpher.

"Excuse us, Michael," Hale whispered, "but Mr. Wachs wanted to see . . . hrrrmmm . . . that is, visit with you."

I could feel Hale's heart go arrhythmic over her slight *faux pas*. I reached out my hand to Grove who scurried over to shake it. If Hale tended toward the obsequious, Grove was downright fawning.

"Oh, Mr. Wachs, how kind of you to think of us in our grief."

"It's Nigel, please. And I am so deeply sorry for your loss." I continued to hold his hand as we talked. My sub-dermal nano-sensors aren't nearly as powerful as those in the exo-suit, but they do have their uses. "I understand that you and Miss Pike were due to be married."

Even without the sensors, Grove's reaction would have been hard to miss, though anyone else would likely have attributed it to grief. He stiffened and flushed and through his skin I sensed a sudden and massive spike in epinephrine levels. He didn't speak for a moment, but it was anger, not grief, that racked him. I bowed my head and leaned in a little closer — the blind are permitted to intrude into personal space in a way the sighted never are — and I took a deep breath as Grove exhaled. It was faint, but I clearly detected traces of cocaine in his system.

"Yes," he finally said, keeping his emotions in check. "It would have been a May sweeps wedding."

We exchanged a few additional, minor pleasantries before Hale walked me back out of the studio. I was through with them all.

For now.

As blessed darkness fell, I donned my second skin and once again claimed The City for my own. I decided to take the NightCycle for a spin, heading north out of The City toward Derleth Sanitorium.

Dr. Outcault, the Director, greeted me warmly. He assured me that Professor Gash was still safely locked away in the maximum security wing. He had, of course, heard about Pike's murder, but insisted that Gash could not possibly have been involved. The good Professor, it seemed, had just begun the painful grafting phase of her re-orientation therapy. Having engineered her treatment myself, I knew that the psycho-genital reconstruction would have left her incapacitated and docile. While it was conceivable that one of her minions had done the deed on her instruction, I dismissed the possibility as unlikely.

My faith in Gash's treatment and ultimately total rehabilitation is abiding.

As long as I was at the Sanitorium, I thought it best to briefly look in on some of the other sick supervillains: The Holy Roller, Black Narcissus, The Eidetic Man, Queen Quincunx. But all were safely ensconced in their cells and respective therapy regimens. Though the night is oh-so-short and I had much yet to do, I couldn't resist the temptation to descend to Derleth's deepest level and check on the status of my arch-foe: Mr. Jouissance.

Jouissance's cell is comprised of three-foot thick walls of solid bedlamite, a shielding substance of my own design and manufacture. Though the walls are transparent, Jouissance's essentially chaotic nature played havoc with the dim light reflecting off of him. Fittingly, it lent to his twisted psyche an equally warped physical manifestation: he resembled nothing so much as a runny finger-paint portrait of a man.

Jouissance is not allowed out of the cell; food and oxygen are delivered and waste products taken away through a multi-shielded, automated system. I'd learned the hard way the consequences of allowing him the opportunity to unleash his fractal forces on mortal humans.

No treatment was possible for Jouissance. No therapy. No rehabilitation,

He was perched on the tail of a Mandelbrot island of his own mental projection. The infinite recursivity of the set was dizzying, even through the bedlamite. I had to recalibrate my visor to compensate for the effect, but it still left me slightly nauseous. My exo-suit quickly prepared and injected me with a seven-percent solution of bismuth subsalicylate.

Jouissance ignored me for several minutes, during which I mused over some of our past encounters: the Interstitial Episode, the Lepidopteran Incident, the Couscous Crusade.

And, of course, the final, fatal battle at Wylie Point in which MaxiMan was tragically felled. Jouissance and his evil crew might have won the day had The White Wham! not recovered his memory at the last minute and saved the day. The Legion of Decency subdued Jouissance and his mutant henchmen, but it proved too late for MaxiMan. That day was as close as I've ever come to intentionally taking a life. Only the restraint of my fellow Legionnaire's stopped me from killing Jouissance on the spot and violating the very heart of The Code.

Max's loss haunts me to this day. Is there anything worse than attending a funeral for a friend?

Jouissance seemed to notice my presence all of a sudden.

"Yx-nay! Y-may old-ay al-pay!"

The Mandelbrot island disappeared, replaced by glowing Koch Curves that whirled off his torso like shurriken throwing stars. I readjusted the visor's filters.

"What brings you here?" he said with a wheezing laugh. "A death in the family, perhaps?"

"What would you know about that?" I asked.

"Or maybe a birth? Birth of a nation. Sometimes a great notion," he said and then sang: "Having my baby . . . "

"Curse you, Jouissance, if I find out you're involved in . . . "

"Hoootie-wooooooo!!" he shrieked as Barnsley Leaves sprouted on his nose and from between his fingers and toes.

"What. Do. You. Know?"

"It's not what you know, Yx-nay, it's who. Hoo-hooo-hooooooo-eeeeeeeeeyoooooooooowwww!!!"

His eyes started to spin in pretzel-like Lorenz patterns and he was gone, orbiting some very strange attractor in his mind that no-one — not even me — would ever comprehend.

I cycled back to The City, disturbed by the encounter with Jouissance. It was unthinkable that he could have found a way to breach the bedlamite, yet he seemed to know *something*. What was all that talk about birth? And about who I know? Was he just playing his chaotic head games with me or was he somehow involved in Patti Pike's murder?

I tried to put Jouissance out of my mind as I pulled up in front of McCay Towers. I secured the NightCycle and scaled the sheer glass wall of the building. I noted the presence of controlled substances in several apartments as I went past, logging the locations for a future report to John.

The lights were still burning in the penthouse suite as I swung over the ivy-draped balcony wall. I heard voices, but detected only one heart beating inside. I took a deep breath, smelled alcohol — Mescal — and bile.

Grove lay on the floor of his immense living room propped up against the base of a leather couch. An almost empty José Cuervo bottle teetered on his chest, and he sat in a pile of his own vomit.

Through teary eyes he drunkenly stared at a bank of video monitors, all offering up the same image: Grove and Patti Pike engaged in sexual practices of the most debased and unnatural kind. I quickly looked away from the perverse images, turning off the monitors with the universal remote in my utility belt.

Grove continued to stare at the dark screens. He didn't so much as blink until I wrenched the liquor bottle from him and tossed it away. He sobbed slightly as it broke, leaving the bloated worm plastered against the wall.

"Too late," he slurred.

"Too late for what?" I whispered.

"Sheesh gone. No more bouncy-bouncy, bangers and mash with Patti-cakes."

At first I thought he was referring to the dreaded Dr. Banger, Then I realised what he meant. "Language," I hissed.

"Huh? Are we on the air? Which camera?"

His drunken breath, tinged with methamphetamine and cocaine, was a mighty offence to me. I grabbed him by the collar and hefted him off the ground. Were my reflexes just a hair slower, he'd have retched all over my exo-suit.

I threw him back down on the couch.

"Why was Patti Pike in Helltown last night?" I growled.

"Bouncy-bouncy up the bum-bum," he sang and laughed hysterically. He grabbed an antimacassar to wipe the telltale vomit from his lips.

"Was she buying drugs for you?" I asked.

"Drugs? For me? Oh, thank you!"

I slapped him hard across the face, twice. He looked stunned, like a toddler who bumps his head, then started to cry. I slapped him again.

"Why was Patti Pike in Helltown?" I repeated.

"Bouncy-bouncy," he said again. Mucous slobbered out of one nostril as he sobbed. "Bouncy-bouncy. Not for Mikey, though. Meeting her *new* friend for bouncy-bouncy."

I raised my hand to strike him again, but decided it was a waste of time. Grove was weak and worthless; a pathetic sot. I'd apprise John of the situation, have his men bust Grove for narcotics possession. The morals clause in his contract with Wachs Enterprises would ensure a quick end to his career as anchor man.

I turned the video monitors back on: up the bum-bum indeed.

I slipped over the balcony rail.

Bartleby was having a go at NyXus with his Dustbuster when I arrived back at the Night Den. I've told him a thousand times that the Den is the finest automated clean-room in the world, but he insists on vacuuming everything himself. He wore a pink apron over his stiff grey livery and happily hummed as he cleaned. I sometimes worry that his sense of servility borders on the pathological.

"A message for you, Sir. The Commissioner. He requests your immediate presence at headquarters."

John. Perhaps the police had found something. Perhaps the case wasn't complicated at all. Maybe Patti Pike simply paid the price for her apparently adulterous ways. I sometimes worry that my own lifestyle tends toward the obsessive, and fear that I see conspiracies where none exist.

When I got to headquarters and talked with John, I affirmed that any such worries are ill-founded.

*   *   *   *   *

73

The Legion of Decency's official headquarters are atop the Raymond Building, the tallest in all The City. Burne Raymond, aka. Metanoman, had donated the tower to the Legion when he co-founded the supergroup with Red Rover, The Glob and Thunder Girl back in '64. Only The Glob remains from the original foursome — Metanoman himself having recently joined up with the Invictors — but the building was deeded to the Legion in perpetuity.

Normally, I would have analysed the chemical sample John had given me at Night Den, but Bartleby had damaged NyXus' molecular scanner — again — by accidently reversing the suction flow on his vacuum cleaner. The Legion owns the only comparable machine.

Though I was officially on leave from the supergroup (Ulti-Madame was kind enough to fill in for me), I still had the run of the place. HQ was quiet when I arrived. I stopped to greet The Quantum Mechanic, who was goofing with a standing wave front experiment, then headed straight for the main lab.

John said that the sample had been taken from Patti Pike's . . . nether regions.

The Medical Examiner had assumed that the stuff was semen, but when he subjected it to DNA-tests he got indecipherable results. No-one at the police lab could make head or tail of it, so John asked me to solve the mystery.

The first run-throughs were inconclusive. The gooey, white substance showed ample amounts of purine and pyrimidine in the nucleic acids, but the hydrogen bonds were arranged in a highly unorthodox matrix. There was a hint of an identifiable genetic code there, but it couldn't be human.

I reconfigured the scope range for the secondary analysis and immediately detected levels of both californium and einsteinium that would be lethal to any human host. I felt a queasy pang in my belly. It got worse when I confirmed the presence of titanium and adamantium fibres along with residual promethium. I had the computer cross-match the sample with known patterns, but it only confirmed what I already knew, though it was impossible to believe. Still, thoroughness is always its own reward.

The Mechanic had disappeared into his wave front, but his sidekick, Gluon Boy, was watching television in the lounge.

"Yo, Night-dude," he said, as I walked by, "a message came in for you."

"What is it?" I asked.

"I don't know. It was encrypted."

I nodded and started toward the communications centre, then stuck my head back into the lounge.

"Since when do get movie channels?" I asked.

Gluon Boy squirmed in his chair, phasing in and out of sight. "Well, errr . . . I . . . that is . . . "

"Theft is theft. Terminate that pirated signal before I get back. And no violent movies until you're seventeen."

I punched a code into the telfax encryption system and spoke my password for a voice-print match. I waited while it translated the message. I had a pretty good idea who it would be and wasn't a bit surprised when the screen lit up with MaxiMan's stern visage, one dark forelock curled, as always, across his forehead.

"The Citadel," he said.

MaxiMan's Citadel of Seclusion floats inside the ruins of an extinct volcano on an island east of Java. I signalled ahead to Bartleby to have NightFlyer, my VTOL Hyperjet, ready for take-off, and found him polishing the navigation unit with a toothbrush and baking soda when I arrived at the secret airstrip. Bartleby pressed me about when I'd be back for dinner, but I shooed him out of the cockpit and entered the launchcode. Within minutes of lift-off the jet was pushing Mach 5.

The flight to the Citadel took less than three hours. I locked in NightFlyer's autopilot and used the flight time to prepare myself for the confrontation ahead. I readied and tested my exo-suit and checked over all the devices in my utility belt. I spent the rest of the trip in tantric meditation, as I'd first learned so many years ago in the Al'aard Kenta valley of Tibet, readying my spirit to be the equal of my weapons.

The autopilot roused me from my trance as the jet approached the Citadel. I raised my shields, prepared for the worst, but a scan revealed no armed weapon systems on the floating fortress. I hovered above the crater in VTOL mode and gently set the craft down on the blinking landing pad. I scanned the area again before opening the hatch, but the door was open and nothing looked amiss.

I dashed out of the jet, across the runway and through the open bay door, sensors tuned to maximum sensitivity. I picked up the signature of Max's heartbeat and made my way down the lengthy Corridor of Justice toward the massive amphitheatre that dominated the centre of the Citadel.

MaxiMan waited for me just inside. He hovered above the floor, elbow propped on knee, head resting on fist, like The Thinker.

At first, I didn't believe it was him. Once, many years ago, The Deconstructed Man fooled me into doing battle with a near-perfect simulacrum of MaxiMan, but floating before me was the real thing. If the lab sample hadn't been proof enough, the scan I now performed on him — to which he silently acquiesced — was the last nail in the coffin.

"How can this be?" I whispered. Fear, awe and rage bubbled inside me in equal measure.

"I know what you're thinking," he said.

"I don't think so."

"Oh, yes. Now that you know it's really me, you're working out scenarios for why I staged my own death. Why I deceived you. It's what I would have done. Before."

In fact, that was exactly what I was thinking. With the help of a live link to NyXus, I calculated a 84.9 percent probability that this was all a piece of some master plan to thwart Max's arch-foes The Hollow Men.

"The Hollow Men have nothing to do with this," he said, as if reading my mind. I twitched at a jolt of line noise from NyXus. "In fact, they're dead. I have their heads and . . . a few other dangly bits in the trophy room."

"Impossible," I said. NyXus sent me a new scenario at probability 99.99 percent. I refused to accept it.

"It's true, old friend. And everything is possible." He smiled broadly and tossed the forelock of hair back off his face in a gesture I'd seen him make a thousand times. "*Anything* is possible once you break The Code."

NyXus squawked at me with what, in a human, would have been gloating, then went silent. The line had been severed.

"It told you all you need to know," Max said.

I stood there gaping at him, disbelieving the sight of my own visored eyes, the words in my own augmented ears. Had the earth ceased to spin on its axis (discounting the influence of Faultline, I mean) I could not have been more stunned. *Breaking The Code!* It couldn't be.

"'*In every instance good shall triumph over evil and the criminal be punished for his misdeeds.*'" The words — the sacred words — rose unbidden to my lips. I didn't realise I'd spoken them until I heard Max's derisive laugh.

"Don't be a sap *all* your life," he said.

I realised then, even without NyXus' supercomputed help, that he'd gone mad. I didn't know how it had happened — how it could have happened — but my duty was clear.

"I have to take you in," I said.

"Of course you do," he smiled. It unnerved me.

"You killed Patti Pike!" I hissed.

"Oh yes," he said. "Miss Pike and I were very close for a while, but she grew tiresome. And overly curious. Reporter's instinct and all that." His smile grew broader. "You know, my *alter ego* had been trying to get into her tight little pants for years, but the dumb bitch would never see past the glasses and slouch. She couldn't wait to drop to her knees for a real hero, though. In brightest day or blackest night, ol' Patti Pike'd do you right."

His use of profanity shocked me almost as much as the confession of his actions. "You're insane," I said.

"Am I? Who's to say?"

"The Code," I whispered.

He laughed. I tensed, ready for the assault, but he was laughing so hard that he bent over double and then had to float down to the floor. "Good one," he said, wiping the tears from his eyes. The sight of his degenerate state nearly broke my heart.

"And who," he asked, "wrote The Code?"

"Who . . . ?" I was flabbergasted. MaxiMan just stood there, arms folded across the blood-red 'M' on his chest, staring at me with the most enigmatic of smiles. As I thought about it, I realised I had no idea who wrote The Code. The Code has always been.

"The Code . . . is The Code." I finally said, but my head started spinning like one of Jouissance's fatal fractals. I felt off-balance, like I'd received a blow from The Aardvark's stun-snout. I tried again to establish contact with NyXus, but Max's damping field held.

"War is peace. Freedom is slavery," Maximan said, circling around me. "Codes are bullshit."

"You're trying to confuse me," I challenged. "Nothing can explain what you did to Patti Pike."

"Do you eat meat?"

"What?" I said.

"Do you wear leather?" he taunted.

"What are you saying?"

"Is there down in your NightPillow? Soap on your NightSink? Eggs in your NyxBasket?"

"Animals . . . " I started.

"Yes!" he said. "There are other Codes, Nyx: '*Have dominion over the fish of the sea, and over the fowl of the air, and over every living thing that moveth upon the earth.*'"

"But . . . "

I gasped.

"Or how about: '*Every beast of the forest is mine, and the cattle upon a thousand hills.*'"

"Hominah-hominah . . . " I stuttered.

"Not to mention: '*He who is unable to live in society, or who has no need because he is sufficient for himself, must be either a beast or a god.*'"

I felt something start to give way in my head. I fought it for all I was worth. "The Code . . . " I said.

"There are many Codes, many ways to live. Who's to say whose is right, which is true? Ours is a breed apart, a breed above. We are sufficient unto ourselves. Are we then to live as beasts? Or as gods."

"You're confusing the issue. Mixing things, mixing me up."

"Shaking things up," Max bellowed. "When you want a steak, do you cry for the cow as you suck its bone? I wanted Patti Pike. I had her."

"She was a human being," I screamed.

"The cow is a cow."

The pressure in my head increased. Something was bending, about to snap. "But The Code is The Code," I pleaded.

"That's what we all thought," a voice behind me said.

I whirled around and gasped. The Grey Archer emerged from behind a shielded section of wall. In a phalanx behind him were Pheno/Genoman, Captain Quasar and Matter Lass. A second section of wall opened up, revealing Dr. Bold, Ectomo and The Never-Never.

I was surrounded by impossibility. Could they all have broken The Code? I briefly considered that this was not what it seemed. An illusion of Professor Projecto's, perhaps. Or somehow the dimensional seal between Earth and Alter-Earth had again been breached and these were not the noble superheroes I knew and loved standing before me, but their Alter-Earth anti-hero evil twins.

"Think of what you've always wanted. Of what you could never have," Max said. "The world is yours."

A third section of wall disappeared. Curled on the floor was The Tigress. Not exactly a criminal, though hardly a model citizen, the Tigress and I had warily circled each other for years, bound in an uncertain orbit by unspoken ardour. I found myself aroused as always, by the Tigress' throaty purrs and deep, furry cleavage, but stood frozen in place until Matter Lass teleported me beside her. Her revealing orange costume embraced her lithesome form like wet paint.

I heard Max's fading whisper: "Beyond The Code, everything you've ever wanted is yours."

I turned around, but the heroes had all disappeared. It was just The Tigress and me in the empty coliseum. She nuzzled me in a spot I'd never been nuzzled before.

In my head, something snapped.

My exo-suit lies within reach, but I choose to pad naked into the waxing night. The Tigress purrs in her sleep, her fur still matted and sticky with my seed. The others have yet to return.

Or perhaps they have been here all along, watching.

The air is clear and clean and I breathe deep of its richness. The sky is a black velvet drape adorned with twinkling diamonds of promise and possibility. I feel a peace and contentment I've long dreamed of, but thought I would never find. I scratch my balls and fart wetly.

I smile.

The night still calls and there is much to do.

I think, perhaps, I'll have a word with Bartleby.

Introduction to "If Happy Little Bluebirds Fly . . ."

I honestly can't remember where this story came from. I never write short-shorts, though I do sometimes worry that my short fiction tends to be too long. I don't think I should say much more about a tale that's only a thousand words except for this: I've always hated the movie *The Wizard of Oz.*

So go figure.

If Happy
Little
Bluebirds
Fly . . .

A NOTHER FUCKING RAINBOW!
It appeared so suddenly, there was barely time to look up.
Selene reflexively scanned the skies, but the smirking, cloudless
blue was clear as mother's milk. She exhaled a tiny puff of relief.

It only takes one falling house to instill a sense of caution in
a person. *Tottering tin men* what a way to go!

With a grunt of exertion she summoned her magic bubble
and with the mousy squeal of a loose fan belt, willed it off the
ground. Following a couple of tooth-loosening, stomach-
churning bounces she was airborne.

Selene wasn't sure why, but she was drawn by rainbows like
a moth to flame. Or, perhaps, like a junkie to the needle.

It was the memories, she supposed. Of when the Sisters
were Three. Ah, wasn't that a time!

Of course, it hadn't seemed all that terrific back then. Quite
the contrary, in fact. *They* had all the laughs, while *she* did all the
work. Wasn't that the lot of the older sister?

Take the Nome King, for example. A strapping hunk of
granite if ever there was one. And hung like a mesa. Hoo-boy!
He'd taken a shine to Selene, too. She could tell by the lascivious
curl of his moraine.

"When I'm Good, I'm very good," she'd fluttered at him by way of introduction.

"But when we're Wicked, we're better," her miserable Sisters cackled. And the King was all over them like short on a Munchkin while she was left holding the wand.

The bubble shuddered and sputtered like Jack Benny's old Maxwell as the rainbow loomed ahead. She downshifted and hovered just above ground level, startling a pair of the little people busy making the beast with two backs just off the old Y. B. Road. Selene politely averted her eyes, but couldn't resist stealing a second glance at their dirty dance in the rear-view.

In the end, the disaster turned out to be the fault of the dumb-as-a-box-of-rocks King. Of course, that awful girl had a little something to do with it, too. What with her damned dog pooping just about everywhere. What the hell was her name, anyway? Gale? Storm? Margie?

Some of the details had faded, but boy-oh-boy, did she ever remember those beautiful red shoes. The King had given them to Artemis, but Persephone had just gone crazy over them. Selene secretly thought that they best accessorised with her *own* wardrobe, but of course she was too *Good* to say anything to the others. So she let her Sisters duke it out over them. And then the sky opened, and house fell, and the girl arrived with the mutt, and the so-called Wizard and . . .

Oy vey, what a mess.

By the time it was over her Sisters *and* the shoes had been lost. And though she was loathe to recall it, she felt no small sense of complicity for the way events unfolded. All those dramatically timed appearances to nudge the girl and her umb-day companions in the right direction. All for a pair of goddamn shoes.

Sweet flattened Artemis,

Poor melted Persephone.

Her sisters had moved on to other realms, fresh incarnations, while she was stuck here doing Good. Reduced to using her wand to work root canal on midgets, and clean up after the friggin' flying monkey people.

The bubble came to a grinding halt at the base of the rainbow, but refused to settle to the ground. Lifting the hem of her shimmering silver gown, Selene jumped the final half-foot, knocking over a small pot of gold as she alit. She ignored the coins, which were only foil-covered chocolate, then sent the bubble on its creaky way.

The seven sizzling bands of colour ploughed into and under the ground in front of her. Their radiant energy set her hair on end and made her nipples hard as rock candy. The air sizzled with the scent of freshly-cooked ozone and the seductive counterpoint of the muzak of the spheres buzzed subliminally around her. In the back of her mouth she tasted grape-flavoured Pez.

Selene reached out toward the arc's polychromous effulgence and thrust her hand through the before-bed-milk warmth of the pulsating colours. Each supersaturated stripe was as thick as an elephant's hoo-hah and triggered a different sensation, a long buried memory of when the Three were One.

Red: kneeling before Pluto to take him into their mouths.

Orange: snatching Iphigenia from the funeral pyre.

Yellow: holding court from Diana's silver throne.

Green: hunting Callisto for her betrayal of virtue.

Blue: suckling Endymion's fifty daughters.

Indigo: devouring an offering of dogs, honey and black lamb at a lonely crossroads.

Violet: driving a horse-drawn chariot into a flaming, ancient evening sky.

The rainbow bound the colours together just as the Three Sisters had once been joined. Ah, for the days when they'd made short work of that persnickety Scottish thane and his over-achieving wife.

Selene withdrew her hand and wiped the tears from her cheeks. She cried for what had been and for what was, for her Sisters and for herself. She looked back across the plain at the tinker-toy array of jagged emerald spires in the distance, then glanced at her watch. She had another root canal in fifteen minutes.

The *hell* she did.

She tore the satiny gown off her body and shed her highly unflattering but ever-so-practical underwear. With a running jump she leapt up onto the rainbow, straddling its raw, sensuous heat between her creamy legs. As she shimmied up the glowing curve, a small flock of chattering bluebirds fluttered along beside her. She reached out to the nearest chick, which obligingly perched on her finger and sang a sweet song.

She closed her fist around it, bit off its head and poured the cold blood down her thirsty throat.

She tossed the dead bird away and continued up the arc of the rainbow. She had no idea where this one might go, but knew that sooner or later she'd find the one that led her back to her Sisters.

Somewhere . . .

Introduction to "Virtual Uncertainty" and "Ghosts of Departed Quantities"

"Virtual Uncertainty" was published in the little-seen, revived version of *Science Fiction Review*. It wasn't a bad magazine, just a little too ambitious for its own good. The editor, Elton Elliott, was very supportive and I wrote "Ghosts of Departed Quantities" as a sequel for him. Sadly, the magazine folded before it could be published and, as the cyberpunk moment had passed, I never bothered to do anything with the tale. Back when I wrote the stories I harboured thoughts of turning them into a novel, but that never happened either. Anybody want to buy a cyberpunk book?

Although the obvious cyberpunk influence is pretty strong (actually, there's no punk here, just cyber) — not to mention the Chandler — I think these stories are most typical of my fondness for mixing genres, especially detective plus what-have-you. My three novels to date are generally categorized as horror, though for whatever gruesomeness they contain, all are rooted in crime/detective structures. My forthcoming novel-length work will move further into straight crime writing, for reasons both aesthetic and commercial. It pains me some to say it, but over the past half-dozen years there has been far better work written in crime fiction than in horror.

Nonetheless, I love reading books and stories which mix and match genres, even if publishers and booksellers hate such queer beasts. I continue to believe that readers are perfectly receptive to such work, but convincing the industry that readers aren't as stupid as publishers think they are is a job for a bigger writer than me (though you'd think the bestselling success of genre mixers like Dean Koontz and Michael Crichton would be evidence enough). A few of the VR elements here, especially in "Virtual Uncertainty", seem a little hokey nearly a decade down the road, but as stories I think both hold up pretty well. And that's the main thing.

Virtual Uncertainty

MCSWEEN WAS SITTING ON A FOLDING CHAIR by the bed staring at the corpse when I walked in. The coroner had been through and covered her with a blanket, but McSween pulled it back below her knees. She was naked, the pale dead skin almost glowing against the black satin sheet.

She was a little thing, made even smaller by death's quietude. Her hands were folded over her abdomen just above the patch of red, heart-shaped pubic hair. A series of small scars marked the skin on her thighs and around the brown nipples of her slight, boyish chest. Her face was as wide as it was long with thin, cracked lips and a crooked nose. Her forehead and cheeks were pockmarked with acne scars and her upper lip showed the bleached fuzz of facial hair.

Linkposts jutted from beneath her squarish ears and I knew there'd be a throughjack at the base of her neck. A Link-rig dangled from the night table beside the bed, still connected to a portable Virtual Access Device that sat on the floor. McSween didn't look at me, just stared blankly at her face. I cleared my throat.

"I see you," he said, his voice as dead the girl.

"And I spy with my little eye . . . a stiff!"

"A kinky stiff," he said and reaching over ran a finger across the scarred skin around her breasts. "Cigarette burns."

McSween let his hand linger on her breast a little too long, but I just went over and examined the VAD. It was a state-of-the-art model that I couldn't afford on ten cops' salaries. It was still powered up and jacked into the Linkline, but the screen was dead and the processor wouldn't even run through basic diagnostics. I powered it down then up again, but it was garbage. It would have to be autopsied by Comp-SID, but I was sure they'd find nothing but seared chips and overloads. I glanced back at the body — McSween was rubbing his thumb over the girl's burned thigh — saw no sign of physical damage. It had to be a flameout.

I sat on the edge of the bed beside the girl's head. I checked the Linkposts and lifted her head to examine the jack, found the connections were all fried, reeking faintly of carbon. I squeezed an eyelid open and saw that the iris had burst violently into the blackened sclera. McSween was tracing the outline of the heart between her legs with his finger.

"Ahh, Mac . . . "

"Hurm?" he said distractedly.

"Ixnay on the iffstay."

"Oh," he said sort of wistfully. "Right. Thanks."

I took a walk around the room, examining the pictures on the walls, mostly reproductions of classic Fishl paintings. "I'd say our Miss Cupid took a little Virtual stroll where she didn't belong," I said.

"Fell asleep in the deadly poppy fields," McSween mused and sniffed tentatively at his finger.

"How's that?"

McSween just shook his head. He stood up and pulled the sheet back over the body. The corpse must have retained a slight charge because it clung tightly to the contours of her form. McSween gently fluffed it and smoothed it out, but the residual static electricity bunched the sheet up again. He gave up and pulled a glassine evidence envelope out of his coat pocket and handed it to me. He sat back down and stared some more at the covered form.

The envelope contained a corporate picture ID in the name of Aimee Dissault. It identified the dead girl as Virtual Design Coordinator for Grundrisse-Rand. Her Virtual clearance was alpha/omega: practically unrestricted. She could legally travel almost anywhere on the Link, and was certainly skilled enough to break security anyplace else she might want to go. It was inconceivable that someone with her status could accidentally trip a burn.

I stared at the tiny holo-image embedded in the corner of the card. She took a lousy picture. I looked back over at the dead shape on the bed.

"I know this name," I said.

"Uh-huh."

I thought for a minute. "Harlan Dissault," I said.

"Uh-huh."

"C.E.O., Grundrisse-Rand U.S."

"Uh-huh."

"Shit."

"Uh-huh."

McSween stood up. He took a last longing glance at the body then walked to the door.

"Where are you going?" I asked.

He paused to inspect the ceiling.

"Retirement," he said and then was gone.

The department's VAD was at least ten times more powerful than my personal unit, but I preferred Linking through my own gear. I had fine-tuned the jump mechanism to maximise concordance with my synaptic structure. It slowed me down a little in terms of accessing and traversing new Virtual sectors, but gave me an edge in jump-outs that could be the difference between a safe Link-off and a fatal flameout on backburn of the type that apparently killed Aimee Dissault. I've been singed a couple-three times, but never damaged worse than a little short-term memory loss.

McSween got clearance for me to visit the dead girl's datastack in the Grundrisse-Rand archiplex. I could have hacked through the Grundrisse security with a little effort — personnel datastacks would be designed for relatively easy access — but having the precise coordinates saved me a bit of work.

The Grundrisse AI had a very traditional picting function. Most of the big Multicorps were as conservative, in their Virtual representations as they'd ever been in their physical trappings. I encountered the archiplex picted as an enormous bank vault with a massive array of safety deposit boxes containing individual datastacks. I jumped in within a central chamber, at the sealed door to a second high-security vault. I was met there by a fabricant curator, looking much like I'd always imagined Bob Cratchit, prim and stiff in a plain dark suit. He sniffled incessantly and was accompanied by an autonomous security program picting as two 150-pound bull mastiffs. The dogs had conspicuously, absurdly large genitals, which led me to believe that someone in corporate programming had a sense of humour.

I followed Cratchit into the small vault where he pulled out a huge ring of keys, mumbling slightly to himself as he sorted through them. One dog stood immediately behind me, drooling slightly on my shoe. I used the wait to access a program I'd frozen in personal-RAM before the jump. The curator finally found the right key and inserted it into the door of a large box, stepping aside as soon as it was open.

After all these years even I don't really understand Virtual, nor, I think, does anyone else. While the basic fabric of the cyberspace is maintained by thousands of Linked AIs and VADS, it is the human interactions that enable the picts to take on specific appearances.

The general contours of the Grundrisse archiplex were generated according to the algorithms of their AI, but no-one else accessing it would see it quite the same way as I did. Where I found safety deposit boxes, someone else might see file drawers; where I saw a couple of ugly watchdogs, another visitor might encounter Burke and Hare.

Or Hope and Crosby.

The stored data was always the same, of course — otherwise the system would be useless — but the Virtual world was quite elastic to personality, despite the best efforts to standardise it.

The variance in picts was one of the joys of travelling in Virtual and the reason psychoMcLuhanism had become so much the rage among analysts.

Inside the box I found a sheaf of papers and photographs which I only needed to touch to fully access, but which I nonetheless found myself leafing through as if they were real: old habits are hard to break. The G-R execs must have assumed that I'd be some dumb L.A.V. cop who couldn't read subtleties in Virtual. Page after page of data had huge chunks blacked out or written over. Photographs had been retouched and airbrushed and in some cases literally (well, Virtually-literally) cut up.

I reached back toward the open box and heard the dogs growl in unison. They were both crouched and ready to spring. I lowered my hand and simultaneously unfroze the counter-security program I had waiting in RAM. With a look of considerable surprise, Bob Cratchit repicted into a female mastiff in heat. The males responded instantly to her odour and with growls of delight padded toward her. Cratchit briefly spun his new paws on the slick bank floor in panic, then tore out of the vault and down the data corridor, the aroused males in close pursuit. It took me only a few seconds to circumvent the hidden security codes on the girl's files and I accessed immediately. I jumped out as I heard two distant howls: one of primal pleasure, the other of distinct discomfort.

I slept for a couple of hours, as usual, after Link-off. I didn't have to — it had been a pretty short jump — but even relatively brief stays in Virtual can leave you feeling like you've driven through a rainy night in a car with busted wipers.

Supposedly, it has something to do with a disruption of basic schema hierarchies, but being a typical techie I've never had the patience for that cognitive-psych stuff. They say there's no permanent damage, but then they used to say fibre would help prevent cancer. All I know is that once, jumping out after 33 continuous real-hours tracking in Virtual, I Linked-off convinced that I was Judy Garland in *A Star is Born*. I've been told that I delivered the 'This is Mrs. Norman Maine' line rather convincingly, too.

To be safe I had dumped the accessed data on Dissault into hard memory before I Linked-off, and although the information was still pretty clear in my mind I Linked into the file to maximise efficiency. Travelling in Virtual changes the way you think: the linear processing capabilities nurtured by old text and screen-based interactions aren't of much use, you have to think omnidirectionally. It's like the difference between standing under a continuous stream of water that's pouring out of a spigot and being dropped into the middle a vast swimming pool. The data is all around you, open to processing and analysis in any of an infinite number of ways. I brought my old friend Jim Beam out of the cupboard and taking a little of his sage advice, began dog-paddling through the volume of data on the dead girl.

As an apostle of history I am always tempted to sort chronologically, believing the past is almost invariably the most reliable predictor of the present, but as a cop I can't help but check one thing first: citizen or player.

My access of the bowdlerised data revealed no criminal record. It didn't figure that a corporate Virtual exec would be dirty in any traceable way. I filtered the censored data and found Dissault was cleaner than a winter's day. As I brushed the field I thought I felt a glitch in the picting, but I couldn't pin it down and went on.

I ran a search down the corporate trail and found that Aimee had been working for her daddy's company since she was 13. She was a computer brat, working her way up through the AI/Virtual division very quickly. She displayed an obvious affinity for cyberspace, logging an astonishing amount of Link-time which continued to multiply as she got older.

I switched to personal data and found she had completed Virtual University by the age of 12 and finished her V.Ph.D only 18 months after that. Her standard test scores were phenomenal, quite nearly perfect. She had published a series of well-regarded articles and treatises as a teenager and had turned down multiple offers for tenured positions at a number of top physical universities.

There was a visual record of her as well and I lapsed the images to watch her develop from newborn to woman. Although she was naked in the imaging, Dissault must have been aware that her file could be readily accessed, because starting from the age of 12 secondary sex characteristics were blocked out with black bands, like the eyes in old pornographic photos. In the final image, picted at age 24 apparently not too long before her death, Dissault looked not much better than she did as a corpse. There was something harsh and cold about her, a visible discomfort with herself or perhaps with her body, though she wasn't strictly unattractive. I also sensed another slight flaw in the picting.

I ran through data on personal relationships, but found very little. Her mother had died of AIDS in HIVe exile when Aimee was three. Unmarried, no children, no indication of long or even short-term romantic relationships. Not even a dog.

I accessed psychographic records and again found nearly textbook scores on MMPI, V-Binet and Rokeach scales.

I checked her physical medical records, saw a perfectly normal medical history: inoculations, standard childhood maladies, a broken finger at age 6.

And another flaw in the Virtual pict.

The file was for shit.

I was about to Link-off when I got nudged by a couple of messages waiting in the mail queue. I brushed them both, saw they were the autopsy results for the girl and her VAD and merged them into a single file for access.

Just as I figured, both human and machine suffered catastrophic synaptic burns. I activated the holo-record of the physical autopsy and watched over the M.E.'s shoulder as she lasered open the girl's head. She cut through the skull and neatly bisected the cerebral cortex, kibitzing with her assistant all the while about her dinner plans.

As the retractor brushed against the thalamus I heard her sudden intake of breath. The assistant was leaning over, too, saying "wow" over and over. I stepped around the slab for a better look inside the girl's head and froze the image: Her entire upper limbic system had been liquified, the thalamus and hyperthalamus reduced to a chunky, grey paste that looked like rancid pea soup. A full chemical analysis would take three working days *with* an expedite stamp on the file.

I had never heard of anything quite like it and a fast scan through the rest of the report indicated it was new to the M.E. as well. I shelled out of the file and Linked into the pathology archive. I sent a Klone out to search for any similar pathology results and shelled back into the autopsy. The M.E. reported that the damage was too severe for any attempt at synaptic reconstruction. She offered a rough guess as to the extremity of the flameout necessary to account for the damage and suggested that a backburn of that intensity could undoubtedly be traced in the Link record.

Everybody's a fucking detective.

The VAD autopsy confirmed the physical: complete burn of all chips and integrated circuitry. It also revealed the presence of a number of designer chips. They were burned as well, beyond any possible diagnoses, and the housings were all unmarked. Knowing Dissault's background I had to assume that they were her own handiwork. They could have been just about anything from sex enhancers to Virtual bodyguards, but I thought I had an idea.

I stored the file and jumped into the central archiplex for Criminal Records. With a master access code I was able to override basic picting and drop directly into Aimee Dissault's datastack. The record matched her file in the Grundrisse archiplex until I implemented a pixel-by-pixel search and found the patched hole I knew had to exist.

It was a clean job, much more neatly sealed than the datastack at Grundrisse, but then the police file was more readily available to general scrutiny. I pried open the patch and dropped a Canary down the hole to test for traps and alarms. It came back alive so I shot a Mole through the line but it had been cauterised just beyond the datastack.

I jumped out and found my Klone waiting for me. There was no record of anyone ever suffering a similar limbic melt-down on a backburn or any Link-related death. I dedifferentiated the Klone and blew a worm back along its trail to eat its trace then swallow itself.

It was time for some old-fashioned *physical* detective work.

The Grundrisse-Rand Building was erected during the brief but unfortunate era of corporate sponsored deconstructivist architecture. There were no right angles visible on the building's exterior and the steel superstructure was deliberately left exposed and unfinished. The entrance was a revolving door hinged on the horizontal axis and the lobby was a mass of suspended catwalks and zig-zagging electric stairs that didn't lead anywhere. The whole place looked like a dyslexic child's tinkertoy and felt like an expressionist wet dream.

McSween had arranged for the visit only by exerting considerable authority and warned me to be on my best behaviour. After three separate security checks I was whisked aboard an elevator — the floor and walls of the cage were just near enough to perpendicular to induce nausea — and escorted to Harlan Dissault's suite on the 77th floor.

Dissault's secretary was a pudgy little man who looked like Lou Costello and smelled like an old lady's sitting room. He sat at a huge oak desk and watched me as I made the long walk across the office. His ultralight Link-rig was still attached, and his slightly glassy look told me he had just jumped out. He ran one final check on my credentials and acting like I'd just insulted his mother pointed to chair in front of a large Link console.

"I'm not tired," I said.

"The *Chair*man," the little man wheezed, "does not see *any*one in person. He has allotted you five minutes of Link time."

Great, I thought, a jump to an alien space with an unfamiliar rig. I'd have no security or surveillance programs and no sure way to read the veracity of Dissault's picting except for intuition. Cursing, for the millionth time, the justice system that allows the rich to write all the rules, I hooked up the rig and made the jump.

I found myself standing in the office where I had just sat down. The secretary, not quite so small or fat here, ushered me through a door which didn't exist in the real room and into Dissault's suite.

Harlan Dissault stood with his back to me, gazing out at L.A. through an immense picture window. The city sparkled in the setting sunlight, the letters of the distant Hollywood sign glowing a fiery red. Of course, the actual sign had been razed years ago, and there was maybe one day every three years when the air was clean enough to discern the outline of buildings more than a dozen blocks away.

"It used to look like this, you know." His voice was whipped cream and gristle. "When I was a kid I used to go skateboarding along the beach at Venice. The water was filthy even then, but the ocean breeze was cool and clean and a day seemed to last forever."

He walked over to the north face and pointed down at the street. "I lost my cherry to a Chinatown whore in a fleabag on the corner of Ord and Hill. Lost my wallet, too."

"Forget it, Jake," I said, but he didn't seem to get the joke.

"I met my wife on a weekend cruise to Catalina and watched her give birth to my little girl in the infirmary in our mansion up in the Palisades."

He walked around the edge of the room to the south facing window.

"When she tested positive, I brought my wife to the Terminal Island HIVe and watched them drag her screaming and begging into the camp."

"Mr. Dissault," I tried, but he cut me off.

"Grundrisse-Rand is the single largest polluter in Southern California. Has been for over a decade. There's not a politician in California of any import who we don't own."

He finally turned and faced me. He was chiselled granite with stainless steel eyes.

"I am the sixth richest man in North America."

We stared at each other for a while then he turned back to the western vista.

"Was there something you wished to see me about?" he said.

I sighed.

"I'm very sorry about your daughter."

"So am I," he said.

He shot me off-Link before the words could echo off the glass, I knew what I had to do, but I hesitated before making the jump.

Ever since the very early days of electronic data storage there's been a lot of paranoia about the security of Virtual systems and the potential for invasions of privacy by the redoubtable powers-that-be.

It's a healthy paranoia.

The 30th amendment is supposed to guarantee certain inalienable Virtual rights, but then the VCIA isn't supposed to run intelligence operations in-country. There are too many data exchanges across the Link every day for full monitoring, but the important stuff — including police records — is backed-up in a covert, highly illegal data space.

Only the mucky-mucks are supposed to know about it and the system — it's called Mrs. Jumbo ('cause elephants never forget) — was designed to be hack-proof. Once stored in it, data can't be deleted or altered, only visited. The system has been in place since the early expansion of cyberspace. It absorbs information yet goes unnoticed only because it is woven into the very fabric of Virtual. It sits like a benign cancer on the spinal cord of the Link, inseparable from it without paralysis to the host. I know about it for one very simple reason.

I helped to design it.

Trouble is I built the system too damn well. The AIs that support the space are so scrupulous in their self-containment functions that they've found the back doors into the system that I'd left for myself and sealed them over. I tried unsealing a door once, but no sooner had I cracked it open than an immense Mighty Mouse came streaking down the data corridor towards me, looking pissed. As he started singing, "Here I come to save the day," I slammed the door shut and jumped out, hoist on my own trivially fetishistic petard.

I could still get in through the front door — my former employers know about me and so far haven't objected to the odd snoop — but my presence would be recorded. I figure I have a limited account with the data space, only I don't know my balance. I thought about it briefly, decided Dissault's case was interesting enough to take the chance on another withdrawal.

Mrs. Jumbo picts as a hotel check-in desk with a wall of mail boxes that runs to the visible horizon. At least that's how I see it. I've only met one other person who's jumped in and he saw it as an immense concentration camp barracks, with the data stacked in endless rows of hard, wooden berths.

Of course, he was a Republican.

An added security function denies direct access to the datastacks. An autonomous AI works the desk, evaluating all would-be users and serving up information at its own discretion. Fortunately, today the AI was picting the fabricant clerk as Franklin Pangborn, who's a bit prissy but much easier to deal with than Edward Everett Horton.

Copying data out of Mrs. Jumbo is a strict no-no, so I brushed the file while Pangborn eyed me suspiciously from a short ways down the desk. The uncensored police record confirmed my suspicions. I found an additional surprise in the classified intelligence reports, but one that made a lot of sense. It told me that Dissault's flameout was indeed no accident and gave me a good idea of where to find the person who had killed her.

I returned the file to the AI just as Pangborn repicted into Throckmorton P. Gildersleeve and then jumped out.

I have a theory about humanity: I call it the Galactic Tribunal Theory. I believe that someday, however far in the future, the human race will be called to task before a jury of our interstellar peers. We'll be required to justify our existence to those species well-established in the cosmic order of things. It'll be like *Stairway to Heaven* or *The Story of Mankind* or one of those other old movies with Ronald Colman defending humanity and Vincent Price or Raymond Massey as prosecuting attorney. Colman will make an impassioned plea in his impeccable British accent and have the jury just about sold. Then Vinny will stand up and clear his throat. He'll bow slightly to Colman and leaning against the jury box, the faintest hint of a smile on his thin lips, say one word that damns the species to extinction: Rubbernecking.

Other races, I have to believe, *don't* stop to gawk at traffic accidents.

I don't like people. I like individuals, but on the whole I find humans to be a mostly unappealing lot. I guess that's a good part of the reason I got involved with AIs and have spent so much time in cyberspace.

But even Virtual, when you come right down to it, is simply another human artifact, ineffably tinged by the flaws of its makers. Like all previous media forms and technologies, it shapes and reflects the minds of its users in about equal measure.

Guttenberg's second book was a collection of 'erotic' poetry.

The third daguerreotype was a portrait of the artist's mistress that might have made a gynaecologist blush.

When Bell connected the telephone and told Watson, "I need you," it wasn't just to clean up the lab.

Virtual isn't only used for data storage and exchange. Given its scope and emancipatory potential it was inevitable that certain individuals would access Virtual venues for less socially sanctioned activities.

It's called the Underground.

I've heard it argued that Virtual couldn't exist without something like an Underground, that in fact it is a natural projection of the AIs themselves, a kind of silicon id. This may well be true, without dark there can be no light, and all attempts to purge Underground picts have only led to stasis: a new sector seems to appear for every one wiped, so maybe the AIs are smarter about this than we are. Heaven knows, at least they're less prudish.

Dissault's record in Mrs. Jumbo revealed a series of arrests but no convictions for Underground activities. She was a suspect in the programming of several Underground facilities as well as in the distribution of access chips. I had guessed that such was the nature of the unidentified circuitry in her burned VAD. Whether the charges were dropped for lack of evidence or as a result of Harlan's influence wasn't clear. But the fact that she jumped below, along with those scars McSween was so fond of on her breasts and thighs, convinced me that the answer to her death lay Underground. If so, I had no objection to a little id-indulgence of my own.

I mean, I may not like people but I'm not stupid.

The very essence of an Underground of any kind is resistance to authority and rejection of social norms. Virtual isn't any different. Underground sectors tended to appear and disappear, moving randomly through different levels of Virtual. It was never hard to find *some* Underground pict, but specific scenes were rarely maintained in any single sector for more than a brief period of time. Fashion, regardless of medium, is ever more fleeting than glory.

Fortunately, the casualness of Underground denizens and their general disregard for Link propriety make tracing specific pict movements through Virtual relatively easy. As the M.E. had suggested, I attempted a Link-trace on the backburn that fried Dissault. I figured whoever triggered the burn would have covered the trace, but to my pleasant surprise a Klone discovered some matching residual char patterns.

The trace led to a blanked sector, but there I was able to pick up the trail of a wandering pict chain. I tried to reconstruct some aspect of the pict from the trace for the sake of preparedness, but I could barely even follow its winding path. I almost lost it a couple of times, but finally caught up with an extant version in a remote and largely uncharted region of Virtual. I made a last inspection of the defence and weaponry, programs I keep floating in RAM and jumped into the Underground.

My simulation program kicked in immediately, picting me in the garb appropriate to this Underground. The setting was 18th century and after a few moments I recognised the picting as a representation based on Hogarth. It appeared to be his classic *Gin Lane*, though there was a jumble of recognisable elements from *The Four Stages of Cruelty* and *A Harlot's Progress* as well. The programming was as magnificent as the horror and degradation were appalling.

It's not immediately apparent when one is in Virtual whether the figures one encounters are simulacra of Linked physicals, or pure Virtual fabricants. I run a constant filtering program to mark who is who, but in this case it proved to be very upsetting, for the atrocities performed by the physicals easily matched and exceeded the exploits of the preset Hogarth decadents.

A lunatic screamed past me catching me in the ribs with a flailing elbow. He had a bellows atop his head and a live child skewered on a staff in his hands. The man was a fabricant, the baby — a broad grin on its bloody face, it's tiny organ tumescent — a simulacrum of a physical. I repressed a shudder and walked on through the squalor.

The mutilated corpses of small animals lay strewn about the street or hanged, some still kicking, from signs and street lamps. Various genders copulated openly in any and all combinations in alleys and doorways and everything stank of blood and semen, urine and excrement. In the middle of the road the fabricant corpse of a woman with enormous, festering breasts lay atop the splinters of her wooden coffin, one thick

plank piercing her abdomen. The simulacrum of a thin man with a sepulchral visage kneeled over her, his face thrust between her decaying thighs. He looked up as I passed and maggots spilled out the corner of his lips. The only thing worse I could imagine was if fabricant and simulacrum had been reversed, but I found a no less upsetting sight a little further down the block.

I tried not to be judgmental: none of this, of course, was 'real', and I tried to convince myself that maybe this had some cathartic value, but it was tough. I had been to sleazy Undergrounds before, but none as extreme as this. I was thinking I was going to have to look a little deeper into the basis of these places sometime soon, when I was shocked out of my reverie by a woman walking out of the Gin Royal tavern.

It was Aimee Dissault.

Only it wasn't.

I recognised her instantly, though she was filthy and dressed as a whore. A leering fat man followed her out and reached around her, running his hands down her body. She turned around and interlaced her hands behind his neck as he cupped her ass. She leaned in as if to kiss him then brought her knee up sharply into his groin. He fell to the ground writhing in agony as she cackled like a drunk crow. She kicked him repeatedly in the face till his teeth lay scattered about him and her shoe dripped a syrupy crimson.

It must have been more than he wanted, for the simulacrum de-picted taking with it even the bloodstains on the ground. Dissault spat grey phlegm at the now empty space on the street and adjusted her skirts.

At least, her fabricant did.

I rebooted the filtering program, but it fed me the same information: Dissault was pure pict, not a Linked-in physical. As she walked down the street I followed her from a distance and accessed a scanning program. I booted it as she squatted to urinate in the middle of the sidewalk. She looked up as if jolted and spotted me in an instant. There was a wild hatred in her eyes as she burned my program before its iterations could converge and I knew she was no simple Klone or monitor left in place for continuity.

Dissault had done what others have only dreamed of . . . a full personality replication maintained off-Link. Her physical self didn't even need to be alive to sustain it.

Virtual immortality.

I remembered that other little piece of information about Dissault I had uncovered through Mrs. Jumbo. Intelligence reports indicated that Dissault had been the subject of some irregular surgical procedures. The suggestion was that Harlan Dissault authorised silicon brain implants in his infant daughter in violation of the AMA's cyber-ethics code. Such implants would go far toward explaining the girl's facility with Virtual and the fact of her present existence.

She started to smile as she walked toward me, the scary obverse of the crocodile's tears. I instinctively backed away, a truly futile gesture in cyberspace. I accessed a disable program but she crashed it before I could even complete the boot up.

"Oh Mr. Detective," she taunted in a sing-song chant. "Did you come to play?"

I tried to access my other attack programs but she had wiped out my personal-RAM. I tried to jump out, but she blocked that off as well. She had a mastery of Virtual unlike anyone else who had ever Linked-on. Hell, she was Virtual now.

I knew what was coming and I tried to stall, hoping inspiration would strike before Dissault did. No-one else on the street seemed at all interested in us.

"It wasn't a murder at all, was it Aimee? It was a suicide."

"Suicide?" she said, "But I'm not dead, am I?"

"You're not alive."

"Who's to say? I don't feel any different than I did before. If anything, I feel better."

I could feel it building around me. The pict was breaking up as the Virtual space started to sizzle.

"You burned yourself," I said and knew I had only one chance. I needed a little more time.

"It was fun. That scrawny old body was a terrible limitation to me. I mean, how many people get to act out their death wish and be nostalgic about it after."

"But why such a major flameout?" I asked. I was almost ready.

"Oh," she said. "There were some funny chips in that nasty head of mine. We couldn't have anybody picking through them. They were starting to fail anyway, so whoosh, I melted it all down. Just like you."

I felt her release the full burn. I smelled ozone and felt the first searing charge in my head. The Hogarth street scene flickered and nearby simulacra de-picted. Micropixels crackled and burst beneath the strain as the very space around me tore like cheap silk and I knew I was a nanosecond too slow.

Then the explosion hit.

McSween was sitting beside the bed when I came to. His face wore the same blank expression he had showed to the would-be dead girl only days before.

"Feds want to see you," he said.

"I'll bet." My head felt like the inside of an earthquake.

"They think you owe them an AI."

"Shit."

"They're a little curious about the 23 simultaneous flame-outs, too."

I closed my eyes. A thousand tiny lobsters danced in my brain, snagging raw nerves in their snapping claws. I thought about the moment before the explosion. Though Dissault disabled my RAM, I was able to spin a Klone out of Virtual materials.

I positioned it behind me on the Link and programmed it to bounce back all incoming data. It was a one-in-a-thousand shot that it wouldn't melt from the overload, but it reflected enough of the burn to mostly protect my physical self. The reflected flameout wiped out Dissault and the Underground and apparently the AI that supported it, leaving me an instant in which to jump out before the burn bounced back again and took me with it. If I had been Linked through any VAD other than my own I would have fried.

I opened my eyes, but McSween was gone. I went back to sleep.

I was in the hospital for a week then home on temporary disability. I got grilled by the Feds and IAD and neither was real happy, but they cleared me in the end,

I thought about the 23 people Linked-in to the Underground who died in the flameout and wondered if I should feel guilty. They were all major deviants and illegally played in the Underground at their own risks, but *physically* they hadn't actually done anything.

Then there was Aimee.

As I lay in bed I tried to figure if anyone could say that I had killed her. I mean, technically speaking she had been dead for two days at the time.

But I just wasn't sure.

I considered the achievement of her replication in Virtual and wondered if Harlan Dissault would repeat the experiment given the price paid by his daughter. It wasn't just her death that was on his head, it was her life. Something awful had driven her to her perverse revelries in that Underground and I guessed her father's literal head-games might explain a lot of it. If he didn't know about it, he was sure-as-shit going to find out.

I suspected it wouldn't come as news, but either way I bet it wouldn't do more than pique the old maggot's curiosity.

Another fucking rubbernecker.

I thought about Aimee and an existence limited to Virtual.

Or maybe *un*limited to Virtual. It is, after all, a universe as potentially infinite as our own. And one in which, with a little time, she could have become something like omnipotent.

I thought some more.

It was unlikely that Aimee would have tied her simulacra consciousness to any single AI; the chance of system crash, accidental or otherwise, was too great. She certainly wouldn't have Linked herself exclusively to an Underground AI, they're the most susceptible to physical intervention, as my little jump to Hogarthland demonstrated. And if she could replicate herself once in a Virtual environment, why not multiple versions?

I suddenly felt very queasy. It had all been too easy: the obvious flaws in the Grundrisse datastack, the open access to Mrs. Jumbo, the hard-but-not-impossible-to-follow pict trail of the Underground. And the fact that my Klone withstood an off-the-scale backburn, saving me to make my report.

I contacted a hacker snitch and sent him Dissault's synaptic prints with instructions to scan the Undergrounds for her. I promised him some highly illegal sex chips if he came through. Though my brain still ached I jumped in to a private, off-Link data space I use as a workshop and fashioned a very special program.

I was hours in my shop and when I finally jumped out the snitch was waiting for me. He had found her in a lesbian-only Underground, the look on his face telling me not to ask how *he* managed to sneak in.

I was dead tired and my brain felt like a turtle baking in its shell, but I was afraid to wait any longer. Dissault might never be so easy to find again and I was afraid to ever attempt another Link-on knowing she was in there, maybe just biding her time for me.

There was no margin for error; if she got any hint I was near she would fry me on the spot. I camped outside the Underground and waited for a jumper. When I sensed a pict forming on jump in I piggy-backed the simulacrum. As long as I performed no conscious action, my presence couldn't be detected, not even by the physical I had attached to. I hated endangering a citizen without her consent, but I had no choice. Before her pict could stabilise I injected the program.

We spent several interesting hours in the lesbian Underground before we found Dissault. I sensed everything my host felt and did and it was a different perspective to say the least. We finally spotted her in a bar that sported an Early Egyptian motif, having sex on a plush divan. As the two women changed positions and I glimpsed her partner, all doubts concerning what I was about to do evaporated.

She was engaged in furious oral sex with herself.

Or was it masturbation?

We ambled up to the bar and the bartender came over wiping the counter in front of us. She was a gay fabricant, but built like a brick AI. We could see the Dissaults in the mirror over the barmaid's shoulder. They were looking around now, as if they sensed something amiss in the Virtual atmosphere.

It was almost time.

The bartender asked what we wanted. As we started to reply I detached from my host and picted beside her. I heard several screams from the other patrons.

The Dissaults looked at me and smiled like it was feeding time at the zoo. There was no delay this time.

"You *ass*hole," they said and the burn began.

"Boilermaker," my host ordered, tripping the program I planted in her pict.

The reason flameouts are so deadly is that you normally never know when they're going to hit or from which direction. But I knew it was coming this time and I was very ready.

A small plasma sac, looking like a hyperthyroid amoeba picted between me and Dissault. As the burn detonated it was diverted into the sac which expanded with the surge of energy. Dissault was surprised by it and raised the degree of the burn, but the sac absorbed the additional power. Dissault was laying everything she had into it now, screaming with fury as the air shimmered with the intensity of the blast. Simulacra cowered in the corners, the AI too overloaded to divert processing for jump-outs.

The sac had expanded to occupy most of the bar when it exploded. A thousand smaller amoebas burst from the sac and spread out through the fabric of Virtual. Two of them immediately glommed onto the Dissaults, expanding to envelop them, before beginning to contract. The membranes were cloudy but transparent and I watched the Dissaults battle futilely against the antibody program.

The sacs got smaller and smaller, compacting Dissaults' picts as they shrank, wiping all synaptic traces of her from Virtual memory just as the other amoebas were doing across all levels of the cyberspace.

It was a gamble, of course. If Dissault had integrated herself deeply enough into the AIs all of Virtual would crash with her. But I was betting that she simply hadn't had enough time to accomplish that since her physical death.

As the last screaming pixel of them popped out of existence and the Underground shuddered but maintained, I knew the bet had paid off. I couldn't be sure that I got every trace of her — Virtual is a big place to hide — but I was reasonably confident that even if some synaptic element survived, she would never be able to re-pict.

If she ever did, I would sure as hell find out about it.

As the Underground stabilised, the other patrons were looking at me with less than welcome delight. I bowed with what small elegance I could muster and jumped out.

The Feds were waiting for me when I Linked-off.

They always are.

Ghosts of Departed Quantities

M Y BRAIN DANCED THE HOKEY-POKEY IN LOOSE galoshes. For weeks a rogue hacker had been reprogramming picts in Virtual Disneyland, augmenting the erogenous zones of some the Magic Kingdom's most beloved critters. When corporate security couldn't turn up anything more than raging hard-ons, the buck landed on my desk with an ugly thud.

The stake-out took three days and the hacker was good. If she hadn't gone back to *circumcise* Goofy, I might never have nailed her. As it was, I Linked-off wanting only a dozen hours of *real* sleep, untroubled by dreams of toothless, saucer-eyed dwarves who ogled each other's rude bits as they sang 'Someday My Prince Will Come'.

I managed almost 45 minutes before the doorbell chirped.

I dragged myself to the door, only half-aware I was humming 'Cruella DeVille', and pressed a bloodshot eyeball to the peephole. McSween waited outside, picking his nose with his pinky. I opened the door and staggered back to the living-room, flopping face first onto the couch.

"Off-duty," I mewled into the cushion.

McSween closed the door behind him and perched on an armrest. He wiped his pinky on the back of my shirt.

"Asshole," I croaked.

"Where's the hooch?" he said.

Against my better judgment, I turned over and pried open a tired eye.

McSween stood by the bookcase, three fingers of bourbon already in hand.

"I just don't get it," he said.

"Well you're not my type so work the other side of the street."

"These goddamn books. You of all people."

"I like 'em, Mac," I sighed. "I like the smell of the ink and the feel of the paper and the endless variation in type faces. I like the sound the spine makes when it cracks and the weight of the volume on my chest when I read in bed. I just like, them, okay?"

"I don't get it," he said again.

I forced myself to a sitting position. "What do you want, Mac? Surely you have better things to do than torture me?"

"Oooh Pancho, I theenk jew must be in trouble."

"*Que es esto?*"

"*Federales, Pancho.*"

"Fuck me with big, noisy power tools why don't they."

"I tell them we don't need no steenking badges, but they no leesten.

"I'm too tired to play today, Mac. What's the deal?"

"You tell me, brother. Sigornic calls me not half an hour ago with orders to roust you PDQ Bach. Must be gnarly, 'cause he sounded like he had a bonsai up his ass."

"Jesus wept."

"Crocodile tears, old son, crocodile tears."

Federal Plaza is a ghastly old building that looks like a pile of unevenly stacked venetian blinds. McSween dropped me at the gate and sped away, cackling, "Off-duty, off-duty," as he disappeared into the smog.

Noboru Sigornic was Chief of the Bureau's Virtual Investigations Division in L.A. Being half-Japanese and half-Polish meant he was smart enough to know he was the butt of a lot of dumb jokes. He waited in his office with a stiff Aryan *ubermensch* in a government-issue suit, and a mousy, fortyish brunette who chain-smoked menthol cigarettes and played at a Gioconda smile.

"This is special agent Pettifore," Sigornic said nodding at the Hitler youth.

"You're kidding," I said.

He wasn't. I make friends everywhere I go.

"And I, umm, believe you know Dr. Silver."

"Hi-ho Lilian!" I sing-songed. She blew smoke in my face.

"We go way back," I explained to Sigornic. I threw her a big wet kiss, but she ducked it.

McSween was right; Sigornic did seem to have something prickly jammed up his rectum. I poured a cup of coffee and gulped it down as we settled in for the spiel.

"You look like shit," Sigornic said. His lip turned up in a fair imitation of Elvis.

"Sweet-talker," I replied.

The curled lip went full-snarl. "Agent Pettifore coordinates monitoring activities for the Bureau in Washington. He's following up on an investigation of some, ahhh, irregularities on the Link. I think perhaps it would be best to let him explain. Agent?"

Pettifore was leaning back against Sigornic's desk, arms folded over his trim gut. He had one of those V shapes that's supposed to be the masculine ideal, but which always makes me think of those anorexic greyhounds they make shlep around the dog tracks. He straightened up and ran a hand through his wavy, plastic blonde hair, and spoke with that faint trace of a southern accent — I made it Kentucky or Tennessee — that he'd never shake no matter how hard he tried. And I could tell that he had tried plenty.

"Thank you, sir. Twenty-three days ago a routine free-sector optimisation program detected an unlicensed processing operation in an unallocated Virtual sector. Twelve tracks in the sector were flagged and a follow-up investigation initiated. Now as you know, small-scale pirate activities are not uncommon, and generally drop off the Link before traces can commence."

Yapita-yapita-yap. Bored already, I glanced at Lilian sitting beside me on the couch. The angle was just right to ogle the delicate lace of her brassiere and I remembered how her skin tasted on my tongue. She caught me staring and blushed down to her lovely cleavage. Same old Lilian, I thought and smiled, and turned my attention back to Albert Speer who was clearing his throat at me.

"As I was saying, the unauthorised operation expanded beyond the flagged tracks. Within three weeks of discovery, the illegal processing enveloped the entire sector. A Link-warrant was signed by a Virtual magistrate and a VID team attempted access, but they were, ah, repulsed by an unknown force."

"Repulsed?" I asked.

"Detached might be more accurate," Lilian said between puffs. "The agents did not return from the Link. We initiated emergency jump-out protocols, but I've been unable to restore synaptic function to any team member. They're effectively brain-dead and sustained on life-support."

So that explained Lilian's presence. As the Bureau's ace cyber-neurologist the veggies would be in her care. She'd no doubt have to hover around the edges in case any further gardening was required.

"Where'd you trace the pirated sectors to?" I asked.

"Well, that's been part of the basic problem," Sigornic said. "We can't seem to complete a trace to a physical Link-port or any supporting AI or network."

"It's a free-floating sector?" I asked, confused.

"No," Pettifore cut in, "it's fixed and expanding. The VID agents that bought the burn were a trace team."

"You're telling me that VID can't even attach a simple trace on a fixed-sector processing facility in free Link space?"

Sigornic looked sheepish but managed to meet my gaze. "It's not exactly a processing program."

"What then?" I said. "Virus? Datastax? What kind of moron would leave property out there like that?"

"No," Pettifore said, "it doesn't act like a virus and we don't think it's an archiplex either."

"I know you don't *think*, it goes with the suit. How could you not know?"

Himmler pursed his weasly little lips, but didn't answer. He left it for Sigornic.

"Because it picts as a total blank," he said. "A great . . . black hole has opened in the middle of the Link and it's slowly sucking up the surrounding cyberspace. We don't know what it is, who's supporting it or where it's headed. It's like staring into a cave at midnight."

"And you need someone to go spelunking," I said, catching on.

Sigornic smiled at last. "God and the Bureau love a volunteer," he said.

The Link is like Gertrude Stein's Oakland: there's no *there*, there. Like the Internet which preceded it, the Link is really nothing more than a collection of individual data spaces connected by shared data thoroughfares. The vital core of the Link is maintained by a small number of massive government and corporate AI networks, but every private AI, data network and Virtual Access Device that joins the Link is required to devote a *pro rata* percentage of processing time to the maintenance of the shared community.

While every private space is designed and picted according to the needs and idiosyncrasies of its owner, most of the Link is not represented according to any specific picting function. That is to say, while I might choose to represent my own space as the Taj Mahal or Yankee Stadium, the electronic avenues that connect my ballpark to your mausoleum do not themselves take on any physical appearance; they simply are.

The point, beyond saving unnecessary programming and processing time, is to discourage loitering. If one does not have specific coordinates and access codes, it is assumed that one does not belong on that bit of the Link and is likely up to no good.

There do exist, however, numerous sectors which are unallocated but formatted for homesteading, and sectors for which licensing has been revoked. These regions retain a basic pict representation which, while spartan, has recognisable physical contours. Sectors are inevitably usurped for short-term, generally illegal and illicit activities like Undergrounds, which is why VID maintains a regular if somewhat inefficient monitoring system. It was in just such a region that Sigornic's black hole had materialised.

I reviewed the Link record that Sigornic provided me on the burned VID team's procedures. I saw that they had jumped right into the affected sector, tripping a burn immediately on arrival. It was damn sloppy technique and I couldn't say I felt too sorry for what had happened to them as a result.

On-link, I booted up a Bloodhound and sent it sniffing around a formatted sector adjacent to the area of infection. While I waited to see if it would trip any hidden burns, I produced a monitor Klone to send into the sector ahead of me. When the Bloodhound came back wagging its tail, I saved it and dropped the Klone in.

I scanned the barren sector through the Klone's eyes. It looked like the inside of a small dome with the floor and curved ceiling painted a uniform grey. As with all such sectors, the invisible horizons gave off a sense of expansive distance even as the featurelessness induced claustrophobia.

As I turned the Klone around I noticed a small dark patch on the opposite wall. I directed the Klone toward the spot, but took only a few steps before tripping a burn. The Klone deconstructed as its program crashed, and even from a distance and through an array of protective filters I was jolted by the force of the explosion. Whatever or whoever this thing was, it reacted only to higher level synaptic activity. Anything that could fool my Bloodhound like that was very sophisticated and double-plus-ungood.

Shaken, I jumped out of the area and headed for the nearest Link depot for a breather. Between the echoes from the explosion and raw exhaustion, I felt the onset of a Krakatoa headache, and much as I wanted to Link-off and get some sleep, I needed to set some gears in motion for my downtime.

There is something truly remarkable about the consistency of human nature. Not good, mind you, just remarkable.

Depots are established at regular points across the Link, just like stations on any rail or bus line. They ostensibly exist to facilitate connections between disparate Virtual locations for low level info-commuters, but in fact serve mostly as hang-outs and pick-up joints for the ever-present low-lifes, grifters, hustlers and bums of virtual reality.

A bus station is a bus station is a bus station, to continue in ein Stein-ian vein.

This particular depot picted as some sort of western way-station, but I suspect the design owed more to John Ford than any real Pony Express stop. A couple of mangy looking horses were tethered out in front and several of the users were decked out in cowboy regalia. The station manager bore more than a passing resemblance to Slim Pickens and though I only heard the bartender's voice, it *had* to have been Andy Devine.

I was rummaging through some files in personal RAM when a wafer-thin dude in green army fatigues with a thousand-and-one-yard stare plopped down next to me. He had stringy blonde hair like old spaghettini and a week's worth of razor stubble. I couldn't for the life of me imagine why anyone would choose to pict themself that way, but it's a free country give-or-take. He looked everywhere but at me, mumbling into his dirty collar: "Nickel-ROMs, dime chips."

He had to be kidding. Even in a Link depot, nobody was stupid enough to be that blatant.

"I got what it takes, I got what you need. Sexcapades. Ultra-viles. Dogs and cats living together."

The little light bulb went on. "Bobo! You Ghostbusting monster! Nice picting. What it is?"

"Stealing my pay check. How's it hanging?"

Bobo was a Ghostbuster, which is to say Virtual Vice. As repulsive a job as anyone could possibly imagine, but I knew no-one better suited to it. "Pretty dull place for a studly vice officer like yourself, isn't it Bobo?"

"Sometimes you got to pick your roses in Spanish Harlem."

I didn't have the slightest idea what he was talking about, but that wasn't unusual. Bobo maintained a hard-guy-cum-psychopath Virtual persona which was effective, but also a crock of shit. He kept a very low realworld profile, but we'd met years before and I knew for a fact that he was a chubby bald guy with a slight lisp. Still, he did his job well and was connected on the Link.

"Hear anything lately, Bobo?"

"Ears I got, pilgrim."

"How about lips?"

"Of what to speak?"

"The kind of stuff that interests me. You know."

Bobo finally glanced at me, and for a moment I caught sight of the fat little bald man beneath the picting. He resumed the thousand-yard stare and shook his head.

"The abyss naps, too," he said and wandered off.

"Thanks a heap," I muttered to his back. He waggled his fingers behind him. I started resorting my files when a klaxon wailed around us. The local flotsam looked around in puzzlement, but Bobo and Slim Pickens quickly acknowledged the crash-call and de-picted. I invoked an emergency, sector-wide jump-out protocol even as the fabric of cyberspace started dissolving around us and individual pixels exploded in tiny mushroom clouds. The walls and ceiling of the depot melted into each other and an immense clock above the main entrance wilted with Dali-esque abandon.

I was still waiting for acknowledgement of override authorisation from the supporting network when the first black tendrils burst through the walls. I heard Andy Devine scream in the background and saw the creeping blackness envelope a toothless bag lady. I caught a whiff of foul odour, like burnt flesh. A lance-like, ebony arm shot toward me from above and a resident fail-safe program yanked me out of Virtual in a last-minute whiplash-inducing jump.

When I came to in my office, I saw that my Virtual Access Device and Link-gear were toast. It was a minor miracle that I'd made it out in one piece. I guessed that some of the others hadn't and was damn determined that it wasn't going to happen again.

I dozed for a few hours on the office sofa, but my sleep was uneasy. I caught fleeting glimpses of strange dream faces and heard choruses of dim, garbled voices, like echoes in a school yard. The horrid smell seemed lodged in my nose, as well. Too much Link-time does strange things to your head, so I shook it off, chalking it up to the unpleasantness of that last, whiplash Link-off. I probably could have used more sleep, but I reckoned Sigornic would be pitching embolisms the size of softballs. The guess was confirmed when I saw the emergency code flashing on my pager in 7/8 time.

Sigornic let loose with an impressive, but not particularly original stream of curses. Fortunately, I'm not the thin-skinned type.

"What did you do?" he finally asked, sounding uncomfortably like my mother.

"Nothing," I mumbled, completing the exchange.

"We've got crashes in three new sectors, with a half-dozen flame-outs and two fatalities. Don't tell me 'nothing.'"

"Listen, Chief," I Jimmy Olsoned, knowing he hated it, "there's something very odd going on here. This thing, these . . . fluxions, have a very sophisticated response heuristic and it's obviously having no problems breaking down Link security protocols. I've managed to get two looks at it now, and barely came away in one piece either time. This Creeping Terror whatever-it-is is goddamn scary."

I could hear Sigornic's heavy breathing and knew by his silence that he was rattled that I was rattled. And I was. Nothing like this had ever appeared on the Link before.

"What do we do?" Sigornic finally asked.

"Well, I'm a little too wired to go back in just now. Do you have a list of the flame-outs from that last crash?"

"Er, hang on a second. Yeah, got it right here. There's about a dozen in all."

"Any local?"

"Let's see . . . New York, Poona, Melbourne, someplace called Shingletown, wherever the hell that is. Wait, here's one: Rebecca Hughes. Address up in Hollywood."

I took down the information, offered Sigornic some patently false comfort and hung up.

The unease I felt in my dreams seemed to have crossed the threshold of sleep and taken root in my waking mind. In the back of my head I thought I could still hear a dim chorus of voices playing like a staticky, subliminal soundtrack. I tried to shake off the cobwebs with coffee and a chocolate doughnut — cop's speedball — but while the sugar rush revved me up, I couldn't quite make the voices disappear.

You gotta love Hollywood. Really. You gotta.

I mean, where else can you buy illegal ROM chips, a first edition of *Brave New World* and a twelve year old boy all on the same block?

Rebecca Hughes lived on Ivar Avenue in an old mock-Tudor apartment building that was right across the street from the landmark house where Nathanael West wrote *Day of the Locust*. I took that as an omen, but couldn't decide if it was a good one or bad. All in all, the neighbourhood probably hadn't changed too much, physically or spiritually, since West's day.

The building's security gate was wide open. I checked the directory and trudged up to the third floor. There were only two units, neither of which had an apartment number, so I knocked on the closest one. After a minute or two, it was opened by a short, twenty-ish woman with closely cropped blonde hair. She looked me up and down and wasn't impressed. Few are.

"Rebecca Hughes?" I asked.

"Who are you?"

"Police," I intoned, flashing my badge. I love that stuff.

The woman made a fish-face — perch, I'd say — and invited me in with a twitch of her head. "Wait here."

The blonde meandered down the hall. I scanned the room, marvelling at the decor. The walls were plastered with posters and stills from various western films. The living room was dominated by an enormous blow-up of L. Q. Jones and Strother Martin in a scene from *The Wild Bunch*. There was a bookcase filled with Louis L'Amour and Max Brand novels and a big wagon-wheel coffee table in the middle of the room. A shiny leather saddle rested on a sawhorse in the corner.

I heard raised voices from down the hall and a minute later a stocky brunette shambled in and sat down on the leather couch. She wore a tattered white bathrobe with pink bunny slippers and a Vancouver Vintners baseball cap. Her hair was a mess and dark bags — more like satchels, actually — dangled under her eyes. I noticed that her sclerae were slightly discoloured, a sign of serious Link use. She started biting her nails, which were already well-gnawed.

"Rebecca Hughes?" I asked again.

"Cop, huh?"

I smiled and nodded. "I'd like to talk to you about the crash yesterday."

She looked at me a little more carefully, squinting and cocking her head. "Hey. You were there. In the depot, I mean."

"That's right."

"You look just like you pict," she said, marvelling. 'I've never met anybody who did that before. What's, like, wrong with you?"

"I'm a simple kind of guy."

"Totally."

"You were Andy Devine," I said.

"How'd you know?"

"Educated guess. You don't strike me as the Slim Pickens type."

"No, Emma was Slim," she said, pointing down the hall with her chin.

"How are you feeling today?"

"How the fuck do I look?"

"Have you seen a doctor?"

She snorted. "Yeah, sure. Like I can afford Link-time *and* health insurance. Get a clue, Nancy Drew."

I let that pass. "I need to know what you saw and felt when the sector crashed. I heard you scream. How'd you manage to jump out."

"I didn't. Like, I barely knew what was going on. One minute I'm making goo-goo eyes at this dude from *Citizen Kane* and the next thing I know the floor is melting and these black, wavy things are coming at me."

"So how did you get off-Link?" I asked.

"It was Emma," she said and glanced down the hall again. "She Linked-off right away and when she saw I didn't follow she cut the Link-line."

"Yikes!" I said and winced.

"Yeah," she agreed. "No shit."

Linking-off without an exit protocol is one of the big no-nos of virtual life. It can be done — as the woman's continued presence demonstrated — but the process entails a very high risk of neural damage.

"Do you remember anything specifically about the black things. Did you get any feelings from them or any sense about them?"

She shook her head. "No, it was just like stark terror time, I thought . . . "

"Go on."

"No. It was nothing."

"Please tell me. It might be important."

"It's . . . I thought I heard something. Voices, like."

She must have seen my reaction, which explains why I always lose money at cards. "What is it?" she said.

"Tell me about the voices. When did you hear them?"

"It was weird. One of these like big arms of blackness swooped down from the ceiling and kind of washed over Mr. Bernstein."

"Who?"

"The, you know, the *Citizen Kane* dude. It just like dropped down right in front of me, but didn't touch me and then he was gone and I was staring at this . . . empty space. Then I saw another wave of black race toward me from across the room. It almost got me when Emma yanked me out. But right before the jump I could have sworn I heard a jumble of voices. I couldn't make any one of them out, though. It was like in a theatre or something before the show starts, you know? Just this all around undercurrent of talking. But . . . "

"Yeah?"

"The thing is that — I know this sounds crazy and it's probably just 'cause of the way I got yanked out and all — but a few times now I thought I could still, like, hear them."

"Maybe in your dreams," I said.

"Yeah!" she said and her eyes grew wide. "How did you know?"

"Did you smell anything?"

"I think I pooped my pants."

I moved right along. "How did you sleep last night?"

"Really bad. My head was totally pounding and I was so tired, but I couldn't seem to fall into any kind of deep sleep. I've been trying to sleep today, I mean I'm supposed to be at work, but . . . "

"The voices," I said. She nodded and slumped back on the couch.

"Can you remember anything else?" I asked.

"Not really. But I've still got the headache. And I'm sort of afraid to get back on the Link. What is this all about anyway? What did I hear?"

"I don't know," I said, "but I want you to see a doctor. Don't worry, it's no charge. Her name is Silver."

I gave her Lilian's number and told her to say that I sent her. Then I tried talking to the roommate, Emma/Slim Pickens, but she wasn't too cooperative. She'd Linked-off right away, didn't actually see the blackness and wasn't hearing any voices. She also made it clear that she didn't much support her local police. I got the feeling she was maybe involved in some Underground activity, but didn't press her.

By the time I wandered back out to my car, exhaustion was starting to set in again. I wanted to go home for another nap, but there was way too much to do.

And, in truth, I was getting to be a little bit afraid of my dreams.

I checked in with Sigornic, who told me that Pettifore had interviewed several of the other crash victims. Their stories were more or less the same, but there was one interesting titbit: two of the subjects reported something about hearing voices after the crash and one mentioned a smell of decay.

With my personal VAD in need of overhaul, I had to borrow a department unit to Link-on. It was slower than my own machine and left me without my usual array of safety programs, but I wasn't about to attempt anything too dangerous or extravagant just yet.

I jumped in to a Link Command Centre to check on the progress of The Creeping Terror, and saw that it had breached two new sectors since my conversation with Sigornic. It was still moving through a largely undeveloped area of Virtual, but was inching its way toward a district of corporate archiplexes. Potentially affected sectors were hurriedly being copied and deconstructed, but the archiplexes were way too big to be emptied in time.

I also noted that the blackness had vacated the sectors in which it first appeared. It wasn't spreading so much as actually moving, as if self-contained. From what and to where it was going I hadn't a clue, but at least I had a place to start. A quick review of Link records showed that the first infected sectors now read as completely clean, and as long as the blackness didn't decide to return to the scene of the crime, I reckoned a visit would be safe enough.

The department VAD wasn't equipped for point-to-point jumps and Link transport was too slow for my cultivated tastes, so I jumped out and reconfigured for a direct jump to the desired sector. I accessed a weak public domain fail-safe program which was better than nothing and punched the code for the jump. However, I found myself diverted to an Operations Fabricant picting as a heavyset, middle aged woman with tortoise shell glasses and smeared, electric pink lipstick. She nasally informed me that I was attempting a jump into an unformatted sector and to please check my coordinates and jump again. I got booted off-Link post-haste.

I tried the jump twice more with identical results. The third time, the Fabricant actually got a little rude, questioning my proficiency in basic Link protocols along with my toilet training.

I went back to the Command Centre and rechecked the status of the affected sectors, but everything read as normal. It didn't make any sense.

I jumped out again and this time reconfigured for a sector that had never been touched by the Creeping Terror, but adjacent to one that had. In an instant I stood in the middle of the blank, formatted sector. I made my way to the sector boundary which picted as a standard grey wall. I pressed my ear up against it, but there was nothing to be heard. It may sound like a strange thing to have done, but there's a certain unpredictability about Link space and you can never be sure exactly what will work.

It was a bit of a risk given the borrowed VAD, but I invoked override protocols to initiate a sector breach. Immediately, a shirtless Bruce Lee, dragon tattoo writhing across his muscular chest, picted in front of me. He eyed me up and down and verified my security clearance, then bounded off in an impossible, chop-socky leap.

Like I say, a certain unpredictability.

I booted up the fail-safe program and crossed my fingers. Then I wove a Mole out of RAM and set it to burrow through the wall as I retreated away from the edge of the sector. I watched and waited as the Mole sniffed around the wall, seeking the point of easiest access. Once it found the spot, it broke through in less than an instant.

I just had time to see the Mole fry as a blast exploded out toward me through the tiny breach. It wasn't blackness that spilled out, though, but pure argent light.

I was struck by a psychic wave of distortion and confusion. I tried to close my eyes, but the light was far too bright. A garbled, sonic boom of screaming voices filled my head like hell's own chorus. I smelled burning hair and melting flesh and realised it was my own.

An unpleasant-but-familiar whiplash jerked me out of virtual with multiple-G force. I managed to disengage my Link-gear and take two steps before collapsing on the floor. My last conscious thought was of sending a big fat check to the author of that shareware fail-safe program.

I was only out for a short while, but my brain pulsed to a salsa-migraine beat. I knew I should go see Lilian for a check-up, but couldn't bring myself to face her smirking smugness. Instead, I begged a ride home and crashed on the sofa.

My sleep was still unsound. I experienced a series of looping fever dreams filled with images and faces that seemed familiar, but hovered just outside of recognition. I felt like a fly in a web, as spiders danced around and over me, wrapping me ever tighter in a cocoon of strange sound and vision. Even as I was enveloped in constricting tendrils of black, a blinding argent light washed over me. My head filled with a dissonant choir of voices, some screaming, some pleading, some laughing.

I woke up in the middle of the night, shivering and drenched in sweat. Though I'd been out for hours, I still felt exhausted and my head continued to throb. I rummaged through the bathroom, dry-swallowed a handful of painkillers and tried to sleep again without success. I took a hot shower then a cold one, but it was still no go. Finally, in abject misery, I forced down a glass of warm milk. But every time I lay back down the dance of painful images and tortured voices would begin to haunt me again.

By the time the first trace of morning brightened the room I had been dozing restively for almost twelve hours, but felt just as tired as before I crashed. I made a cup of jasmine tea and sat by the kitchen window in my bathrobe. I sipped the steaming liquid and watched the day arrive, trying to empty the slowly dimming sounds from my head.

I took another shower in attempted revivification. I started to shave and, as always, flipped on the radio. Upstairs, I heard a neighbour turn on her hair-dryer. It interfered with the radio so I reached to turn it off, but froze in mid-motion.

The sound had gone mostly white-noise static, but there was also a blur of voices and music as the signals of several stations overlapped one another. I listened to the jumbled voices and stared at my reflection in the steamy mirror, watching my fuzzy image shimmer in the haze. The thin sheen of shaving cream lent my already pale features a positively spectral visage. The muddle of frequencies was harsh to the ear, but it sent an epiphanic shiver down my spine.

My neighbour turned off her hair-dryer and the jumble of voices reformed into a single, clear frequency. The steam dissipated and I saw my reflection clearly in the clean quicksilver. I finished abluting as quickly as I could.

I dashed off to the closest virtual rental store. The Nintendo VADs were all crap, but I didn't need anything fancy. I dragged the unit home, snapped in some of my own chips and punched a very unusual code. In an instant I was on-Link and standing at the door to Mrs. Jumbo's place. The voices in my head had grown louder again on-Link, but I did my best to ignore them.

Mrs. Jumbo is a massive, ultra-confidential data base that maintains the permanent Link record; sort of *The New York Times* of AIs. I only had access to it thanks to some disgustingly low friends in embarrassingly high places. There seemed to be some quirk in the picting that day, though, because while I was sure that the Fabricant at the desk was based on Bob Denver, I couldn't tell if it was specifically Gilligan or Maynard G. Krebs. The matter was settled when a coconut suddenly appeared and dropped on his head while he was verifying my authorisation.

Once approved, I accessed the Master Link record. Standard records, even at Sigornic's level, can be fudged quite readily, but Mrs. Jumbo is tamper-proof. I called up a Link trace for the affected sectors and soon found what I was looking for. Contrary to what Sigornic thought, the sectors had been more than homesteaded. They'd been used and reformatted, with the other Link records wiped clean.

I Linked-off with the voices still in my head, along with a strong theory as to what was going on.

I tried to insist that she take my pants off for the examination, but Lilian was having none of it.

"Lie back and shut up," she said.

"And enjoy?" I cajoled.

She tried to glare at me but, as always, it just made her look like a petulant little girl.

"You're still an asshole," she finally said. "After all these years."

"Isn't it comforting to know that some things never change?"

Between cigarettes, she ran her usual battery of tests — everything from EEGs to a full Synaptic Integration Series — but they all came up A-OK. I thought Lilian actually seemed a little disappointed by the results. She took another look at my eyes and gave me a small bottle of drops. I squeezed a bit of the stuff into each weary socket and yowled when it burned like hell. I couldn't see her, but I could tell she was laughing behind my back. Lilian had long ago mastered the silent snigger and was still trying to hide her glee when my vision cleared.

"They look like fried eggs you know. You're going to be looking at transplants, not to mention through them, if you don't cut back on your Link-time."

"Just doing my job, ma'am."

"Oh," she said, "*there's* a new refrain."

"Please Lilian. It's toxic waste under the bridge."

"You got that right."

We sat in silence for a minute, me trying to be good, her poring over the results again. No doubt looking for a malignant tumour or a small but deadly haemorrhage she might have missed.

"Lilian . . . "

"What?" she snapped.

"Truce, truce," I said, holding up my hands. "We need to talk business here. Did the Hughes woman come to see you?"

"Yes. She kept asking if the exam was 'like really free'."

"What did you find?"

Lilian shifted into professional mode. "Nothing special. I didn't run anything very exotic, but then she didn't seem to know what you wanted. All synaptic activity was within normal parameters, though her eyes looked even worse than yours and there was a very slight trace of an old burn. She doesn't seem to have any medical records so I couldn't run comparisons."

"Did she tell you about the voices?"

"She told me about the crash and said she *thought* she heard voices in her sleep. Didn't make it sound very unusual. Of course, a little virtual seepage isn't really out of the ordinary. Why?"

"What if I told you I was hearing voices, too?"

To her credit, Lilian actually looked concerned. She even took the cigarette out of her mouth. "*Are* you telling me that?"

I nodded.

"In your sleep?" she asked.

"In my sleep," I said. "And in my wake. And now, even as we speak."

She walked back over and looked at my eyes again. I don't know what she expected to see.

"What do they say?" she whispered.

"It's not like that. It's more a constant murmur, like background noise on a busy street. I can't sort it out, but it's not pleasant. It's louder when I sleep, but I'm hearing it almost all the time. It's a bit like an angry fly that keeps circling my head."

"I'm going to rerun the Integration Series."

She did, but the results came out the same as the first time. She started to call down to set up a VMRI, but I stopped her.

"Lilian," I said, "I think I know what it is."

She held the phone away from her ear and looked over at me. I could hear an annoyed voice on the other hand saying "Hello? Hello?"

"Do you believe in ghosts?" I asked.

Judging from Sigornic's expression, the bonsai up his ass had sprouted fresh growth. He squirmed in his chair as I recounted what I had seen and heard and proffered a theory to account for events. Pettifore was there, too, standing in the corner and looking confused.

"Ghosts?" Sigornic said.

"Well," I said, glancing at Lilian, "I'm using the term loosely, of course. I'm not suggesting anything paranormal here, but there's something . . . haunting the Link and I think that these fluxions may actually be a collection of dissociated, residual neural patterns."

"You buy this?" he asked Lilian.

"Let's just say I'm leaning his way," she forced herself to say. "I V-conferenced with a friend of mine named Prokop at Cornell. He's the guru of Massively Orthogonal Processing and he's been doing some interesting work on artificial neural nets. His group has found some evidence for the notion that user neural patterns are being permanently inscribed on the Link. He hasn't been able to isolate the circumstances, but he thinks that neural traces get burned into Link sectors. It's akin to the situation that existed in some pre-digital video technology; extremely bright or persistent images would be permanently burned into vidicon tubes."

"Or like radio waves," I said, musing on my bathroom epiphany.

"How's that?"

"All those signals just floating out there into space, overlapping each other. The moment of origin is long gone, but

130

the traces drift along forever. Maybe they drift on the Link in the same way. Ghosts of departed quantities."

"Huh?" Pettifore said.

"So why have they come together like this?" Sigornic asked. "Why in this particular place and time? And why is it crashing sectors across the Link."

Mercifully, the voices had grown dimmer in my head and were barely more than a distant whisper now. But I remembered the fury of the moment when I breached the affected sector wall. The pain that accompanied the argent flash.

"I think these patterns have been drifting out there for some time and are trying to reintegrate," I said. "I checked the Link Command record with, ahhhh, sources and found that it's been altered."

"Impossible," Pettifore said.

"VCIA," I retorted with a grim smile. "My sources suggest that the origin sectors of this thing were used in a black-op about thirty months back. Remember, this was the extreme fringe of the Link at that time. Anyway, something nasty went down; I still don't know exactly what, but personnel were lost. The whole region was deconstructed and reformatted as part of the cover-up, but some records don't get erased. Nor, apparently, do some neural patterns."

Pettifore started to ask me how I could know this, but Sigornic — who knew — shushed him and told me to go on.

"I think the patterns are traces of the lost ops team, and that somehow they've found a way to reintegrate. We know that the patterns have consistently moved toward higher levels of neural activity, from empty sectors to active. For instance, when the patterns crashed the Link-depot they went straight for the human Simulacra, reaching for the most powerful sites of neural activity. I went back and reviewed the record, and the patterns attacked the Simulacra first and only went for the lower level Virtual Fabricants afterward."

"This is nuts," Pettifore said.

"No," I continued, "I don't think so. I think the voices some of us have been hearing are a result of proximity to the recombinant patterns. Our brains worked like radio receivers open to the jumble of the ops team's scattered neural frequencies. Just as the traces have lingered on the Link, some of them are still bouncing around in our heads. Hopefully with less permanence."

"I agree," Lilian interrupted. "And I think these dissociated patterns are seeking an architecture through which they can reform. They went for the nearest human brains on the Link because a complete, familiar structure was there for them. Lacking that, they're trying to reshape aspects of the Link to accommodate their need."

"Can't we just sever the Link around them?" Sigornic said. "Not just deconstruct, but permanently remove all the affected sectors and reroute the Link?"

"I'm sure it could be done," I said, "but do you really want to?"

"Why not?" Pettifore asked.

"When I breached that sector wall, I thought I was tapping into a blank sector — that's what the Link record said, after all — but it wasn't blank at all. Something was there that even Link Command couldn't grok to. I was overwhelmed by that incredible light and whatever was behind it. It's all been swimming around in my head since then, sometimes blending with the voices, but bits of it make sense to me every so often, like an object I can half-see out of the corner of my eye. I think that sector was a kind of womb and the argent maelstrom was the chaos of something . . . in formation."

That shut them up. So after a suitably dramatic pause, I added: "And I wonder, if we sever it, would it be murder?"

Even though we'd been, you know, together and all, I had never been on the Link with Lilian before. Neither of us was much on cybersex — it's messy, and definitely *not* in the good way — and we'd always striven to keep our work lives separate. It's a silly thing, but I was secretly pleased to learn that she, too, picted on the Link exactly the way she looked in real life. Right down to her lousy taste in clothes and a dangling cigarette. It was enough to remind me what I used to see in her.

"Say," I asked her when we jumped in, "was you ever bit by a dead bee?"

"What?" she said. Which is, of course, the wrong answer. The search for the perfect woman goes on.

We'd argued with Sigornic for hours about what to do. The Creeping Terror, as I'd called it, was wending its way ever closer to proprietary corporate data space and Sigornic was feeling pressure to act fast. I argued that a few lost archiplexes were nothing compared to the phenomenon that might be at hand, but Pettifore, living up to expectation, was all for instigating a final solution purging the affected sectors. In the end, Lilian came to the rescue with the big idea.

"Helluva hunk of cheese," I said, admiring the unfolding program. Millions of angel-hair filaments spiralled around and through each other across the breadth of the mega-sector. At various points of intersection, tiny flashes of luminescence shimmered like fat snowflakes in moonlight.

"Let's just hope the mouse is hungry," Lilian said. She consulted again with the Klone of her professor friend, Prokop, and made a few final adjustments on the software for the neural net. "That's it. The net is at 97 percent. We have to get out of here to complete construction."

We'd been huddled inside a protective sphere within the mega-sector and jumped over to a monitoring station I'd assembled in what I hoped was a safe region. It had taken several days to get everything together and realise the programming. Five more sectors had crashed and Sigornic was sweating bullets from the heat, but he promised us our shot and remained true to his word. Pettifore griped almost constantly, though, so I had Sigornic send him out for an order of wild goose to go.

"How does it look?" Lilian asked.

I activated the monitoring program and a schematic of the area picted around us. The advancing pattern sat in a processing sector, presumably attracted by the vast neural activity. While it was there, we severed as many Link connections as we could without entirely disengaging the region from the supporting networks. The only remaining Link paths led to the mega-sector Lilian had programmed with the artificial neural net. The hope was that the pattern would advance toward the artificial net, but there was no guarantee. Several times, now, it had forged new Link paths where none existed before. If it happened again, the whole region would have to be purged and all affiliated AIs disempowered. The data loss would be staggering, but nothing compared to the potential of leaving the pattern free on the Link. It was the deal we'd struck with Sigornic.

"You're clear on what to do if it goes for the net?"

"Duhhh," I said and drooled a little down my chin. I materialised a naked pixie with a paper towel to dab away the line of saliva.

"That's not funny," Lilian scolded. "We can't afford to waste processing power on that kind of nonsense."

"Yes, dear," I said, eyeing her cigarette and saying nothing.

"Here goes," she said and a large, open electrical switch picted in the air in front of her. Lilian looked at me suspiciously, but I raised my hands.

"Not me," I said. "That's out of your head, Sister."

Lilian sighed and shrugged and threw the switch that activated the neural net. For a second, I thought I saw sizzling arcs climb a Jacob's Ladder behind her (along with an Igor-ian cackle), but it faded quickly and might have come from either of us.

The Creeping Terror or the pattern or whatever-the-hell-it-was reacted immediately. We watched it surge in the direction of the artificial net, and as it moved I quickly severed the Link passages behind it connecting to the core of Virtual.

"It's working!" Lilian yelled and redirected processing from our AI to maintain support for the sectors that the pattern was departing. In the event it left behind any more proto-patterns, like the ones I had previously tapped into, we wanted to try to support what might grow there. The idea was to isolate the main pattern and any residue in a self-sufficient cyberspace and then fully disconnect from the Link. Prokop had offered use of the university AI to maintain the space in exchange for exclusive rights to study the thing. We weren't sure his limited network could generate sufficient processing power, but it was the only viable option. Even so, Sigornic had practically kacked up a hairball before agreeing to the plan.

I carefully cauterised the remaining paths to the Link and monitored the isolated sectors, while Lilian charted the adaptation of the pattern as it entered the neural net. Everything seemed to be going well when a panicked message came through Prokop's Klone that the network was overloading and a systems crash was imminent.

"It hasn't settled in, yet," Lilian said

"Damn," I said, "there are still some open links." I tried to cut them as fast as I could. Prokop's Klone was positively apoplectic, its head spinning around in Linda Blair dervish whirls.

"Just another minute," Lilian pleaded.

"Too late. We've got to dump the other sectors," I told her.

"But . . . "

Lilian's "but" hung there like a wet willow branch while Prokop's Klone bounced up and down, screaming bloody hell. The picting started to go all wonky around us. Just as I made the decision to lose the other sectors and jump us both out, a blinding argent light exploded around us, enveloping the sector in a searing, heavenly embrace.

"It's in!" I heard Lilian yell. "Christ, what's that smell?"

"Uh-oh," I said.

And darkness was upon the face of the deep.

I came to in a black void, with no idea where I was and only a queasy certainty about who I was. The second matter resolved itself within a few moments, but I quickly decided it would have been better not to know.

"Lilian?" I called out. No response.

I unsteadily got to my feet, but either dizziness or the disconcerting effect of an utter absence of light, or both, sent me back to my knees. I tried to reconstruct my final moments of consciousness, recalling the flash of light and Lilian's exultant cry as the pattern integrated itself into the neural net. I remembered the sudden darkness and deathlike stench and realised that fail-safe protocols should have yanked us off the Link. If not . . .

"Uh-oh," I said.

I tried to access my personal RAM-space, but it simply wasn't there. No software. No jump-out protocols.

No nothing.

"Uh-oh," I said, with somewhat greater feeling.

I sought out emergency Link routines, but got no response. I reached out for any trace of Link Operating Systems: pict transformers, local compilers, even cursory BIOS.

Nada.

I tried to reason out my situation. I existed, somehow and somewhere, in a virtual space. I was apparently isolated from Link Command and any available software. But since I was here — wherever *here* was — the space was being maintained by some external processor. Either my own VAD, which was highly unlikely, or . . .

"Oh-ho!" I said.

I willed myself to drift through the darkness of the unformatted region and after a while started to rise off the ground. I briefly panicked and plummeted downward, but controlled my thoughts and again began to ascend. It was like floating in a heated pool, all comfort and warmth. Womb-like. Or so I imagine, not actually possessing prenatal memory.

I don't know how long I floated like that. I just sensed a steady upward drift, as if borne by a knowing current. Without volition, I came to rest, still in darkness, but feeling much more secure of my position. I could hear a low humming nearby, smooth as a Rolls Royce engine.

I reached out for the compiler. It had a terribly awkward interface, but this entire cyberspace proved exceptionally malleable and I was quickly able to reshape it. It took hardly any time at all to partition off some RAM-space and from there I was able to confirm that I was inside Prokop's AI, and established a link with the CPU. It was configured according to ASCII-AI guidelines, but for some reason I had considerable trouble executing even simple commands.

With a thought, I shed some light on the situation and saw that I was amid a vast, well, *vastness*. I stood on a featureless expanse of plane, extending endlessly in all directions without even a horizon line to break the monotony. I was naked, but there wasn't much I could do about it. I tried to execute a jump, but found that commands which had worked only moments before were not being executed. I took a deep breath and noted that the air smelled exceptionally clean. Almost like breathing pure oxygen.

I started to walk.

For a long while there was nothing to indicate any measure of progress through the wasteland. Then I saw a speck of colour in the distance and began running toward it. There was a figure, lying on the ground, curled in a fetal position. I ran harder, practically flying, and stopped on a dime as I was suddenly on top of her.

She looked about thirteen years old and just from the way she lay I could discern a sweet adolescent awkwardness. Her dark hair was trimmed in a terrible page boy cut and her face ran with too much make-up. She, too, was naked and I felt a brief pang of shame as my eyes dashed across the pale skin of her slightly budding breasts. I suspected that this gangly young girl represented her most deeply held self-image and I half-smiled through the pain.

I lifted Lilian's lifeless form and pressed her to me. She had no weight at all and after a moment simply evaporated in my arms, till all I held was the empty space around me.

I pressed on through the wasteland, for hours, days, centuries.

Or perhaps a few nanoseconds of CPU time.

They weren't waiting for me, but they didn't appear surprised by my presence. When the faces turned my way, the expressions seemed simply to say, "Oh, it's you."

The faces bubbled up from the ground all around me, expanding like balloons then contracting just as fast. Their features were imperfectly formed and they came and went so quickly that I couldn't really identify any one. Some of them lacked noses or mouths — some had too many — but all had eyes and they focused intently on me.

I tried to talk, but couldn't find a voice. I squatted on my haunches and reached down to touch the nearest face, but it squirted away from my touch, reappearing a dozen feet away.

My head rang with familiar voices, but I still couldn't make out any of the words. The voices were inharmonious, but less discordant than before. As if they'd agreed on a common key, if not the same song. And I thought I heard a small, new voice.

After a while I caught on to some of it. The message wasn't received on a linguistic level, but emerged through sight and smell and taste and touch. I understood that the wandering patterns had indeed come together and recombined in the neural net. The process was still going on, I sensed, and somehow Lilian had been drawn into it. Why I hadn't been absorbed as well, I had no idea. Perhaps it was just proximity. Perhaps the attraction was more fundamental.

Or just dumb luck.

I was certain that Lilian was gone, though. I knew there could be no disentanglement from that chaotic, embryonic new being. I had a suspicion Prokop might not be able to access his machine again, either. My feeling was that this . . . thing had its own intentions, or at least instincts, and they had little to do with the rest of the Link. At least for now.

I stood up again and the voices faded. The bubbling slowed and the faces disappeared. As the last few melted back into the ground I was pretty sure that one of them smiled at me.

Lilian's smile.

Then it just disappeared. And so did I.

When I came to, the first thing I saw was Lilian's corpse. She was sprawled on the floor, Link-gear dangling, her body tucked in a gangly and hauntingly familiar fetal curl.

I drew the hair back from her face and kissed her goodbye.

Introduction to *"Sous Rature"*

I have to admit to a particular fondness for this story. You see, I was an academic once upon a time. That dissertation I mentioned earlier earned me a Ph.D. in 'Communication Theory and Research' from the University of Southern California. Add a couple of bucks to one of those and you can buy yourself a cappuccino. Some joints even throw in a little square of chocolate, no extra charge.

Academia wasn't all bad: I got paid for screwing-off for four years. I met my wife; I can legitimately call myself 'Dr.' when the mood suits me (or when I'm talking to banks); I got to live in Los Angeles . . .

Damn, I always go one too far on these lists.

I can, in fact, remember a time when academia was exciting to me, when the pursuit and study of ideas seemed a hell of a nice way to make a living. And while there were brief snatches when that notion was realised, too much of the reality of university life consisted of barbed spite and petty politics of the most perverse kind. I've been out of academia for nearly ten years, but I can still, at the slightest provocation, work up an astonishing fury over my grad school experience. There are professors out there who (to steal my old office mate's line) better never be crossing the street in front of me when I'm in my car.

My area of expertise largely concerned applications of theories of postmodernity to aspects of popular culture. Like many genre writers, I am a devotee of movies and television and comics and all manner of pulp fictions, and that love figures rather prominently in my work. The main thing I learned as an academic was that I liked writing such fictions vastly more than writing about them. "Sous Rature" — while containing a healthy helping of postmodern gibberish (if that isn't a redundancy) — manages to combine a little bit of both.

(A deeply digressive footnote: one of the great regrets of my life is that I once had a chance to buy Jacques Derrida a beer and didn't do it. He was visiting USC and, attended by a *coterie* of

VIPs and hangers-on, turned up at a bar some friends and I hung out in. Though I thought about it as I went up to order a round of drinks, a failure of nerve prevented me from buying a beer and dropping it on the table in front of him. So, Jacky-boy: this deconstructed Bud's for you.)

Sous Rature

WHEN THE PHONE RINGS IN THE MIDDLE OF the night, most people think: who died?

I know it's only Klein.

"I don't understand this *sous rature* stuff, Steve. How the hell does the bastard get away with it? I mean, he just crosses the bloody words out and then leaves them there on the page like squashed bugs. Doesn't that bother anyone? Isn't there a law? Doesn't it drive you crazy?"

Our apartment sits just off-campus, in a neatly appointed professorial ghetto. The phone rests on the floor across the room from the bed because the cord won't reach to the night stand. I don't know why we haven't just bought a cordless — or moved the bed — but that's the way it is.

Elaine sleeps right through the calls. She used to bolt awake and roll off the bed, grabbing the receiver in one smooth motion. It amazed me how she could answer in a crisp, businesslike voice. As if it wasn't the middle of the night; as if she hadn't been stone dead to the world two seconds earlier.

Now she doesn't even turn over.

"It's because he's French, isn't it? They get away with *every*thing. I can live with Baudrillard's bullshit, and even that crazy Virilio. But this *erasure* thing is too much. I mean, it's up there with Jerry Lewis and Jean-Marie Le Pen. It's, you know . . . *God*, it's brilliant. It fits."

I knew I'd regret lending Klein the Derrida books. I knew it would mean a lost night's sleep.

"Klein . . . "

"I just, I can't fully make sense of it. Steve, this is your field. You've got to explain it to me, I . . . I think I see where it fits — it's *so* bloody fractal — but I just can't quite . . . I'm afraid I'm going to have to really learn French for this guy, Steve. I mean, not just that oo-la-la crap that got me through Foucault. He's . . . "

"Do you know what time it is Klein?"

"Uhhhh . . . hold on."

"No, Klein . . . "

Too late. I glanced at Elaine. I wondered if the little bug inside her was awake or asleep. The duvet had become twisted around her slightly swollen belly. A thin line of saliva trailed from her mouth, watering the faded flowers on the pillowcase.

"It's almost three-thirty."

"Klein . . . " I sighed and stared vacantly at Elaine's heavy breasts.

"You really have to go back to Heidegger," I began.

I started having doubts about fractals and such the day one of my undergrads — a gaunt, black-clad cultural studies major with the unlikely moniker of B. Bronski — came to class wearing a t-shirt emblazoned with the Mandelbrot set on the front and 'I ♥ Chaos' on the back. This same kid handed in a term paper with the title: 'The Prosthetic Aesthetic: Fractal Postmodernism in the Cyberpunk/Splatterpunk Imperative'. After that I figured it was only a matter of time before old Benoit himself performed a turn on *Oprah*.

Not that I entirely understand the stuff. If poked sternly with a pointed stick I can creditably acquit myself with an explication of strange attractors and sensitive dependence on initial conditions — God knows, I've heard Klein go on about it enough — but it's still something of a strain for me. A lifetime in comparative literature departments has taken its toll on a scientific aptitude which wasn't terrific to begin with. Once upon a time, I dreamed about becoming an astronomer — next best thing to astronaut — but Cs and Ds in physics and calculus quickly stymied such fancies and sent me running for the shelter of Chaucer's little helpers.

Still, my interest never entirely waned. I kept up with Drexler on nano-technology, and was hyping VR and cyberculture *long* before *Wired* magazine. Barnsley and Gleick and all the others opened up new worlds for me even as I completed my doctorate in English. I sprang for a top of the line PC and high-res monitor when that kind of stuff still cost an arm and a leg, and played with fractal-generating software, staying up into the wee hours, reliving the 'star-gate' sequence from *2001*.

And I re-channelled my interest from science to science fiction, cajoling the department chair into letting me teach a graduate seminar by throwing a little Pynchon and Lessing in with the Dick and Ballard. I set to work on the *definitive* study of Olaf Stapledon and even scammed some funding to organise a small conference on popular science and science fiction.

Which was where I met Klein.

"Klein call?"

I nodded and gave Elaine a mug and a kiss. It was a morning ritual and sort of unwritten contract that I get up first and bring her tea in bed. I like it. The ritual, I mean. Like any red-blooded American — even a Yank at (well, near) Oxford — I hate tea.

"He wake you? I didn't see you stir."

She took a series of quick, tiny sips, the way the dog laps his water, and leaned back against the pillows.

"No," she said, "but I dreamed of bells."

"Wedding bells?"

"Don't be a cheek. What did he want this time?"

I stood at the mirror adjusting my tie. My sole sop to respectability. I ran the back of my fingers under my chin and decided maybe I should have shaved after all.

"He wanted me to explain deconstruction to him."

"Aauuuughhh," Elaine laughed and darjeeling sprayed out her nose. She dabbed at it with her nighty, still giggling. "What in the world for?"

I stared at my face in the mirror. A nasty zit was blooming in the crease between my nose and cheek, and my hair had visibly thinned again during the night. Where did it go?

"You know Klein. He's onto another of his big ideas. Something about a relationship between deconstruction and chaos theory. Really, the bastard already knows it better than I do. You remember Derrida's notion of *sous rature*, putting things under erasure?"

Elaine half-squinted at me. "Ehhhhh . . . "

I sat on the edge of the bed, softly rubbing her belly. I often do it without even thinking. "You know how he writes a word, then crosses it out, but leaves the crossed-out expression in the text?"

"I think I vaguely remember. It's been a while, though, and I could never stomach any of that crap."

"Yeah, it's all a bit of a con. Or a decon. But erasure's meant to indicate a concept or idea that's under question or whose meaning is to be doubted. An idea that's been negated, but not dismissed. By placing it *sous rature*, it can be there and not there at the same time. Well, that's a nasty simplification, but you get the idea."

"Uh-huh . . . "

"So Klein thinks this somehow ties in with fractal geometry. After reading some Derrida, he's decided that deconstruction is, and I quote, ' . . . a chaotic philosophical function'. And he claims that the process is dangerous because it has fractal contours. Something about gamma matrices approaching a threshold in maximum likelihood models."

"Sorry?"

"I know, I know. He explained it to me for an hour, but I didn't get it, and it was four o'clock in the damn morning. Anyway, he's all excited about it, so we're going to meet for lunch. But you know Klein."

"We all know Klein," Elaine sighed. I kissed her again and headed out the door. I thought she said something and stuck my head back in the room.

"How's that?"

Her hands were folded over the empty mug resting lightly on her bulging stomach and she stared at the wall with her head cocked slightly to one side.

"I thought I heard bells again," she said.

The student union is the oldest building on campus: a massive gothic structure embraced by thick tendons of ivy and perched at the edge of Library Slope. The Senior Common Room offers a stunning view of the valley below and a sparkling expanse of water to the northwest. The place was packed, but Klein had already secured seats. The canteen food was your basic preprocessed, post-industrial gruel, but the university subsidises the prices so there's always a queue.

Klein looked his usual dishevelled self, every bit the absent-minded professor. He wore a creased, sky blue shirt that was a couple of sizes too big, with the cuffs flapping loose and the buttons fastened all the way up to his chin. His black polyester pants nearly matched the shade of his peeling Hush Puppies, but he wore them at high tide depth and they didn't go at all with the brown socks that drooped around his bony ankles. Klein's kinky red hair was thin across the top, lending him an unfortunate Bozo the Clown look exaggerated by his overlarge nose. The bags under his eyes were thick and dark as war paint, and magnified by a pair of cheap glasses that were filthy beyond belief.

Klein hadn't shaved and had his usual odour about him. It was the smell of someone who's just come off a lengthy flight: not dirty, exactly, but musky and tired. Klein works odd hours and on more than one occasion I've been around when his wife — a truly stunning redhead named Margaritte — has had to publicly scold him about bathing. Klein never gets embarrassed; he just forgets such mundanities.

"You see the paper?" he said by way of greeting.

"Let me guess: rationing on soap and water."

Klein looked puzzled for a moment, then unself-consciously sniffed at his armpit. An elderly administrative type at the next table snorted, but Klein didn't notice.

"Oh," he shrugged. "Sorry. I've been working."

"What's in the news?" I smiled.

He handed me a copy of *The Guardian*, folded over to the Style page.

"You fashion beast!" I said. He grinned like a kid and pointed at the lead item.

It was about a new line of women's clothing. The patterns were to be fractal-based and there was considerable to-do about how they mirrored nature's own true design, with some outrageous pseudo-scientific doublespeak about chaos theory and complexity.

"Old B. Bronski's ahead of his time," I mumbled.

"Heh?"

"Nothing. Yeah, so what? You could have predicted something like this. I think people already have. Christ, the bookstore sells fractal postcards."

"Read the sidebar."

I skimmed the accompanying article. It was about the manufacturing process that had been devised for producing the clothes. The process was also rooted in fractal concepts, so that a standard assembly line could be employed, but every item produced would be subtly different. The idea was to create complete uniqueness within the confines of mass production. The engineer who designed the system was quoted as saying that his software package was going to revolutionise every aspect of assembly line manufacturing.

"Interesting," I said, digging into my salad, "but also a little scary in that zany, fin-de-millennial way."

"Scary how?" Klein's eyes were alight.

"If this is right, it maybe changes — or changes again — the definition of 'unique'. If you can mass produce singularity, then what does it mean? What possible value could be left for such a notion?"

Klein nodded approval and handed me the business page with a short item circled in red. Grundrisse-Rand had commissioned Frank Gehry to design their new EU headquarters in Bonn. It would he the first corporate commission of a piece of deconstructivist architecture, and one of the few major deconstructivist designs to be realised.

"Yeah, I heard about this the other day on Radio 4. I thought the deconstructivist thing was yesterday's news, but I guess someone's interested. Gehry's still hot, at least."

"But what do you make of it?"

"I can't say I much care for it, at least not the sketches I've seen. The stuff makes me sort of dizzy with all those odd angles and exposed superstructure. Very Weimar, somehow. Decadent. The kind of thing that's fun in theory, but awful for the poor saps who'll have to live and work in it. But then I don't really know much about architecture."

"Bloody hell!" Klein said, slapping his palm on the spread out paper. "I'm talking about two articles on the same day in the fucking *Guardian!* Fractals and deconstruction!"

"Yeah?"

"It's the ideas, Steve. Don't you see? The ideas."

"Yeah?" I tried again.

"It's what I was talking about last night. You know that there are very precise mathematical models for how things are diffused in culture? It doesn't matter what — VCRS, compact discs, AIDS — they're all the same in these models. Threshold criteria and critical mass levels determining rates of adoption. It's all very calculable and occurs along an exaggerated S-shaped curve, with a small number of people adopting early on, then an explosion during which most everyone else climbs on the bandwagon."

"Sounds reasonable."

"Well, the thing is that it works for ideas and concepts, too. And what's more, I think that when certain ideas — in the form of the things we call theories — fulfil those critical mass requirements, they become something more. Something . . . substantial."

"Don't know if that's true, but it sounds neat," I said. "I can't even balance my cheque book so I don't know from math models, but . . . well . . . what do you mean substantial? You mean accepted, right?"

"No, Steve. I mean substantial. Palpable. Real. And it's dangerous as hell."

I was shaking my head. "You said that on the phone last night — this morning — but I still don't follow."

"There's a very thin line separating conception from reality. From the idea of something being true to that selfsame thing becoming physical law."

"Ahem," I said.

"Okay, look. You know that everything we do, everything we build, the entire design of the Western world is more or less based on parameters set forth in Euclidean geometry."

"I suppose I know that somewhere."

"Exactly. Well, mathematicians have always known that Euclidean geometry is itself based on certain approximations of reality — lousy approximations, it turns out — but they've always just brushed that little matter aside and stuck it under the label of 'assumptions'. They've gone ahead and said it doesn't matter.

"But Euclid is the law for most of us. For two thousand years we've regarded those Euclidean approximations as realer than Coca-Cola. For the vast multitudes, for *you* to take an example, those assumptions about the logic of space and geometry aren't ignored, they're completely *unknown*. Let me ask you something. What was the world like before Euclid?"

"I don't know. It was . . . simpler, I guess. Smaller, more compact. Less technological, certainly."

"Yes!" Klein practically jumped out his chair. His glasses flew off his face and bounced on the table. He grabbed at them, smearing the lenses with butter, but stuck them right back on his nose.

"Before Euclid this wasn't a world of science and technology, it was a world of gods and magic. Euclid came along and reshaped geometry, yes, but at the same time he reshaped an entire *cosmology*!"

"Whoa, wait a minute. Correct me if I'm wrong, but Euclid dates back to what? 300 or so B.C.? That cosmology of Greek and Roman gods survived him by centuries. And even then you're talking, what, hundreds of years more before things really caught on."

"Of course!" Klein shouted. "Because it took that long for the Euclidian conception to approach its critical mass. You couldn't pick up a paper in ancient Rome and read about how Euclid redefined the world! There was no Page Three girl to help spread word of the invention of this neat new geometry. There wasn't any CNN to tell the masses: Greek gods dead, film at ten."

Klein was sort of bouncing up and down as he spoke and alternately enthralling and intimidating me. Generally excitable, he was now at the edge of something more extreme. The room had emptied out, but those still around eyed him with nervous apprehension or undisguised mirth,

"There were no mass media. It took hundreds of years for ideas to be made real. Now it happens in no time. Or practically no time. The first work to see chaos for what it was appeared barely three decades ago. Within a few years we have theories of fractal geometry and complexity, and philosophies of deconstruction. And now it's on Yves Saint Laurent's bloody knickers."

"Take it easy, Klein. Sit down."

Klein looked around. He was breathing hard and his glasses were so filthy he might as well have been wearing shades. He stood still for a moment, ran his tongue over his dry lips and flopped back into the chair.

"Two thousand years ago Euclid killed the gods. What's going to happen this time?"

I had no idea, but strongly suspected that Klein didn't have it quite right. The other diners went back to their affairs. I started to proffer a counter-argument when Klein's already ashen pallor went even whiter.

"Shit," he said and got up. I turned around and saw Margaritte eying us from the door. Klein ran over to his wife, but she didn't look happy. They started arguing almost at once, then she stormed off. He trudged after her, pressing his glasses to his face with one hand and I heard their rising voices carrying on down the hall, Shaking my head and smiling at the onlookers with a 'well-what-can-you-do' kind of grin, I gathered up his books and papers and took them with me. I didn't know what to think of Klein's theory, but I was frankly worried for his mental health.

Rightly so, as it turned out. For I would never see him alive again.

Klein called at 4:02:35. Ah, the priceless precision of the digital age.

I grabbed the phone on the second ring. Elaine never moved. I'd neither seen nor heard from Klein for ten days following our lunch, though I'd tried to call him. In the interim I'd come across an article in *The Spectator* decrying the dangerous political correctness of the deconstructive influence in schools, and seen two TV news features relating to chaotic processes on the Internet. One even featured a sound bite from Mandelbrot.

"Hi, Steve."

It was a most un-Kleinlike greeting. He sounded tired and hoarse and out of sorts.

"Hey, Klein. How are you?"

"It looks bad, Steve. I'm frightened."

"What? Of what? What's wrong?"

I glanced over and saw that Elaine was awake and watching me. I spoke softly, but there was an edge to my tone that must have got though to her. She looked groggy but concerned.

"I've been running the models, Steve. Exact calculations. Thousands of iterations before the equations converged. Soon that won't work any more, you know. Iterative processes are doomed. But for now, for a little while longer, maximum likelihood estimates don't lie. Though I wish they did."

"Klein . . . Have you been drinking?"

Elaine's eyebrows leapt up like grasshoppers. I'd never known Klein to imbibe anything stronger than tea with lemon.

"A little. Margaritte keeps a supply you know."

I didn't wonder. "Are things, you know, okay with you and Margaritte? After the other day and all?"

There was a lengthy pause with only line noise and Klein's deviated septum to fill the silence.

"I . . . that is, Margaritte . . . we're approaching a threshold, too. It's all gone to turbulence, now, and I can see the edge. I can feel it, Steve. I . . . I know it doesn't matter. In the bigger picture, I mean. The equations, the models they prove it. But still. Shit, Steve. It still, you know, it hurts."

There was another staticky silence. I hesitated, but with my eyes fixed on Elaine's, decided to go ahead.

"Listen to me, Klein. You can't always . . . depend on the numbers. They're like you were saying with Euclid, you know? They're not quite real. They're just representations and they're different from people. Abstract. People aren't fixed things. Even when you think they are."

"I don't know, Steve . . . "

"What I'm about to tell you, I've never talked about before and I . . . we don't like to think about it. Especially now. But I'm going to tell you. All right?"

I was talking to Klein, but looking at Elaine. She nodded back at me.

"My first teaching position was back in the States, right out of my doctorate. It was a shit hole of a department in a dull Midwestern town and it was horrible. Elaine was miserable. She had left behind her job and all her friends because it was the only position I could get and we were committed to staying together.

"Well, let's just say that things got bad. Real bad. I had a killer teaching load and the town was full of overqualified faculty spouses, so Elaine couldn't find any work. I'd come home tired and mean and she'd be angry and bored. For a while we communicated through grunts and yells."

"Steve . . . "

"Just listen, Klein. It was the end of the semester and we hadn't . . . been together for weeks. I was starting to browse the classifieds for studio apartments. So it's right around finals time — and you know, I've got a couple, three hundred undergrads and it's just pure chaos, you'll pardon the expression — when this perky little sophomore comes to see me. She's a total airhead, but with one of those teenage bodies that won't quit. And she's failing the course and the door's closed and she *knows* what she's doing and I'm unhappy and . . . I don't know, Klein, I just figured what the fuck, you know? I just . . . it was just an idea, Klein.

"I hated myself for it and I still do. I figured for sure it was the end for us and probably my career. Hell, I thought maybe that's why I did it. And I won't lie to you, Klein, it got pretty bad. But it also brought stuff into focus. There was a lot of pain, but we found a way through it. Eventually. And my point is this: in the end I . . . we decided that it was all just a moment. Just an *idea*, you see? And we rose above it. We *made* healing tractable. An idea isn't real unless you make it so. *Choose* to make it so. Otherwise it's *only* an idea; only an abstraction. I mean, isn't that what we were talking about?"

There was silence, and then there was laughter. Distant, dim and very scary.

"*Just* an idea. Just an *idea.*" He said it over and over and was still laughing when he hung up the phone.

I tried to call him back, but the line was engaged. I crawled back into bed and kissed the tears off Elaine's face. I tried to go back to sleep, but I kept hearing Klein's laughter in my head.

I don't know what time the phone rang.

Elaine had gone to bed early, but I stayed up to watch *The South Bank Show*. Melvin Bragg was interviewing Derrida.

At about half eleven, Elaine staggered out of the bedroom clutching her belly. Her face was white as milk, and blood oozed down her thighs. She was crying and moaning and collapsed to the floor before I could get to her. I thought about calling an ambulance, but couldn't bear the wait. I lifted her up and put her in the car, then sped to the local hospital in a panicked daze.

Elaine lost the baby, but it was worse than that. Her uterus had become malformed in the pregnancy. It was actually touch and go for a while, although the surgeon didn't tell me that until later. The doctor also said she had never seen or heard of anything quite like it before, and asked if Elaine had ever worked around radioactive or toxic substances. I couldn't make any sense of it then, but of course anything and everything is explainable now.

I left the hospital confused and exhausted, but satisfied that Elaine was going to be okay.

The police were waiting for me when I got home. A detective accompanied by a pair of PCs. I immediately assumed something had happened to Elaine.

"Steven Rich?" the detective asked.

I managed a nod.

He mumbled his name, but I didn't catch it. "Do you know a Dr. Paul Klein?"

Another nod.

"When did you last have contact with him?"

"Week or two ago. Why? What's going on? Is this about Elaine? Is Elaine all right?"

The detective glanced at one of the constables who started back toward the car. "I don't know about any Elaine, Sir. But Dr. Klein killed his wife and took his own life early this morning. Your phone number was found on his person. Did he call you at any time last night or early today?"

I never thought of myself as a fainter, but things went black around me. I felt like Dorothy caught up in the twister and carried over the rainbow into some alien landscape. Fortunately the cop caught me by the arm and helped me to a sitting position on the front steps.

I told him in rambling terms about Elaine and what had happened the previous night. That I knew Klein and Margaritte were having troubles, but that his news was an utter shock. He clucked sympathetically and tried to look interested.

"Okay," he said. "We may want to talk to you some more, but that can wait. Why don't you get some rest now."

The cop helped me inside and guided me to the living room sofa where I collapsed. He closed the front door softly as he left and I fell quickly and deeply asleep.

Neither of us thought to check the blinking light on the answerphone.

Our answering machine is an old model — it works well enough that I never saw any reason to buy a fancier one — but it only gives you sixty seconds to leave a message.

"I've been running the equations for days, Steve, but they won't converge. The iterations will go on forever now.

"I was grading exams the other day, you know? The first-year class. A girl wrote out elaborate calculations for a problem that didn't require it, a problem with a simple answer. In the end she just put a big 'X' through it all and gave up. I saw it as *sous rature* and gave her full credit.

"It's coming now, Steve. Almost here. I thought I should warn you. We're at the base of the S-curve, but the explosion will happen soon. The numbers don't . . . didn't lie . . .

"I put her under erasure. Margaritte. I thought it was for the best. The only thing I wish . . . "

Sixty seconds.

I remember ~~Klein~~ once told me about something called luminiferous aether. It was an early, discarded notion in physics, like spontaneous generation or phlogiston. Aether was supposed to be the medium which filled all unoccupied space and was the mechanism for transmission of magnetic and electrical forces. ~~Klein~~ said that there had been some promising work verifying its existence and the idea was catching on until Einstein disproved it all with relativity. ~~Klein~~ always repeated the same thing when the topic of relativity came up.

"Hell of an idea," he would say.

Elaine came home from the hospital after a week. We talked about the ~~baby~~ and about ~~Klein~~ and ~~Margaritte~~. She cried a lot and told me she understood if I didn't want to stay with her now, but I just told her to hush and held her tight. I didn't let her hear the phone message, nor did I voice my suspicions, but after a while she pieced it together herself.

The curve is on the rise: ~~Klein's~~ explosion has started to detonate and the world has begun to change. It's hard to keep up with because it's hard to know what's ~~real~~, what you can count on to remain solid, consistent from day to day.

The world doesn't meet at right angles any more. All the assumptions that we've depended on for so long have crawled out of the rotten woodwork of our lives. The old formulae don't add up and the new ones are still a mystery. I know it's what ~~Klein~~ suspected, but I'm also sure that it's less awful than he feared. It is ~~certain~~ that he overreacted; living *sous rature* is still better than dying under it.

Like bugs or fish that spend their lives in the darkness, this sudden flash of bold light has sent all of us scurrying in turbulent new directions. It's scary, but it's sort of interesting, too. At times it's even wondrous. ~~God~~ knows, it's ~~chaotic~~, but not without its own subtleties of ~~order~~.

Mostly, it's a hell of an idea.

Introduction to "Waltz in Vienna"

This is another story that sold to a magazine that promptly folded, and then took its time before finally seeing print in *Dark of the Night*, the first Pumpkin Books effort. It's a story that worried me some when I wrote it, because I feared it might be read as misogynistic. I took some reassurance from a prominent female editor who read the story (but didn't buy it) and who didn't see it that way at all. Of course, one of the pleasures/traumas of writing is discovering just how differently people read what you have written. I know that 'reception theory' is a whole tradition devoted to the study of this phenomenon, but as ever, there's nothing quite so eye-opening as first-hand experience of the difference between theory and practice.

"Waltz in Vienna" is one of two Holocaust-related stories in the collection, and it is rather more angry (and perhaps didactic) a tale than "Lily's Whisper" which follows. The basis of the story is my unending dismay over what I regard as a dangerous view of history which seeks to explain the destiny of the many by the actions of the few. To this day, it seems, there are those who want to explain human evil — like Nazi Germany — as a function of the actions of one person or a small group of individuals, without reference to the multitudes who allow it to happen in their name. This 'Great Man' perspective seems a pernicious idea to me, though an obviously comforting one. In this view, what the German people did is not their fault, but the fault of Hitler and his immediate circle. The same view pervades to this day, creating villains like Saddam Hussein and Slobadon Milosevic (though villains they very clearly are) without taking account of the cultures and people which nourish them. Milosevic is an utter monster, but the Serb people are paranoid, fascistic shits. Hussein deserves to be gutshot and left for rat food, but he is merely one of a multitude of petty tyrants in a part of the world which has been blissfully resistant to even the ideas of democracy and equality for centuries. And lest anyone accuse me of racism or small-minded xenophobia, the same rule holds for western leaders and peoples. The fact that most Americans are ignorant of the atrocities carried out in their names in places like El Salvador and Chile, makes us no less culpable for those actions. We just have the biggest and bestest guns and (so far) haven't been called to account for what we've done/allowed to be done.

"Waltz in Vienna," the immediate inspiration of which was a Leonard Cohen song based on a Garcia Lorca poem, is about the futility of trying to escape the past. Lots of my work is about the same thing. If that makes you mad, well . . . good!

Waltz in Vienna

MAGDA TOUCHED HER HAND TO THE WEATHERED stone, felt its warmth seep into her skin, her blood. The building stood on the north side of the Karntnerstrasse and basked all day in the frail afternoon sun. A bitter November wind stabbed its icepick finger through her long leather coat. Pedestrians moved quickly, spurred by the sharp edge of the cold, as newspaper pages and cigarette wrappers bounded across the streets and sidewalks like tired birds fleeing toward their winter rest. Magda shut her eyes and pressed herself against the wall of the old café wishing she could melt into it, become a part of its warmth and strength, and gaze out forever on the timeless Vienna street.

A lean teenaged boy came up and asked if she was all right. She admired his tousled blond hair and strong Aryan features, his eyes as clear and blue as the autumn sky. She thought of the boys she had known so long ago with that same hard and dangerous, but beautiful look. She smiled slightly and nodded at him. He grinned back and bowed like a gentleman from some other age, then put his headphones back on and hopped off down the street. Her gaze followed him until the crowd swallowed him up again, and she thought: *In a few years they'll be fighting to sleep in his bed.* And then: *Perhaps they already are.*

She pressed on up the avenue and crossed the street to the Hotel of A Thousand Windows, where a brightly dressed doorman with a purple feather in his hat ushered her in with exaggerated politeness. She shrugged off her coat and fingered the gold locket draped around her neck. It was 5:15 pm and she was slightly late. She stood directly beneath a noisy heating vent and allowed the dry, warm air to caress her as she caught her breath. She sauntered through the pristine lobby with its antique chairs and plush divans. A massive stone fireplace with a broad, carved mantle dominated the room. Tiny cameos had been hand-cut into the rich mahogany. The carvings were worn, but the faces looked tortured, crying out for release. The sight made Magda uneasy. The fire that roared beneath conjured the image of souls burning in Hell begging, if not for an end to their torment, at least for some measure of forgiveness. She tried not to glance at the mantle as she went by, but the faces penetrated her self-conscious peripheral vision, and she walked faster.

She was pleased, took it for granted, that heads still turned as she passed. She looked a good decade younger than her near seventy years, though she felt her age more often than she cared to admit. Her skin was still remarkably soft and unlined, her fine hair gone not to grey but a rich silver: a storm cloud lit from within by lightning. She moved with the smoothness and grace of a dove on the wind. Her clothes were tailored and expensive, befitting her age and bearing; simple and perfect.

She pushed at the massive oak door which led to the hotel bar, sniffing the odours of tobacco and sweat that wafted through the long room. Light streamed in from a wall of multicoloured glass at the far end. Each pane was separately fitted into an elaborate, labyrinthine pattern that was dizzying to look upon. It fractured the light into a delicate array of soft brightness and deep shadow that bathed the room in a mysterious, romantic glow.

Magda was mesmerised for a moment by a curl of smoke drifting slowly through a shaft of setting sunlight, the deep amber haze rising like an angel's wing.

She scanned the bar and dim booths for her daughter, but couldn't immediately pick Hannah out of the late afternoon crowd.

She strolled toward the far end of the bar, squinting a little against the windows' glare. Two silhouettes sat face to face at the end of the bar, the wall of glass at their backs. Magda recognised Hannah's profile. She was talking to a man, tall and broad with a large nose and jutting brow. They were laughing, and Magda saw the man lay his hand atop her daughter's, but as she approached he abruptly stood up. His face hung in shadow, but there was something familiar, something disturbing about his shape. She could tell from his posture and the nimbus created by his shock of thick hair that he was a young man. For a moment, it seemed, he was looking right at her — right *through* her, she thought — and she felt an inexplicable queasiness. Just then a woman with a frilly hat stood up in front of Magda, briefly obstructing her view. As Magda's field of vision cleared she saw the man disappear out the door. She caught a glimpse of his back, of the long brown hair tucked into the collar of his heavy coat, and then he was gone.

Hannah had been watching the fellow depart and didn't notice her mother approach. As Magda called her name she turned slowly, as if torn from some vision. The glassy look on her daughter's face made Magda uneasy. She felt sure she knew the man from somewhere and the connotations were not pleasant. She sat down and kissed her daughter lightly on the cheek. The bartender appeared and she ordered a coffee and brandy. Magda asked Hannah who she was talking to.

"Just passing the time," Hannah said, "waiting for you. He's another guest here."

The dreamy lilt in her daughter's voice added to Magda's discomfort. She sensed something more than casual conversation had passed in their exchange, but knew better than to make an issue of it.

"He knows a lot about Vienna. He was telling me all about this section of the city and about the history of the hotel. Did you know that Garcia Lorca used to come here before the war? He lived in one of the suites upstairs, maybe even the one we're staying in."

"Dago faggot," Magda said.

"Mother!" Hannah chided. "Anyway, he said that Garcia Lorca used to drink in this bar, and he danced in the ballroom every night. He even wrote a poem about it. Isn't that interesting?"

Magda shrugged. "You should be careful who you talk to," she said. "Especially a strange man in a bar."

"Really, Mama," Hannah teased. "Do you fear for my virtue?"

Magda snorted derisively,

"Besides, he was perfectly lovely. And such beautiful eyes."

Magda felt suddenly dizzy. *His eyes*, she thought, *his eyes were . . .*

The bartender set the drinks down in front of them and the spell was broken. The moment and the memory were gone, but Magda's unease remained. As she sipped from the steaming mug, Hannah told her about her day and Magda's sense of discomfort began to lift as well.

But not completely.

Magda stood on the balcony of their suite, leaning into the cold, staring out at the ever-present stream of activity on the Ringstrasse. A cigarette burned down in her hand as she thought about the city of her youth. She had been back to Vienna only once since the war, for her honeymoon with Hannah's father. The girl had been conceived in the city, in a small pension on the other side of the river. Her husband had made a small fortune in the re-industrialisation of Germany after the war, but died in a car crash when Hannah was still a girl. Magda had taken many lovers in the years since his passing, but nothing equalled the passion of that week in Vienna.

During the war, of course . . .

She didn't like to think of that time, preferring to mark the start of her life from the day she met her husband. The war years had been painful, for *everyone*, she thought, not just the Jews, though it seemed to her that was all anyone ever talked about anymore. People found themselves doing things that they never would have dreamed of merely to survive. Young girls did what they had to. They . . .

Damn it, she thought, *no reason to summon what has been forgotten*. This Vienna, this Europe was a phoenix cleansed of old ashes. She had been in the city for several days now and not once had the cruel images of the past played through her thoughts. She had carefully buried them years ago when she began her clean, new life. Why should they suddenly return?

That man, she thought, *the one at the bar*. It was so familiar, like the name of a song you can't quite recall but whose tune you find yourself humming over and over. There was something about him being here in Vienna, something that pricked at ancient wounds.

She yelped at the sharp pain in her fingers and tossed away the hot stub of the cigarette. The end of the day winked at the horizon as Magda took a final glance at the city. She thought she could see a plume of smoke rising in the distance and she shuddered, recalling a day long before when flames were all around. She squinted into the deepening darkness and realised it was only a rain cloud catching the last stray rays of the sun. She suddenly felt very cold and went back into the room.

Hannah came out of her bedroom tugging at the zipper of a short leather skirt that might as well have been painted on her body.

"God in heaven," Magda said. "Do you think you could display a little more of yourself?"

Hannah smiled wickedly and Magda shook her head. Hannah didn't much resemble her mother; she was slight and boyish with short raven-black hair and big green eyes. She wore a scarlet silk blouse open to mid-chest, and as she bent to put on her boots Magda could see most of her slight breasts. She clucked disgustedly and walked over to Hannah, securing two buttons as the girl stood up.

"Oh, Mama," she said and giggled, pushing Magda's hands away, slipping one button open again. She went to the door, but hesitated at the threshold.

"Are you sure you don't want to come down with me? I don't think it will be too loud."

"No, no," Magda said. "You go on. I'm too tired tonight, I think I'll just read for a while."

"This is supposed to be a holiday, Mama. You're supposed to have fun."

"This is fun for me."

"Who knows, maybe you'll meet a man," Hannah taunted.

"I've had enough with men, thank you. You just go and have a nice time." She smiled, but the image of the man at the bar bled back into her thoughts. Her smile wavered.

"Are you sure you'll be all right?"

"Go already!"

"Okay, but if you get bored or change your mind, come downstairs."

Hannah blew her a kiss and went out. Magda stood for a moment staring at the closed door, the uneasy feeling from the afternoon rising up through her belly. She tried again to jog the memory of the silhouette, but it was like catching a breeze in a jar. She poured a brandy and sat down with her Ezra Pound. After a while she took her pills and turned out the light.

She was asleep within minutes.

The ballroom was called The Gallery of Delights and the glassworks featured detailed etchings of a nineteenth century Viennese winter. Soft light spilled from antique lanterns set along the walls. The band was outfitted for rock and roll, though several classical instruments fitted with electric pick-ups rested on stands at the rear of the stage. Hannah walked in as the musicians were going on a break and the conversation level rose to fill the sudden quiet.

She ordered a glass of white wine at the bar and strolled the perimeter of the great ballroom. Hannah saw several sets of hungry male eyes tracking the sight of her short leather skirt and muscular thighs. She avoided several attempts at eye contact, smiling slightly to herself when one fellow tripped over a chair, spilling his drink as he tried to sidle up beside her.

Hannah completed her circuit of the room in time to order another drink. Before she could speak a warm voice behind her said, "A bottle of champagne, please."

She turned around and looked into the sparkling brown eyes of the man she had met earlier. "I trust that is satisfactory with you?" he asked.

"Very much so," she said through a smile.

They sat at a small table in a quiet corner of the ballroom. His name was Paul Opfermann and he had come to Vienna, he had told her, to visit an old friend. They exchanged small talk for a while, of their homes and backgrounds and of her vacation with her mother. He listened attentively. The conversation was light, but pleasantly unforced. Hannah found herself doing much of the talking as the champagne bottle emptied.

"So you've not seen Vienna before?" he asked.

"No, I've wanted to come for years, but my mother always dissuaded me."

"Oh?"

"Yes, she lived here during the war and I guess it wasn't such a nice place to be."

"Not many places were," he said softly, staring down into his glass.

"I guess," Hannah said. "I've never really thought about it."

"And what have you thought about?"

She looked at him quizzically, not sure whether or not to take offence. He started to say something, stopped, then went ahead with it.

"Have you ever asked her about that time?" he said. "What it was like? Did you ever wonder how it was to survive such horror?"

She looked over at him with surprise. He suddenly appeared very serious, the small flecks of gold in his eyes blazed like tiny bonfires as he ran a finger along the wet rim of the glass. It emitted a low squeal, the sound of an animal caught in a trap.

"What difference could it make?" Hannah shrugged. "It's all in the past and best forgotten."

He continued to blankly look at her in silence. He was making her uncomfortable. And a little angry.

"It's not like any of that stuff is my fault," Hannah said, "or even my parents'. I mean they were just kids back then, my mother was like eighteen or something."

"That's not so very young," he said.

"Hey," she said quite loudly, "she wasn't a Nazi or anything, she was just another person, you know, trying to get by."

Several people glanced over and Hannah blushed, but Paul seemed not to notice.

"Trying to get by," he echoed, staring back at his drink and nodding slightly to himself. Hannah was now feeling very defensive.

"What about you? What about your family?"

He lifted his finger from the edge of the glass. "They were all killed in the war," he said and made a fluttering gesture with his hand. She returned his gaze defiantly at first, but had to look away. He was too intense.

The silence grew awkward between them and Hannah thought about making her excuses when the band came back to the stage. The leader, a small blonde woman with spiked, banana-yellow hair, was tuning an electric violin.

"We are obliged," she said, "if only by tradition, to play at least once a night, a real Viennese waltz. So in the spirit of the past we offer you now an old folk song that goes by different names in different places. We like to call it *Cheap Violin Waltz*."

As the music started, Hannah saw Paul's expression soften. He tilted his head slightly and closed his eyes as the sweet melody unravelled. He smiled at her and held out his hand.

"I'm sorry," he said. "Please, always I am too serious. Especially when it concerns what has passed in the past. Forgive me with a dance."

Hannah hesitated, still unnerved by the harshness of his inquisition.

"I would feel like Garcia Lorca," he said, the warmth of his magical eyes melting any lingering coldness. She felt again the electric charge she had experienced when they met earlier and she took his hand.

He held her close, and as they danced the floor turned to water and she floated like a leaf on the calm sea of his disguise.

Magda dreamed uneasily of the past:

She is seventeen and the Nazis are still in Vienna. The war is winding down to its obvious *dénouement* and the Germans fill the little time they have left indulging all vices. Magda works in a once elegant whorehouse on the Hauptstrasse. The brothel services German officers as well as what's left of the city's elite. Her striking Aryan features have made her a favourite among the German officers. She has survived the ravages of conquest with little more than her virtue and dignity despoiled.

Two girls perform on a crude stage while a dozen or so customers — Viennese businessmen and a couple of very drunk Gestapo officers — watch from divans arranged in a half-circle around them. Magda sits beside a pale, nervous young man from some ministry or other. She nuzzles his unshaved neck and intermittently runs her fingers over his crotch. The Gestapo sit to their left, a girl kneeling on the floor between them, her mouth bobbing over one man's lap then the other. The Nazis have their arms draped about each other's shoulders, and occasionally bring their heads together like lovers to whisper and laugh.

The door behind them crashes open and two more drunk officers stagger in holding between them a large, young man who has been severely beaten. Several of his teeth are missing and blood seeps from a deep gash over his right eye. One officer grips his arm, the other holds him by a handful of his thick dark hair. Despite the injuries, Magda sees that the prisoner has stunning brown eyes with flecks of gold that glint like spinning coins in the reflected light of the crackling fire.

The young man is dragged to the front of the room as the naked girls are chased from the stage. The new arrivals exchange a few words with their fellow Gestapo, and then the one with a shaved head climbs up on stage with the prisoner. A single spotlight illuminates the pair in a hot, white circle. Magda cannot tell if the man is a Jew, a homosexual or a member of the resistance, nor does she suspect it much matters. He is handsome, though, and his eyes seem to possess great power.

She feels the man next to her tense up and start to breathe heavily through his mouth as the German begins to speak. She thinks he is frightened, but as he reaches to return her hand to his stiffening member, she understands his excitement is about something else entirely. Still holding onto the prisoner's hair, the officer forces the man down into a chair and addresses the group.

"My dear friends, I present here to you an enemy of the Reich. We have it on the best authority that he has been passing information to the resistance. He claims, of course, that we have made a terrible mistake and that as he is Austrian we have no right to arrest him."

The Nazi smiles.

"I have explained to him that we are nothing if not fair and that to prove this to him I would leave his fate to the good people of Vienna."

A wicked jeer goes up from those present. The prisoner's head begins to droop and the Nazi yanks back on his hair. Magda sees the man wince and try to blink blood out of his swollen eye.

"So. I say this to you, my friends, if one of you — just one — will stand up and speak for this man I will let him go."

A sudden, nervous silence takes hold. One of the other officers begins to chuckle and takes a swig from a bottle of brandy.

"Just one word. A simple '*ja*' and I will release him to your tender mercy."

Still there is only silence. Magda stirs slightly and her companion glances at her with panic in his eyes, his erection fading. As she starts to open her mouth she can feel the man try to distance himself, cower into the opposite armrest and hide his face. She sees the German look over at her, his tongue poking slightly through his narrow lips, his eyebrows raised.

"Do you have something to say, little whore?"

Magda wants to speak but freezes, shackled by the Nazi's anticipatory gaze. She looks at the prisoner, but can only shake her head.

No-one else says a word.

The officer jerks the prisoner's head toward him and grins. "You have been found guilty by a jury of your peers. Sentence to be carried out immediately."

The officer glances around the room again then points a finger at Magda and beckons her to the stage. She doesn't want to move, but the others grab her and force her to her feet. They push her to the stage where the bald man lifts her up. He sets her in front of the prisoner and pushes her down to her knees. She feels the heat of the spotlight on the back of her neck.

The German tears open the prisoner's pants, slices the material with a large serrated blade. One of the Viennese in the audience points at the man's exposed, shrivelled penis and yells "*Juden, Juden,*" and the Gestapo laugh. The officer grabs Magda, pushes her face toward the man's crotch. She looks up into the prisoner's amazing eyes and sees no fear, only exhaustion and contempt.

Magda gags as she takes him in her mouth. The German holds her hair, forcing her head up and down, but she shrugs him off. With a whore's resigned disinterest she plies her expertise. She hears the customers and other girls laughing and clapping behind her.

She releases him from between her lips and gently strokes his thigh with a soft hand. As she does so she begins to hum a small tune, an old Viennese waltz. She looks up and sees recognition in the prisoner's eyes, and for a moment she thinks she hears him hum along as he responds ever-so slightly to her touch. Then there is a blurry glint of steel before her eyes and the world turns red.

She falls backward, her face covered in a sticky warmth. She teeters at the edge of the stage and wipes the blood from her eyes. She sees the prisoner frozen in a crouch, his mouth open, his eyes gone wide. A fountain of red spews from between his legs as the German tosses his severed penis on the floor next to her. The audience applauds.

Magda doesn't want to look. She focuses on a point on the wall behind the dying man, locks on the sight of his frozen silhouette: the broad shoulders, the fuzzy penumbra of his mussed, thick hair. A large crack in the plaster bisects his shadow almost in half. He finally collapses and she sees only the circle of light on the bare, white wall.

Magda woke up screaming.

Not even Valium could ease Magda back to sleep. She laid in bed, sweating beneath the covers, watching the digital clock painfully advance a digit at a time. She focused on the lines of the numbers until they became abstract patterns and she could fill her mind completely with the blinking dots that marked the tedious passage of seconds. The long-suppressed memories pounded at the doors of her consciousness, but she concentrated on forcing a blank state of mind.

It was not until she heard a sound at the front door that she became aware of how much time had drifted past her troubled vision. She hadn't realised that Hannah was still out, had assumed the girl was asleep in her room. It was very late, and the dance had surely ended long ago.

Magda heard the door slam shut and two sets of feet noisily stumbling through the reception room of the suite. She listened as the door to Hannah's bedroom creaked open followed by another crash and what could only be a man's voice cursing lowly. Then a padded thud and the creak of rusty bedsprings.

Magda got up and pressed her ear to her own closed door. She could hear the low rumble of the man's voice and Hannah's drunken giggle, but she couldn't make out any of the words being spoken. Her heart pounded in her chest and though the window was open and cold night air swept across the room, she had to wipe sweat from her brow.

Magda hesitated a moment, then carefully eased open the door to the sitting room. She winced as it squeaked on its hinges, and tentatively peered through the narrow opening. She saw light streaming from Hannah's bedroom, heard another high laugh and a few slurred, incomprehensible words.

Then a loud slap followed by silence.

Magda threw open the door, ignoring the screaming hinges. She gasped at a second sharp sound of flesh against flesh, and felt a burning in her bladder and sick taste in her throat. There was no laughter now, only a thin mewling from her daughter that threatened to become a cry.

In a state of near-terror, Magda approached Hannah's room and as she peered inside, fell to her knees. She stuffed a balled fist in her mouth, but didn't register the stream of urine that ran down her legs into the thick carpet.

Hannah was sprawled on the floor, bent back against the side of the bed. She was naked, her torn clothes strewn about her, the leather skirt twisted around one ankle. Deep red welts pulsed across her face, the outline of four thick fingers running like bars down her cheek. She looked dazed, her movements sluggish, her eyes teary and red and half-closed. Standing with his back to the door, towering above the drunken girl, was the figure Magda had earlier seen in silhouette at the bar.

It was the shape that she knew from her dream, escaped from an ancient memory; frozen for an eternal moment in a blinding spotlight on a cracked white wall.

Magda wanted to scream but she couldn't. Like on that night so long before, she wanted desperately to raise a hand, waggle a finger, speak a single short word.

Her lips opened, her tongue pressed against her palate, a vibration began in her throat. Then the man glanced over his shoulder at her and she looked into those unforgettable eyes.

"Do you have something to say, little whore?" he asked.

She tried to speak, to move, but she had become a thing of stone, trapped in the present by her past.

She saw the terrible, black shape slap and maul and hurt her daughter. She watched him brutally enter her over and over; from the front, from the rear, in the mouth.

He never looked back at her.

Blood ran down Hannah's thighs staining the sheets and the rug. Magda heard her daughter's drunken whimpers, soft and weak as a dying bird's. She still could not move as the shape passed her by again. He hovered briefly behind her, his breath gently rustling her mussed hair. She thought she heard him hum the first notes of an achingly familiar tune, but she would never be certain.

As the front door opened she felt a rush of cold air and looked up.

He stood in the doorway. Light from the hall washed across the threshold, capturing his silhouette on the far wall. Reality merged with dream and memory as past and present met in the shape of a shadow.

Then he was gone, leaving the door open behind him. A breeze gently stirred the curtains that billowed across a clean, clear Vienna dawn. The smell of fresh pastry drifted in the air.

Magda listened to the echo of her daughter's hoarse cries.

She stared vacantly at the wall's stark, accusing whiteness.

Introduction to "Lily's Whisper"

I reckon this is my favourite of all the current stories. It's the least typical, most personal and most satisfying to me. An early version of it is one of the first things I wrote when I decided to take another shot at fiction writing, after not having done any such thing for half-a-dozen years. That first version was written and submitted (to Ellen Datlow at *Omni*) in 1989. Following a dozen rejections in the intervening years, the present, not all-that-different draft, was published in *Dark Terrors 2* in 1996 and then reprinted (by Ellen Datlow!) in the subsequent *Year's Best Fantasy & Horror*. Ellen told me that she didn't remember having read the story before, but in fact she had sent me the nicest rejection letter I'd ever received. At the time, not yet having sold a story, it went a long way to reinforcing my faith in my work.

Lily and Sally were real people, and though much of the story is pure fiction, the heart of it is based on actual events. At least, events as I understand and remember them. I still don't know the full version of Lily's story, though thanks in part to having written "Lily's Whisper", I'm hoping to learn more. Family histories are peculiar things, shaped as much by the haze of time and self-delusion as the truth of experience. I barely knew Lily in life — she is, indeed, little more to me than a very fuzzy face — but I feel an inexplicable, perhaps, even undeserved, identification with her.

Even if my writing career does not amount to anything more than it has to date, I will have been happy just to know that this story was told.

Lily's Whisper

SOMETIMES, AT THE EDGE OF CONSCIOUSNESS, on that unsteady divide between my waking and dreaming life, I'll hear her wonderful little song. The spectral voice of memory, I suppose. All in my head. But then, isn't everything?

An orderly asked if anything was wrong. *A lot*, I thought, but I told him I was fine and forced myself to walk on in. I'd been standing, frozen with dread, outside the door to my grandmother's hospital room. I stared at the small white paper with her name in blurry type: **Bernstein, Sally**. No middle initial. When I was little I used to ask her why it was that she had no middle name. She always answered with the same joke: 'We were too poor to afford one.' It drove me crazy because it didn't make any sense, but now I smiled thinking about it. *Okay grandma*, I thought, *let's get this over with*.

My aunt Lily died when I was a kid. She was actually my great-aunt. My mother's aunt. Grandma Sally's sister.

Although she didn't live far away from the house where I grew up, I never knew Lily very well. Once or twice a year someone would bring her along to a family gathering — she couldn't drive — where she always showered the children with fruit candies and cheap but wonderful presents. Unlike my mother's other seemingly born-ancient aunts and uncles, Lily seemed not just to like children, but to understand them. To think like them. Even though she was the only one without kids of her own.

I never much cared for those other relatives, who were somehow sort of scary to me in their sere way, but I was always

174

happy to see Lily. It wasn't just that she treated us differently or better (though she did), she somehow seemed utterly apart from her siblings. Her face betrayed the same harsh, Eastern European stock, but there was a gentle quality to her that none of the others possessed. A humour in her eyes and playfulness to her touch which made the cloying affections of her shrewish kin all the more glaring.

I suppose I realised that there was something unusual about Lily — something secret — from the way the others talked about her. They always lowered their voices when Lily's name came up, as if she was something to hide or to be ashamed of. If not for the fact of our Jewishness, I think they would have crossed themselves at the mention of her name. Even when Lily was in the room the others spoke about her as if she wasn't there. Or as if she was dead. Perhaps the reason the children identified with her so closely was because, among the other adults, she was treated as if she, too, was of no real consequence.

Hospital rooms are like shopping malls in their dislocated uniformity. Stepping into one, whether in Los Angeles or West Palm Beach, removes you from the normal fabric of local time and space and into the antiseptic, spiritually liminal realm of the sick and dying.

The bed nearest the door had been stripped of linens and I had the sudden ominous sense that the last person to occupy it had not walked out on their own. A tall plastic curtain had been drawn around the far bed, the elongated shadows of the guard rails silhouetted like prison bars on the laminated barrier. As I got closer I could hear raspy breathing. The curtain hadn't been pulled all the way around, and as I reached the foot of the bed I saw my grandmother for the first time in almost ten years.

Sally had always been a short, plump woman, but age and illness had shrunk her down so that, lost under her covers, she looked like an old ventriloquist's dummy. She stirred in uneasy sleep and I saw that she was little more than a bag of withered flesh. The sight of her reminded me of a balloon you'd find behind the couch two weeks after a party, limp and wrinkled and only vaguely suggestive of its original shape. Her skin had stretched and sagged beyond the capacity of her diminutive frame. As a child I had always marvelled at my grandmother's upper arms; they were fatty and thick and dangled like jowls, jiggling wildly with every gesture she made. Now I saw that the folds of skin remained, but the meat beneath them had dissolved and the flesh hung limp as a ghost ship's sails.

Her stained dentures swam in a plastic cup on the formica night table and her hollow mouth drooped open. A glistening thread of saliva trailed down her chin and tufts of thin, colourless hair dotted her mottled scalp. In fact, the sight of her made me feel a little queasy and I started to walk back out when her eyes opened, nailing me to the floor.

She stared at me, but I wasn't certain she could see me or if she could, that she recognised who I was. The last time I'd seen her had been at my mother's funeral almost a decade before. Despite her numerous illnesses and various surgeries, I had spoken with Sally only once since then, when she had called on my birthday. It was a hellish call in which she quizzed me accusatorially about my lack of contact with her.

Like all good New York Jews, she and my grandfather had retired to Florida when I was a kid. As a result I had never been particularly close to her — from an adult's point of view, I never knew her at all — though I still carried a certain latent guilt over having ignored her so in her declining years.

Especially after first her husband, then my mother died.

It was primarily that lurking guilt (along with my father springing for the cost of the air fare) which had served to bring me all the way from my home in Los Angeles to her Florida hospital for this reunion. A reunion for which Sally had hysterically and inexplicably begged.

The silence was broken only by my grandmother's fractured breathing. She scanned me up and down, but her only movement was the slight rise and fall of her chest. I shifted nervously and cleared my throat. I was about to identify myself when, with a low moan, she pulled herself up against the pillow and slowly lifted an arthritic hand.

"Brucie," she said.

I came around the side of the bed and took her hand. It felt as light as a styrofoam coffee cup, the skin hard and cool to the touch.

"Hi, grandma," I croaked.

She left her hand in mine for a moment then drew it back beneath the covers.

Her eyes never left mine.

"You're so thin," she said and coughed. Then she farted wetly. I felt slightly embarrassed, but she didn't seem bothered. "And a beard, yet."

"Yeah," I said, scratching my chin. "That's right."

She didn't reply. The tension could have been cut with oh, say, a small sword: six-foot blade.

"So," I said, posing the stupidest question of all time: "How are you?"

Here is everything that I knew about Lily's life:

She was the youngest sibling of the large Petrowski family, something like eight or nine children in all. They were dirt poor and lived like sharecroppers in seriously anti-Semitic Poland at the turn of the century. Neither my great-grandparents nor any of their children were educated and they all worked at maintaining the subsistence-level farm.

Most of the family emigrated to America in the early years of the century with the great human tide that fled the miseries of the Old World. A couple of the older siblings stayed behind, but the rest, including Lily, settled in Brooklyn.

While the various children who became my mother's aunts and uncles started families of their own in America, Lily never married. She lived out her drab life and died, alone, in the basement flat of a Brooklyn tenement. In the end, no-one even knew exactly when she died. Her body was found by a stranger because of the stench rising from her corpse.

I only really remember three things about Lily. Once, when she came to visit, she brought along a new puppy. It was a mad, brown ball of energy. In what even at the time I recognised as pure Lily style, she had named it Wolfie. My cousins and I spent a wondrous day chasing the dog around the small yard of my parents' suburban New York house while Lily watched and clapped along in delight. She seemed, I remember, not to handle the dog very well, as if she didn't understand that it was a living thing and not a toy, but her pleasure in its company was clear. A couple of weeks later I overheard my mother tell my father that Wolfie had been run over by a car.

I also remember a simple little song Lily used to sing to us. My mother knew it too — had probably learned it from Lily — and often sang it to me as a lullaby. Lily would sing in Polish mostly, but sometimes in English. My mother only knew the English version. It went:

> Meet me at midnight, my sweet one.
> By the tree in the garden,
> Where the white roses grow.
> Meet me at midnight, my darling.
> But don't let anyone know.
> Never let anyone know.

The song had a tender, happy/sad melody and to this day it summons, however fleetingly, that childhood feeling of utter safeness and security that simply doesn't exist in maturity.

The third thing I remember is not so much about Lily as about myself. It concerns her death and I recall it, even after all these years, with some shame.

I was maybe eight or nine years old and my best friend and I were playing in the house one day when the phone rang. My mother picked it up in the kitchen while I eavesdropped (as usual) from the hall. Sally was on the line and I heard my mother start to cry. I understood that it was because Lily had died. I knew Lily was my mother's favourite aunt. I stood there listening to her cry when my friend came down the hall to see what was up.

As soon as he looked at me I began to laugh. He kept asking what was go funny, but each time I tried to tell him the laughter grew more hysterical. I couldn't stop myself. We retreated to the safety of my room and I told him what had happened. I don't think I'll ever forget the look on his face.

In the years since I've tried to rationalise my behaviour without real success. I've told myself that the laughter was a child's nervous response to the mystery of death or a cathartic emotional release. Hell, maybe it's even true. For a time I thought that I'd blown the incident out of proportion, but years later, that same friend and I were talking and he asked me about that day and my laughter. It had stuck with him, too. I managed to change the topic of conversation, but I've never forgotten the shame.

I leaned against the hall's cool tile waiting for a nurse to finish helping Sally with the bedpan. I heard the gulping flush of a toilet and a moment later the nurse came out and nodded at me.

The room stank of shit and piss, but I pretended not to notice. I pulled a chair over next to the bed and as I sat down I saw that Sally had put her teeth in. Her eyes looked a little clearer, too. Her wasted body still suggested the proximity of the scythe, but she seemed more alert and, I hoped, able to explain her desperate need to see me.

"I know you don't care so much for me," she began and seeing my burgeoning protest held up a finger. "No, no, you don't have to say. It's all right."

I sat back in the chair and exhaled a deep breath. I felt desperately trapped, like being stuck in bumper-to-bumper traffic at the entrance to a long tunnel.

"I know also you're only here because your father insisted, but this I don't care either."

That was true as well. Not only had my father paid for my ticket, he had seriously guilted me into making the haul from California at all.

"I have something to ask you, but first I have a story to tell. It's to do with your aunt Lily, I don't know if you even remember."

I nodded, suddenly more interested. Though Sally didn't ask, I recited the outline of what I knew and remembered. I didn't mention how I laughed the day that Lily died.

"What you say is right. I don't remember from a dog, but with Lily it could be. Always she did such things. But this is like the skin of the apple what you know. The fruit is underneath, but I'll tell you now and you should understand, it's not so sweet.

"Lily we always hated," Sally said. She stared past me, out the window as she spoke. "When she was born she was too small, like to die, and mama was very sick. They have what to call it today."

"Premature," I said.

"Yes, I think. Always weak Lily was and so tiny. For a long time she didn't walk or talk. A terrible burden she was on us. We lived all of us then in a little house, like you don't know. Always Lily had to have special and we all had to make do with less so she could get. Terrible jealous it made us.

"My father came first to America and sent back money for the children to go one by one, but mama died soon after we all arrived. But this you probably know. Lily was then a big girl already, but still she was . . . not right. Slow, she was and difficult. But with mama gone Lily wasn't special anymore and terrible mean we could be to her, like how we always wanted."

My grandmother laid back against the pillows and closed her eyes. Her breathing became shallow and even and I thought perhaps she had dozed off, but then she opened her eyes again and stared up at the ceiling.

"When Bella died . . . "

"Whoa! Wait a minute. Who's Bella?"

Sally shook her head. "I forget, Brucie. These people, some you never met. But to me it's all like yesterday. Bella was the oldest sister. She married and stayed yet in Poland."

"You know, I don't think I've ever even heard her name."

Sally only nodded, but somehow communicated to me: *such is the sad nature of time and memory.* She went on:

"Bella died from the typhus, left alone a husband and a little boy. Such could not be in those days and something had be done. We saw then a chance to get rid of Lily. Lily had no husband and who would ever marry such a thing? Bella's husband we knew from before. A hard man. Like only in Poland you find. We knew it was a bad thing to send Lily to him, but jealousy is . . . " — Sally shook her head — "She went, you know, it was not so long before the war. We didn't know then from Hitler, but even if we did, I can't say sure that we would have done different."

"Christ," I muttered. I'd never heard *any* of this before.

"What happened, who would have thought? Lily married to Bella's husband and took the little boy to her heart. And she was happy. The life there wasn't easy, but Lily made for herself a place. The baby she thought of like her own and Bella's husband she even maybe could love. Who can say?"

Sally laid back again and I could see she was exhausted. She could barely keep her eyes open.

"Maybe you should take a little nap, grandma," I said, though I was intrigued by her story and puzzled as to where it was leading.

She nodded and offered me a little smile. She was asleep before I could get out of the chair.

I waited around the hospital for a while, ogling the student nurses and drinking bitter coffee from a machine. I saw a nurse go in and out of my grandmother's room and ran after her. She told me that Sally would probably sleep for a few hours at least.

"Can you tell me . . . " I started. I felt a little silly asking, actually.

"What?" the nurse asked.

"What, exactly, is wrong with her?" I knew from my father that Sally had undergone some treatments for cancer a while back, and that at least one hip had been replaced fairly recently, but I didn't actually know why she was hospitalised now.

"Some heart trouble. Bad circulatory problems. Mostly, she's old," the nurse said. "Just plain worn out." She must have seen I wasn't too thrilled with the answer and sort of shrugged. "You're Brucie, aren't you?"

"Bruce," I said, clearing my throat.

"She's been going on and on about you."

"Really?" I asked. "Do you have any idea why?"

"No, she wouldn't say," she said. She started to walk away then half turned around again. "Though maybe if you called her once in a while, you'd know."

I scraped my lower jaw — and my pride — off the floor and walked out of the hospital.

West Palm Beach ain't exactly the thrill capital of the world. That is to say, if you aren't up for a round of Bingo or a day at the *jai alai fronton*, there's not one heck of a lot to do. There is the beach, I reckon, but living in Los Angeles pretty well spoils you for such things.

So I went to visit my cousin.

Beth owned a condo in one of those godawful, prefab developments which litter the Florida landscape like broken shells on the beach. She worked for a bank and wasn't married, which is the extent of what I knew about her life. I had to call my dad to get her address.

I don't even know how long it had been since I'd seen Beth. We'd been close as children — we were born just two months apart — but that was ancient history. She was my mother's sister's only child and had somehow come to serve as kind of caretaker to Sally after my aunt passed away. Neither of us had even bothered to attend the funeral of the other's mom. I didn't even think I'd he able to recognise Beth, but when she opened the door I was pleasantly surprised to find the face of the little girl I remembered etched inside the older-than-her-years lines of the woman I didn't even vaguely know.

I hadn't bothered to call or write, but she wasn't surprised to see me. "Grandma said you'd be coming," she told me. "I didn't believe it though."

"I'm not entirely sure why I'm here," I told her.

We tried the small-talk thing for a while, but it didn't go too well. I found her life in banking as dull as she found mine as a teacher. Neither of us was too keen to talk over good old days which didn't exist, so all that was left was Sally. Beth told me about the old woman's physical decline in rather clinical, unemotional terms. I got the strong feeling that Sally's glacially slow deterioration had worn Beth out. She basically told me what the nurse had said about Sally's health.

"A tumour here, some angina there. Old age everywhere." Beth shrugged between chain-smoked cigarettes.

"And you don't know why she's been so adamant about wanting to see me?" I asked.

"Not a fucking clue," Beth said.

I could hear the resentment in her voice, got the feeling that my seeing Sally was somehow treading on territory Beth thought of as her own. I couldn't blame her, really. I wasn't the one who'd been changing the old bag's diapers these past years.

"Apparently it has something to do with Lily," I told her.

Beth coughed out a cloud of smoke. "*Aunt* Lily?" she choked.

"Yeah. She started telling me all about her before she dozed off. I haven't a clue as to why, though."

"Unbelievable," Beth whispered, shaking her head.

"What?" I asked.

"I've been trying to get her to talk about Lily for years. I've asked her time after time and she'd never tell me a goddamn thing."

"Why did you want to know about Lily?" I asked. But somewhere a memory stirred in the back of my head.

"My mom used to talk about her a lot. She always thought there was something important about Lily. I wanted to make a film about her. Once."

I remembered. I remembered from years before that in our very practical and deeply unimaginative family, Beth had been an 'artsy' kid with dreams of being a filmmaker. I never quite got it straight how she ended up working for a bank. Looking now at her tired face and nicotine-stained fingertips, I didn't want to ask. A hint of a smile formed at the edge of her lips.

"She was in the camps, you know," Beth said.

"Excuse me?"

"You don't know do you?" Beth shook her head. "Lily was in a concentration camp for a while during the second world war."

"No," I said weakly. This was quite the day for family tales. "I didn't know. How did . . . how could she have been in the camps? Who told you this?"

"My mom. But she didn't know much more than that, either. It was something no-one ever talked about, apparently."

"I'm not surprised," I said. But I was trying to picture the sweet old lady with candy who I remembered superimposed into one of those archive-issue black and white images of Dachau or Treblinka that we all have stowed in our heads. I couldn't suppress a shudder. "What happened?" I asked. "Do you know?"

Beth got up and rooted around for another pack of cigarettes. She let me dangle while she fiddled with the wrapper, searched for some matches and oh-so deliberately lit up the smoke.

"You'll tell me what this is all about? Why grandma wants to see you? What she says about Lily?"

"Of course," I said. "Why wouldn't I?"

Beth shrugged and I realised it was information she would hoard.

"Come on," I said. "Please?"

"I don't know that much, really. But I guess it's more than *you*." I realised of a sudden that there was some deep resentment happening here, but I didn't have a clue what it was all about.

"You know that Lily was in Poland right before the war? She went back to like nursemaid her brother-in-law or something."

"Grandma was just telling me about it. She said that Lily married a dead sister's husband. And there was a kid, too."

"Yeah," she said and hesitated again. I summarised what Sally had told me in the hospital. Beth listened and nodded, seemed to think about it for a little while.

"I don't know the details," she finally said. "I don't think any of the family really did. But Lily got rounded up by the Nazis at some point. Just for being Jewish, far as I know. They all got herded into the cattle cars. Lily was separated from the husband and the kid, but apparently she still had American papers or something. Anyway, she was in a camp for a while. I don't know which one. Not a death camp, obviously. But they let her go."

"I didn't think they ever let anyone go."

Beth shrugged again. "Who knows? A U.S. citizen, a woman. They probably just didn't give a shit. Or she was just fucking lucky."

"What about the brother-in-law — the husband, I mean — and the little boy?"

"Soap. Lamp shades. Ash. Whatever."

I winced at the harshness, the casual tone of my cousin's response. "Jesus," I said.

"I don't think old JC was involved," Beth said, sucking in the last of the smoke. "But you never know."

"Do you know anything else?"

"Apparently she waited out the war in Europe. Don't ask me where or how. She waited for the others. She never found them, of course."

"How did you find all this out?" I asked again.

"My mom. She told me the whole story once when she was stoned." I must have looked at Beth oddly, because she laughed and quickly explained. "You never saw her during her post-menopausal hippy phase did you?"

"Uh, no," I admitted.

"Far out. Literally. I'd get home from work and we'd share a joint. Man, you ain't lived till you've had it out with your mom for bogarting a roach."

"I can only imagine," I said. But remembering my aunt as a suburban housewife, I really couldn't. Beth lit up another cigarette and neither of us said a word for a while.

"What must it have been like?" I finally said. Beth raised an eyebrow. "For Lily, I mean. Growing up hated by her brothers and sisters. Treated like a piece of shit. Finally finding a family only to lose it to the . . . you know. What would that do to you?" Beth didn't have any answer, but for the first time since I arrived, some of the hard edges fell out of her face.

"It's too bad you never got to make your film," I said.

She turned away, ostensibly to reach for another cigarette, but through the swirl of cigarette smoke I'm sure I saw a tear in the corner of one bloodshot eye.

I got back to the hospital just after six that evening and walked smack dab into chaos. Sally had become hysterical wanting to know where I was. It seemed they could only dope her up with the mildest of sedatives and she fought it tooth and nail. She had just dozed off again when I arrived, much to the relief of the third floor staff. I chatted with a couple of nurses who told me Sally had been driving them nuts for weeks. They all seemed to know who I was; Sally had been ranting to them about me and about Lily, though the connection was unclear.

I went back to Sally's room to wait until she stirred. I stared out the window as a thunder squall broke apart the still hot Florida evening. I listened to the sizzle of the warm rain on concrete and to Sally's graveyard hack. I looked over at her as she began moaning lowly in her sleep, her drawn face contorting.

Suddenly, her eyes shot open and her face took on a frenzied expression. She started to yell, then saw me sitting by the window. The wildness went out of her eyes and she settled back against the rumpled sheets. I asked her if she was all right and she nodded.

"I went to see Beth," I told her.

"A good girl," Sally said, nodding. But her face suggested she didn't entirely believe her own words.

"We talked about what you were telling me. She said that Lily was once in a concentration camp. That she lost her family there."

My grandmother looked up sharply, but wouldn't meet my eye. She nodded again, but looked down into the sheets as she spoke.

"This is true," she said. "Terrible. Terrible." She seemed to want to say more, but I don't think she could.

"So what happened?" I prompted.

"Lily we brought back to New York after the war . . . "

"Wait," I said. "What happened to . . . "

Sally just closed her eyes and started to shake her head. Like a little kid throwing a tantrum. I half-expected her to stick her fingers in her ears and yell 'blah-blah-blah' to drown me out. I got the message.

"Lily came back," she continued, "and she was like a child again. We all thought she would be different maybe, but she barely could take care of herself. So a tiny apartment we found for her, cheap but close to where we lived. We took turns bringing her food when we could and your mother . . . " she paused here, choking on the words. I felt a coldness roll through my bowel.

"Your mother liked to go over to Lily and play. She kept Lily company and Lily would sing to her."

I thought I saw Sally's eyes moisten and felt a pang myself. I imagined it was the Polish lullaby that Lily sang to my mother.

"It was later yet that the troubles started. We hadn't been to see Lily for a while and your mother wanted to visit. I made a *kugel* to take her.

"We knocked on her door, but she wouldn't open. Inside we could hear Lily, talking and laughing, but to us there was no answer. I knocked and knocked and your mother called out to her. We heard her voice, but still the door was shut.

"I began to think something is terrible wrong, so I went to get the Super and I made him to open the door."

Sally paused for a moment, her eyes open wide. She seemed to be someplace else, looking at a picture from the past.

"Inside Lily sat at her table, all set with the best china and a beautiful dinner. Two other chairs also she had there and she was serving food and laughing."

Sally looked right at me, now, streaks of moisture cutting across the deep crags in her old face.

"Who was she talking to, grandma?"

Sally shook her head, "Dolls. Two dolls, like made from *shmates*, she sat up in those chairs. She talked to them like they were people. She never looked at us, never saw. The Super, he didn't say a word, just ran away fast as he could.

"I tried to talk to her, but Lily had not to hear. She just kept serving the food and talking to the dolls. One I heard her call Joseph and the other Avram. Such a coldness I felt, you shouldn't know. My heart still doesn't beat like it should when I think about it."

"Were those the names of the husband and the boy? The ones who'd died?" I asked. Sally nodded, painfully.

"For days, only to the dolls Lily would talk, and never to leave the house. We all went, but she didn't see through her eyes. We left her food and cleaned a little, not that she noticed. Finally, one day your grandpa and me went over and the dolls were gone. We tried to ask her about it, but she made like she didn't know. Like a stone she was. Like a golem.

"Long after she would go funny like this. Everything fine, then suddenly she went away to that other place. To be with the dolls."

There was a long silence. I thought about the horrors of Lily's life, of the terrible loss and the place her mind must have fled to escape from her memories. I thought again of my laughter that day so many years before and felt a rush of self-loathing. The nurse came in then and asked me to step out while she changed Sally's IV. I went into the men's room to piss and wash my face, but I couldn't look in the mirror as I stood at the sink.

I settled back into the chair, saw the nurse had smoothed the sheets and fluffed the pillow. Sally still looked uncomfortable, but a fresh glass of orange juice with a flex-straw sat on the tray by the bed.

"Why are you telling me all this now, grandma? Why did you want me to come here after so many years?"

"It's Lily," she said. "Lily needs you."

I exhaled slowly and deeply. I had no idea how to deal with this, wished more than anything that I was back home in Los Angles with only earthquakes and riots and semi-literate student essays to worry about.

"Lily's dead, grandma," I said as softly as I could.

"I see her, Brucie," Sally said. Her eyes took on the most life I'd yet seen. "Every night she comes to me. I see her. Every night she tells me what it is has to be done. It's Brucie, she says, he's the only one who can do it."

I didn't know what else to do but humour her. "Do what, grandma?"

Sally looked away from me, turned her head toward the tall curtain. She spoke without once looking back my way.

"This what I tell you now no-one knows. Your grandpa and the others are all gone. Only me now. Your mother I never told and I don't want you should say to anyone else. Especially not your father."

I was puzzled, but told her okay. Still she wouldn't look at me.

"Before Lily went back to Poland, there was a man. She was a foolish girl, Lily, but not so bad looking. This man, he . . . took advantage. You understand what I mean?"

I swallowed and nodded. I may have blushed.

"There was a baby, but Lily we knew couldn't take care on her own. So we all decided that someone else had to look after the little girl, this child without a father and no kind of a mother.

"It was agreed your grandfather and me should be the ones to take care of her. Always like our own we treated her. Never we told her the truth. We sent Lily away not just for Bella's family in Poland, but for ours. For yours. For your mother."

Senility, I thought. Or drug-induced fantasy brought on by a lifetime of guilt over the mistreatment of her sister. Surely, that explained Sally's belief that the long-dead Lily came to see her.

And this other grotesque fantasy.

I was tired and annoyed that this was what I had come all this way for, inconvenienced my life about. Until Sally turned and faced me and I looked into her eyes.

And I knew, I just knew, that it was all true.

"Oh Jesus, grandma," I said. "Jesus Christ."

"A terrible thing this has been to keep inside so many years, but it was the only way. Before the war it was a thing that was done. And after . . . "

I was in shock. The thought that Lily was my *real* grandmother sent me into new paroxysms of guilt. I looked back out the window. The rain had stopped and a setting sun made its final appearance of the day.

"What does Lily want me to do?" I asked, mostly to fill the deadly silence, intending sarcasm.

Sally didn't seem to notice.

"Lily wants you should find her son," Sally said.

I'd already seen the in-flight movie, but sought refuge in it again to avoid my troubled thoughts. After an hour I surrendered and stuffed the cheap plastic headphones back into the seat pocket and stared out at the clouds.

I thought of poor Lily — *grandma*, for Christsake — and the nightmare of her life. I racked my brain till my head ached trying to remember something more about her: the details of how she looked and dressed, the inflections of her voice, the things she said.

Anything.

But it was no use.

It came down, every time, to that damn dog, my hellish laughter and her sweet sad song.

Back in the hospital, Sally had told me that every night it was the same. She'd wake with a start and though she could feel the hospital bed beneath her, hear the blips and bleeps of her various monitors, she could also see her old Brooklyn apartment.

The door would open and a youthful Lily stood there, naked and pregnant with the daughter that Sally would claim as her own. Lily would drift in like a balloon and float around the room. Sally would reach out for her, but Lily always bobbed out of reach. As she wafted through the air she rubbed at her swollen belly and tears streamed off her troubled face.

Lily told Sally how her adopted son had survived the Nazi killing machine, had been adopted by a Christian family not very far from the Sobibor death camp which had claimed his father. The boy was a boy no longer, Lily said, but he was in terrible trouble. He lived now, not in Europe but in Montreal, where his adopted parents had emigrated. Her grandson — me — she told Sally had to go to this place to save him from some terrible thing. What it was, or how it was to be done she would or could not say. But the son of the daughter she had been denied was the only one who could act. Only through the daughter that was stolen, could she redeem the son who had been lost.

As Sally told me the story and no doubt saw my dubious expression she grew increasingly frantic. I tried to convince her that it was just a recurring dream, but she'd have none of it. She insisted it was real and that her nights had become a kind of torture. She clutched at my arm and dug her nails into my flesh, pleading with me to honour Lily's wishes and make good the offences of her past. She gasped for breath like a runner at the end of a marathon and her voice became a shrill chalkboard scratch as she begged me to promise to fulfil Lily's plea.

"What do you expect me to do?" I yelled at her. "What do you expect? Am I supposed to scour a foreign city to find some old Polish guy and tell him his dead mother sent me to be his guardian angel. This is crazy!"

"No," she told me. "His new name Lily told to me. Wajda. Stefan Wajda. And where he lives even. You have to promise me, Brucie, you have to!"

I tried to protest again, but she started to scream. I couldn't believe, frail as she was, that the old lady could muster such intensity. The IV was slipping out of her arm and spittle and mucous exploded from her lips and nose. I feared she was about to stroke out.

"Promise," Sally shrieked, "promise, promise!"

"I promise," I finally said in desperation. "I do, I promise." She calmed down as soon as the words passed my lips and collapsed back onto the bed.

Yeah, I thought in the merciful quiet, *I promise.*

And I love you and the check's in the mail and I won't . . .

I promise, I thought again, silently mouthing the words as the plane descended into the Christmas-tree fantasy of lights that is Los Angeles.

Shit.

I awoke to the starkest moment of terror in my life. I've always been jealous of people who can remember their dreams because I never do. At most I usually recall an image or a feeling that melts like a vampire in the morning sun. This dream, though, was as real and solid to me as my own name.

It was Lily, of course. In what had to be the horrid Brooklyn tenement where she spent her life after the war. I saw her sitting at a rickety table heaped with plates piled with bones and gristle and rotten fruit. She stood between two high-backed chairs, each with a midget-sized rag doll perched on it. Sawdust stuffing spilled out of gaping holes and button-eyes hung off torn faces by frayed, black threads. One doll had an arm of real flesh with a bluish-black number etched into the peeling skin. The other was slighter, but no less ragged. Lily forced sharpened spoonfuls of greyish meat between their tightly sewn lips. I tried to move toward the table but hung suspended, like an insect in amber, condemned to watch. I looked at Lily, and for a moment, saw my mother's face ripple across her countenance like a slight Florida wave lapping across a sandbar.

Lily looked up at me. Tears of blood flowed from her soft eyes and ran down her cheeks in jagged streaks. She opened her mouth and through blackened teeth the horrid sound that emerged was the world's sorrow.

I woke with a start and dashed into the bathroom to throw-up. I ran cold water over my wrists and splashed my face, rinsed my mouth. I stumbled back to bed, but sleep was out of the question. I lay awake thinking and shivering, though the night air was quite warm.

As the first grey finger of dawn poked a hole in the darkness, I got up and went to the phone. I looked up the Montreal area code in the phone book and dialled the number for information. In a voice as dry as a perfect martini I asked if there was a listing for Stefan Wajda, apologised for not having an address. The line was quiet for two unendurable moments. "Thank you," a computer generated voice said, "the number is . . . "

Fresh doubts assailed me as the plane hit turbulence near Salt Lake. I thought again of the crazy phone call that sent me packing, considered the possibility, the likelihood, that the Stefan Wajda I was going to see was a mere namesake of Lily's lost son. Was Wajda the Polish equivalent of Smith or Jones? Still, I was so shaken by the reality of *someone* by that name in the city of which Sally spoke that in a less than rational moment, I booked the flight. I didn't have a clue what I was going to do when I got there.

I thought again about Sally and about Lily and my terrible dream. I kept coming back to that brief moment in the dream when my mother's face flashed across Lily's and knew that this was about her as much as anything else. My mother had died, rather horribly, of cancer while I was at college, drinking and screwing and having fun. I hadn't wanted to face the horrors of her condition. Just as, at a younger age, I found a way not to face Lily's death, and more recently had avoided dealing with Sally's decline.

The promise I'd made to Sally, I knew, meant nothing in and of itself. I could tell myself that it was the reason for this insane excursion, but in that deep mental pit where we live with our unspeakable truths, I knew that this was about my mother. It was about a kind of expiation, a purging. About the debts — and respect — we each owe to our past.

Ain't guilt grand?

*　*　*　*　*

I had called an old college friend named Dornan who lived in Montreal and met me at the airport. He was a bit puzzled by the sudden visit, but had happily agreed to put me up for a few days. He seemed to sense that I had something on my mind, but didn't pry. We reminisced some about the good old days as we drove back to his apartment. He already had a date arranged for the evening, invited me — sincerely — to tag along, but I told him no, that I had something to do.

I was exhausted physically and mentally, but grew restive shortly after Dornan went out. I snooped among his many bookshelves. I found the city white pages on the third shelf, wedged between copies of Max Weber's *Protestant Ethic and the Spirit of Capitalism* and Art Spiegelman's *Maus*. I briefly puzzled over his organisational scheme, but my head hurt too much already.

There was only one **Wajda, S** in the book. The address listed was for Rue Saint-Cuthbert. A quick look at a map showed it to be a street within walking distance of Dornan's place. I stuffed the map in my pocket and carefully shut the door behind me.

Wajda's street was yuppy-ritzy with lots of black Saabs and BMWs parked in front of restored brownstones. It was quiet, with only the omnipresent background rush of the city to break the silence. The house matching Wajda's number stood at the end of the block. A great maple tree by his gate whispered in the warm night breeze and through a small square of leaded glass in the front door I saw the glow of a dim yellow bulb. The rest of the house looked dark and empty. I leaned on the gate to the entrance path and stared at the door, unsure of what to do. What the hell was I *supposed* to do? It was almost eleven o'clock at night. I could hardly go up and knock at this hour. What would I say? I must have looked pretty damn suspicious lurking out front, but there was no-one else on the street and not a single car passed while I waited.

What the fuck am I doing here, I thought. I suddenly felt ridiculous and was prepared to turn around and head back to

Dornan's place, discounting the whole trip as temporary insanity, when I noticed the sound of an idling automobile engine. I glanced around at the parked cars, but they were all dark and lifeless. Cautiously, I opened the gate at the front of the house and took a few steps up the path.

The low rumble grew slightly louder.

I found my way around the side of the building and saw that there was a garage in back that opened onto a narrow alley running the length of the block. I pressed an ear to the corrugated steel door and heard and felt a deep bass reverberation from within.

I stood there for a minute, listening to the steady throb of the idle. I tried peering under the garage door, but no trace of light filtered out from inside. I glanced down the dark alley, but like the street, there wasn't a sign of life. Just a long row of locked garages.

As I stood there, a sick feeling overcame me with the suddenness of a heart attack. A sheen of nervous sweat oozed from my pores and my tongue went thick and dry in my mouth. I started to knock, then pound on the garage door and called Wajda's name at the top of my voice. When there was no response but the engine's throaty hum I began to kick at the door with all my strength. I saw some lights go on in nearby windows, but I ignored them.

I tried to turn the handle, but the garage door was locked and wouldn't budge. I kicked it again, trying to force the mechanism. Someone next door leaned out the window and yelled at me in French, but I didn't stop to respond. Instead, I dashed back around the house and leapt up the steps to the front door. I tried the knob, but of course it, too, was locked. I pounded on the door and stabbed repeatedly at the bell without result.

I stopped and thought carefully about my choices.

If I was wrong Dornan would likely be bailing me out of a Montreal jail and I was going to have to make up one hell of a story.

But if it was what I feared . . .

I saw a small garden spade among the shrubs and used it to break the thin square of glass in the front door, knocking jagged shards into the hall. I snaked my arm through the window and opened the locks, cutting my elbow on a tiny piece of glass.

I dashed about the house looking for the way in to the garage. I ran madly from room to room until I realised that I was one floor *above* the level of the back alley. I tried every door I came to until I found a flight of steps leading down. I couldn't feel the light switch and crashed into a second door at the bottom.

I flung that door open and smashed it into the dark headlights of the idling car. I was nearly overcome by the noxious carbon monoxide fumes. A bare thirty-watt bulb suspended from the ceiling had come on when I opened the door, illuminating the narrow garage. I gagged and covered my mouth and nose, peering through the smoke toward the driver's side. Slumped over the wheel of a Mercedes I saw the wan outline of a figure, one hand dangling out the open window.

Coughing and retching I ran around to the driver's door, but I could only open it a few inches before it scraped against the garage wall. I tugged at the limp body but he was too heavy for me to pick up. I touched his hand. It felt warm, but I couldn't find a pulse. Not that I ever could.

I switched off the engine then squeezed past to the back of the car. At the base of the garage door I saw that sheets and towels had been firmly wedged into all the gaps. I kicked them aside and reached for the handle, The door opened readily from the inside. I heaved it open as far as I could and took a deep gulp of the fresh night air. I hurried back inside and released the car's emergency brake. Then I went around front and bracing myself against the garage wall, pushed the car backwards with my legs.

It rolled slowly, but the garage floor was on a slight grade. With another shove the car picked up speed and scooted out of the garage and into the alley until it crashed loudly into a solid brick wall across the way. I ran out behind it gasping for a clean breath.

In the alley, several neighbours had come to investigate the ruckus. Through blurry eyes, I saw a thin man in a red bathrobe pull Wajda out of the car and start to administer CPR. I heard the sound of approaching sirens even as I dizzily fell forward, the Mercedes' hood ornament looming in my vision like a harvest moon.

I sat in the back of an ambulance while a uniformed policeman interviewed me and a paramedic dressed the cut on my arm and a small gash in my forehead. I gave them Dornan's address and told them Wajda was a friend of a friend who I didn't know but had been told to look-up while I was in town. The cop asked me what led me to check the garage or even suspect that anything was wrong. I glanced away, shook my head and told him the truth.

"I don't know," I said. "Just a feeling."

The cop didn't look happy, but he had one of those faces that probably never did.

The crowd started to disperse as the ambulance sped off. I made eye contact with the man in the red bathrobe and went over to talk to him, He nodded as I approached and cinched his belt. He had bony legs. We watched for a moment as the last of the police pulled out of the alley, then introduced ourselves.

"Hell of a thing this, eh?" he said.

"You have no idea," I said.

"You're a friend of Steve's then?"

"Relative," I said with a half-smile.

"Is that right? So you must know what this was about then." *A-bewt*, he said, like a good Canadian.

I shook my head nervously. "*Distant* relative. Several times removed, you might say. And then some."

"The wife and kid, I figure," my new friend nodded.

"How's that?" I asked, my gut starting to roil. "What about his wife and kid?"

"Don't you know?" he asked in that special voice reserved for the perversely joyful presentation of lurid news. "Killed. Just a couple of weeks ago. Car accident, don't you know. The boy was quite young. I mean, considering Steve's age. Terrible thing. Just awful. I suppose it was all too much for him."

I must have visibly blanched because the man asked if I was all right. I nodded and mumbled something about the effects of the evening. He clucked sympathetically and patted me on the shoulder as we said goodnight.

I walked for a while — a few hours, actually — until I didn't know where I was and eventually found a cab. I started to give the driver Dornan's address, but suddenly changed my mind. I told him to take me to the hospital. I wanted, needed, to know how Wajda was. To make sure he had made it okay.

I wanted to see him again.

I emptied my mind as we drove, too numb to think or try and understand what had happened, how I got here or what it meant that Sally had really known about what was going to happen. I pressed my bruised forehead against the cool glass of the air-conditioned cab and let the lights of Montreal dance and shimmer in my fuzzy vision.

At the front desk I was told that Wajda's condition was listed as 'guarded', but that I would have to wait until morning for more details. I got his room number and thanked the receptionist. Then for reasons I can't entirely explain, I snuck around to a deserted hospital entrance. I tried to appear officious as I walked the quiet halls, but no-one even looked at me twice. I hesitated outside his room. With a quick glance around, I eased the door open.

Wajda's wrists were secured to the guard rails as a precaution and an IV dripped into his left arm, I looked carefully at his thin, ashen face in the faint fluorescent glow. It was crazy to expect him to look like Lily — he was, I reminded myself, her blood nephew, not her son — but I thought I detected a trace of the family genes in his sharp-ridged cheeks and deep-set eyes.

He seemed to be breathing well and I somehow felt sure that he was going to be fine. That my bizarre journey of redemption, a trip I could never hope to truly understand, was over.

I started to sneak back out when my cousin's eyes opened and he looked up at me. I froze as I saw a mixture of puzzlement and fear cross his face. I was tempted to bolt, but he dragged his tongue across chapped lips. I really didn't know if he should have water, but there was a cup and pitcher beside the bed so I figured it would be okay. I poured out two fingers' worth and held the cup to his lips. He lifted his head slightly and dabbed at it gingerly with his tongue. I put the cup aside and he smiled at me and for ever so slight a moment I thought I saw my mother's face in his.

I don't know what made me do it, it certainly wasn't a conscious thing.

I started to sing Lily's song.

With the second note, his expression went as wide as a western sky. As I sang, I saw tears pool in his eyes, felt them fall down my own cheeks.

When I got to the last line he sang it, too, in a voice as slight as a rose petal:

Never let anyone know.

I fell asleep almost as soon as I got back home to L.A. And I dreamed. At least, I think it was a dream. It was strange, because I could sort of make out the familiar contours of my bedroom in the background.

I found myself staring at Lily's apartment again, but this time the light was bright and soft and the air rich with the oniony smell of good home cooking. The table had been set for one, the plate heaped with steaming potato *latkes* and sour cream and a big bowl of *borscht*. Lily stood in the kitchen fussing over the stove, sweetly humming her little tune. She looked up at me for a moment and passed a wisp of a smile. Then she turned back to her cooking.

The telephone woke me up. I mean if I was asleep. The smell of fresh *latkes* seemed to linger in the air and it made me wonder.

I stumbled over to the receiver and mumbled a hello. It was my father calling from New York. Where had I been, he demanded, he had been calling all night. I made up a story about visiting friends in Santa Barbara and staying over when I hadn't planned to. What was the big deal, I asked. He yelled a little more then calmed himself down.

He was calling, he said, because he had some bad news: my grandmother had died in her hospital in Florida. I didn't bother to correct him about her identity, but I asked what had happened.

Nothing, he said. She died during the night.

Peacefully.

In her sleep.

> *The red rose cries, 'She is near, she is near',*
> *And the white rose wells, 'She is late',*
> *The larkspur listens, 'I hear, I hear',*
> *And the lily whispers, 'I wait'.*
>
> — Tennyson

Introduction to "Sullivan's Travails"

Which brings us to my dear friend Marty Burns.

Marty is the closest thing I have to an *alter ego*. To date, I've written two novels about him (a third, *Greed & Stuff,* is in the works) and three short stories, of which "Sullivan's Travails" is rather the longest. And, I think, the best. The short stories stand alone, but are also part of a thematic sequence dealing with different aspects of the movies.

The full back story on Marty can be found in *Celestial Dogs,* his début to the world. Although it was the second novel I wrote (*Blood* came earlier), it was the first novel I sold. Marty's biography, as an ex-child star-cum-private eye whose fortunes rise and fall like Paris hemlines, could not have less to do with my own life experiences, but allowing for some artistic licence, his voice is pretty similar to my own. At least, the voice that sounds inside my head. Perhaps others hear me differently.

The events in "Sullivan's Travails" pick up after Marty's adventures in *Burning Bright.* After many years of living on the scrap heap, Marty is once again starring in a network television series and living the (pretty) good life. The thing is that Marty is an attractor for serious strangeness, a kind of supercharged nexus for otherworldly oogy-boogy. The Marty stories are a major attempt to blend detective, horror, fantasy and comic fiction in one big, entertaining package. The response I've received about them has been overwhelmingly enthusiastic, which is gratifying, but the truth of the matter is that it has been a titanic struggle to get the books out into the market in a visible way precisely because the publishing industry is so resistant to that which cannot be readily pigeonholed. So while future Marty short stories will continue to be mixed genre pieces — and there will be more stories to come; that's a threat — the new novel and any subsequent ones are going to sit more squarely in the mainstream of detective fiction. You can only bang your head against the wall so long before you stop and say "Ouch." Ironically, *Celestial Dogs* was originally intended as a straight detective novel — the demons sort of wormed their way in — so maybe I'm just coming full circle.

Oh, yeah: *Sullivan's Travels* is one of my favourite films, and I've been in love with Veronica Lake — one of the great, tragic Hollywood figures — ever since I first saw the movie. It probably shows.

Sullivan's Travails

THE OLDEST JOKE IN THE BUSINESS HAS TO BE the one about the movie starlet who's so stupid she sleeps with the writer. The ethnic version makes her Polish to boot, but the point remains the same. The jibe is supposed to be at the expense of writers — as if counting Joe Eszterhas among your number isn't joke enough — but has anyone ever considered it from the actress's point of view? How is the poor, dumb thing supposed to feel the morning *after* she's balled the writer? At least *he's* bagged a babe.

Not to mention how awful she might *still* be feeling fifty years down the road.

The first day of a shoot is always a bit of a laugh and a lot of a waste of time, even on a TV series. It's like the first day back at school after summer vacation — everybody's busy catching up with what (and who) all the other kids have been doing, trying to figure out if the rumours and gossip they've heard could possibly be true. For example, in the four month hiatus between wrapping up the modestly successful first season of *Burning Bright* and starting work on the who'd-have-thunk-it second, both Kelly Garner and Greg Kite, my co-stars, had been romantically linked with Jenifer Aniston in the tabloids. That Kelly and Greg were both happily married, *to each other*, had little effect on the rumour mongers, and none whatsoever on our crew members, mature gentlemen that they are, who fake-coughed "Jenifer" into their fists all day in efforts to get a rise. I have to admit I snuck a peak at Kelly when the best boy hacked up a phlegmy "Aniston" — Kelly's always struck me as just a tad butch, especially for Greg — but she laughed it off, flipping him the bird.

Needless to say no-one linked me with the divine Ms. A. Or with anyone else, for that matter. The only rumour I'd even caught a whiff of during the off-season hinted at penis enlargement surgery in Tijuana.

I wish.

If the first day back is a party, the second is pure and holy hell, precisely because you're already a full day behind schedule as a result of pissing away most of the day before. By lunchtime, the A.D. is snorting lines of coke and the producer is sipping maximum strength antacid from his industrial-size bottle. (Normally, at least two affairs will also have been consummated by the end of the second day, but this doesn't become clear until several weeks later when the first D&C of the season takes place. I won that pool last year with a long shot bet on a mousy-looking script girl with big tits and a penchant for paisley; call it detective's intuition.)

The season opener had something or other to do with a kidnapped heiress, a religious cult and a whore with a heart of gold. Very *Barnaby Jones*, I know. Then there was some sub-plot about beach volleyball — the *Baywatch* factor — but to be honest, I don't pay all that much attention to the story lines. I did at first, but I kept getting into arguments with the creative consultant, a big hairy guy with pointy little teeth and a goatee, who totes a copy of *Hero With A Thousand Faces* wherever he goes. He insists that there has to be a 'mythopoeic' underpinning to every episode and reads me bits from the book to prove it. I still don't have a clue what he's talking about, but I've learned to hate Joseph Campbell.

I was waiting for my call, sipping a frosty Anchor Steam and reading about the latest Dodgers bullpen fiasco, when I heard the kerfuffle. This week's director was a gangly prick with Spielberg facial hair, Jan de Bont charm and Michael Winner talent. He'd made his name shooting a controversial tampon commercial — the Clio award-winning centrepiece of the campaign was an image of a bleeding, stuck pig — but now he was screaming at the top of his voice at an elderly bag lady. Actually, he was screaming at the actress *playing* the bag lady, but she was still only a little grey-haired thing, half his size and three times his age. Spittle flying, he bellowed every obscenity in the book at her — I gathered she'd blown a cue, and not for the first time — full in the face. The old woman just stood there, taking it, though so fierce was the director's onslaught that I thought I could see her hair billowing behind her like some character in a comic strip or a Memorex ad. When he ran out of expletives, the director just unleashed an inchoate roar. As he finally strode off, he spoke the words uttered more often in Hollywood than "I love you" and "*no hablo ingles*" combined:

"You'll never work in this town again," he spat.

The set had gone still-life quiet, everyone hungrily taking in the scene. The crew stood in their places, silently waiting and wide-eyed watching, like jerk-off bandits at a quarter-a-throw peep show. Even after the director had wandered off, the old lady just stood there. The thought flashed through my head that if only we could achieve this level of drama when the cameras were rolling, *Burning Bright* might really have something. But then there's the difference between television and real life. (Well, that and the credit sequence.)

The old woman glanced sternly off to one side and I thought perhaps she was trying not to cry, but as I studied her, she seemed more distracted than upset. I tried to follow her gaze, to figure out what she was staring at stage left, but there was nothing in particular to see. Still clutching her sacks of prop rags, the actress finally shook her head and walked slowly — and with enviable grace — off the set. She paused once, to glance again at that same vacant spot, then left the building. Everyone silently watched her go and only when she'd passed out of the still blaring lights and into the darkness beyond did activity resume. The stage was quickly filled with the buzz and bumble of white hot gossip and spite.

It was only as the bright lights winked off that it occurred to me that I could have — *should* have — done something. The director may be the boss on the set, but he ain't the star. Of course, even a year into this gig I still don't quite *feel* like a star, but that's no reason not to have acted. I felt embarrassed and ashamed, though a glance around the set suggested that I was the only one.

I went out looking for the old lady.

I passed the director who was being attended to by his coterie. How does a man whose fame is built on feminine hygiene products come to have a coterie, you might ask. Whose bright idea was it to build a big city in a desert and on a fault line, you might just as futilely ponder. He nodded at me as I walked past, but I ignored him. The nice thing about television is that directors are only marginally less insignificant than writers; that's why they turn into such fabulously hideous monsters if they graduate to features. I pushed open the heavy sound stage door and blinked into the harsh afternoon sunlight.

She was sitting on the kerb, smoking a cigarette and rocking back and forth, looking every bit the part she'd been dressed for. Seeing the deep crags in her sallow cheeks, I realised she was older than I'd first thought. Though somewhere inside those hollow cheeks I sensed a distant, not entirely vanquished beauty. Just then a pair of network Suits came walking by.

"Christ, they're fucking everywhere," one of them muttered. "How do they get past Pete at the gate?"

"Have a heart," the other chided and pressed a five dollar bill into her hand. I knew which of the two of them wasn't headed for the top of the executive ladder.

The old woman held up the money and started to protest, but the Suits had walked on.

She unfolded the note, held it up to the sun to inspect it — it *had* come from a network boy, after all — then stuffed it in her pocket. She looked up and saw me watching her, and I could see her trying to concoct an explanation.

"Keep it," I said, sitting down beside her. "It's the least they owe you."

She smiled a thin smile at me, and went back to her cigarette.

"Are you all right?" I asked. "That was really uncalled for in there. I'm very sorry it happened."

The old woman leaned back and studied me briefly, genuinely puzzled I think. She snuffed her cigarette out under foot and drew herself up a little straighter.

"That's very kind of you, Mr. Burns. But it's all water off an old duck's ass, believe me. I've known much worse. I once worked for Fritz Lang."

"Really?"

"The little Nazi used to jab you in the stomach with his finger when he wasn't happy with a take. And he sharpened his nails, too. Or sometimes rabbit punches to the back of the head. I knew a fellow ended up concussed after two weeks work on *Beyond a Reasonable Doubt*."

"Still, that doesn't excuse the way Tampon Boy went at you in there. It's . . . it's not right."

The old woman laughed out loud, then slapped a hand to her mouth. "Oh, I'm sorry."

"What? What's so funny?"

"It's just . . . "

"Say it," I insisted, smiling.

"Mr. Burns, it's very kind of you to take the time to come out and talk to me like this. Really it is, and I appreciate it. But you know, I've been in The Business for almost sixty years now . . . "

"No shit?"

"Yes, indeed. I've been performing all my life: movies, TV, dinner theatre, you name it . . . " She again looked off to her left in a distracted way, shook her head, before turning back to me. "In all those years, I've yet to meet anyone, *anyone* in show business who *ever* did the right thing." After a pause she added: "Myself included."

She briefly looked me in the eye then glanced on down the street again. What the hell was she looking at? She'd smiled when she caught my eye, but the smile turned wryly sad as she looked away, as if she was studying the ruins of a long and very lonely life.

"Call me Marty," I said, and held out my hand.

Her name was Olivia Sullivan. You won't find it in any film encyclopedia or reference book, not even those sad cult magazines with endless photos of skewered eyeballs, David Duchovny, and jumpsuited *Star Trek* babes. But, as Olivia told me later, she'd worked on over two hundred movies, almost always as an extra. She started in 1939 with *Water Rustlers*, starring 'Singing Cowgirl' Dorothy Page. ("Not much of a voice," Olivia told me, "but a great set of lungs, if you know what I mean." You bet I do; some things never change.) She had no idea how many TV shows she'd done, but reckoned it was at least half again as many as her movie parts. She claimed to have worked on no fewer than thirty episodes of *Bonanza* alone. ("Hoss was just a dear, but that Hop Sing was always undressing you with his eyes.")

"So westerns were your thing, huh?" I asked her.

"Hell, no," she said. "I've done a good forty, fifty musicals — had a helluva set of gams in my day, hard to believe now I know — and probably near as many horror flicks. Hollywood moves in cycles, dearie, and I went with the work. For a good long while it was westerns were the ticket — lord, I do miss them sometimes — so I'd slip on a hoop skirt and bustle and bonnet and play another milling townswoman."

Movie extras are a funny breed. There are quite a few who make a living at it, if you want to call it living, and for what little it's worth they do have their own union. An extra does whatever is asked and never complains. At least, not to anyone official. An extra might work a sixteen hour day, standing out in the freezing cold in a bathing suit or the desert sun in a parka; whatever the shot, and director's ego, calls for. All for fifty, sixty bucks a day plus all the shit they can eat. Extras get treated worse than animals — the ASPCA watches out for them, at least — and, befitting their title, are regarded as entirely expendable.

Why do they do it?

Ask the guy who walks behind the elephants at the circus.

I walked Olivia back into the sound stage and made sure that she got to complete the scene that she'd been bawled out for blowing. The director wasn't happy about it, but a Suit had wandered on set — a Suit *so* high up that he didn't even have to wear a suit — so he couldn't make a fuss. Olivia didn't actually have a line, just a reaction shot, but she picked up her cue on the first re-take, so it was smiles all around.

I had a couple more scenes to get through, and sort of forgot about Olivia in the eternal struggle of trying to remember my lines. We ran a little over-schedule — you can practically see the dollar bill signs flash in the crews' eyes when overtime kicks in — and it was dark by the time we wrapped for the day. The great thing about Marty Burns playing Marty Burns PI is that I don't even need to change out of costume at the end of the day. Though I do sometimes get depressed when the pretty girls I pass on the street don't track me with the same dreamy, bedroom eyes that the ones on camera do. Mark another highly significant difference between TV and real life.

As I left the set, I saw Olivia waiting out in front. She'd traded her bag lady outfit for white slacks and a frilly blouse. She looked ten years younger, but she still wasn't going to need photo ID to get the senior citizen's discount at Denny's. She timidly waved at me when I looked her way, so I walked over to her.

"Hey, Olivia," I said.

"Hi, Marty. I wanted to thank you again for your kindness today."

"*De nada.* Professional courtesy."

Yet again, as we talked, I noticed that she was looking somewhat askance, focusing on some invisible point in the distance. I think they called it the thousand-yard stare back in the 'Nam. At least they did in *The 'Nam*, a Vietnam movie I appeared in. It was disorienting at any rate.

"You okay, Olivia?"

"Hmmmm?" She turned her attention back on me. "Oh,

yes, thank you. A little tired, though. It's been a long day and I'm not as young as I used to be."

"Dick Clark's the only one who is," I joked.

"Not the only one," she muttered, sounding very serious indeed. Something about her manner worried me.

"I was just about to go grab a bite. Nothing fancy. Would you care you join me? My treat."

She was looking over my shoulder again and I half-turned, fearing Charlie might be emerging from the tree line. No-one there.

"Hmmmm?" she said again. Then my question seemed to register. "Oh, no. I couldn't impose."

"Don't be silly. I'd love the company. Consider it an apology from the show for what happened."

"That's really not necessary."

"C'mon," I urged. "I want to hear more about Dorothy Page's tits anyway. Was she any relation to Betty?"

It felt vaguely risqué saying 'tits' to an old lady like that, but she seemed to find it flattering.

"Thank you, Marty," she said, but she was searching the invisible tree line again. "We'd like that."

We? I thought.

But I let it pass.

As you do.

Word of advice: Don't.

I thought about taking her to the Smoke House for a juicy steak, but the last couple of times there I ran into Tom Snyder and I didn't want to risk it again. Olivia didn't seem like the type who'd go for the trendy joints — which made two of us — but I reckoned that working for extra's scale she didn't get *too* many good meals out, so I took her to a nice-but-quiet Thai place on Ventura Boulevard out toward Sherman Oaks. I'd never collided with any industry types there before, but fuck me with a satay stick if the babe who plays Xena's dyke buddy didn't saunter in with her entourage (don't confuse it with a *coterie*) two minutes after we'd sat down. Fortunately, the Amazons were well-behaved, though I did keep a nervous eye peeled lest Hercules wander in and flash his pecs.

"The Yum Yai is yum-yum," I pronounced, perusing the menu, even though I already knew what I was going to have. "And the steamed dumplings are top notch. But please order anything you like."

Olivia had the menu open in front of her, but her head was half-turned and she was peering at something from the corner of her eye. I thought she was checking out the Greek chorus, but she was definitely watching an empty table in the corner and shaking her head ever so slightly. I might have thought she had Parkinson's or something, but she hadn't been doing it before.

"Olivia?"

"Hmmm? Oh, I'm so sorry, Marty."

"It's okay. Just . . . are you still upset about what happened on the set? It's really not worth fretting about, you know. That director is a total jerk. I predict he'll be back in the feminine hygiene game before you can say 'toxic shock syndrome — the movie'."

"You're very sweet, really you are. But no, I'm not awfully bothered by that. Like I told you, I've encountered tons worse in my time."

The waiter brought our drinks and took the order just then. Olivia was only going to have an entree, but I made her go for soup and an appetiser and ordered a couple of extra veggie dishes for us to share. She was still glancing back toward the empty table.

"Would you rather sit over there?" I asked. "I don't mind."

"Haaah? Oh god! I'm so sorry. How horribly rude. You'd think I might have learned some manners at my age. I do apologise. This table is fine. It . . . doesn't really matter."

Okay, I thought, *young actresses are all crazy because they're so attractive, so it only figures old actresses will be even crazier, either because they're not pretty anymore, or because they got so in the habit of being crazy when they were young, that they don't know anything else. Deal with it, Marty.*

"You always been nuts?" I asked.

Olivia had been drifting off again, but that caught her attention. She looked mad for a second, then saw the cheeky glint in my eye — you don't want to know how many hours I've had to practice in front of mirrors to get it right — and broke out laughing.

"Maybe so," she said, dabbing her eyes with the corner of her napkin. "Or maybe just since 1937."

"Okay, I'll bite," I said, as the waiter set down our appetisers. He looked at me oddly. "What happened in 1937?"

She hesitated, taking another long, mournful look at the empty table in the corner before staring me square in the eye. "You'll think I'm crazy."

I rolled my eyes and gestured at her with an egg roll.

"No, I mean *really* crazy."

"Hey, babe, go with what works for you."

She hesitated again. Another glance into the void and a slight shrug of her shoulders.

"I'd come to Hollywood to be a star. How many stories, do you think, start with those same foolish words? I was seventeen, the prettiest girl in Johnsburg, Illinois — or so I was told — and sassy as a brass saxophone. All of which got me as far as the scarf counter at Bullock's Wilshire after six months of knocking on doors and seeing nothing but the casting couch behind the few that even opened."

"The more things change . . . "

"I worked at Bullock's six days a week, earning just about enough to pay for a room in a boarding house off Vermont that Nathanael West wouldn't have slept in. I used my lunch hours to visit agents' offices and read at open calls and do anything else I thought might land me a foot in the door. All it got me was fired from the scarf counter for taking too many long lunches.

"Enter Preston Sturges, stage right."

"Preston Sturges the director?"

"No, Preston Sturges the kosher butcher. Of course, Preston Sturges the director! What the hell business are we in?"

"Sorry," I said. And slunk back to my Yum Yai.

Olivia shook her head and clucked, but went on.

"Of course, he wasn't a director yet. In 1937 he was still an up-and-coming writer, but he was determined and smart and charming, and knew it wouldn't be too long before he got to direct. He'd already been a success on Broadway and made a fortune out of that lipstick . . . "

"Excuse me?"

"Didn't you know that Preston Sturges invented kiss-proof lipstick? It didn't smear no matter *what* you did. *Believe* me."

I think I may have blushed a little at that point.

"His mother owned a cosmetics business. That's where his money came from originally."

"Wait. How did you meet him?" I asked. "Certainly not at the Day of The Locust boarding house."

"It could have been a movie," she sighed. "I was sitting in a little luncheonette downtown, treating myself to the luxury of a doughnut and coffee and debating whether or not I should swallow my pride and catch a bus back to Johnsburg. He happened in and sat down beside me. We got to talking and before you could say 'The Lady Eve' we'd hit it off."

"Wait a minute," I interrupted, "that *is* a movie." I literally felt my jaw drop. The waiter came by to refill the teapot just then, and I half-expected him to lift it back up for me. "Sullivan's *Travels*."

The look on her face at that moment should have been photographed and put into Webster's to illustrate the definition of *bittersweet*.

"He wrote that script for me," Olivia said. "The day we met in the luncheonette was the inspiration for the story. About the would-be actress on her way out of Hollywood, rescued and brought to public attention by the dashing, but disillusioned movie director. See, he wrote the script for me, to make me a star. And him, of course. It was going to be his first film as director."

"It wasn't though," I said, thinking back on my admittedly haphazard knowledge of cinema history. "Not for either of you, from what you told me before. Not unless there was a singing cowgirl with big hooters in the script."

"No." Olivia was now staring so intently at the empty table that I turned around in my chair to see what she could possibly be looking at.

Nada.

I turned back to study the old lady. "So what went wrong?"

She snorted like Mr. Ed, then shook her head. "Ask him," she said, nodding in the direction of the empty table.

"Heh?" I said. I looked behind me again, but there still wasn't anyone there. *Huh-boy,* I thought. I took a deep breath and slowly turned back toward Olivia. As I did so, for just a fraction of a second, I could have sworn on a stack of Leonard Maltins that I caught a glimpse of someone, a man, sitting there at the table, staring back at us. But when I double-took back to check — again — the table was plainly deserted.

"What the . . . ?" I muttered.

Strange shit. My middle name. *That's what you get for taking a crazy old actress to dinner*, I thought.

"No good deed goes unpunished, does it?" I said. As much to myself as to Olivia.

"I don't know, Marty," she replied. "But I can tell you one thing for certain: you pay for the bad ones for ever and ever."

Preston Sturges didn't get to make *Sullivan's Travels* as quickly as he'd hoped. In fact, he would direct three other pictures first, and none of those until 1940.

"*Hotel Haywire*," Olivia told me.

"Beg pardon?"

"Preston had just finished the script for it when we started our affair."

"Never heard of it."

"Be thankful for small blessings. It starred Leo Carillo — god, I still love saying that name; it just rolls off your tongue — but it was meant to be a vehicle for Burns and Allen. The studio had other ideas though and massacred the script. Preston was so furious he went and wrote *Port of Seven Seas* for Metro. He did go back to Paramount in the end, of course."

I'd been sneaking glances back at the empty table myself, occasionally using my spoon as a mirror in an effort to be less conspicuous about it, but I didn't see a thing. Olivia finally touched her fingers to the back of my hand.

"He's gone," she told me.

"What? Who?"

"Preston. He's gone."

I swallowed hard, the chilli sauce from the sizzling chicken coagulating unpleasantly in my stomach.

"Preston," I said.

"Mmmm."

"Preston Sturges was sitting at that table."

"You saw him didn't you?"

"I don't think I care to say."

"It's all right. He's often around me."

"Preston Sturges?"

"Yes."

This time I did turn around a take a long, hard look. Xena's girlfriend was strolling back from the toilet and winked at me. The *maître d'* was seating a party of six at the table. One of them waved — just a fan, I reckon — and I nodded in reply.

"Isn't Preston Sturges dead?" I asked.

"Oh, yes. He died in 1959."

"But he was sitting at that table?"

Olivia pushed her plate away — she'd barely eaten — and sighed. "God, I need a cigarette," she said.

"It's no smoking."

"I know. I hate California."

"Take a number," I said. She smiled and half-shrugged. "So Preston Sturges is dead."

"Yeah."

"I'm no great logician — hell, I can't even do the damned Jumble — but isn't there a slight contradiction here. I mean, him being dead and all, and sitting there in the corner?"

"He's been haunting me," Olivia announced, just as the waiter came to collect the dishes. He looked at her and then at me.

"Haunting you. Okay. Has this been going on for long?"

"Since 1973."

I nodded. "Yes, that is quite a long time."

The waiter's eyes went wide. I saw a big tip coming. So, I think, did he.

"It's a hell of a thing," Olivia said.

The waiter scurried off. I scratched my head.

"Anything special happen in 1973?"

"Oh, yes."

The waiter returned, holding out dessert menus.

"And what was that?"

Olivia took a very deep breath. "That was the year that Veronica Lake died."

"How could I forget," I said. I looked up at the waiter. "I think we'll just have the check."

He seemed to understand entirely.

1973 was a cusp year for me; one in which I passed over that dark threshold from could-have-been to has-been. *Salt & Pepper*, the series in which I'd become a child star, was four years gone and even the network casting directors didn't want to see my glossies any more. I did a couple of soft-core/druggie movies and began my final descent into 'whatever became of' territory.

1973 was also, indeed, the year that Veronica Lake shuffled off this mortal coil.

I drove us back up Ventura toward the studio lot where Olivia had left her car. I like driving in L.A. at night, after the rush-hour mania has passed and a hint of clean, crisp breeze reaches into even the San Fernando Valley. Olivia had rolled down her window and trailed a hand outside like a little kid.

"It's my fault, you know."

"What is?" I asked.

"What happened to Veronica Lake."

"You killed her?" I joked.

"In a way," Olivia said.

"Umm, you want to explain that?"

She pulled her arm back inside the car and began rubbing her hands together. She took a very deep breath.

"Preston got me a bit part in *Hotel Haywire*."

"This is back in '37?"

"Yes. It was just a few lines, but it was still my first real acting job. Then he saw what they did to the script and went crazy. They banished him from the set and since I was his girlfriend, they sent me packing too. I did one day's shooting, but they scrapped it and got another girl. Funny thing is the director, a guy named Archainbaud . . . "

"Never heard of him," I said.

"That makes everyone then. Funny thing is I worked for him again as an extra years later, not that he knew or would have remembered. He ended up directing set-bound westerns for television in the fifties. Water finds its own level, as they say.

"So Preston started writing *Sullivan's Travels* as a vehicle for me. He figured he'd get me a couple of smaller roles first and then insist that the studio could only have this brilliant script if they'd take me as the star."

"I think feel a 'but' coming on," I said.

"But . . . Veronica Lake."

"What about her?"

"Preston couldn't do our story right off the bat. He knew it was his best work, but he wanted to direct it himself and knew he had to work his way up to doing justice to it. So he wrote some other scripts and convinced the studio to let him direct some of the them first. *The Great McGinty, Christmas in July, The Lady Eve.*"

"So you were in those?"

"No," Olivia said, very coldly. "He dumped me."

"Oh," I said.

"We were at it hot and heavy for almost two years. I got some small roles, was building a little bit of a name. And Preston's star just kept rising and rising. He kept saying that the time was almost, *almost* right for *Sullivan's Travels.* We even went shopping for engagement rings in Beverly Hills, and looked at houses in Pasadena. And then he met her."

"Veronica Lake."

"Moronica is what they used to call her around town, you know, and did she ever deserve it. Though her real name was Constance; Constance Ockelman, can you imagine? When Preston first mentioned her, started talking about her, I figured it was just about the work: a new picture, a rising starlet. I couldn't believe that anyone as brilliant as Preston could be interested in someone . . . like her. Of course she was pretty and all . . . "

I shot her another look, which she caught.

"So she was gorgeous, I admit it. But how could he have fallen for her? We used to go to the theatre, to the opera, to the galleries. You know where he would take her? To the pier at Santa Monica. She liked to listen to the music from the merry-go-round and eat cotton candy."

"He told you all this?"

"He told me he didn't love me anymore. That he loved her. He said she understood him in a way no-one else ever had or ever could. And that he was going to cast *her* in *Sullivan's Travels.*"

"Ouch. That's pretty cold. Even for this nasty old town."

"I was heartbroken. It was supposed to be *my* story, *my* movie. It was going to make me a star and be a monument to our love.

"But here I am, fifty years later, still an extra. Still alone."

We'd arrived back at the studio lot. Olivia pointed out her car and I drove us over.

"*Sullivan's Travels* was made, what, around 1940?"

"Forty one."

"So to cast off suspicion you waited . . . " — I did the mental math; these things can take a while — "thirty two years? Fourteen years after Sturges died, and then you killed Veronica Lake in spurned lover's revenge?"

Olivia looked down at her hands, one tight fist folded inside the other, and smiled a sad smile.

"I didn't *physically* kill her, Marty."

"Phew! Saved me having to haul you down to the station house. And me without my detective's 'cuffs."

"I shouldn't have told you all this. It's . . . ancient history and no-one cares. Not even me, not anymore."

She opened the door and got out. I followed her.

"Wait," I yelled. "I was only teasing there. I want to hear the rest of what happened. Really. You haven't told me about the haunted bit. The table at the restaurant."

She already had the door to her own car open and was halfway in. She wouldn't look up at me.

"It's all in my head, Marty. The only ghosts are in the minds of those who live in regret. Take it from a very foolish old woman. Thank you for dinner."

"Wait," I called again, but she closed the door, started up the engine and drove off without another word.

"Shit," I said. I pounded a hand on the roof of my car, watched her taillights disappear into the dark. "Asshole!" I called myself.

Feeling very small indeed, I got back in my car and stared out the window for a while. I turned the radio on and off, and felt generally shitty without being entirely sure why. Olivia was obviously a little bit goofy, but I kind of liked her. I didn't mean to offend her, should have realised that there are things about people you can't, and shouldn't, make fun of. *Christ*, I thought, *when would I grow up and learn?*

"Wouldn't we all like to know!" a voice said.

I gasped and spun around, but there was no-one else in the car. I looked all around outside, but there was no-one and nothing to be seen. I checked the radio, but it was definitely off.

"You're losing it, bud," I said to myself.

I did one more survey of the terrain, then started up the car and pulled out of the lot. I turned onto Ventura Boulevard, where traffic was light. I was driving a little fast and came up on a yellow light, deciding at the last minute that I'd better hit the brakes. It wasn't the smoothest manoeuvre of all time. I nervously glanced in the mirror to check if I'd screwed anyone coming up behind me. Like, say, a cop.

The road was clear, but a blurry figure glared at me from the back seat.

"What the heck kind of driving is that? You want to get us killed?"

This time I definitely screamed.

I'd like to claim it was my unparalleled powers of detection, honed over many years of mean-streeted private eye-dom, that enabled me to locate Olivia Sullivan so quickly. I'd really like that.

What I did, though, was call my producer, who called his PA, who woke up the casting director, who sent her PA scurrying to the office to dig out the accounting records and call me with the address.

Celebrity is not without its perks.

Olivia wasn't too surprised to see me when she opened her front door.

"I was afraid it might be you," she said. Christ, if I had a nickel for every time someone has said *that* to me . . .

I offered a wry smile and gestured over my shoulder with my thumb.

"So ya gonna let us in or do we gotta stand out here all night?" the gravelly voice complained.

"I gather you are already acquainted with Mr. William Demarest?" I asked. "The very late and generally irritable Mr. William Demarest."

"Late, early, what's the stinkin' difference? What are ya, a time clock? How long is a person supposed to stand out here on the sidewalk anyhow?"

"Oh, dear," Olivia said.

But she let us in.

"This dump could do with a good cleaning. Uncle Charlie wouldn't have stood for this, I can promise ya that."

Demarest was running a spectral finger across various surfaces, performing a hereafter variation on the white-glove test, griping as he went, while Franklin Pangborn, who had been pestering Olivia when we arrived, supervised from over his shoulder. Demarest didn't seem to much like his partner in incorporeality — "Get out of my way, ya big sissy," Demarest shouted — but Pangborn took it in stride. Demarest had hardly shut-up since first appearing in the back seat of my car.

"Are they with you *all* the time?" I asked Olivia.

"No," she said, "thank god." The two ghosts shot her a look at mention of the almighty's name, then went back to their fussing. I wasn't sure what it meant. Olivia slumped even further in her chair and shook her head slowly back and forth. "They come and go. I think they can only stay for so long before they have to return to . . . wherever. I thought I must be mad. All these years."

"Because you saw them?"

She nodded. "But you see them, too."

"I do. Though it's the listening bit, I find less appealing."

"Hah!" Demarest said. I thought he was responding to me, but he held up a fluffy dust bunny he'd removed from atop a hanging picture frame. Prissy Pangborn pointed at it and 'tsk'-ed.

"You know, I actually auditioned for *My Three Sons*," I said. "When they added Ernie. To this day I have a hard time accepting that I lost out to Barry Livingstone."

"He tested *much* better than you," Demarest said. "Plenty cuter, too."

"Why are they here?" I asked. "Why these guys?"

"It's not just them, though I do see a *lot* of Bill Demarest. Jimmy Conlin, Bob Grieg. Rudy Vallee once in a blue moon. He's very nice, I have to admit, so polite. And all the others."

"Sturges' stock company," I said, nodding as I remembered the movies. *The Palm Beach Story, Hail the Conquering Hero, Miracle of Morgan's Creek.* Of course, Demarest and Pangborn were in almost every one. Jimmy Conlin, too (the weasly little guy). "Oh, man: Eddie Bracken doesn't show, does he? That guy makes my throat itch."

"I think he's still alive, Marty."

"That's a relief."

"I'm not complaining, but you seem to be taking all this very calmly. I've had years to get used to it. To the extent that I have, I mean."

Pangborn and Demarest were bickering over the placement of knick-knacks on Olivia's mantelpiece. Demarest kept trying to rearrange them, but Pangborn slapped his hand every time he tried to move something, until Demarest finally took a poke at him. Pangborn simply popped out of existence and Demarest did a forward somersault when his blow met empty space. "Criminy!" he complained, from somewhere on the floor behind the sofa. "I always forget about that."

"I've been around the otherworldly block once or twice myself," I explained, massaging my temples. "You might not believe me at this particular moment, but there's worse than this . . . out there."

"My," Olivia said. I don't think she believed me.

"Was it these guys who were distracting you earlier tonight? At the studio and back in the restaurant?"

She shook her head.

"It really was . . . "

It wasn't the least bit cold, but Olivia crossed her arms tightly over her chest and issued a little shudder. She stared down at the floor and swallowed hard.

"Preston," she whispered.

I nodded. "These clowns are still working for him, aren't they? Still his stock company."

"We happen to be an *ensemble*," Pangborn trilled from across the room.

"Ensemble my Aunt Fanny, " Demarest said. "We're a team!" He's just gotten up off the floor, took two steps toward Pangborn and tripped over a telephone cord, going down with a loud crash. Pangborn emitted another sibilant 'tsk'.

"Maybe you'd better tell me the rest of the story," I said. "The *whole* story."

Olivia, suddenly looking all of her years and then some, nodded in agreement.

"Maria Ouspenskaya," Olivia said. She'd spent a good few minutes sitting there, collecting her thoughts while Demarest and Pangborn continued their tag-team antics. Both ghosts froze when Olivia spoke. If they'd had any colour in their semi-transparent faces it would have drained out. They looked at each other, then simply disappeared with a sound like a plastic cork popping out of a bottle of Cold Duck.

"Well that's a neat trick," I said. "Where'd they go?"

"I've tried asking but they never say. Ouspenskaya's name scares the bejesus out of them, though."

"The actress? What's she got to do with it?"

"Just about everything."

"She was in a mess of horror flicks. *The Wolf Man*, right? The old gypsy woman."

"Maleva."

"Of course! Wait, how did it go? 'Even the man who is pure in heart, and says his prayers by night . . .'"

". . . 'May become a wolf when the wolf-bane blooms, and the autumn moon is bright,'" Olivia recited.

"Yeah! Great stuff."

"I don't find it quite so charming as I used to."

"Hmmm, I can imagine. So what happened?"

"Ouspenskaya always played those spooky old women. Which was fair enough, because she *was* a spooky old dame. She really was Russian and claimed to be descended from Baba Yaga."

"Baba Yaga? Isn't that where the Nazis killed all the Jews outside Kiev?"

"I don't think so," Olivia said. "She was some kind of Russian witch or something. Anyway, Ouspenskaya claimed to be a witch-woman herself by lineage. She used to sell charms and amulets, and would cast spells for a fee. Especially after the acting jobs started to dry up."

"And you knew this because . . . "

"I was an extra in *Frankenstein Meets the Wolf Man*. She was pretty heavily into black magic by then. Some people thought she was just very serious about getting into character — sort of pre-Method — but she was more than living the part. She believed."

"Huh," I said.

"Preston had already made *Sullivan's Travels* — I couldn't believe he didn't even change the title — and moved on. He and Lake were still having their affair, and the pair of them were on top of world. Do you know that Lake was so popular that the Defence Department asked her to change her peek-a-boo hair style? So many women copied it that accidents in defence plants were getting out of hand. Can you imagine?"

I nodded. I could imagine how Olivia might have dreamed that she was the one who should have had all that fame.

"I was so bitter. Sturges won an Oscar for one of his scripts. He's opened that restaurant, The Players, which was the hottest spot in town. I couldn't even afford to eat there. Lake's picture was in every newspaper, on every magazine cover; staring down at me big as a house from billboards on Sunset Boulevard.

"And there I was: an extra in a B horror picture. Back in a West Hollywood boarding house with a hall toilet while Preston burned money like kitchen matches and flew to Paris for dinner with Moronica."

She was still slumped in her chair, but a tension had taken over her body. She had a white-knuckle grip on the armrest and her eyes seethed with fury. And only fifty-odd years after the fact.

"What did you do, Olivia?"

She crossed her arms over her chest. She offered a very cold smile.

"I put a curse on them." The smile quickly faded. "Rather, I paid Maria Ouspenskaya to do it."

"You're kidding."

She gave me a look.

"You're not kidding."

"Cost me every penny I had. The old hag was miserly as Scrooge. And that was the price of the curse: everything I had. And then some. But, you know, it didn't seem like all that much at the time. And I was so angry, so . . . vengeful that it felt like no price to pay at all. Which, I gather, is how these things work."

"I wouldn't really know."

Olivia raised an eyebrow.

"My expertise," I explained, "such as it is, rests in other realms of the Great Googly-Moogly. My knowledge of curses doesn't extend beyond the ten and twelve-letter variety. Actually, I know a sixteen-letter one, too, but I think it's hyphenated."

She nodded.

"So this hex . . ."

"Curse. Ouspenskaya said that the shape and nature of it would be determined by my own feelings, my anger, and that she was just the channel. After the . . . rite, after she did it, she told me that she never wanted to see me again. She looked a little rattled, like maybe it was more than she bargained for. Or charged for. She looked scared."

"Yikes."

"I know. I told you I was bitter. What happened, what Preston did to me, had been eating me up, tearing at my insides like chunks of swallowed glass. But the curse took that away. And out on the two of them."

"How so?"

"It took time — Ouspenskaya warned me that it would; that the curse was like a dark snowball that would grow and grow — but it even started with a bang. Lake threw Preston aside. She took up with Howard Hughes for a while, then married André de Toth. Preston was shattered. He managed to ride his career high for another year or two, but as the curse built up a head of steam, it affected that, too. His movies flopped, his career fizzled, the restaurant went bust. He started drinking. Finally, in desperation, he left the country. Moved to France."

"And Veronica Lake?"

The cold smile briefly flashed across Olivia's face. "Her career went into a tailspin at exactly the same time. The parts stopped coming. Her marriage fell apart. She lost all her money. It was *wonderful*."

I felt a chill go through me and repressed a shudder.

"When the old hag laid that curse in 1943, Sturges and Lake were on top of the world. Within ten years both their careers and lives were ruined. Preston died penniless in 1959, barely even remembered in Hollywood. And do you know what happened to Lake?"

I sort of did remember the story, but Olivia didn't give me a chance to speak.

"Some hack found her working as a barmaid in a sleazy hotel in the sixties. She lived on tips. Can you imagine? From being asked by the Pentagon to re-style your hair to fending off groping booze-hounds in a New York City dive in less than twenty years. That Ouspenskaya was amazing."

"I seem to remember that Lake made a bit of a comeback, though."

Olivia laughed. It was a nasty sound, far more frightening than the ghosts I'd seen in the room a few minutes before.

"Yeah. She did a couple of movies. *Flesh Feast*, ha! Then she died of hepatitis the same week she was offered a role in a David Lean picture."

"The curse," I said.

"It had no end. Has no end."

"I don't understand. They both died miserably. What else could there be?"

Olivia Sullivan leaned forward now, perched on the edge of her chair. The bitterness, the remnant of vengeance I'd observed on her face had all gone. She looked merely . . . sad. And old.

"I was happy, Marty. I had no regrets about the curse. I felt like they both got exactly what they deserved for what they'd done to me. And when I heard about Moronica, how she was working in that bar, I felt vindicated. Because I was still in Hollywood, still in the business, still working. Maybe I'd never made it beyond being an extra, but I'd outlived, out-survived the both of them. No mean feat in this horrible business.

"But only after she died did I realise the strength of the curse, the depth of bitterness that Ouspenskaya — that I — had put into it. Because it didn't end with death. It just goes on and on."

"I still don't understand," I insisted. "What is the curse? Why are these clowns, why is Sturges still haunting you?"

"Because they're still apart," Olivia cried. "Even in death, the curse is keeping them apart. Preston and Veronica. They were *supposed* to be together, *meant* to be together. But in my fury I destroyed that for them in life. And now, even in death, their souls can't be as one. Which is what they were destined to be. I see that now, Marty, I *accept* that. And Preston and his buddies, Demarest and Pangborn and Conlin and all his players, are haunting me. Ever since Lake's death I've been seeing them. Preston never says a word, not in all these years. He just comes and stares. Shakes his head. Punishing me for what I've done. Torturing me for torturing him."

"There's got to be a way out," I said. "Something you can do to lift the curse."

Olivia was actually in tears now. "No, I've tried. I've gone to psychics and healers and witches and crazies all over town. None of them have helped. You've seen for yourself that they're still here, still haunting me. There's nothing I can do."

"Yes," a voice from behind me said, "there is."

I spun around to see a dapper looking fellow with sad and anxious eyes. He had bushy dark hair and a thin moustache. He wore a swanky, if old-fashioned, double-breasted jacket, and a cigarette holder dangled from lips. I could see through him, but I could also see his pain.

Olivia literally fell off her chair, mouth agape and tears spilling from her eyes.

"*He* can do it," Preston Sturges said.

A very ghostly finger pointed straight between my eyes.

I drove, Olivia sat in the front passenger seat. I don't know how many of them were in the back, but I felt like I was chauffeuring the clown car at the circus. Their faces would blend and merge and pass through one another as they elbowed and argued for space. Demarest was there — he still hadn't shut up — as was Pangborn. Robert Dudley, who I remembered so well as The Weenie King from *The Palm Beach Story*, flitted in and out, as did Conlin and Grieg. Brian Donlevy and Akim Tamiroff showed up briefly and argued about the quality of the car's upholstery, and as I glanced into the rear-view approaching my exit off the Hollywood Freeway, I could have sworn I caught just a glimpse of Diana Lynn. I've always had a bit of a crush on her. I almost missed the turn-off.

Sturges, himself, had vanished again.

Olivia just stared straight out the windshield, seemingly oblivious to the fuss and bother. Or perhaps simply numb.

"Whaddaya mean ya can't stand *My Three Sons*?" Demarest demanded yet again. "You gonna tell me ya didn't like *Wells Fargo* either?"

Pangborn just sniffed. I've never heard anyone — living or dead — inject such manifest disdain into a mere exhalation.

"Aaaaahhh, whatta you know? You're crazy, ya big powder puff."

I saw Olivia finally cast a nervous peek behind her.

"And they've been at this since 1973?" I asked.

"Never like this though," she said. "I've never seen so many of them at once. It's never been this . . . intense."

"I think that's a good sign."

"Really?" she asked, a bit desperately.

"Absolutely," I insisted.

I didn't have the first fucking clue.

I turned on the radio to try and quiet the crowd, but it only started a fresh set of arguments about what we should listen to. Demarest wanted Easy Listening, but Jimmy Conlin was strictly AOR. Go figure. In the end, I flipped the damn thing off.

I followed the signs to Forest Lawn. Not that you can miss it: the cemetery is positively immense. It's a funny thing, too, because there don't seem to be any other cemeteries in L.A. Most everyplace else in the world you stumble across the odd churchyard burial ground or little bone yard tucked away on a quiet road. But that's never happened to me in Los Angeles. I know that people die here — and I don't just mean their careers — but somehow the youth-above-all culture of the city seems to extend unto death. Even Forest Lawn is as much a tourist attraction — come visit Marilyn's bones — as Universal Studios. A bit creepy if you think about it. But then you're not supposed to think about anything too hard in this town.

Being the middle of the night, the cemetery was, of course, closed so I had to park on the outskirts of the grounds. Demarest immediately started to gripe, but I told him to go to hell. Amazingly, this shut the lot of them up. It struck me that that particular instruction might carry special weight for those who've passed beyond.

Fortunately, the outer fence provided no serious obstacle. Olivia had a little trouble hauling her bottom half over the top, but with some delicate indelicacy, I managed to help manoeuvre her caboose up, down and onto the grounds. I followed her over and watched with annoyance as the Sturges Players simply passed through the barrier.

From studying my Thomas Guide, I knew that the cemetery was broken into a series of connected memorial grounds. A sign, just legible in the light of the full moon, indicated that we'd landed in Ascending Dawn. I saw a flicker up the path in front of us and felt my heart leap into my mouth fearing that we'd already stumbled into a night watchman. But as the flicker approached — Olivia issued another little gasp — I saw that it was only Sturges. He nodded to indicate we should follow him.

I held Olivia's hand as we made our way through the grounds, Sturges a steady half-dozen paces in front, his now visibly cowed and quiet colleagues three paces behind. There wasn't so much as a breeze that night, nor a sound to be heard beyond Olivia's and my nervous footsteps. The ghosts appeared actively more . . . ghostly in the moonlight, their forms glowing and flickering as they went. They kept reaching out toward the rows of tombstones on either side, touching at things I could only guess at. It all felt very solemn and somber.

But then graveyards are like that.

We passed from Ascending Dawn through Enduring Faith and Murmuring Trees — I didn't hear them — and into Twilight. It was there that Sturges turned off the path and crossed the lawn. I hate walking on graves. It's stupid but it always gives me the creeps. There, in Forest Lawn past midnight, led and followed by ghosts, I thought I could feel my toes burning with every sacrilegious step.

Sturges stopped in front of a modest (by Forest Lawn standards) marble tombstone and pointed down at it. Olivia and I caught up with him and I heard Olivia issue a little groan as she read the name on the stone:

MARIA OUSPENSKAYA

1876-1949

"More things in Heaven and Earth . . . "

The others gathered in a circle around us, looking very worried indeed. We all stood there for a little while, just taking in the sight. Then Sturges and his company looked up at me as one. Olivia followed suit.

"What?" I said. "What do I do now?"

Sturges didn't respond; he just stared at me.

"No, no kidding. I haven't got a clue. You've got to tell me."

Nothing.

I glanced at Olivia — she had tears in her eyes — but all she could offer me was a slight shake of her head.

They were all staring at me now, waiting. Demarest was squinting. He pursed his lips and started to shake his head, disapprovingly.

I was at a loss.

"Betcha hind quarters Barry Livingstone'd know what to do," I heard Demarest whisper to Pangborn.

Then it hit me, though I still don't know how or why.

"Even the man who is pure in heart, and says his prayers by night . . . "

From the corner of my eye, I saw Sturges nod.

"May become a wolf when the wolf-bane blooms, and the autumn moon is bright," I completed.

A sudden gale took shape like a mini-twister. I felt my hair flop off my bald spot, saw leaves and mown grass whoosh up around us. The ghosts broke-up a little, like a fuzzy TV picture, in the face of the wind, struggling to maintain their forms.

As the gust subsided, an alabaster figure hovered in the air above the grave.

"Finally," the ghost of Maria Ouspenskaya said. "Finally."

"'At's the way to do it, kid," Demarest growled. Even Pangborn seemed impressed.

Sturges looked ecstatic.

The sea was rough, though we were no more than fifty yards from shore. The little motor boat rode unsteadily atop the white-tipped waves, and Olivia looked as nauseous as I felt. Though whether that was from the surf or everything else that was going on, I wouldn't care to guess.

Ouspenskaya insisted that we had to be on the water to lift the curse. I did ask why, and she said it was because Veronica Lake had been cremated and her ashes strewn in the sea. I then suggested the Hollywood Reservoir as the nearest bit of water to Forest Lawn — just the other side of Mt. Cahuenga, in fact —

but Ouspenskaya insistently shook her head. It had to be a *natural* water source. I started to ask why, but she set those spooky alabaster eyes on me, so I threw up my hands and accepted that there was nothing to do but go along for the full ride.

Actually, *I* had to do the driving to Santa Monica.

The nice thing about L.A. is that, no matter the time of day or night, you can get just about anything you want if you've got the dough. The bad thing about L.A. is . . . nah, don't get me started. I managed to rent the boat off a boozy old character at Will Rogers State Beach. I *think* the boat actually belonged to him. In any event, it got us out on the water.

Sturges stood in the prow staring off at the moonlit horizon, while his stock company floated in the air around us. Olivia sat on a bench in the middle and Ouspenskaya sat beside me. Who's a lucky boy, then?

I cut the motor and let the boat float along on the waves. The only other vessel out there was a massive oil tanker, heading for Santa Barbara most likely, its twinkling lights just visible in the distance. The wind whipped around us, lashing spray into our faces. In fact, I was pretty well soaked, but Ouspenskaya just sat there, eyes closed, fingering a set of phantom beads that dangled from her pale, ghostly throat. She murmured to herself in a foreign tongue that sounded to me like some thirties, Curt Siodmak scripted approximation of Romany. Or gibberish.

Olivia was shaking. It was cold out there, but I don't think her shivers were a result of the temperature.

The wind picked up in intensity as Ouspenskaya chanted, and the waves crested that much higher. I felt it was a close contest whether I was going to puke or pee my pants first. I do remember telling myself that this was why you should never talk to extras on the set.

Just when I felt that I couldn't stand another minute out on that choppy sea, the wind dropped away and the water grew calm. I could have sworn, too, that the moon suddenly faded, as if on some cosmic dimmer switch, but of course that's impossible.

Ouspenskaya stopped her chanting and Olivia gasped. Sturges was now floating just above the prow and pointing across the water.

"Constance," he whispered.

I followed his finger and saw a roiling and bubbling in the otherwise dead-calm sea ten yards off to port. Something glowed beneath the water, rising slowly to the surface. A hand emerged from the frothy surf like the Lady in the Lake. (In this case, perhaps, the Lake in the lady.) Then an arm and a golden crown of hair. A head and shoulders, a body draped in shimmering gold, twinkling more magically in the moonlight than the sparkling sea itself. She wore a dress made of stars. (More stars than there are in heaven, I'd be tempted to say, had Sturges stayed at MGM.)

Veronica Lake, in all her youthful, peek-a-boo splendour, rose from the depths, until she stood atop the ocean, her delicate, slippered feet floating millimetres above the silvery surface.

"Zowie," I said.

I looked at Olivia, who was now shaking so hard that she rocked the boat. Her gaze zipped back and forth from Sturges to Lake. The ghost of the great director tried to move toward his beloved, but he appeared frozen in place above the prow. Lake then tried to walk across the water toward him, but she too was constrained by some invisible binding. The other wraiths hovered silently around us, but they all looked worried.

"What gives?" I asked the Gypsy coot.

Ouspenskaya ignored me. She stared hard at Olivia, still shaking, but now looking down at the bottom of the boat.

"Girl?" Ouspenskaya said. (I wondered how long since anyone had addressed old Olivia so.)

Olivia reluctantly looked up and I saw the fury in her eyes. Though she continued to shake, I began to realise it was as much with anger as with cold or fear.

"Olivia?" I asked.

"It is for her, now," Ouspenskaya pronounced.

And she simply disappeared.

"Olivia?" I repeated.

She reached inside her blouse and pulled out a locket that hung on a thin chain from her chicken-flesh throat. She opened it up and gently removed two locks of hair.

"I hated you," she said to Sturges. Then to Lake: "I hate you still."

She placed the hairs in the palm of her hand, one dark brown, the other blonde. I think, maybe, they belonged to the cursed lovers.

"I could hate you forever," she said. Then she looked over at me. "But I won't."

I let out a deep breath, very relieved.

"Perhaps we've cursed each other," she said, turning back to the ghosts. "And now, I think, maybe it's time to forget." She added: "And maybe, I don't know, forgive."

Olivia stood up. She held her palm up to the moon. "I set you free," she whispered.

And a gust of wind came from nowhere and blew the locks of hair out of her hand and into the sea. Without so much as a glance back, Sturges leapt off the prow and flew across the water to Lake. It happened so fast, you could barely see, but in the instant before they vanished in a flash of argent, I'm sure I saw them in each other's arms, exchanging an embrace and a fevered kiss that was — as a movieland PR would surely have it — fifty years in the making.

And they were gone.

As were the Players. It was just me and Olivia, both — though for different reasons, I suspect — with tears in our eyes, on a once-more choppy sea. Though I *think* I heard a gravelly voice whisper: "Uncle Charlie couldn't a done it better."

It took some haggling and foot-stomping on my part, but I got the network to agree to make Olivia a semi-regular on *Burning Bright*. The Bag Lady became one of my 'sources on the street', a cranky but lovable old dame who knew everything that was going down in Marty-Land. The creative consultant helped me sell it to the big boys.

"She's the classic 'helper' figure, don't you see?" he explained. "Perfectly, perhaps even ideally Proppian!"

"My thinking exactly," I said.

I'm still trying to find out what 'Proppian' means.

Olivia was the tougher customer.

"I think it's time I gave it all up, Marty," she told me. "My day is done."

"Don't be ridiculous," I said. "You're a terrific actress."

"How would you know that? I didn't even have a line in the episode I shot."

"I scrounged up a copy of *Water Rustlers*. You've got potential, kid. Though you ain't got Dorothy Page's rack."

She laughed, but wasn't convinced. So I took my best shot.

"The show can really use you," I said. "The audience will love you. It's all good entertainment in the end, that's the main thing. A laugh, a cry, a little action with some T&A for the boys. It may not be much in this cockeyed caravan, but you know, it's all that some people have."

She shook her head and shed another tear, but she agreed. She bought it.

Boy!

Introduction to "City of Angels"

Now we get to the nasty stuff.

Occasionally, I get referred to as a splatterpunk writer, almost entirely due to "City of Angels". I have enormous affection for it, mostly because it is the first story I ever sold. The wonderful Jessie Horsting bought it for *Midnight Graffiti* and loved it so much that she immediately sent it to Paul Sammon, who bought it for his somewhat infamous *Splatterpunks* anthology. As it happens, the antho appeared before the issue of *Midnight Graffiti* (ah, life in the small press . . .), so that volume marked my world première. For those who care, *Splatterpunks* is still in print from St. Martin's Press.

And the story has stood me well. Short as it is, "City of Angels" seems to be one that people remember. Some years after it appeared, Gordon Van Gelder asked to see (and eventually bought U.S. rights to) my first novel, largely because he remembered my name from "City of Angels". Some might say that the story is only memorable because it is so extreme, so disgusting. And I can't really argue with that: it is thoroughly disgusting. I certainly wouldn't write anything like it again, though that's mostly because I'm not the bitter and angry person I was when I wrote it. While 'splatterpunk' was a blessedly short-lived craze, there's still plenty of splattery or 'extreme' fiction out there, but — call it conceit — I don't think the absurdly over-the-top gore is what makes "City of Angels" memorable. Okay, it's not *just* the gore.

See, I think of this as an incredibly romantic story, and for all its excesses, it prefigures an important component in my work in that regard. So think of it as a love story. Which can only mean that — Lord have mercy — L.A. must be my lady. Don't tell my wife!

City of Angels

"I'M GONNA CHEW ME A NEW ASSHOLE," PORQUAH kept mumbling.

He'd been repeating the line for hours, ever since Demodisk got the big laugh with it over by the crumbling shell of the observatory. Demo tried to correct him at first — "Chew *you* a new asshole, asshole. Chew *you*. *You* . . . " — but Porquah's shit-eating grin just got a little wider and he thumped himself on the chest with that big, meaty thumb of his and said it again: "Gonna chew *me* a new asshole."

Once Porquah gets an idea in his head there ain't no turning him away. Like just the other day with the baby. We was up around the old Hollywood sign, 'cept all that's left of it is the H-O-L-Y, and we find this little black girl and her baby living in the remains of a DWP shack hidden in the trees. Viridiana, she don't cotton much to dark meat, so she slits the girl from cunt to tits before Demo and me can even get our dicks hard. Well, Demo, he says he ain't real particular and pink is as pink does, so he sort of mashes her together and goes to plugging that new slit. I thought about doing her mouth, but I seen her teeth were crooked and sort of blackish and fuck me if rotten teeth ain't a fierce turn-off.

So I leave Demo to his belly-fucking and see Porqy and Viridiana tussling over the baby. It's a scrawny brown thing, but its making a screeching and a wailing like a rocket coming 'cross the sky. Porqy's got the thing by the feet and Viridiana's holding it by the head and they're like to playing a mean game of tug o' war. I walk on over and grab a hold the midsection like to take charge and damned if, just for spite, Viridiana don't twist that screaming head so's we hear a clean, crisp snap.

Viridiana, she's acting real contrite and sorry, but I can see the smiling in her eyes down underneath. Porquah, he's all upset and ready to cut Viridiana in half with that 9mm Browning he's always waving around, but just then Demo walks back over, smiling and humming to himself, stuffing his bloody dick back in his pants and he says, "Let's cook 'em," and everybody settles down.

Porqy, he's got this thing about the balls and how they're the 'bestest part', which is fine because none of the rest of us ever developed a real hankering for 'em. Old Porqy's been talking about baby nuts for days, just bitching and whining about how he's gotta have some.

"I figure," he says, "they got to be more tender. Tastier, like lamb or baby corn."

Like I say, once the *Porqmeister* gets an idea in that bullet-shaped head of his there ain't no living with him till he acts on it. So 'fore I can even set a pot of water to boiling old Porq he rips them nuts right off that dead little sucker. They're tiny goobers, they are, and raw but Porq, he pops 'em in his mouth like wet jelly beans and sets to jawin' at 'em. A streak of dark fluid starts oozing down his chin, but Porq just dabs at it with that tiny brown scrotum and smacks his lips.

"Well fuck my momma bloody," he says. "They's even tastier than titty tips."

Demo, meanwhile, he's been scrunched over the girl, grunting and puffing and slashing with that big blade of his, and while Viridiana's hacking up the wee one he tosses something pink and hairy and dripping red onto the ground between us.

"Anybody want to eat a little pussy?" he says and screeches with laughter.

Well that Demo he's a card, ain't no doubt, and Porqy and me start rolling on the floor, howling like horny dogs. But Viridiana, she acts offended or something and clucks her tongue, like *she's* never eaten pussy before or things one hell of a lot worse. Then Demo, he picks up that flap of flesh and slaps it over his mouth and starts a yammering through them hairy lips, calling himself a chatterbox. That's too much even for the frost queen and she starts to laughing with the rest of us. So we slice up the meat and cook us some dinner and settle in for the night, 'cause the day's fading like an old pair of jeans.

We were sitting all quiet just watching the sky go purple, like a big old lilac growing out of the rubble of the city. I was sort of liking the silence and the heavenly colours of the twilight. I knew Porqy'd been wrestling with something, 'cause he hadn't said a word since dinner and he was scratching at his head and staring off even blanker than usual. Finally, I guess, he hit a brick wall in that little hunk of grey matter 'cause he started spouting some damn funny talk about pregnant ladies and unborn babies and such.

After a while Demo got sick of it and he said, "Elvis-on-the-cross, Porquah, just tell us what you're driving at here."

Porqy got quiet for a minute and stared down at the dirt. "I was just wondering," he says. "Them nuts on that baby was tender, but wouldn't they be even better fresh out the oven?"

I looked at Demo, heard Viridiana cluck again.

"I mean," Porqy went on, "if we could just find us a pregnant lady, we could rip that young 'un right out her belly and I bet you there's nothing that would taste any finer than them fresh baby balls."

Porqy looked up at us like a little boy who'd just peed his bed and was waiting for his punishment. Viridiana had been resting against a tree sort of dozing, her arms folded tightly over that big bosom of hers. She opened her eyes and leaned forward, mussed Porqy's thinning hair with her three-fingered hand.

"What the hell's wrong with you, Porqy," she said in that motherly tone. "Where in the name of Ronald Reagan are we gonna find us a pregnant lady?"

Porqy nodded and looked kind of sheepish, but for two days after all we heard was talk of baby balls. So in a way it was kind of refreshing when he started talking about chewing himself

240

a new asshole. But after a day and a half of that, I was almost missing all that chatter about nuts.

Always did like talking about food.

The Docworker told us for sure but I already knew we was getting worse. Porqy's face was all puffy and red, the skin peeling off his cheeks and arms in long shiny strips. He was complaining about his knees, too, how they was crunching and grinding with every step and it sure enough sounded like a bunch of marbles rolling around in there, bouncing off each other.

Viridiana, now, was oozing from every which way. Them pustules on her face and neck was dripping grey and white and the crimson stain on her crotch seemed to spread a little bigger and smell a lot nastier every day. Finally, I seen her standing off to the side of the camp with her shirt rolled up over her chest. She's prodding and poking at those bulging boobs of hers, cursing like a sailor with the clap. I called her name and when she turned toward me I saw she was dabbing at some sticky-looking fluid running from her nipples. I ain't never seen nothing that colour come out a human being before, but I didn't say nothing to her. She looked up at me with kind of sad, hound-dog eyes and I could see she wanted like to cry, but she was always trying to show how she's tougher than the rest of us. I couldn't think of nothing else to do, so I just walked away.

I had gone kind of runny in some damned funny places myself and truth is it was more than a mite unpleasant. Demo wasn't looking too bad, but I knew it was hurting him, too, mostly inside. He was acting more squirrelly all the time, talking in nonsense or forgetting our names or even what to call the grass or the sky. His eyes would go a little wild now and again and he'd take to chewing on the rotted things that were always underfoot. But then he'd come back to himself and be the same old joker that kept us going so well.

Anyways, the Docworker — he didn't look so good neither, what with gunk running out an empty eye-socket — he used that scanner of his and told us it was probably just a matter of days now. The others, I believe, knew it too, but Porqy didn't want to admit it. He was still talking about chewing assholes when he grabbed the Doc and went like to bite away a piece of the man's belly. He only got a tiny chunk of flesh 'fore we pulled him off and the kindly old Doc didn't hold it against him.

"Us Angelinos got to stick together," he said hopping back into his little golf cart. "These are interesting times for us all."

Viridiana was steamed as hell and said it was time to do Porqy, but Demo and me talked her out of it. We just agreed that we'd have to take the things Porqy said a mite more literally from now on.

We decided that come morning we'd head down into the heart of it. Figured it didn't make no difference now anyways so we might as well see what it looked like in the centre of the old city. I tried to remember from before, but it was all hazy and distant. I thought about the freeways and the stores and the pretty people and the noise and the Mexicans selling oranges and peanuts on the street corners and all that was gone. I pictured them tall, skinny palm trees what I always meant to learn the proper name for, but I never did and reckon now I never will.

I remembered back to that day and the awful, bright flash and the searing winds. It was funny how when it came it seemed so natural, so inevitable. I remember how I used to think about it before, abstract like, trying to imagine the *after*, thinking it would be all romantic and adventurous, like in some of them neat movies with crashing cars and fancy leather clothes.

I can't believe, sometimes, when I make myself think back, that it ain't hardly been two years. It seems like decades or centuries and I feel like I must be the oldest man in the history of the earth. And then I fish out that crinkled old driver's license and look at that stranger's picture and remind myself: that's me.

I realise that I'm thirty years old and ain't never gonna see thirty one. And sometimes at night, when I'm not really asleep, but like in a dream, I see my Janey's face. I wish more than anything that I could feel her again, bucking on top of me, or just look at her while she laughed at one of her TV programs. I can't believe how much I miss them dopey old shows now that they're gone.

Then I see that bang-gang all around her in our kitchen and I hear her scream as they get inside her from every which way. And they're cutting her into little chunks of meat with that electric carving knife, laughing and dancing in the blood like Gene Kelly in the rain.

And I think, *when things change, they change and that's all there is to it. Ain't no sense or reason and tears is just so much salty water. There's no going back, no unringing a bell, no living for the dead.*

And I'm glad it's just a matter of days.

Wouldn't you know that screwy idea about baby balls would be the death of Porqy. We could tell from the shapes on the ground that we was close to the centre. I'd always heard about them, but never had believed it before. They were everywhere, though, blackened silhouettes of people who was standing too close to ground-zero, their bodies vaporised, their shadows burned forever into the cracked concrete.

Demo, silly as always, pulled out his flashlight and did hand-shadows, making like the silhouettes had dicks and tits and talked like Mickey Mouse. It was funny, I have to admit, but no-one did much laughing. The end was too close and we was all feeling it real bad. My skin was itching so's I felt like ants and roaches was crawling over every inch of me, biting and stinging as they marched. Parts had gone kind of mushy, too, and I was afraid I'd bust right open like an old tomato if anyone pressed too hard.

Porqy was running like an ice cream cone in the desert sun. The skin on his face and arms was all peeled off and the pink muscles and tendons glistened like liver in a butcher's window. He was breathing real hard and walking like a three-legged dog with a hangnail, ranting and raving about preggo women.

We turned down what might once have been Wilshire Boulevard when Porqy saw her lying on the ground in a pool of

Elvis-only-knows-what. I could hear the bones snapping in his legs as he ran toward her. I made to stop him but Viridiana held me back and shook her head. I watched as Porqy flipped the bloated corpse over and dug into the bulging belly with them massive claws of his.

There was a low ripping sound, like an enormous passing of wind as his fingers broke the blackened flesh and released the gurgling gasses within. A thin geyser of murky magenta spewed out of the decaying husk dousing Porquah's flayed cheeks. Porqy seemed not to notice, though, and scooped out handfuls of brackish grue, sifting the corrupt tissue, I reckoned, for some sign of a baby. He grasped a small, roundish object — a shrivelled kidney, maybe — and shovelled it into his mouth, chewing happily.

"Balls," I heard him say through a mouthful of grey. "Baby balls, yum-yum."

Suddenly, his eyes went all wide and he started to gag with a noise sounded like a backed-up drain. Then he went quiet and pitched face-first into the messy corpse. The body splattered like a rotten pumpkin as soon as Porqy fell into it and we knew old Porq was dead as could be.

I figured to just leave him lying there with his nose buried in what once might have been a sweet bit of bush, but Viridiana of all people, had a fine idea for a memorial. Demo sliced Porqy's balls off and we boiled them over a small fire. Demo and I split one and left the other for Viridiana. We ate in that unnatural silence, and I thought, wherever he was, Porquah would be right touched.

My eyes felt ready to burst out of my head and my tongue was like a hunk of splintery wood in my mouth. We found a patch of mutant wild flowers and marvelled at the flowing, surreal colours that glowed in the setting sunlight. The thin clouds looked like paisley against the silky, mauve sky and for a flash I thought I remembered something about what beauty was.

Demo was off on one of his crazy jags, but it hardly mattered now. I looked over at Viridiana and I don't know what it was —

maybe the dimming light, maybe just the way she cocked her head — but for I minute I thought I saw her just how she must have looked as a little girl, all pretty and bright and full of dreams.

I walked over to her and put my hands on her shoulders, felt the bones grind under my touch. She looked real wary for a second, but then she stared into my eyes and seemed to understand.

We took off our clothes, trying to hold on to as much of our skins as we could and laid down in that bed of soft colour. She was a goopy, dripping mess and I don't suppose I looked a whole lot better, but she opened her legs and I laid on top of her and got inside. I slipped in a little further than seemed right or natural and I didn't much care for the slushy noises we both was making, but it was good and it felt right, in the way that it always had and ever should be. Viridiana was making some mewling sounds and I think they was happy noises. Myself, I've always been sort of a Silent Sam in the sack, but I was liking it, too.

At the end, I closed my eyes and I thought about Janey and what had been and I do believe it was the best I ever felt.

I rolled off of her just as Demo strolled over to us, something bulky in his hands. He stood right over Viridiana's head, looking at her all upside-down with that toothy smile of his, and fired two ten-penny nails square through her eyes from some sort of pneumatic gun. It must of been battery-powered and Elvis-alone-knows where Demo found it.

Viridiana didn't make a sound when it happened, she just sort of stopped breathing as crimson tears flowed out the sockets and ran down her cheeks.

I looked at Demo, but he just grinned a little wider. I got up and slapped him playfully on the back of the head and he giggled, but I felt something shift inside his skull so I didn't do it again.

"I guess we both nailed her, huh?" he said.

I laughed and we walked off in the direction of the ocean, toward the setting, decaying sun.

That Demo is a pistol, I tell you.

Introduction to "Down"

Not a lot to say about this one. It, too, dates from older, splatter-filled days and has more to do with a state of mind than a devotion to narrative. Traces of the same attitude figure into *Blood* my rather graphic, revisionist vampire novel which seems to be too nasty for American publishers. (But available in British and French editions. What does that mean?)

Down

STONE DUDE, RIDING SHOTGUN AND SHITTING bricks. Marquis, cool as Eskimo Pie, steers with two fingers, a menthol Dunhill dangling from his mouth.

Marquis flicks the stick out the open window, shoots a glance at Stone Dude.

"Don't go nelly on me, Stone."

"M'all right."

"You white as a nigger's smile, sunshine."

"I'm down."

Hard left. Tires squeal, horns blare behind them. Glass breaks, Doppler shifts.

Marquis' hand snakes to Stone Dude's crotch. A rough squeeze and gone before the Dude can even move.

"Fuh . . . " Stone Dude starts, cups his balls.

"Just checking to see if they still there."

Stone Dude rubs his crotch.

"Stone?"

"Hmmmm?"

"Dude!"

"Yah."

"Down?"

"Mmmmm."

"DOWN?"

"I'm down, all right?" Practically a whisper. "Down."

"Mint."

Marquis floors it.

Malibu beach house. Marquis holds the key, as always.

"Comes with the drop," Marquis explains, smiling, ugly as old roadkill.

Oil for the hinges. Cutters for the chain. Quiet. Marquis is a ghost, a tapped 'mute' button. Stone Dude follows, shoulder grazing the severed door chain. Tinkle, tinkle of an ankle bracelet on a young girl's leg.

A silent snarl from Marquis.

Marquis points. Stone Dude waits. Marquis floats up the stairs. Not a creak.

The Dude counts. One motherfucker. Two motherfuckers. Three motherfuckers . . .

"Down!" Marquis from above. Twenty-three motherfuckers. Damn!

Stone Dude on the move. Twelve steps, seven creaks. A loud swish as his vinyl jacket brushes the jamb at the top. Marquis leaning out a door, shaking his head, baring his teeth, tapping his ear.

The bedroom, big and warm. Wall to wall carpeting, framed art prints — Kandinsky, Mondrian, Dix — fresh cut flowers and old photos in silver frames on an antique dresser. Stone Dude eyeballs himself in a wall-length mirror, the bulge in his pants big as a subway rat.

Windows first: blinds drawn. Stone Dude slips a gloved finger between the slats: window open. Marquis smiles and nods as the Dude silently slides it shut.

A king-sized bed, covers stripped. The man on his back, no rise to his chest. White jockey briefs stained at the crotch, pubic hairs sprout from the elastic like withered clover. The bottoms of his feet are dirty, the toenails short and jagged.

The woman awake, wearing a long night shirt with a bunny on the front. Jumbo titties. Hands behind her back in plastic restraining 'cuffs, sharp wire wrapped around her ankles drawing beads of blood. Eyes wide, trained on the gun pointed at the head of the child lying face down at the foot of the bed.

Marquis hands a syringe to Stone Dude. The woman struggles, but Marquis waves the gun. Her eyes capture the Dude's as he approaches. A plea.

Stone Dude's hand shakes, he misses the vein.

"Again," Marquis demands.

Again.

Again.

Speckles of red form a connect-the-dot puzzle up her arm. The shape of a scythe.

Marquis nods when the Dude gets it right. The woman convulses, dies.

"Mint," Marquis chuckles.

Stone Dude flips the kid over, the body already getting cold, turning colours. Marquis makes him practice injecting air bubbles into the tiny dead form.

Marquis checks the pulses. Always careful, always sure. Stone Dude starts to lift up the woman's shirt. Marquis slaps his hand away.

"Just want to look," Stone Dude whines.

Marquis shakes his head. "Ain't in the contract, it ain't down."

"Ain't down," Stone Dude repeats and nods. He follows Marquis out, glancing back at the bed, at the woman's chest as he goes.

Marquis watching every move, holding his breath.

"Ah, ah. Too fast, Dude. Got to take it slow, till it's . . . Watch that knife!"

Stone Dude in the kitchen, *Turban of sole mousseline*. Stone Dude doesn't even like seafood.

"That's it. Nice and easy. Beat the cream in. Slowly. Let it get absorbed. It's an art, Dude."

"Fucking piece of fish, man. Goddamn, fucking trout."

"Sole, Dude. Sole."

"Fucking fish! I'd rather have a burger."

Marquis shaking his head. "Attitude, Dude. You got to think it. Always got to think it. Treat the fish like life, bro. Treat your life like pussy. Work it slow and easy, take your time. When the moment comes, you add the sauce."

"Shit. Fish is fish. Pussy's for pounding. Stick it in, shoot it off and go to sleep."

Still, he slows it down. Adds a dash of tabasco, picks up the nutmeg. Marquis, mouth open, "Enough" forming on his lips, Stone Dude taps in just the right amount. Marquis smiles.

"We gonna make a renaissance man out you yet, Dude."

Later: dishes soaking, Marquis in his chair, *Jeopardy* on TV. Stone Dude on the floor, on his knees.

"Who is Alexander Nevsky," Marquis asks Alex Trebek.

"What is *The Wise, Little Hen*?"

"What is . . . shit. Where is Kuala Lumpur?"

Marquis glances down at the Dude. "The fish was a little dry. Try a cooler oven next time. And . . . mmmmmmm, *down* Dude . . . remember to watch your . . . huh! . . . flame on the sauces."

Stone Dude doesn't respond. Renaissance man doesn't talk with his mouth full.

Marina penthouse apartment. Full moon floating like a Chinese lantern over the harbour. Too high up to hear the crashing surf.

Marquis, holding on by the wrist, walks to the kitchen. A roach scurries across the bright tile floor with the flick of the light. Marquis is faster. SPLATT!

The arm is severed just above the elbow. Frayed flesh drips slow red, the broken fingers splayed like broken breadsticks. Marquis tosses it in the microwave, punches the buttons: **2:15** on the digital display.

"Check it out, Dude."

Stone Dude leans over, peers through the mesh glass in the tiny door. Marquis stands behind him, arms crossed, smiling like the cat that fucked the canary.

2:00

The arm spins on the platter like an old 33.

1:48

The thin blonde hairs start to singe.

1:32

The sallow skin bubbles, red and grey liquid oozes from the gaping wound.

0:54

The busted fingers turn black, curl into a defiant mockery of a fist.

0:26

Seared tissue peels away in dark, paper-thin strips. Fingernails burst off, knuckles go like Jiffy Pop.

0:01

The arm explodes. The window smeared with crimson and grey chunks of liquified flesh. A small hunk of blackened bone ricochets, pierces the reinforced glass, leaving a hole perfect and neat as a BB shot.

"Timing, Dude," Marquis says, pointing at the read-out, picking the bone pellet off the floor. "Timing is everything if you want to be down."

Stone Dude figures no-one will notice if he leaves the ice tray in the sink. He stacks the frozen dinners on the left, the veggies on the right. Checks out the ice cream — Ben & Jerry's: Chocolate Chip Cookie Dough — sees a frozen glaze across the top. Stone Dude hates that. He slips the carton into the rack on the freezer door, sets the head in the middle, propping it up against a box of Sara Lee cheesecake.

"Front and centre, boy!"

Stone Dude gently closes the door, stops, goes back and fills the ice tray at the sink, wedges it back in its place in the freezer.

Marquis in the living room of the Beverly Hills mansion, watching another game show on the wide-screen. Marquis *loves* game shows.

The man sits stiffly in his easy chair, back to the Dude. Stone Dude waits for the commercial. Quietly.

Marquis watches through the end of the credits, flicks off the screen. Walks around into the man's field of vision. Stone Dude falls in behind.

The man is obese. His rubbery, jaundiced skin is Krazy-glued to the Naugahyde chair. Fat man's tits hang down like an old lady's, his doughy belly almost obscuring a shrivelled, undersized cock.

Marquis has cut away the eyelids. Bulging eyeballs sit like poached eggs on a flabby red face.

Marquis points to the sloppy, uneven cuts.

"I got mad, Dude. He didn't want to watch the show. You see what happens when you work with your heart and not your head?"

Marquis removes the gun from his case. Police-issue .38, hollow points. The barrel sight is sharpened to a razor edge, Marquis runs the honed sight up the fat man's cheeks to the corners of his eyes, drawing lines of red tears.

Marquis looks at the Dude, smiles. Plunges the sight through a filmy eyeball, sending a grapefruit spurt a foot in the air. Marquis rotates the barrel twenty degrees right then left, back and forth, working it deep into the socket until the jerking — and screaming — subside, and the waves of flab stop jiggling. Stone Dude eyes strips of skin glued to the chair.

Marquis pulls the trigger once, turns, points a finger at Stone Dude.

"*That*," he says sternly, "is a Sarajevo Skullfuck."

Nob Hill mansion. Dawn a cunt-hair at the horizon. Extension cord hangs from a thick wooden beam. Cathedral ceiling. High pitched shrieks of agony.

The baby dangles by its feet. Marquis watches as Stone Dude makes the cut. A thin trickle of blood embraced by gravity. A hollow sucking gasp like a dying dustbuster. Marquis looks up from his work on the gagged boy.

"Christ, Dude, when are you going to learn? You caught the fucking windpipe and missed the carotid again."

Stone Dude makes it right.

Marquis stands to the side and watches, occasionally glancing out the bay windows at the expansive view of the Lower East Side.

Stone Dude riding an adrenaline high. The rush in his ears like two conch shells strapped to the sides of his head. The lighting is dim, but every object and surface seems to glow, as if bathed in high-powered Kleigs. He eyes the naked woman on the floor, feels himself grow hard again. Wishes it were an open contract.

Stone Dude has trouble igniting the acetylene torch. It lights, sputters, lights, sputters. He glances at Marquis who doesn't move. Doesn't blink.

The torch catches.

Stone Dude wonders what they did to deserve this. The contract never says, but this one is gruesomely precise about the treatment. Marquis had to carefully go over the specifics of a Beijing Blowjob, asked if Stone Dude wanted to wait until next time to solo.

"I be down," Stone Dude answered.

The Dude adjusts the flame. Straddling her chest, he grabs a handful of long auburn hair, slick with sweat. She tries to shake him off but the bindings are too tight. Stone Dude applies the torch to her nose and the screaming begins again. The chiselled cartilage melts like a cheap candle, sealing off the nostrils. She struggles for air, gasping through her broken teeth.

Stone Dude goes back to the boyfriend, picks up his severed cock and balls. He winces slightly at their feel, hopes that Marquis doesn't notice. He forces the bloody organ through the woman's open lips. She gags and shakes as Stone Dude rams it down her throat, stuffing the testicles in after, making sure the air passage is thoroughly blocked.

He steps back and watches her twist and shudder, turn white then blue. It takes a good while, the body lurching and convulsing, the mouth still open.

He re-ignites the torch and squats over the body. He plants a knee in her chest and forces the jaws shut. The lips sear crookedly closed, the stench of burnt flesh thick as blood. A final twitch and it's over.

Stone Dude packs up the gear and walks over to Marquis whose face is a blank. Stone Dude heads for the door, but Marquis blocks his way with an iron arm, stares him down.

Gives him a thumbs-up.

Stone Dude at the drop sight. It smells wrong but he can't see it. Two gorillas appear behind him as the dark limo pulls up. The conversation is brief, two packages change hands. Stone Dude sweats, nods, tries not to piss his pants.

The car is gone. Stone Dude alone on the street.

Shaking.

Scared.

Excited.

A condemned motel near Anaheim. A light in a second-floor room, a silver Honda parked around back. The Magic Kingdom visible in the distance.

I'm going to Disneyland, Stone Dude thinks.

Marquis turns, eyes blazing. Stone Dude spoke aloud without realising. Glances down, avoiding Marquis' gaze.

They glide up the steps, Marquis leading. A delicate job; a *very* exacting contract.

Marquis points and Stone Dude takes up a position below the lighted room window. Marquis silently opens the door to the adjoining room. "Ten motherfuckers," Marquis has told him. "Then in."

"One motherfucker," the Dude counts and opens the unlocked door.

"Two motherfuckers." Nods at the gorilla inside.

"Three motherfuckers." In position.

Marquis comes through at "eight", taser in hand, rolling low according to the book, directly into the tangle of razor wire. Must hurt like a serrated cunt, but Marquis is a pro. Never makes a sound. He fires the taser at the gorilla even as flesh is ripped from his body. The electrode hits the target, but can't penetrate Cermet body armour.

Marquis goes for the gun. Doesn't see Stone Dude behind him. Never sees the knife till the point of the blade bursts through his belly.

Stone Dude spins his mentor around. Marquis' eyes are wide with shock, a flap of skin, torn by a razor, hangs comically from his chin like a goatee.

"Ten motherfuckers," Stone Dude says and blows Marquis' head apart.

The gorilla nods, pats Stone Dude on the cheek and heads for the door. The Dude grabs his arm, holds up a finger. The gorilla growls, crosses his arms.

Stone Dude grabs the body around the waist and tosses it onto the bed, face down. He yanks the knife out of Marquis' back and slashes at the trousers. Dude pulls a Baretta 9mm. and screws on a silencer, jams the barrel as far as he can up Marquis' gaping, cold asshole.

Five muffled pops.

"Kuwaiti Cumshot," Stone Dude tells the gorilla.

"Not in the contract."

"No extra charge," the Dude smiles.

The gorilla nods, turns, leaves.

Stone Dude admires the sludgy trail oozing down Marquis' chubby white thighs. Pats the wad of cash in his pocket along with the instructions for the new drop. Thinks about grabbing a burger, heavy on the grilled onions, double cheese and bacon. *Fuck* renaissance.

Stone Dude is *down*.

Introduction to "Undiscovered Countries" and "Revenge of the Zombie Studpuppies"

If you read short horror fiction even a little bit, you will realise that everyone has a *Book of the Dead* story. Or two. These are mine.

John Skipp & Craig Spector did a great job with *Book of the Dead*, a theme anthology based on George Romero's "Living Dead" film trilogy that would seem to suffer from terminal limitations, but which featured two brilliant stories — by Joe Lansdale and Ed Bryant — and plenty of other fine work. The sequel, *Still Dead*, consciously shed some of the extremity of the first volume, but at the cost of the thrills. It's still a pretty good book — "Undiscovered Countries" appeared in it — but nowhere near as memorable, or successful, as the first. As to the debacle concerning the would-be third and fourth volumes of the series, the less said the better. Rest in pieces.

"Studpuppies," which I have since revised a bit, was my first submission to S&S for *Still Dead*. They turned it down. I then wrote the considerably more subdued "Countries" which they bought. I think "Studpuppies" was exactly what they didn't want for the second book, but it's a story I still like. The Lansdale influence is a little too obvious, but the tale is serious low-budget, late-night, cable-viewing fun. It's a classic case of all-themed-up-with-no-place-to-go, and I never bothered to submit the story to other markets, especially when it seemed you couldn't swing a zombified cat without hitting yet another leftover BOTD tale. The two stories provide an interesting contrast in tone and approach, and make a kind of case, I reckon, for the malleability of themed collections.

Undiscovered Countries

T HE TOP OF THE SKULL WAS ATTACHED WITH velcro. Hodge shuddered slightly as Dr. Chari thrust two fingers beneath the scalp and tore back the dark skin and wiry hair.

"Come over here and look through the magnifier," Chari said.

Hodge walked the long way around and leaned over the body till his forehead brushed Chari's.

"See these striations within the sulci?" Chari asked.

"They look more like furrows," Hodge said. He adjusted the magnification and focus. "Jesus, they're goddamn trenches."

The brain was severely desiccated. The velcro seal was hardly airtight, and dark blotches had formed across the pale grey surface of the cerebral cortex.

"What about the pattern?" Hodge asked.

"Nonspecific so far as I can tell. You can see that initially the striations followed the fissures of the sulci before branching off. Like starting a pathway at a natural clearing in a thicket."

Hodge nodded. The furrows formed an intricate concentric design, which spiralled like a staircase through the meninges and down into the cerebrum. Chari had driven a plastic, surgical shim between the right and left hemispheres, neatly bisecting the *corpus callosum.*

"Now look at this," Chari said.

She snipped at a line of sutures that ran along the base of the cerebrum and slid a retractor underneath. She pried up a thin layer of tissue, then cut away another line of sutures and raised up the entire cerebrum just enough so that Hodge could get a good look.

"Jesus, Mary and Joseph," he said. Chari allowed herself a smile.

The pustules hadn't been at all visible through the thick, vascular *pia mater*, but seen from beneath, it was clear that the cortex was rife with a thin layer of tiny purple lesions, growing like wild mushrooms.

Below that, the cerebellum and brain stem were positively *alive* with the bubbling pustules. They were slick and puffy and attached to the ridged brain surface like weeping sores. Chari prodded them with the flat edge of a scalpel and they gurgled slightly, roiling like overcooked, rancid oatmeal.

"Look here," Chari said.

She let the cerebrum slip back into place, and forcefully worked a syringe through the tough, fibrous *dura* and weblike arachnoid. She eased back the plunger until a viscous, mauve fluid spilled into the hypo, then withdrew the needle.

"Suhh . . . no, it can't . . . " Hodge shook his head, but Chari was nodding.

"Cerebrospinal fluid," she said, and laughed nervously. "And you ain't seen nothing yet."

Chari handed the syringe to Hodge then walked over to the far wall.

"Girls," she said, flicking off the lights, "you'd better hang on to your boyfriends."

The fluorescent ceiling lamps had been the room's sole source of illumination, but now a faint purple glow emanated from the syringe in Hodge's hand. The fluid was phosphorescent, and bright enough to cast Hodge's face in twisted, expressionistic shadows. But there was another light as well.

Hodge looked down at the body, saw the same violet glimmer spilling dimly from the opened skull. Hodge gasped as he watched the pulsating legions flicker like Christmas bulbs across the peeled-back cerebral cortex, fed by racing currents of the radiant fluid.

"I haven't the slightest idea why it does that," Chari said.

She turned the lights on again and walked back toward Hodge, who was still gaping at the exposed brain.

"And now for the big finish." Chari rooted through a tray of surgical instruments. "Where the hell is the . . . oh, screw it."

She leaned over and carefully but firmly grabbed the protruding edge of the shim between thumb and forefinger and, with a clean jerk, yanked it out of the brain.

Instantly, the corpse's eyes opened wide, the dilated pupils irising down to pinpoints and focusing on Chari.

The jaws mechanically opened and closed and a bloated, blackened tongue distended and flicked obscenely at the doctor. The stench of rotten meat wafted from its maw. It tried to lean forward, but Chari had disabled all motor function below the neck.

Hodge shrank away from the corpse, but Chari held her ground, watching the frantic gurgling of the purple lesions with something like awe.

She looked up at Hodge then, her face set in the widest smile he'd ever seen.

"I call him Mort," Chari said.

Hodge sighed deeply when he saw that his wife was watching the Zombie Channel again. She sat stiffly in a high-backed chair she'd dragged in from the dining room, swinging a cigarette back and forth between her lips and her ashtray in a regular, almost metronomic motion. Her head was tilted back against the top of the chair at an uncomfortable-looking angle, as if she was waiting for a shampoo.

Hodge came up behind her and planted a lifeless kiss on her forehead. Keiko was sweaty, and breathing hard. Her skin tasted of garlic and nicotine.

She didn't look up from the screen.

Three soldiers in Cermet body armour were circling around a gangrenous zombie in a ramshackle hut. Most of the action was Third World, these days, and the African footage consistently scored the highest ratings.

The perspective switched back and forth between cameras mounted in each soldier's helmet. A blinking digital read-out in the corner of the screen marked time to the hundredth of a second. The rapid cross-cutting made Hodge slightly queasy, but Keiko didn't seem at all bothered.

The zombie was in bad shape; one eye was gone and a row of fractured, grey ribs poked out through its bloody chest. Hodge saw that the soldiers could finish it at any time, but were dragging it out for the sake of a little drama.

"I don't like you watching this," Hodge said.

Keiko took a final drag on her cigarette, then snuffed it out and blew the smoke in Hodge's face.

Two of the soldiers had snared the zombie's arms in razor-wire lassos and pulled in opposite directions while the third, whose camera was active, circled slowly around them. Dark fluid spurted from the zombie's formerly bulging biceps as the wire dug through the mushy black flesh.

"I said . . . "

"Michael had an incident today."

"What?"

The circling soldier meticulously fired a couple of dozen rounds of tiny magnesium charges into the zombie's body. Each charge impacted with a sound like overripe fruit dropped from a great height. Keiko grabbed the remote and turned up the volume.

"What kind of incident? What happened?"

Keiko didn't answer. Hodge stepped directly in front of her, but her eyes never moved, as if she could see right through him to the big screen.

"Talk to me, goddammit."

Keiko stood up slightly, turned the chair ninety degrees to the left and sat back down. She turned on a second wall screen with the remote, then touched another button: each screen displayed the point of view from a different camera.

Half the room was now alive with video as the zombie began to smoulder. Thin streams of smoke rose out of the tiny holes in its body as it started to jerk and spasm. The soldiers holding the creature closed the snares, severing the arms cleanly above the elbows. The zombie frantically flailed its stumps.

Hodge grabbed for the remote, but Keiko was too fast. She punched another button and a third screen, on the wall opposite to the second, lit up.

Three walls, three screens, three camera angles.

"His implant went haywire."

"Jesus Christ," Hodge exhaled.

The soldiers stepped back from the action. Camera one was in long shot, and camera two in medium, while the third held the creature's contorted face in brutal close-up.

Keiko punched the buttons, rearranging the images so that the close-up appeared on the largest, centre screen. She was practically panting now, and dime-sized drops of sweat trickled down the side of her face.

Plumes of dark grey smoke billowed from the zombie.

"He was in class," she gasped, "when the corpse-men burst in. The teacher verified that he hadn't died, but they had to shoot him up and take him in."

"Procedure," Hodge said, nodding.

Keiko took an extra deep breath and held it.

The zombie threw back its head and then exploded. Dark grue spattered two of the lenses, spoiling the picture, but number three was a pro. He tracked the head as it detached from the torso, and kept it in frame as it hurtled through the air. Blood blossomed from the open mouth, and the remaining eye was blown out by the pressure.

Keiko exhaled with a throaty moan as the head ricocheted off the ceiling. All three screens went to close-up now, and slo-mo kicked in as the head spiralled down, cracking open on impact with the floor.

Keiko lit up another cigarette.

"They diagnosed the malfunction and put in a new implant. The doctor said it's a better model than what he had, and told me it was a lucky thing he happened to be in a roomful of witnesses, or . . ."

Hodge ran a hand through his thinning hair, and finally sat down on the futon. He stared vacantly at the one wall without a screen.

"Lucky," he said.

"Anyway, he's still in the hospital. They said he won't be conscious for another few hours, but they wouldn't let us see him anyway. Not for twenty-four hours."

"Procedure. Why didn't you call me?"

"How do you know I didn't?"

The soldiers finished prying open the skull and fried the brain with electric prods. Hodge could now make out the characteristic furrows, though he had never noticed them before. He could even see some of the tiny lesions as they sizzled.

You had to know what to look for, he thought. Like the old lady and the young girl in the optical illusion. You only see one until someone points the other out to you. Then you can never *not* see it again.

"Let's fuck," Keiko said.

"This is crazy," Hodge said.

"That's what Mr. Hyde said to Dr. Jekyll," Chari quipped, but Hodge didn't laugh.

We should at least bring in some security.

"Oh, yes. And let's have CNN cover it live, too."

Chari was stooped over Mort's open brain case, looking through the magnifier. Her gloved hands deftly manipulated the laser micro-scalpel. Hodge stood by as *ad hoc* scrub nurse, passing her the odd instrument and looking nervous.

"What if . . . "

"Look, Bill. I will stop if you want, but I thought we'd been through this. Mort's a quad, guaranteed, so there's no real danger. And seeing how we've already trounced over at least a dozen CDC regs, I don't see where one more really matters. Besides, what Phaedra Pharmaceutical doesn't know can't hurt them."

"But *I* know, and *I'm* supposed to be responsible to them."

"You're young. You'll find other work."

Hodge still wasn't laughing, but he gave Chari the nod anyway. "Middle-management lackey destroys world," he mumbled.

"Courageous administrator approves immortality project," Chari corrected. "Besides, it's Frankenstein that everyone remembers, not his supervisor."

"But everyone also thinks that Frankenstein is the monster."

Chari didn't seem to find that amusing. She restored the last of the severed links in Mort's neural network and withdrew the laser. She then turned off the surgical lamp. Spreading tendrils of glowing mauve fluid were immediately visible as they raced through the brain.

"Better than barium," Chari said, marvelling.

Within minutes a ridge of violet pustules, big as jujubes, had sprouted along the outer surface of the *dura mater*. Mort's entire brain expanded and contracted within the skull, the heavy folds of the gyri randomly inflating till the organ began bulging beyond the confines of its bony casing.

"Jesus, what the hell is happening?"

Chari shook her head. A number of the pustules had burst, spewing the thick, fluorescent fluid up in tiny purple geysers that stained Chari's lab coat.

"Make it stop, Ilona, make it . . . "

The corpse's eyes shot open. Its jaw dropped and the creature started to moan, the swollen tongue mercifully muffling the monstrous sound. The small volume of air in its lungs was quickly expended, but its mouth hung open, the eyes still wide with terror as it tried to express its agony.

Its eyes were like capers floating in bloody milk. They darted left and right, settling finally on Hodge's astonished face.

Hodge didn't want to look, but he couldn't turn away. The creature had fixed on him as it continued its voiceless scream. With great effort the corpse managed to move its head and peered down at its decayed and useless body.

Mort looked back up at Hodge, its features twisted in desperate panic. Hodge saw its lips start to move, but just then the creature was racked by a series of spasms. A great spray of glowing liquid splooshed out from the open skull.

Chari said something but Hodge didn't hear it. His eyes were glued to the creature's shuddering lips.

Chari grabbed a shim from the table beside Hodge and brutally rammed it into Mort's brain.

The spasms ended and the eyes went dead, but the lips remained twisted in what Hodge believed could only be a curse.

When he finally turned to Chari, he saw she was back at her desk, frantically scribbling notes on a legal pad.

The man's sweaty, jaundiced face was in excruciating close-up on the screen. His eyes bulged out of their sockets, magnified and contained, it seemed, only by the thick lenses of his welfare-frame glasses. His eyebrows bobbed up and down like silverfish.

"For the Lord sayeth, 'If a man die, shall he live again?' And I say to you the answer is upon us, brethren, and the answer, most righteously, is yes. Yes, I say to you."

The camera pulled back a bit. A silent, robed choir stood behind the preacher, nodding vigorously at his every inflection.

"But man dieth and wasteth away: yea, man giveth up the ghost, and where is he? Where, you ask? Where? *Here* is the answer.

"He discovereth deep things out of darkness, and bringeth out to light the shadow of death."

Hodge glanced away from the Right-to-Undeath preacher, and looked at his son. The only movement was the slight rise and fall of Mikey's chest facilitated by the respirator. Hodge eyed the cardiac monitor the way a nervous broker might eye the ticker on an October Monday.

An infection from the new implant caused the fever, which had raged for a week. It was just one of those things. Antibiotics had no effect, and Mikey's brain activity was near zero. When the last tiny spike disappeared from his chart, they would be legally obliged to decapitate.

The voice drew his attention back to the screen.

"I will ransom them from the power of the grave; I will redeem them from death. O Death, I will be thy plagues: O Grave, I will be thy destruction."

Hodge remembered when his father had been in the hospital, with wires and machines hooked up every which way just like Mikey. Hodge had been in the room when the cardiac distress alarm went off.

He remembered how doctors and nurses came running from every direction, with crash carts and defibrillation paddles and grim determination. They had worked on his father for forty minutes before surrendering to the inevitable.

"I am He that liveth, and was dead; and behold, I am alive for evermore, Amen; and have the keys of hell and of death.

"To him that overcometh will I give to eat of the tree of life."

Hodge was on constant edge, waiting once again for the shrill peal of the alarm. He knew the reaction would be different now. No doctors and nurses, only armed guards and an emergency autopsy team.

It was too risky to permit anyone more than their one chance to live.

"He *shall* rule them with a rod of iron. I will not blot out his name out of the book of life."

Hodge was sobbing to himself. A nurse walked in the door, but turned quickly around when she saw him.

"Be thou faithful unto death, and I will give thee a crown of life."

The preacher's eyes, nose, and mouth completely filled the screen. A small piece of gristle dangled from between his yellowed front teeth.

"And *yes*. I said *yes*. I will. *Yes*."

*   *   *   *   *

"Mort's dead," Chari said.

Hodge tiredly looked up from his paperwork. "Yeah . . . ?"

Chari stood in the doorway hugging the jamb, one foot in, the other outside of Hodge's office.

"No, I mean he's really dead. Dead again. For good. Probably. I'm waiting on decapitation, just to be sure."

Hodge leaned back in his chair and gestured for Chari to come in and sit down but she continued to slow-dance with the door frame.

"What happened?"

"I'm not sure. The virus didn't survive in the forebrain. It's funny, it seemed to be taking until I reactivated the neural network. Then, well, you saw."

Hodge flashed back on the look of horror on the corpse's reanimated face. He nodded.

"I'm thinking," Chari went on, "that it just got fried in the cortex. The electrical charge in the forebrain is slightly higher than in the brain stem. They're both so slight that we normally wouldn't worry about the difference, but to an organic substance that was growing there, it might be like walking along the third rail as somebody suddenly turns on the juice."

"What does it mean for the project?" Hodge asked.

Chari finally let go of the door and came into the office. She could hear the trace of desperate hope in his voice. She stood behind a leather armchair, stroking the headrest with the back of her hand and shaking her head.

"It's a big step back," she said with great deliberation. "The regeneration in brain tissue is only promulgated under the influence of the virus. Without successful regeneration of higher-level functions, I just don't see any means for maintaining control. I don't know, the gentech section has some new ideas. Maybe between us, we can make sense of things."

Hodge raised an eyebrow.

"Yeah," Chari said, "the report's written and filed. Don't worry, your lackey ass is covered."

They sat in silence for a while.

"You want to hear something stupid?" Chari asked.

"What?"

"I'd sort of come to like old Mort," Chari smiled demurely, but the look reeked of artifice.

"Never give them names," Hodge said.

"I know, I know. I've always done it, though. When I was a grad student, I used to name all those dopey lab rats. I'd end up all teary-eyed when it came time to fractionate them."

Chari plucked an old styrofoam coffee cup off the armrest, and swirled the rancid dregs. "You know, after rat brains have been centrifuged, they look exactly like that chocolate diet drink stuff. It's been the ruin of my figure."

Chari put the cup down and headed back out of the office, stopping for a final turn with the jamb.

"I thought we had something there for a minute," she said. "It's terribly unobjective, I know, but for a second or two after the reconnection I thought I saw a trace of, ummm, intelligence on Mort's face. Did you get any sense of that?"

Hodge was again staring down at his papers, but he saw in his mind the corpse's expression as it glanced down at itself. The terror in its eyes, the burgeoning plea on its lips.

"No," Hodge lied.

"Probably just a reflex," Chari said, and went out.

"Ilona . . . "

Chari ducked her head back into his office. Hodge forced himself to meet her gaze.

"Do you believe that there's dignity in death?"

Chari was about to say something smart, but caught herself. She thought about Hodge's son in the hospital, and all the possible responses, including the one she knew that Hodge wanted to hear. She settled on the truth.

"No," she said.

"Me either," Hodge said.

*   *   *   *   *

The barbed wire and cyclone fencing was really unnecessary at this point, but it seemed to make people in the area feel better, so they left it up.

The guard at the gate was pretty much a formality as well, but his presence was still mandated by law. Although appearing to possess all the cunning instincts of a retired bank guard, he was always pleasant enough to Hodge. Hodge suspected the man welcomed any living visitors he could get.

Other than the guard and Hodge, the cemetery was deserted, both above ground and below. Bright rectangles of thick, new sod stood out like hair-transplant plugs atop the graves, although a goodly number of the plots had yet to be reseeded.

The corpses that hadn't dug their own way out of the ground in the first few days had later been exhumed and torched during the long and ongoing cleanup process. Many of the headstones were charred, and a number had been broken or vandalised and not replaced. The cemetery hadn't been razed, however, though many had favoured such a solution.

Hodge spent a great deal of time at the bone-yard now, taking great comfort in the isolation and quietude. He had tried several times to get Keiko to accompany him or at least go on her own, believing it was what she needed. But she spent her days staring at the screens, bingeing on the endless loop of violent, final death.

It all made Hodge quite ill.

He never went directly to Mikey's plot. He preferred to walk slowly around the cemetery, stopping occasionally to read the chiselled inscriptions, still playing the game of finding the oldest grave.

Sometimes he didn't visit his son's grave at all. He just walked a slow circle around the yard — or sat in the grass and stared — and tried, most of all, not to cry.

Near the end, he had begged Chari to look at the boy. She was loath to get involved, but didn't know how to refuse.

"The organism," Hodge had entreated. "What if it were introduced into a living subject? Into Mikey?"

Chari was horrified but not surprised.

"No, Bill," she said. "You know that we aren't even close to that stage of the program. Human subjects are . . . Think of Mort."

Hodge did, but the memory no longer mattered. Mort had at least returned to life, and his son was about to die.

"For God's sake, Ilona. They're going to chop his head off. They're going to cut my son's head off."

Chari tried to reason with him, but it was impossible. She mollified him by agreeing to perform the spinal tap. "Exploratory," she told him.

Knowingly, she insisted that Hodge remain in the room as she drew the fluid. The boy never moved or made a sound as the thick needle penetrated his lower back.

With the sample still in her hand, Chari went over and closed the blinds. Hodge was stroking his son's feverish brow and didn't notice until she turned off the lights.

An ever-so-faint mauve glow shimmered slightly in Chari's shaking hand.

And he knew.

The autopsy team took the boy away within the hour.

Without even realising it, Hodge found himself standing at the foot of Mikey's grave, not that the boy's body was actually buried below. The laws were very strict about that. They had merely buried some ashes, along with a photograph, and the boy's favourite stuffed animal: a purple-and-yellow cow that Mikey had unaccountably named Becky.

Few people even bothered with burial these days, but Hodge had insisted on it. He couldn't explain why at the time, but thought that perhaps he somehow knew how important it would be to him to have a grave to come to later.

Even in a world where death's undiscovered country held inconstant borders, there was an odd sort of peace to be found in such a place.

The day was almost gone. Clouds in the western sky radiated a majestic purple that sent a shudder through Hodge's body.

In the background, he heard the faint rattle of the guard's key ring, and knew the man was getting ready to lock the cemetery up for the night.

Hodge wasn't ready to go. He wasn't ready.

As night fell, Hodge cried, but no sound emerged as his bitter tears fell on an empty grave.

Revenge of the Zombie Studpuppies

1

MY DICK WAS REDDER THAN A HORNY DOG'S. A couple of open sores just below the head were oozing blood and pus, and I was still looking at stall 7. Old #7 had a cunt like a scouring pad and just didn't quite seem to grasp the gravity of her situation. If you'd asked me just a few seconds before, I'd have said no way Jose that I could raise the Titanic again.

Wouldn't you just know the Old Lady would pick that moment to come strolling down the walk. I swear, the way she stickled for rules was worse than the zees themselves. We all do what we have to to keep off the dinner plate, but some go beyond the call.

I remember seeing pictures of collaborators from WWII and how they got their heads shaved afterward so everybody'd know who they were and what they done. I don't know if there'll be an after, this time, but if there is I mean to be there to shave the old bitch right down to the neckline.

Number 7 sort of groaned when she saw me, but this was no time for subtlety.

"Open the garage door, honey," I said. "Time to park the pink Pontiac."

By the time the grizzled biddy came into view I was pumping like an oil rig.

It was like fucking a power sander.

The Old Lady watched for a while, making notes on her goddamn clipboard.

"Nice rhythm," she said. "I give it an 84."

I reckon I left more pus than jiz up #7's love chute, but the Old Lady seemed satisfied. That's more than I can say for #7, but it kept us out of the Yards for another day.

That's all that really matters here.

2

They say that sooner or later he who calls the tune's got to pay the piper, but you never see the bill till it's far too late.

When they first showed the pictures on the tube, we all figured it was some sort of gag, like that old invaders from Mars hoo-ha the fat guy with the sled done on the radio way back when.

The fact of the situation got manifested all too soon.

Those first few days were right good fun, though. The zees were slower than frozen honey and dumber than Hollywood blondes. They just shambled along waving their arms and flapping their gums and a one-armed, blind man with a twitch could have blown their dead brains out.

They took their prizes, to be sure, adding to their ranks as they went — you'd be surprised how many damn fools never took advantage of their god-given right to keep and bear arms — but between the police and the army and the national guard and an appropriately outfitted citizenry, we were putting them down and having ourselves a reasonable fair time in the process.

Looking back now, I realise it all started to go sour that day I was out hunting with Bobby Goodman and Joey Navinsky.

It was what you might call a microcosm for everything that was to come.

We were working our way up the Post Road east of Taft when Bobby spotted a dead one thrashing around in a half-empty swimming pool. The zee couldn't have been more than a half-dozen feet from the side, but it clearly didn't know how to swim because it was flailing away like to drown if it weren't already dead.

We walked on up to the edge and Bobby pulled out his .45. He started to squeeze the trigger extra slow, like he always does, but Joey swiped at his arm, sending the bullet wild, deflating a grinning Freddie Kruger wading tube.

"What the hell?" Bobby said, fit to be trussed, but Joey had gone all slack-jawed, a thin strand of saliva glistening in his open mouth. He just kept pointing at the zee.

"Hot damnation," Joey said.

"Jesus on toast," Bobby murmured.

I wasn't paying real close attention — dead is dead, near as I can tell — but as Joey picked up a long pole with a hook on the end, I took another look and saw it was a girly zee, and a pulchritudinous one at that. She made an extra hearty thrash and the little light bulb went off.

It was Hilda DeLisle.

Now, Hildy was trashier than a used paperback romance, but I could see how in the wee hours of a Saturday night at the Two Drops O' Scotch, a fellow might allow the . . . immensity of her physical assets to cast a dark shadow on his better judgement.

Joey, of course, had always had hot pockets for Hildy. Unfortunately, even Hildy drew the line someplace and that turned out to be right above Joey Navinski's John Henry.

By now Joey had grabbed onto — or more like into — Hildy's leg and was pulling her toward the side of the pool. Me and Bobby traded glances and head shakes, but Joey started screaming out instructions and we figured it was best to humour him and it'd been sort of a slow day, so what the hell.

As Hildy pulled herself up on the ledge, Joey flipped the pole around and smashed the blunt end into her mouth. She fell back in the water but held her grip on the side, and being dead and not all that bright to begin with, just started pulling herself right on out again.

Joey gave her more of the same, till her teeth were floating like dead bugs on top of the water. When she final dragged herself out of the pool, Joey said the word and me and Bobby blew her knobby knees apart.

Joey rolled her over with his foot.

Hildy's tits were a tad ripe and she was overall looking generally waterlogged. She tried to drag herself toward us with her arms and chin, but Joey pulled out his hand axe and hacked off her hands. The stumps oozed a bit, but really it smelled worse than it looked.

Joey hesitated then and me and Bobby exchanged another look: it was the story of Joey's life.

"Go ahead," Bobby finally hissed at him and Joey went for it.

He ripped the wet clothes off old Hildy and pinned her flat with his knees.

He mounted her like a twenty-pound trout.

It was rough-going at first — I expect Hildy was somewhat lacking in the lubricatory frills — but don't you know God watches over drunks and horny fools. Hildy was clawing at Joey with her stumps and damn near gummed him to death, but had nothing to show for her efforts but a bunch of pus-covered hickeys on Joey's neck.

Joey'd reached the top of the ladder, and Elvis was about to leave the ballpark when they sprung the ambush.

Half-a-dozen of them came out of nowhere. Moving fast, too, not at all like the zees we had seen so far.

Bobby was the quickest. He started shooting and shouted out a warning to Joey who was finally adding his cream to Hildy's coffee. Joey looked up and tried to pull out, but Hildy locked him up with her nether-muscles and wrapped her stumps around him in a big old bear-hug.

Joey was screaming and pounding the back of Hildy's head into the concrete walkway, but before I could make a move, two more of the bushwhackers were on him. I saw one reach into Joey's mouth and yank his tongue out like toilet tissue off the roll. Then I had to take notice of the pair that were advancing on me.

One came low from the right, the other high from the rear. I was holding a 5.56mm mini-MAC, with the M16 slung over my shoulder. 'Course, I kept a snub-nose .38 speedloader in an ankle holster, but there wasn't time to reach for it.

They were quick, but dead still ain't like alive. The one charging from behind was a tall, gangly fellow, with gaping holes in his chest and belly, and a bit-off nose. I ducked left just as he made his leap and flipped him on over me with a roll of the shoulder.

I took two extra tumbles and almost landed in the pool, but braced myself against the diving board. I sprayed back along my path with the MAC, catching the other zee across the knees, sending her sprawling. She was a squat little thing, covered with shit and missing a tit, but she moved darned fast for all that. She tripped over a rusty Hibachi and did a jackknife into the shallow end that would have scored a '10' even from the Romanian judge. She hit bottom with a sound like a cherry bomb in a garbage can.

The tall zee was almost on top of me again, so I tossed the spent MAC and went for the .38, but it must have slipped out of the holster when I did my tumbling.

Did I mention the .22 in my pocket?

I often don't, cause it really ain't but a toy. Still, I do load her up with hollow points, which proved to be a right smart thing, because it took three shots before that sucker's dead brains went out the back of his rotten skull.

I shoved the .22 back in my pocket and grabbed for the M16.

Incredibly, the bitch in the pool was dog-paddling her way toward me, though her head was all flat on one side, sort of like an open grand piano.

One shot later she was impersonating Natalie Wood.

I quickly turned toward Bobby, but he had done just fine. One headless zee was dangling from a low tree branch, while Bobby stood on top of another, them big tuna boats of his planted firmly on its chest. He was digging through its eye sockets with his bayonet, scraping out the brains and wiping grey chunks off on the dead grass.

"I hate you," he'd say, and scoop some brains.

"I hate you a lot." Another scoop.

The zee was still squirming a bit, letting out a screechy yowling, but Bobby finished up by prying off the top of its mushy head.

"I hate you a lot," he concluded.

I looked over to Joey and saw it was too late. Bobby'd taken out the last two bushwhackers, but Joey'd been done. I walked on over and found that Bobby hadn't quite finished Hildy off. Her lips were perched where Joey'd always dreamed, but I don't expect this was quite the way he'd wanted it.

Hildy had managed to crack Joey's nuts open and was sucking up a wormy mass of tubes and veins like them clear Chinese noodles in a sweet and sour sauce. Just then Bobby started to stir and I didn't know if he was still alive, or dead and come back, but this wasn't any time to find out.

Me and Bobby did a one-potato, two-potato for the honours. He won — as usual — and opted for skewering Hildy's head with a picnic umbrella.

That left Joey for me.

I retrieved the .38 and did him with that.

It's best to keep in touch with all your weapons.

3

That pretty much marked the beginning of the end as things worked out. The zees sprung their traps just about everywhere. Seemed they were a whole lot cleverer than they'd let on. They were scheming from the git-go and the fresher they were, the smarter they were.

It was a matter of simple arithmetic: There's a lot more accumulated dead folks in the ground than live ones on top of it. For a while it was pretty much smorgasbord city as the zees swarmed like hungry cousins at a bar mitzvah. The whole world was their Viennese table.

But they were deliberate, too. They heeded the old adage about leaving the table a little hungry. They were careful not to eat every last bit of what they caught, leaving just enough intact to bring a new set of choppers into the program.

And they got organised.

They introduced some sort of hierarchy, though I still ain't figured out exactly how it works.

They evolved some sense of order and a weird kind of decorum.

And they built the farms.

4

Officially, this is West Zone Fertilisation Centre #4, but calling an asshole a cunt don't make a bent man straight.

It didn't figure to me, at first. I mean, I couldn't make any sense of what they were doing.

Or why.

We used to talk about it quite a bit up in the bunk-house. It was really just an old railroad car turned on its side that they locked us up in at night, with a busted chemical toilet in the corner and a bunch of silverfish-infested mattresses on the floor. Somewhere along the line somebody'd hung a big sign on the door that said: STUDPUPPY LODGE. It had been up as long as anyone could remember. The zees didn't pay it no mind and we'd all just sort of picked up on the name.

The Farm was divided into three zones: the breeding areas, including the henhouses, birthing buildings and the Studpuppy Lodge; the zees' living quarters (you should pardon the expression); and the Yards for the Herd, which took up most of the grounds.

The whole complex was ringed by triple-fencing, with barbed-wire and watchtowers and back-from-the-dead Dobermans running between the fences.

And, of course, the Crumbsnatchers.

At least, that's what the Pups call 'em. They were the zee hordes that milled around all day along the outside perimeter of the farm, just hoping that a snack might fall their way.

The 'Snatchers were mostly made up of your lower grade zees. These were the real shamblers, rotted almost beyond resurrection, mean as horny sailors in a pussy shortage, and beyond the control of their brethren.

They waited out there night and day, squeezed up against the fences, desperate for anything living that so much as shook its dick.

Sometimes it got so crowded out there that the 'Snatchers would be stacked eight and ten deep against the fence. They'd press in so tight that the ones closest to the fence — particularly the *really* ripe ones — would get squeezed right on through the steel mesh like Velveeta through a red hot grater. The fence would sizzle and sparkle and the smell of seared, rotted meat would sit thick in the air.

There was this one Pup in the lodge when I first came in. He didn't hardly say nothing, but he stuck out like a turd in a punch bowl. He was older than the rest of us, maybe 35 or even 40. I didn't think nothing of it at the time. After a while I understood that the wear and tear on the equipment makes this something of a young man's game. It don't matter how far or straight you can shoot, only the number of bullets you got in your gun.

Anyway, the Pups were jabbering on, as usual, about the zees and what they were doing and how we was going to break on out of here and all, when Vince — this older fellow — started in laughing.

He was lying in the corner, twirling the armband that we all wore for identification. His laugh was sort of eerie and the rest of us quieted down right fast. The laugh seemed to echo on a while through the silence.

"You *boys* don't know shit," Vince said, after a while. Those were the first words we'd ever heard him utter.

"So why don't you go ahead and educate us, Grandpa."

It was a big fellow named Karl who spoke. Karl was pretty happy at the Farm. He liked hurting the Hens and though I didn't particularly care for him, I didn't much fancy a scene.

"How do you figure it?" I asked Vince. "I mean, what the hell are they going to all this trouble for? They must have something in mind."

"They ain't got no minds," someone else said.

"They must have something," I said. "My daddy worked for Oscar Mayer up near Chicago and the system they got here is near as slick. But what do they want? What could they be after? I mean, it's not like they need the food, being dead and all."

"What's that got to do with it?" Vince said, sitting up.

"It's . . . they're . . . I . . . what do you mean what's that got to do with it? *They're dead.*"

"So?" Vince asked. "You're alive, so-called. Why do you do what-you do? Why'd you get up in the morning? Why'd you go to work? Why did folks get married and have kids and live their boring lives? Why did the Gettys and the Rockerfellers and the Gates and others with all their billions keep on working and hustling just to get more? There wasn't any point to that either. They were going to end up just as dead in the long run. They just did it 'cause that's what they did. It's what they knew."

"Shit," Karl said, "that don't mean you ain't gonna live right while you can."

"Sure. Isn't that exactly what we're still doing? Do you have any illusions that you're not going to get eaten alive, then wake up and eat someone else? Doesn't matter though, does it? You do what you can, while you can."

" Ain't the same . . . " Karl started.

"Is the same," Vince said. "The zees aren't any different. Near as we can tell all they've got is their hunger. To them eating is living. *Eat-o ergo sum.* It's all that *they* know and it makes them happy. Or so I reckon. To us, happiness is always set against the fear of dying. We know that everything we do is up against a life-clock. The zees don't have *that* problem. As long as they've got food, they've got what they want. It doesn't matter why, it just is. And as long as they've got us they've got food. Sounds like zee heaven to me.

He laid down again and went back to twirling his armband, None of the rest of us had an answer to him. Even Karl kept his mouth shut, though he looked kind of mad.

Vince disappeared the next day. I reckoned he wasn't meeting his quota.

The next week, they brought a new kid in to take Vince's place. He was a talkative type, with a shock of bright red hair and a face covered in zits. He was chock-full of ideas about what was going on and what was going to happen.

We all just told him to shut the hell up.

5

"Fuck me. Fuck me *now*. My pussy's so hot and dripping. I want your big cock in me. Just fuck me hard. Ram it in me. I want your cum. I love your cum. Your cock's so big and beautiful and I want it inside me. Fuck me. Please, please fuck me, fuck me, fuck me."

Number 17 was getting a mite desperate. This was her last chance before her status changed from Breeder to Stock and they moved her on out of the henhouse. She'd had her time to get pregnant and wasn't cutting the Gulden's. I'd even slipped an extra dose of fertility drug into her IV, but she was still as barren as a Saturday night in Tulsa. She wasn't a bad gal and I felt for her and all, but I'd done her just the day before and had my own schedule to think of. Besides, this was the Old Lady's shift and no time to be taking chances.

She screamed for a while after I walked past, but it faded to a whimper quick enough. I went on down to #12 to see the new girl.

They were still fastening her into the stall. A Techie opened the clamp on the tube that'd been fused to her femoral artery and the blood zipped through the tangle of plastic tubing like chocolate milk through a crazy straw. I watched it disappear into a small hole in the floor, then come back down from a tube in the ceiling a few seconds later. It filled-up an IV sac swinging above her head. Another line coiled down and was plugged into her forearm with a long, dirty needle.

The security system was a damned nuisance. It was always putting kinks in the tubes or dislodging the needles in the heat of the moment. But the zees insisted on it, so what was a Studpuppy to do?

I guessed that she was maybe sixteen with big silver eyes like spinning dimes. Her hair was matted and tangled, but even in the dim light I could see its corn silk lustre. She had thick, dark lips to match the colour of her swirling blood and high, angular cheekbones. Her skin was pale, but smooth and rich as French ice cream.

The Techie checked the flow then walked on out behind her zee minder. She sort of scowled at me as she went and I wondered where she got off displaying such a haughty attitude. I ignored it, and turned my attention back to #12. She was a little woozy from the initial loss of blood, but she'd get used to that soon enough.

The girl was powerful pretty. But more than that she looked fresh. Most of the others had ridden to hell and back on busted tricycles and every inch of the ride was etched in their faces. This one had an unspoiled look about her, though, and I guessed she'd been hidden away real good.

As she started coming around, she cast her eyes up into my own steely blues.

I just about melted.

I maybe ain't no hard guy, but I'm no soft touch, either. I've seen stuff to kink a Chinaman's hair and thought no more of it than the sky thinks of blue. But something in that little girl's eyes sent me all jellylike from tits to toes.

I never believed in love, much less love at first sight, but if this little girl was the church I was willing to take a leap of faith.

My expression must have been about as hard to read as a tube of toothpaste, because the Old Lady flashed her false yellow choppers at me and swiped the needle out of #12's arm.

I grabbed for it, but she pushed me away with the business end of her Uzi.

"Little Miss strikes your fancy, does she?" she snarled. I didn't say a word, just glanced from the corner of my eye at the IV tube, swinging like a pendulum and slowly dripping her life's blood away.

"Tell you what, Loverboy: you do me *and* the Prom Queen before the Hawaiian Punch runs out, and maybe you and Junior Miss here get to make bouncy-bouncy again some time."

The Old Lady had rubbed up against me a few times, but she'd never tried anything like this. I ran my gaze up and down her gnarled frame and suppressed the Godzilla of shudders.

"You wouldn't dare," I said. "The zees would never stand for the breakage."

The miserable crone just smiled. "Accidents will happen, it's only hit and run . . . "

"Shit," I muttered, and dropped my drawers.

An old bitch who could sing Elvis Costello like that was capable of anything.

The Old Lady's tits were like wrung-out athletic socks, and her breath smelled of dead violets. Her cunt was smooth as a bag of broken glass, but I kept my eyes locked on that little girl's argent orbs, and miraculous as Jesus making all them tuna sandwiches, I managed to spurt a loving spoonful into granny's cranny.

I don't think she got off or nothing cause she didn't make a sound the whole time. There was blood when I pulled out, but I couldn't tell if it was hers or mine or both. I didn't know how I was gonna manage to get it up again for my little love goddess.

"Tick, tock," the Old Lady said, scratching herself and sniffing her fingers. She gave the IV tube an unhelpful squeeze.

I did my best to wipe the Old Lady's crusty gunge off my love rocket and climbed up on top of #12. She was looking scared as a big-eyed doe frozen by headlights in the road. There wasn't time to be delicate, but I held her in a soft embrace and ran my filthy hands through her hair.

"You got to do what you got to do here, darling," I whispered. "You got to pretend it's just you and me and forget all the rest. Now close your eyes."

I could barely believe it when she did. I felt a bit of the stiffness drain out of her and planted a gentle kiss on those full, red lips.

I was shocked to discover a big old erection percolating its way to near grandiose tumescence. My little baby took me in her hands just then, and I damn near had to struggle for basic containment.

She worked me inside her with pained moans and gritted teeth and we made the motion of the ages. I ain't about to make any extravagant claims here, or expect anyone to believe that I was able to provide my baby with anything like a religious experience, but excepting for the moment the unpleasantness of the circumstances, it wasn't a totally terrible first time, either. Better than some I'd known — and I'm talking before the zees came along.

I gave my girl a big wet kiss on the forehead. Her eyes were still closed and I believe I detected the track of a tear on her porcelain complexion. I climbed on down.

"What do you think of that?" I said with a shit-eating grin, but I never got to find out.

The Old Lady clocked me across the bridge of the nose with the rifle stock. I crumbled down into the thick pool of my baby's ichor and the world started to fade like a busted picture tube.

But the last thing I saw was the Old Lady hooking that IV back into #12's arm, and even as the blackness grew complete, I knew things were going to be all right.

6

I woke up in the Yards. My armband was gone, and a brand had been tattooed on my thigh.

This was not a good thing.

The sun was just taking its final bow behind the curtain of mountains to the west, so I figured I must have been out near half the day. It was getting cold fast, the way it always does in the valley, but there was no lack of body heat by which to keep warm.

The Yard was packed tighter than new Crayolas in the big box of 64. Folks were laid out on top of one another in a long daisy chain tangle of arms and legs. There were a few that insisted on milling nervously around, stepping on hands and feet and faces, and occasionally there'd be a yelp or a flailing fist on account of it, but most of the Herd just sat there, looking to escape into sleep and dream, or staring blankly at a sky fading faster than their hopes.

There was no pity on the farm. The zees weren't capable of it, of course, and no-one else could afford it. The Hens sure didn't pity the Studpuppies, and the Pups, well, we never gave the Herd so much as a passing thought, except maybe to say a prayer that we weren't yet part of it.

The Herd was too far gone to even take pity on themselves.

I remember how back in school, in the history lessons, we used to learn about the other camps, the ones back in Europe. I remember how, like everyone else, I took an almost sick fascination in every detail about them, trying to imagine what it must have been like.

The thing I could never figure out was why the prisoners never rose up against the bastards. Why they just laid back and took it, and waited to die. Seemed like they hardly had anything to lose.

There was probably five, six hundred of us locked in the yards, and another couple-three score humans wandering out in the camp 'twixt the Pups and the Hens and the Techies and such, and there couldn't have been more than fifty zees in the whole place.

But after sitting with the Herd for a spell — and it wasn't even a long spell — I came to see that it didn't really matter how many of them and how many of us there were, or about the 'Snatchers outside the gates, or even about the fear of death — or undeath — itself.

It was more like a sickness that took hold of your brain. Something in the very air that was infectious and weighed you down, like when you catch a fever and can't for your life imagine getting out of bed, even if a locomotive came tearing down the hall at you.

You couldn't see it or smell it or touch it, but you could taste it deep down in your gut, where it sat like a big old fat guy.

It was a kind of mental surrender; the realisation of just how thin and fragile a veneer humanity is, and how once that fine, soft surface has been scratched, there's just no way to repair the damage.

The zees could treat us like animals and put us in the Yards, because animals is what we'd become. It turns out that 'civilisation' is no more substantial than a juicy pimple on your chin. One little squeeze and POP! The Herd was the pus that got sprayed on the bathroom mirror.

The zees up in the towers were perched like gargoyles.

The Crumbsnatchers were moaning their song of the damned. A Chinky-looking 'Snatcher was eyefucking me, opening and closing it's rotted hands and working its dislocated jaw. Its little pecker pointed straight at me, hard as a good man is to find.

I exhaled a weak sigh, elbowed myself some room in the cold dirt, and went to sleep.

7

It was my baby that saved my miserable life.

It was my tenth day in the Yards, and I knew the end was coming soon. Transfers happened every couple of weeks, and the cattle cars were a tad overdue.

I was standing by the feeding troughs picking through the gruel for chunks that weren't too veiny or hairy and provided no more than the recommended daily allowance of maggot, when I saw her.

They were moving her from the henhouse into the birthing quarters. She was strapped down to a gurney, with the Old Lady riding shotgun.

I started to call out to her, but I couldn't seem to make my voice work. Even so, I saw her glance over my way so I jumped up on the trough and waved my arms over my head. I thought I saw her lean forward some, so maybe she saw me, but then the whole party disappeared behind a shed and out of view.

I was so thrilled just to catch a glimpse of her sweet face that the meaning of it didn't hit me at first.

Moving her.

The birthing quarters.

I was going to be a father.

"HOOOO-EEEE," I screamed, suddenly finding my voice. A couple of the guards looked down at me and snarled, and I remembered where I was. I jumped down off the trough and landed hard on the ankle of an emaciated woman.

"I'm gonna be a Daddy," I proudly told her.

She let loose with an enormous, wet fart and spat something grey, but pretty Lady Luck was flashing her tits at me that day, 'cause the tubercular lugie missed me by an inch.

I was high as a tightrope walker on airplane glue thinking about the miracle of what had occurred. They tested the Hens once a week and my fertile little darling had rung the bell first time out. I took comfort that she'd be all right for a while, 'cause the zees know where their bread is buttered, and are right mindful of mommas-to-be.

Even though we'd only had the one chance to play land-the-shuttle, and surely another Pup had taken over my shift, somehow I was just sure that the little dude sprouting in my honey's belly would prove to be the product of my own seed.

287

I was determined that come hell or the carving knife, I was gonna figure a way to see him pop on out.

I pushed my way to the best vantage point I could find in the Yard so as to survey the situation and set the grey matter to stewing. The high ground left me out near the lodge, and I spotted the Pups heading in at the end of their rounds.

I tried waving at them, and I knew that they'd seen me, 'cause a little dude named Jimbo who'd taken sort of an odd shine to me started to wave back. But Karl, that Nazi bastard, growled at him, and Jimbo hurried into the lodge, though I thought I saw him eye me again as he passed out of sight.

I couldn't really be mad about it. I'd done the same many times in the past. You were either with the living or you weren't, and there wasn't time nor strength to waste on the likes of the Herd.

I sat and sat, and thought and thought, but the fact of the matter was that I didn't have a cunt's hair of an idea for a plan.

And as the cold and the darkness settled like a fat woman in a warm bath, I heard the whistle of an approaching train, with its long stream of cattle cars, and its one way ticket to the cafeteria.

And I knew I was out of time.

I heard the whistle blow again.

And again.

And I smiled a big old smile, because just like that I had a plan.

It had about as much chance as a boner in a dyke bar, but it was a plan just the same.

I was ready to rock and roll.

8

It was surely a sucker's bet, but I had a funny feeling that moment when me and Jimbo made eye contact that opportunity was wiping its big old feet on my welcome mat, and getting ready to rap its knuckles on my door.

Like I say, I'd had my suspicions about Jimbo. He did his studpuppy service sure enough, but I sort of sensed his heart wasn't completely in it.

I reckoned that he didn't always say howdy to the girls by way of the front door.

It was nothing in particular, just the way you'd catch him glancing out the corner of his eye at you at funny moments, or the fact that no matter how ratty the lodge got, Jimbo's bunk was always just a bit neater than all the others.

And Jimbo just hated using the old toilet in the lodge. I knew that most every night he snuck out to do his business in private in the dark.

I was cold and tired, and weak from eating gruel, but the train would surely make the Farm by morning so I slapped myself awake and kept a wary watch.

I could practically smell first light, and figured I was destined for the serving platter all because of a case of constipation, when I heard Jimbo pry open the emergency exit in the roof of the lodge, and squeeze on out. I knew he always headed for the dark cul-de-sac behind the lodge, and he didn't disappoint me.

As he started to squat, I whistled at him.

It was a big chance, 'cause the yards were quiet as a lipless librarian. The zees got extra cautious near shipping time, and the guard in the towers was doubled.

I didn't know if Jimbo could even hear me, or if he'd respond if he did. If he'd been a regular Pup, he wouldn't have given me a second thought.

Fortunately, Jimbo was just a might on the irregular side, and though I saw a spark of fear in his eyes, he scurried on over.

I was huddled in a corner where two cyclone fences were crudely welded together. It was as close as I could get to Jimbo's private privy. We both laid flat on our bellies, and I had to practically whisper my spiel into the dirt.

He didn't say anything at first, didn't even move. We were talking so low, I thought maybe he didn't hear me, but in the glow of the searchlight that passed over us, I could tell that the little wheels were spinning in his brain.

"What's in it for me?" he finally asked. It was a hell of a stupid question, but I paid it no mind.

I put on my best come-hither look.

"Me," I said.

It was a hell of a stupid answer, but it was the only one I had.

He seemed to like it, but he wasn't ready to admit it.

"Never work," he said, shaking his head. I didn't say a thing. "Million to one shot. Hell, ten million."

The way his head was moving back and forth, he should have been perched in the back window of a Studebaker, but he hadn't got up and left.

"How about," I said, "a little gesture of good faith on my part. No expectations, no obligation."

He cocked an eye at that, and I did the vice-versa. That's when I knew I had him.

I took a quick glance around. The eastern sky was turning the colour of robin's eggs, so there wasn't much time. I shimmied out of my dirty skivvies and got on my knees, I backed myself against the fence till I felt the cold metal digging sharp into my butt cheeks. I look a deep breath and tried to relax. I laid my face against the dirt and grabbed two handfuls of the loamy dark soil, squeezing tight.

I waited what seemed like forever. I was afraid to turn around, for fear that Jimbo had took off, and just about as scared he'd still be there. I thought for sure I'd misjudged the whole situation, when I felt the tip of his cock tickle my asshole.

Instinctively, I tensed up and he pulled away. I was afraid I'd spooked him, and tried to relax. I heard Jimbo spit a couple times and knew he was still with me.

I squeezed that dirt so tight it spurted through my fingers, and I dug my nails deep into the flesh of my palms. I gritted my teeth till my jaw popped like the cork on a bottle of Andre's, but I didn't tense up again.

And after a spell, he was in.

There really ain't much more I care to say about the experience, except that it wasn't the worst thing I've ever done.

Which don't exactly make it April in Paris.

It was over quick, anyway, and when he shot his load, Jimbo made a sound like a baby's toy that you squeeze to hear the little squeak.

I pulled up my pants and turned around to face him. His peter was still hard and hanging out his fly, and he stroked it absently. His pecker wasn't nearly so red and runny as my own, and I felt slightly embarrassed.

"So?" I whispered.

His eyes were closed, and he opened them slowly, unwilling to let the hard morning light intrude on his dreams. He looked at me, and sure as the Pope shits in the woods, at that moment I didn't have the slightest idea what to expect.

"God, I want a cigarette," he said. And we both smiled.

9

I felt like I was smoking a stogie, only we were both lit at the wrong end. I mean, my butt was sore as a spinster with trampled azaleas. The way I was walking, you could have drove a Fiat between my legs and still had room to pass.

The train was right outside the gates of the Farm. The tracks actually ran right on into the Yards, but the triple-gate system was rigged to keep the 'Snatchers out while the zees inched the train on in. There were always a few that managed to sneak through, but the zees posted a ring of guards and persecuted trespassers with something more than extreme prejudice.

I kept my eyes open for Jimbo, but didn't spot him. I guess I was looking for some reassurance, but in the end I knew either he'd do his bit or he wouldn't. There was nothing I could do about it either way.

The Herd was in a state of agitation, just like any animals in the slaughterhouse at killing time. Some even squealed like sows.

The first three railroad cars had been let inside the Farm and the zees were getting the Herd together with cattle prods and leather bullwhips. I forced my way to the edge of the surge, near as I could to a fence that ran across from the birthing quarters. I had to squeeze my way through the meat without looking too conspicuous or upsetting the movement of the Herd.

Two more train cars had rolled on in when I heard a commotion, and felt my heart try to leap out past my teeth. I almost made my move right then, but I saw it was just a couple of 'Snatchers that had climbed up on top of the train and tried to jump over the ring of guards. One got blown clean out of the air like a fleshy skeet, and the other was so rotted that the big bones in her calves exploded right on up through her knees when she made contact with the ground. She tried to slither toward the Herd, but a guard kicked her in the head till her brains popped out through the hole. A second guard squished them with his heel.

Only the caboose remained outside the Farm when the sharpshooter in the tower spotted me laying back along the fence. I saw him point at me and figured it was now or never.

I crouched down and sprung up into the air, grabbing as high as I could reach on the fence. I got one hand over the top and snagged it in the barbed wire.

Over my shoulder I saw the guard raising his rifle.

I bit my lip as the rusty razors sliced through the flesh of my fingers and palm, but I hauled myself higher even as the first bullet ricocheted off the fence post between my legs.

I glanced over and saw the last car clearing the first fence. I threw my leg up into the barbs and felt a painful tearing across the right side of my body.

A second bullet went wild below me in the Herd, ripping through both cheeks of a mouth-breathing old man and lodging in the spine of gaunt looking, once upon a time surfer-dude.

The train car was past the second fence.

I managed to stretch a gap in the wire with my bloody hands. Little flaps of skin tore loose and dangled from the barbs, but I hauled the rest of my body up till I could straddle the fence.

I looked up and saw that the sniper had me in his sights.

I looked down and watched the caboose clear the final fence.

I stood up as best I could and flipped a bloody double bird to the zee in the tower.

"Top of the world, motherfucker," I screamed and jumped.

It all happened in less than half a second, but the way I heard it and saw it and felt it, it might have been forever.

The sounds first: the crisp crack of gunfire, the harsh splinter of splitting wood. The frightened screams, the hungry squeals.

The images: the recoil of the rifle, the surprise on the sniper's face, the tower teetering, then crashing to the ground in gravity's bittersweet embrace.

The feelings: raw fire as the bullet tore the fuck-you finger off my left hand in a splay of crimson. Holy joy as the tower thundered down across the triple fencing, opening the way for the Crumbsnatchers.

I could hardly believe it, but Jimbo'd done his thing.

There'd been some old telephone cable and empty spools from Lord knows when sitting out behind the coops. I reckoned that with the right leverage the cable could be attached to the tower and the train, with a spool rigged as a pulley. The moving train served as the engine to drag the whole thing down.

It was a simple enough get-up, but I never truly reckoned Jimbo'd make it work. I don't know how he set it up without being seen, but then the Pups, being cocks of the walk, pretty well had free run of the Farm.

Amazing what a motivated man can do.

I landed in a flayed heap, my clothes and skin in tatters, my hand hurting worse than my ass. I found the top two knuckles of my finger on the ground, but decided there wasn't anything to do with them.

There wasn't much time, but I had to pause to take in the scene as the 'Snatchers poured in through the busted gate and went on a feeding frenzy amidst the Herd.

The zees tried to stop them at first, but soon realised that there was no hope, and joined right on in with the orgy.

There was some scattered gunfire from the remaining towers, but once the guards saw what they were missing they gave it up and leapt into the fray.

Hearts and minds were flying like Frisbees in the park on a sunny afternoon. In a matter of minutes, strings of intestine were draped on fences like tinsel. Eyeballs were plucked out of sockets, and ears ripped off and munched like Lays potato chips. How can you eat just one? More cock got sucked than at a cathouse fire-sale. Screams tore the air as men and women were pulled apart, their blood spraying thick and heavy as crimson rain.

The Herd was packed in too thick to get away. I looked for Jimbo by the train, but spotting anyone was hopeless in the chaos. I saw several of the other Pups squeeze out of the lodge through Jimbo's secret exit, but a pack of particularly putrefied 'Snatchers were waiting for them. The boys put up a good fight, but they were still meat in the end.

It was like a movie and I couldn't take my eyes from the screen. Blood gushed from my hand, and raw wounds pinched me from head to toe, but for all the horror, I couldn't make myself look away.

It wasn't until I heard the screams from the birthing rooms that I came to my senses and went looking for my baby.

When I burst on in through the nursery, I feared the worst. The zees had given up all pretence of control and were stuffing their dead faces like speeding bulimics. Babies were wailing and mommas were shrieking like broke-dick banshees.

I saw a heavy-set Mexican zee pull a suckling infant right out of its momma's arms and stuff its tiny head completely inside his mouth. The zee tore that baby's head clean off with one jerk of its neck, rolling it around his cheeks like a big plug of chewing tobacco, before crunching down and spitting out the soft bones.

The momma screamed bloody murder but another zee plunged a hand into her mouth and yanked her jaw off. Two more set on her and ripped her milk-laden tits apart in a geyser of blood red and creamy white.

Similar scenes were going down all around me as babies and new mommas were shredded like lettuce in a Cuisinart. Most were strapped down and helpless, and the zees had so many to chose from that I managed to dart through the ward without hardly attracting any notice at all. I even managed to grab a cattle prod that must have been tossed aside by one of the guards in the heat of desire.

I barrelled on through the last few yards of the birthing room. I was breathing hard, trying to ignore the pain in my finger and side. The air was thick as old Pennzoil with the stench of blood and death, making me a little light-headed.

As I tore down the hall toward the maternity ward, the Techie who had snubbed me in the henhouse came lurching out of a doorway, a tattooed forearm gripped in her teeth the way a momma cat carries a newborn kitten. She'd gone over to the other side.

Her dead eyes seemed to light up a bit when she saw me and the chunk of flesh dropped to the shiny tile floor with a wet splat. She came rushing at me, growling like a grizzly. Her jaws were snapping like rabid turtles.

There wasn't even time to think.

I started running toward her full speed. I can't be sure, but I think I was screaming at the top of my lungs.

Just as we were about to hit, I scrunched down low and took her in the gut with the top of my head. She bent near double around me, and I felt her spine crunch between the crown of my skull and the wall.

I tumbled on down to the floor. I gingerly fingered my scalp and felt where it had gone kind of soft. A little circle of robins were flying around my head, but I shooed them off and shakily got to my feet.

The zee was lying beside me, twisted all funny in the middle like one of them squiggly bits of pasta. She was trying to get up, but couldn't find any leverage. She started dragging herself toward me, busted spine and all.

I flicked the switch in the cattle prod and let her inch closer, shaking off the last of the cobwebs. As she got within an arm's length, I thrust the prod right on through a big brown eye.

"Take that, Miss High-and-Mighty," I gloated, and zapped the power on and off, fricasseeing her grey matter till she stopped convulsing.

Screams from the maternity ward brought me back to reality.

I yanked the prod out of her skull, wiped the goo off on her shirt, and hurried down the hall.

As I turned into the doorway of the maternity ward a bullet took me full in the right shoulder, blasting me back out into the hall. I hit the wall hard with the back of my head and felt something go dead in my right arm.

I crumpled to the floor and started to shiver some. As I lay there shaking, the picture that had been exposed to my eyes in the second I stood in the doorway developed in my mind, and I practically had to laugh.

The Old Lady and her Uzi had been standing with the dozen or so girls in the ward against the zees.

I heard two more shots and pulled myself up along the wall. I fingered the gaping shoulder wound with my four-fingered hand. The bullet had gone clean through.

"You stupid old bitch," I yelled. "I ain't dead yet."

I heard a wondrous screech from inside the ward, and recognised my baby. It was enough to get me moving.

"I'm coming in," I yelled.

I didn't have time or energy for any slick moves. I stumbled through the doorway, fully expecting to take a fatal round in the chest, but as I staggered in I saw the Old Lady was busy with a gaggle of zees that were tearing through the chicken wire that covered the windows. A clip had jammed in the Uzi and the Old Lady was smashing the gun against a table trying to pry it out. She just managed to slap a new clip in and spray the glass with bullets when I saw a mess of zees shambling down the hallway right behind me.

"Gun," I screamed, and damned if she didn't toss it to me in a smooth motion. I did a tuck and roll and came up with the blazing hot Uzi poking out between my legs like the spurting, steel phallus it is. I let loose with a short, controlled burst and three zee heads exploded like overripe pumpkins.

A couple of 'Snatchers came crawling in behind them, and I emptied the clip at knee level, creaming their heads into paste the colour of vegetable curry.

I tossed the Uzi back to the Old Lady who slipped in another clip smoother than a greased tampon. I started to get up when I got knocked back over by a blonde cannonball. I was half-reaching for the cattle prod before I realised it was my little angel, planting kisses on my puss and squeezing me tighter than a midget's jockstrap.

"Babycakes," I said, holding her close.

"Hey, Loverboy," the Old Lady snarled, keeping an eye on the windows. "Got any bright ideas?"

I got us up on our feet, my half-dead right arm draped around my baby's sweet shoulders, her face buried in my neck.

"Ammo?" I asked.

The Old Lady bared her teeth in the smile I'd learned to hate and slapped the clip in the Uzi.

There wasn't much time. More zees would smell our fresh meat or simply stumble onto us in a matter of moments.

My baby was fussing with the hole in my shoulder and I hurt so bad I could barely stand. Outside, the Herd's seemingly endless screams sounded a painful underscore.

I looked around the ward.

I smiled.

"Let's make us some noise," I said.

10

I watched the plume of thick, black smoke get smaller and smaller, till it looked like nothing more than a razor-thin crack in the deep blue mirror of the afternoon sky.

I was sitting on top of a cattle car, the setting sun barely warming my neck and back through the stiff northerly breeze. We hadn't quite figured out how to shift the engine into second, or however the hell these locomotives work, so we couldn't muster more than about fifteen miles an hour, but it was good enough. I reckoned we'd put about thirty five miles between us and the ruins of the Farm, and knew we'd have to stop soon, and risk the rest of the way on foot. There was no way of telling if word had got out about us, and besides, it was none too hard to track a slow moving train through this big, empty valley.

I heard a grunt behind me and spun around, the cattle prod instantly in my hand.

It was only Jimbo hauling himself up on the roof.

"Easy, partner," he said and pointed at the prod. "Plenty of time for sex games later."

I started to relax, then scrambled back to my feet, almost sliding off the roof.

"Who's running the train?" I yelled.

"Take it easy, for Christ's sake," he said, sitting down beside me. "Darlene's handling it."

"Darlene?"

Jimbo pursed his lips and shook his head at me. "Number 23," he said. Then he chuckled.

"What's so goddamn funny?" I asked.

"Darlene."

"Yeah?"

"She's a Sister."

"A nun?" I gasped.

Jimbo rolled his eyes. "A Sister of Sappho, Dr. I.Q."

"Sappho who?" I asked.

Jimbo looked exasperated. "She's got a closet full of flannel shirts, if you know what I mean."

"Ohhhhh," I said, and started to chuckle myself. "Hey, wasn't she in your . . . "

"Yup," Jimbo said.

Number 23, that is to say Darlene, had been in Jimbo's roost. He'd probably porked her two dozen times, and chances were she was carrying his baby.

"Funny thing is, I'd always sort of wondered how it'd be to have a kid, and Darlene always thought the same, so . . . "

"Mazeltov," I said, and we took in the scenery for a while.

The maternity ward had been outfitted like a regular hospital, including oxygen tanks beside every bed. Flammable as hell, those suckers are, especially when they're ignited by Uzi fire.

We used two tanks to blow out the back wall of the ward and scorch anything waiting outside. We loaded the rest on gurneys and then just rolled them out ahead of us, setting them off with the Uzi as we went, roasting dead meat every which way.

Me and the remaining girls bowled the tanks, while the Old Lady scored the strikes. She was one mean old bitch, but damn, could she shoot.

We burned a path right to the engine car of the cattle train. The zees might have learned some smarts, but like the animals they were, they never got over their fear of fire. A few, wearing the tatters of official uniforms, tried to stop us, but most were too busy bingeing on the Herd, to give a damn.

We lost four of the girls along the way, which made me sort of sad, but it was still better than I ever could have figured.

Jimbo — God bless his bent little soul — was waiting for us at the train. We climbed aboard and hightailed it on out of the camp.

Jimbo and me sat there quietly for a while, feeling the wind in our faces and watching the sky turn to evening grey. Jimbo rested his head on my shoulder, his grungy beard scratching at my neck and ear. I absently patted him on the cheek.

"She's right pretty," he said after a spell.

"Darlene?"

"You know who I . . . " He saw me smiling and punched me playfully on the shoulder, but it still hurt, so he rubbed the pain away.

"Yeah," I said, thinking of my baby's sweet face sleeping in the car below us. "I know she is."

"Think we'll make the ocean?" he asked.

I shrugged. "Not on this old wagon."

"It'll be cold in the hills."

"That it will," I said.

The plan was to head for the coast near Santa Maria. I knew the coves around there and figured we could steal a boat somehow and head for one of the Channel Islands. I knew we had to get off the mainland, and since the islands were used as test ranges, I reckoned they'd likely be deserted, though I didn't really know.

It was a plan, anyway.

We sat in silence for a while longer. Neither one of us wanted to move because we knew it would mean starting the next, dangerous leg of the trek.

"How do you figure the Old Lady?" Jimbo finally said, stalling really.

"Don't," I answered.

The Old Lady had got us through. Between my dead arm and blown off finger, I never could have fired the Uzi. But she hit every one of those goddamn tanks, and with single shots.

We had almost made it to the train when a hunk of shrapnel from a just-blown tank caught her square in the face. Took the top half of her head clean off.

I wasn't exactly sorry after all she'd done to me — I'd planned to whack her once we got out of the Farm anyway — but it did give a fellow pause about the vicissitudes of human nature. I was happy that at least she'd never make a zee.

"Don't," I said again.

Jim nodded slightly, then made to get up.

"Hey," I said.

He paused and looked at me.

"You still ain't explained why you waited for us like that. You could have pulled the train on out long before we got there and been safe and sound. Should have done. Hell, you couldn't even figure we'd make it. It was one of hell of a chance to take."

Jimbo turned his back to me and stared into the soft pink of the western sky. He turned his head in a slow pan, taking in the imposing sight of the approaching mountains.

"I told you I would," he said, without looking back.

He walked to the end of the car and started down the ladder. He disappeared out of sight, then poked his head back up above the car.

"Besides," he said, "you got one perky little ass."

His throaty chuckle echoed behind him.

I stared into the spreading eastern darkness and shook my head. Here I was, fleeing a world of flesh eating monsters on an old freight train with nothing but a cattle prod, seven pregnant babes and my new gay lover.

Just then I heard a sound that I couldn't quite place. I cocked my ear and listened hard before I realised it was singing coming from below.

I hadn't heard singing in far too long. Jimbo was leading the girls in a raucous chorus of 'Over the Rainbow'.

I recognised my baby's sweet voice carrying the heart of the melody.

I turned my back on the darkness and started to sing along.

Jay Russell: Afterword

WHAT CAN I SAY ABOUT JAY RUSSELL IN AN Afterword that hasn't already been said, in words with very few syllables probably delivered well past the deadline, by Michael Marshall Smith in an Introduction?

By now, unless you're one of those truly rare (ie: borderline psychotic) individuals who picks up a book and turns first to the Afterword, you'll have read all the stories, so I don't need to tell you about them. Good, weren't they? Impressed, aren't you? Even the splatterpunk gubbins had major redeeming factors, right? The money was well spent, wasn't it? The prevailing wisdom in book publishing goes that people don't buy short story collections, so you elite types who have invested in this one — or stolen it, which is fine since there's still a royalty payable, or borrowed it from a library, which means a few pence of Public Lending Right dribbling through in January when it is often welcome — can also rack yourself up some smug points for having good taste. Chances are you'll be familiar with Russell already, from his excellent novels, those featuring showbiz PI Marty Burns (I always imagine Mark Hamill) and *Blood* which doesn't.

You'll note that above, I refer to the author as Russell. That's not because of some English public school attitude whereby lifelong friends never use each other's christian names, but because in real-life writin' whizz Jay Russell is secretly mild-mannered, bespectacled sometime academic Russell Schechter (rhymes with Lecter), whom I see most Friday lunchtimes at a theatre pub in Islington, where a select group of underemployed literati gather to complain about publishers and other writers before decamping to one of the district's many fine hostelries for a generous repast and even more complaining.

It is in this regular forum that the real Russell shines. Unlike most authors, Russell is as good a listener as he is a writer. Sometimes, as he will admit after having been backed into a corner in a pub and subjected to full-bore tedium from 'that guy I always get stuck with' (his words), he is too good a listener. If you ever want to hear the full inside story on the members of Pat Cadigan's family she would like to leave in the woods without a map, or get the lowdown on what Paul McAuley's publishers have stuck on the cover of his latest and just what exactly Paul thinks about it, or indeed the state of my semi-permeable kitchen roof, then Russell has probably been taking notes and can read them back to you, through his trademark gritted, pained grin.

This ear for what people say and the way they say it is a distinctive feature of Russell's work (to get back to that), and if you think hard of the stories you've just read you'll see what I mean. There are tales here linked by theme or character or setting or style, but each has its voice, which can be street-level callous, affably academic, hardboiled but panicky or sincere and affecting. He brings to his work his own enthusiasms, for baseball and Preston Sturges (and all old movies), for pulp and high literature, for sexual mutilation (I'm guessing on this one) and superhero comics, but never as a name-dropper or a showoff.

You've finished the whole book now. You can remember or re-read at leisure. You have fifteen chunks of Jay Russell lodged forever in your memory cells. Don't you feel better? You should.

— Kim Newman
Islington, Monday 14, June 1999.

So tell me, class, what was the main theme of Waltzes and Whispers?